THE DALE

Michael Parzymieso

NFB
Buffalo, New York

Copyright © 2025 Michael Parzymieso

Printed in the United States of America

The Dale/ Michael Parzymieso/ 1st Edition

ISBN: 979-82186925-3-7

Fiction>Supernatural Thriller
Fiction>Thriller>Psychological
Fiction>Occult Horror
Fiction>Horror>Small Towns
Fiction> Horror>Religious
Fiction>Mystery>Supernatural
Fiction> Female Driven

This is a work of fiction. All characters in this novel are fictitious. Any resemblance to actual events or locations, unless specified, or persons, living or dead is entirely coincidental.

No part of this book may be reproduced or transmitted in any form by any means, electronic or mechanical, including photocopying, recording, or by any information storage and retrieval system without permission in writing by the author.

NFB
<<<>>>
NFB Publishing/Amelia Press
119 Dorchester Road
Buffalo, New York 14213

For more information visit
Nfbpublishing.com

The Dale

For my wife

Part I

One

May 1985
Cold Springs, Massachusetts

Caroline Sullivan halted two steps before reaching the edge of the glassy, dark water. Standing there, she had decided that the secret William Lane and Daniel Wilson kept from her might not be worth telling anyone in seventh grade.

At her feet, an abandoned road wound out of the thick forest behind her and disappeared under the Quabbin Reservoir before her. She swatted away a swirl of gnats rising in the heat of the clear May afternoon. She glanced behind her. Only a couple of small, squarish, collapsed, broken homes sat on one side of the road.

On the other side of the road, a ruined chapel rose out of the surrounding brush. This hamlet wasn't supposed to be here. This place, the place both boys called The Dale, was presumed to lay one hundred feet below the water with the four other sunken towns scattered deep in the Quabbin basin.

But only the boys knew, and now she knew something nobody else did. This insignificant hamlet, The Dale, wedged into a narrow valley as to be unnoticed for almost fifty years, survived untouched and abandoned.

Caroline squinted, mitigating the dazzling reflection of the sun off the blue water in front of her. The low shape of Mount Prescott rose in the hazy distance. She decided that even from a boat, The Dale would be impossible to see. Heavy, steep forest and the odd angle of the road hid it from the water. Since boats were restricted in this area, and forbidden to land, nobody from the water would ever see this place.

For some time she smiled, and a wave of delight rolled over her. She was here. William and Daniel let her in on their most guarded secret.

She stared past the ruined chapel, focusing on the narrow steep valley behind her. As she did, another less comfortable emotion flared from deep inside her chest.

"Something wrong?" asked Daniel Wilson, thick shouldered and sporting an unwieldy shock of blond hair.

"Maybe Déjà vu?" she replied, trying to drive away the rising unformed tension inside of her.

Daniel nodded. "Backwards or forward… past life or one you haven't lived yet?" he asked.

Caroline shrugged, inexplicably irritated by Daniel's question. Like he poked a nerve she didn't know was raw. "Dunno." She tried to pivot away from the anxiety. Caroline turned away from the valley and back toward the reservoir. "Why today? Why did you show me this today?"

It had taken both boys the better part of spring and half of summer to agree to let her in on their secret. Daniel had been the first to offer to show her their secret place. A place they hiked to and fished while leaving her behind. William would not hear it. Since William and Daniel had made a pact, Daniel had to go along.

"You are leaving for most of the summer," said William with a grin. "It's a going away present."

Joy rallied for a few moments and then faded, leaving Caroline awash in a troubling final emotion. It wasn't Déjà vu. Instead, a vicious wave of inexplicable dread rolled over her. Maybe she had tapped into a worry of leaving Cold Springs for the summer. She had never been on tour with her father and mother in the past. Maybe she just did not want to be away from the two best friends she ever had. Maybe it was not the sheer, dark valley behind her filling her with dread. Caroline decided, as the terror crept from her chest outward to her fingertips, perhaps she should not tell anyone in the seventh grade about this place. Perhaps, she should not have come here at all.

"What do you do when you are here?" Caroline wandered closer to the chapel. The blackened weather worn wood clapboard exterior held no paint. Sunlight glinted off a broken stained-glass window. The steeple leaned to the left. However, the simple act of running her hand along the warm wood of the chapel steadied her. By the time she walked past the dozen pews and headed back outside, the fear had subsided.

"Fish," replied William.

Both William and Daniel brought their fishing poles. The value in which the boys placed on them Caroline did not understand but accepted. She watched as William cast his line into the narrow finger of deep water in front of them. He avoided the dead tree limbs poking out of the water.

They all watched as the small spinning lure at the end of his line jinked and flashed as he reeled it in. Then, as the lure rolled over a sunken stone wall, a small fish darted out and struck the lure.

"Smallmouth bass?" Daniel asked.

"Nope," replied William.

"A brook trout." Caroline marveled as the fish flopped to shore. She worked her way from the chapel to the shoreline thirty feet away to get a better look at the fish. Its orange belly flared under the olive flanks speckled with yellow and brown. William held it up. Daniel gazed at it in wonder. "It doesn't belong here. Water's too warm." Caroline knew the water of the reservoir had already warmed up to the point where rainbows and brook trout drifted down to the deep, cold water of the Quabbin in the afternoon.

"Maybe not." William pointed out the sunken rock wall. Three small dots drifted above the sunken wall shaded by a dead tree standing above it. "There's more over there."

Caroline knelt to touch the fish before William released it. The cold water had to come from somewhere to hold them. The fish squirmed out of her grasp, splashed once, and zipped back toward the sunken wall. Caroline hopped back with a squeak erupting from her mouth, followed by a giggle.

Caroline frowned as the fish retreated into the safety of the cove. She wanted a better look at it. But something else caught her eye. The water where the trout swam looked slightly darker, like a narrow smoky column made of thousands of tiny strands of dark and light liquid swirled together. She traced the path of the flush of color back to shore. Then, she walked off the narrow, crumbling road on which they stood, past the chapel, and almost to the wood line. She bent down; her short, petite frame blended in among the ferns and scattering of granite boulders.

Caroline reached down farther between the rocks and then quickly yanked her hand back. "It's cold," she said, holding up her hand. A clump of brown hair from her short bob stuck to her forehead.

Daniel and William stopped fishing and ran over to her. Caroline watched Daniel quickly clear away dead leaves and vines that clogged the area where she found the cold water. His thick muscles bulged under a sweat-soaked tee shirt. His efforts revealed a deep pocket of cold water. A hidden stream. One that led directly to the trout. But she did not look out into the cove. Her eyes were called upstream—into the forest. The dread which rolled over her minutes earlier now had a home.

"You are leaving for six weeks, Caroline," said William. "We really should see where this goes before you leave."

Caroline nodded, not sure if she wanted to go further. The three of them worked to remove the debris that clogged the narrow watercourse. The chilly water ran along a path that led directly to the cove edge. "That's why the fish are here. This water is cold enough for them," said Daniel.

"But only in that spot."

"I'll bet this goes all the way up into the valley," William said.

Caroline felt certain he was correct, yet she quietly resisted the magnetic fear, which led her toward wherever the spring-fed stream burst from the ground. "Maybe we don't follow it," she said meekly.

However, the boys' curiosity won out, and she joined them as they followed the creek up a steep grade. As the grade rose, the creek narrowed and deepened.

Further upstream they discovered a low stone wall. "Just like the sunken wall in the cove," said William.

Except for the middle of the wall, thought Caroline, where water in the now-clear path of the stream rumbled through. It appeared as if a giant hand had smashed the lichen-covered boulders outward. A pile of them lay strewn out in a reverse "C" pattern.

"What would do that?" asked Caroline.

"Dunno," replied William. The three of them kept close together as they strode into the darkening, thick forest.

There were two other smaller stone walls blocking the stream—both blown out in the middle. As the grade of the streambed steepened, the water flowed freely in a five-foot-wide brook that wound between increasingly larger boulders. Caroline dreaded the silence as she trudged along with the boys' relentless curiosity.

Finally, they reached the source of the water. A sheer wall of sandstone rose thirty feet above them. Water rained out of the sandstone, down the face, and finally to the base of the wall and formed a swimming pool-sized pool of water.

Daniel looked up at the rock face. "It's like the whole rock wall is the spring."

Caroline barely heard him as she closed the distance to the pool at the base of the waterfall.

"I don't think anyone has ever been here before," said William.

"No," said Caroline slowly, her voice no more than a whisper. She pointed.

Rising from the center of the pool, and breaking the surface, lay a pile of stone. The rocks shuffled into a mound, and around the mound lay a perfect circle of single stones—each of them identical to the next. Crowning the mound lay a set of four glassy black obsidian rocks. Each of the rocks were the size of a bowling ball. "A person had to have done that."

Daniel and William worked their way to the pile to touch it.

"Don't," cried Caroline before she knew what she was saying. "Let's go," said Caroline, hurrying back down the streambed. Just the sight of the pile of stone rattled her. Her chest squeezed tightly, a hot, hard knot at the center of her. Fiery anxiety overwhelmed her.

"We just got here," protested William, in awe of the sight. He took several more steps and reached the center of the pool, his face aglow in pride, and reached for the obsidian crown of the pile.

Daniel glanced back at her. Her mouth agape, hands in front of her, no more words coming out, must have stopped him. "Let's go."

William stared at the pile for a long moment and then turned away. "Fine."

The boys headed back toward Caroline, and she let out a long breath. She made sure both were next to her before she headed back downstream. The fear drained away as they headed downstream. But all she could think about was the perfect circle of rocks crowned by obsidian stones at the center of the pool. A single phrase burst forward in her mind. *Don't touch the stones.*

She wanted to touch them very badly. So badly, it hurt to leave.

Two

Red Rock Amphitheater, Colorado
June 1985

Caroline Sullivan sat with the T-shirt rumpled up in her hands. Her mother scowled and snapped out her next words.

"Well, don't you want the T-shirt?"

Caroline nodded and gazed back teary-eyed at her mother. "Yes."

"Good." Her mother sat down across from her in the large custom RV. "Just remember this is hard on me. You're young and will get used to this pretty quick."

Caroline could not understand her mother's sudden perky optimism. Divorce swam in disaster and nothing more. No positive spin could exist in the new truth in her life. Allyssa Sullivan told her that she was leaving but could not articulate a clear reason why—other than, "It's better this way."

She craved more, something that would explain why her world had just collapsed. Twenty minutes ago, Caroline only needed a T-shirt with a sparkling unicorn emblazoned across the front. Her name could be stamped on the back. Then, she thoughtlessly barged into Niles Sparrow's trailer to find her mother intimate with him. Caroline froze in stunned silence. Her mother calmly stood up, adjusted her clothing, followed Caroline out of the trailer, and asked why she had come in.

Caroline numbly replied that she wanted a T-shirt, and her mother walked her through the bustle of preshow activity and bought her the shirt. She added that they didn't have time to get her name on the back of the shirt.

Now, back in their own larger RV, she could only focus on her mother's beautiful oval face. Caroline looked at her in a desperate search for some break in her will to leave.

She found nothing. Even when Caroline cried and even, a surprise to herself, she threw a lamp across the trailer, smashing it and the glasses that broke its fall.

"Caroline," she shouted. "Those glasses are part of a collection." Allyssa pointed at the shattered glasses and bent lamp.

"You are leaving—WHY DO YOU CARE ABOUT THE GLASSES!"

Allyssa took a breath. Caroline didn't know whether it was to calm herself or collect her thoughts. "Because they belong together."

"We," whimpered Caroline, "*belong together.*"

Caroline flopped into the small bed tucked into the side of the RV. Her legs dangled off the edge of the small bed.

"Not anymore." Allyssa pulled a bag from underneath her bed. "It's seven thirty-five," she said. Caroline could hear no warmth or kindness in her voice. Not even a tender word for her. "The show starts in five minutes. You just told me we belong together. I'm making that happen. It's best if we leave now. Your father has a show to play. I've left him a note that explains everything."

"What?"

Allyssa cocked her head. "Haven't you been listening? I'm leaving your father. So are you."

The realization slammed its way forward. Not only was her mother leaving her father, but she was also leaving the rest of her life. "I… don't want to leave anyone. Stay!"

"Caroline. You have to make a choice, and I can't imagine you staying with *him*."

Caroline sat up; her mother stared at her, waiting for an answer. Outside, she heard the activity pick up to a frenetic pace. The crowd in the amphitheater less than a hundred yards away roared. A large strobe light, first in a sequence of events that introduced the band, rose from the center of the stage.

Caroline did not want to decide. Leave her father and lose him, Daniel, William, home, and her friends in Cold Springs. Happiness. Leave her mother…her mother was leaving regardless. Just a month ago she had been coasting to the end of the school year, dreaming about grade eight, when William and Daniel showed her The Dale. And now, she thought, and now everything is over.

A loud firework exploded over the stage. Three minutes to showtime. The preshow video, a montage of pictures and snippets of film from the history of the band, would start any second.

"Caroline," demanded her mother. "You have to choose."

She stood and looked out at the door. The crowd roar intensified. She knew it would get louder until her father played the first notes on his guitar—notes almost nobody ever heard. The crowd generated noise she would be able to feel in her chest.

The house lights went down. The video ran, and an instrumental guitar piece played underneath it. "No," she replied. "You can't leave. You need to talk to him."

Caroline bolted out the door and sprinted for the stage. She dodged the roadies and the dozens of backstage workers who all knew her as she headed directly toward the left side of the stage where the preshow huddle would be. Niles, the bass player, would be there. He was the problem. When her dad knew, he could fire Niles. The solution drove her forward, running effortlessly toward the stage only yards away.

Caroline worried her mother would catch her. Two security guards stood at the entrance. She stopped to dare a quick glance behind her to see her mother. She paused on the stairs; her mother was not there. In the distance, she could still see her standing in the doorway of the RV. She looked at her mother, and her mother turned away. Another hurt.

One of the guards handed her earphones to cancel out the noise as she worked her way up the steps. "Hurry now, Caroline," he added. She put them on.

Nobody knew?

The world just exploded, and nobody did anything different.

Enraged, she bolted forward. She had to stop this and stop it cold. Fire the bass player; sweep her mother off her feet again.

Caroline swung around the corner, and the preshow huddle did not look like it normally did. They should all be together, arms around each other, waiting for the cue to run to their spots. But now, Niles Sparrow already stood on his spot, stage right. The drummer sat behind his kit, his eyes darting back and forth, the keyboardist bobbed his head with the introductory video. She could not find her father.

Then, she saw them. He had his arm around the waist of the band's publicist, Sherry, and then Caroline knew.

Her father was cheating too.

Her heart shattered as Caroline dropped to her knees, shameful tears burning down her cheeks.

Her father looked over and spotted her; he quickly pulled his arms away from the publicist. He walked two steps toward her as the curtain came down and the band hit their notes—except him. He continued toward her as the crowd thundered.

Caroline, her chest tight and eyes red, could not bear to look at him and turned and ducked off the stage and into the crowd.

Three

Cold Springs, Massachusetts
June 1985

CAROLINE TRIED TO SHAKE off the memory. Her anger, a fresh bloom, refused to lose its colors. Her world twisted inside out as the smug new reality lit the fire inside. A fire that raged and consumed her.

Opening the trailer door in Colorado to find her mother kissing the shirtless bass player, Niles Sparrow, had ripped her world apart.

Her father had found her hidden under the stage, scooped her up, and buckled her into their rented Ford Explorer. With no luggage and only the money in his wallet, they'd headed east toward Cold Springs.

She had not wanted to return to Cold Springs without her mother. Each mile her dad had ground away in the driver's seat pushed Caroline further from her. The daylight content world painted green, auburn, and sky blue had whipped by as she stared out her passenger seat window. State by state, distances measured by region had stretched out between them. Each mile had hardened her new reality.

Allyssa Sullivan had left them. A loss that hung heavy. The pain of it steadily colored the world around her until she did not want to do anything but try to close her eyes for some relief.

After two days in her room, refusing to speak to her father and only accepting food left outside of her bedroom door, she ventured outside. William and Daniel lived in the two houses across the street, but she didn't want to see them yet.

She couldn't.

Caroline first took a walk as much to pass the time as to dispel her anger. When it was done, the flames of resentment hadn't cooled. So, she took another walk. This one evolved into a long trek. Restless unanswered questions spun in her head.

Soon enough, she had ventured all the way to the town common, the long grassy oval on which the entire town centered. She had been walking for forty-five minutes. She wandered in the small town center longer than she expected. In front of Cold Springs Town Hall, she crossed the street and walked past the monuments on the south end of the common.

Then, she ended up in the place she least expected. She stood in front of a house in which she lived a long time ago. The one before her father had rocked the music world with his band. Before the band had toured stadiums during summer.

Before the bass player.

The yellow house on the common. Caroline lived here with her mother and her dad and a few guppies. She lived here long before William and Daniel were more than barely seen boys in another classroom at Cold Springs Elementary. Those were the happiest times of her life. Time before the world showed its teeth.

She walked up the steps to the front door. Now here, she hesitated. She glanced around as her hand hovered over the doorknob. Lights glowed dimly through the windows in other houses along the street. However, her old house lay dark. It had a reputation.

She had once lived in a haunted house.

She did not believe it, at least not when they lived there. Caroline wondered about the sanity of the neighbors. If they really thought the house next to them held captive ghosts, why didn't they move? Maybe ghosts obeyed a set of rules, rules that bound them to a place. Cursed to stay within the boundaries of the walls where they shrieked and bawled in their damned afterlife.

Her dad thought ghosts drifted through the home, or at least, he used the legend to scare her. To her, the house on the common wasn't even mildly uncomfortable.

Most haunted houses looked the part. Caroline envisioned a place with ragged doors which clanked in the wind, rooflines that sagged into frowning window eyes. This one looked like a normal large, yellow Victorian. On the east side of the two-story house, two gables poked out of the steeply angled roof. She noticed the neatly mowed grass. Perhaps a neighborly offering to placate whatever spirits dragged their irons through the moldered attics and vacant hallways.

Her dad told her that the house's problems started in the late forties. A young man went insane, and he and his mother mysteriously vanished. "Be good," he would say, "or we're moving back to the haunted house on the common!" It would have been a far more effective threat if she believed in the haunting. Her steady disbelief did not stop her dad. Nothing stopped him. Not even a haunted house. Except now. Losing her mother. Her relentless refusal to speak to him. Those two things stopped John Sullivan cold.

Still standing on the long lower porch, which stretched around the front of the house, she wanted to leave for home. Instead, on a whim, she turned on her heels and grabbed the door handle—and it turned. Without thinking, she walked inside. The dim light from the fading sun filtered through the dirty windows and cast the rooms deep in shadows.

The home still had furniture. She could see dishes in the sink and children's toys strewn on the living room floor. A small blanket and a stuffed frog lay stretched out near the front door. Perhaps dropped by a child as panicked parents rushed them out of the house. Scared enough to leave a stuffed Muppet and blanket two feet from the front door.

She sat down in a chair. Somehow, it felt good to be here. Caroline leaned her head back, her eyes half shut. She did not feel fear in this place. For the first time in days, she felt happy. Then, overcome by a wave of exhaustion, she closed her eyes for just a moment.

The Quabbin Gate 5A
Cold Springs, Massachusetts

Caroline Sullivan vanished, and William Lane decided they needed to find her. They decided not to tell anyone where they were going.

Minutes after Assistant Police Chief Glen Chevalier came to their homes to ask where she might be—a question both he and Daniel Wilson answered with a lie—they left the house to search for her. He did not know for sure that Chevalier believed them, but the risk was worth it. He had heard the name Dumont as it crackled out from Chevalier's shoulder mounted radio—a name that left William Lane cold.

Henry *Lee* Dumont. Dumont was missing as well. William had seen him just once—at the Cold Springs Fair early last September, and there he was, shuffling and bobbing between the crowd, weathered, gaunt, and wiry. Their paths merged at the crosswalk between the common and Caroline's old house on common, Walnut Street. Dumont halted with a grunt then glared at him, eyes fiery against the carnival lights. A set of hands, William's father's, jolted him along into the crowd hard enough that he'd dropped his fried dough. But, as he looked for the fried dough on the ground, his eyes were drawn to Dumont who never broke his gaze—feral and murderous until another cluster of families swept by blocking his view.

Months later the image still rocked him. William Lane knew where to look for Caroline and certainly Daniel did too. Caroline Sullivan liked to go to a secret place.

Their secret place.

A place they found—once just a legend in the town that they had discovered two summers ago. This summer, they showed Caroline just before she left to go on tour with her father. Only they knew of it.

And all three of them liked to be there. Especially Caroline. A place in the woods. A safe place to be alone.

One possibility: Caroline was there.

The other possibility: Dumont had Caroline; that *terrified* him.

If they could find her there, then all would be well. Dumont would go back to being Chevalier's problem. Their secret place and Caroline would be safe and nobody else would have to know.

They turned north, walking along the boulder and stone beach. Fifty feet of stone and gravel shoreline separated the edge of the forest and the waterline of the Quabbin. Questions beyond Caroline's disappearance rumbled through Daniel Wilson's mind.

Truth or fiction?

Truth: Caroline was maybe, probably, or possibly in The Dale.

The Dale had been lost to history, just a small part of the story of the Quabbin Reservoir. The larger story was taught to everyone in the Commonwealth of Massachusetts since first grade. Boston needed water, and the Swift River created a perfect source for Boston's water supply. The Swift River would be dammed, and billions of gallons of freshwater would fill the valley behind it. Four towns had been demolished and drowned but not everything had vanished. One place survived, long rumored but never found, a secret place far into the woods.

A place they called, The Dale. William assumed if Caroline had a bad day, she'd go there.

Caroline changed him. By the middle of the first summer she had lived on the street, what had once been just a pair, he and Daniel Wilson, now became a fellowship of three. Caroline, to their surprise, tromped through the woods as a natural. So, this spring he and Daniel had told her about The Dale. They had shown her, and after two walks there, she could lead the way. While they lost interest in the creek which ran behind the ruins and led to the forest and the high waterfall at the end of it, Caroline did not.

They had been to The Dale three times before she left on tour. Each time she begged them to return to the source, the pile of stone crowned by four obsidian stones. Even when she pouted, they had not.

The creek or brook was not even fishable and thus didn't need to be explored any further. But Caroline stayed in the Dale and even sat in the ruined chapel. She drew it and mapped it out and even measured the distances to make her map correct. He saw the way she looked upstream. Odd, he thought, especially since she had been spooked by it the first time. He shuddered thinking about it.

Daniel led and walked head down in his search for tracks.

"Tracks," said Daniel. He appreciated the distraction from the increasing tension.

"Hers?"

"Maybe," offered Daniel. "The dirt is still wet."

William and Daniel walked upstream on the right-hand side of the narrow watercourse. They followed its meandering path until they crossed the remains of a road. They had walked for a little over three-quarters of an hour and stood on a ridge. There they could see a bit of The Dale below them. The steeple of the chapel poked up, partially obscured by the branches and leaves.

William started to yell out for Caroline, but Daniel grabbed his arm and squeezed it hard enough that William winced.

Daniel pointed and waited while William's eyes searched The Dale for what he needed to see. A light mist rolled off the reservoir, making it hard to see in the fading light of day. Daniel slowly lowered himself as William plunged to the ground next to him.

Standing in the doorway of the ruined church stood a man. And he looked in their direction.

The House on the Common
Cold Springs, Massachusetts

Caroline Sullivan opened her eyes to the all-encompassing darkness. Her lethargic brain struggled to catch up. She'd fallen asleep in her old house on the common. A thump sounded from the basement. In horror movies, monsters swallowed those who wanted to know what went on in the night-shaded basement. Caroline stayed put, then she heard a soft gurgle in the dark. The sound, so low and soft, vanished in the sound of her breath. She stopped and held her breath and heard it again.

Perhaps a spirit did haunt the house on the common. Alone and in the dark's stillness, the warmth that she'd felt when she entered the house rushed away. She stiffened in the phantom cold front which replaced it.

Her dad had once explained to her how people became ghosts. There were three ways. The first occurred when a person died before they had completed a crucial task. Second, when a person perished so quickly, they didn't know they were dead. The third way relied on an event so traumatic that it left an imprint on time and space. Here in the house on the common and sitting in the silent dark, it seemed far more possible that a young man went insane and murdered his mother. Caroline stood up to leave. She had enough for the night. She no longer cared whether the house was haunted. Knowing for sure plummeted to the bottom of her priorities.

Click.

She did not need to turn around to know the front door had locked. When her eyes adjusted to the dark, she realized it looked nothing like her old comfortable home.

"I'm in the wrong house," she whispered, feeling the sudden weight of the dreadful situation. Caroline looked to her left and through the windows. She'd sat not in a house but a crumbling wooden building. Her surroundings, a wide and open room with decaying gray wooden floors. Then, another sound rumbled through the house louder than the first two. It took a second for her to place it. The sound of breathing. It came from the back of the structure. The breathing sounded guttural, halting, and louder. She teetered forward, hoping for a back door, but that move required her to venture closer to the sound. She suddenly realized why people in horror movies did stupid things—they were rabbits, just running rabbits.

She looked around for another exit from the house, but even the windows vanished. Dark, save for a dimly lit hallway. The walls of the hall were not sagging; they were moving, synchronized with the breathing; the pulsing shuddering sound now loud enough it shook the whole structure.

Still, she moved deeper into the hall and toward a more brightly lit small room. Once inside the room, she peeked around. To her right stood what looked like a large closet. As she stared, the doors moved in rhythm with the breathing—in and out, ready to burst under the strain.

A gust of hot air blasted her, and the doors blew off their hinges, knocking her down. She could not be sure if the blood draining into her eyes was her own. From the floor, she could almost see into the closet. A dark shapeless mass smashed out at her from the dark.

The very last thought she had before it grabbed her was *Venus flytrap*.

Daniel Wilson stared at the man for some time. Both he and William hunkered down in the ferns and soft pine needles behind a moss-covered log blackened by rain. The rail thin, weather-beaten man surveyed the area for what had made the sound in the thick trees and heavy brush. After a while, he turned away mumbling as he drifted back inside the church.

"What's he doing here?" whispered Daniel stunned by the sight of Henry Lee Dumont.

They had never seen another person in The Dale and now the town boogieman haunted the chapel. "Don't know. Do you think she's in there?" asked William.

His nerve endings flared hot, and his brain desperately tried to balance competing urges. He needed to both run away and charge forward. The first urge started as a soft, steady tap on his heart. Now it raged as a barely contained compulsion. The only thing which kept him here was Caroline, and the desire to keep Dumont away from her reigned over the impulse to run.

"We can't leave until we know for sure," William said and leaned to his left for a better view.

"If she's in there," said Daniel, "we need to figure out how to get Henry Lee Dumont away from the church."

An idea burst forward in his mind. Daniel explained it to William and then squeezed his friend's arm, who gave him a thumbs up. Daniel always reacted quicker than William. On the baseball diamond, William would sense a batter slightly shifting his stance, and Daniel moved to where the ball would go. William would see a pheasant taking flight, and Daniel would have his sixteen-gauge Mossberg 500 raised and ready.

They stayed stock still and Henry Lee Dumont had not reemerged from the chapel.

Then Daniel sprinted to the ruined chapel. He channeled the fear and willed it into action. Once he touched the side of the building, he paused and looked back to where William hid under cover and nodded. Seconds later, a fern swayed slightly, and a twig popped up on the twenty-foot ridge overlooking The Dale.

Ding-Dong-Ditch. That was the plan. He tracked William's movements on the ridge.

Daniel slunk around to the back of the chapel. He arrived at the corner, raised his fist to pound on the building, but stopped short. That had been the plan, knock and run. Get Dumont to chase him and lure him away from Caroline. Daniel was the faster sprinter of the two.

Dumont stood at the back of the church and confronted Daniel.

Daniel spun around, hop stepped twice, and drove his feet forward and down, prepared to sprint. He hoped to run far enough away that William could do his part and grab Caroline from the church if she was there.

Daniel Wilson slipped when he turned, and Dumont grabbed him by the wrist only two steps from the chapel. Their plan ground to a halt. Daniel dropped to his knee and twisted to the right and drove his shoulder forward and flipped Dumont. Dumont thudded to the ground.

Out of the corner of his eye, Daniel saw William flying through the forest toward the chapel. Dumont showed no mercy and hauled

Daniel down to the ground, which propelled all the wind out of him. Dumont straddled Daniel and grabbed his shirt, pulling him up off the ground. He moved his face close to Daniel, who gasped for air.

"Leave her alone," he rasped. The words jolted a shot of adrenaline into Daniel's veins, and in a single burst, he jerked free.

She was here; the electric words crackled through Daniel's mind. *Leave her alone!* His freedom lasted half a second. Henry Lee Dumont slammed him down onto the forest floor. He pummeled Daniel with heavy fisted blows to his face and body. The man's sour breath cascaded across Daniel's cheek. She was here, but he could do nothing other than desperately try to ward off the flurry of blows. He turned, twisted, and whipped his body left and right, but Dumont adjusted to every move. Although he looked frail, Dumont's hands and arms moved with astonishing speed and his punches landed with will-breaking power. Daniel's cheek blazed with pain, his entire world engulfed in the flames of the all-consuming rage which the man thundered down on his face and head. Daniel faded to the edge of passing from consciousness to a welcoming white haze when a rock whizzed by and smacked the side of the man's head with a wet *thunk*.

Dazed, Daniel wondered why the hell William didn't throw like that in the bottom of the seventh inning. The blow stunned Dumont for a second but not long enough for William's flying knee-elbow combination to hit its mark. Dumont easily parried it, and Daniel watched helplessly as William cartwheeled by and hit the ground, rolling to a stop in an awkward heap. As his eyes tracked William's movements, Daniel struggled to focus on Henry Lee Dumont's position. He recoiled at the sight of the crazed Dumont with a large rock raised; neck strained and veins pulsing.

Daniel lay, arms limp and drained. He had always imagined if it ever came to it, he would fight to his last breath. Now reality crashed into fantasy. Daniel gasped for air, looking up at a gray rock flecked with green moss flopping outward, as the football-sized mass began its descent toward his head. He finally raised his arm in a wobbly attempt to keep Dumont's fury from taking him. He flinched at a thundering crack from behind him. Dumont jumped and lost his grip on the rock. Two more loud pops left Daniel curled up and nearly deaf. His eyes locked onto Dumont as he jerked violently once, then twice, and finally, a third time before he dropped , crumbling to the ground with nothing more than a muffled groan as the rage flickered out of his eyes leaving them cold, wet, and lifeless. In the last moment Daniel saw something else, and it confused him. A second or two of complete peace reigned in Dumont's eyes as if he welcomed what would come next.

Daniel lay still on the ground eye to eye with the man. He shut his eyes to block out the horror. When he reopened them, he saw William standing frozen and Assistant Chief Chevalier stepping out of the woods joined by four other policemen. Chevalier worked the bolt on his rifle and jerked out the spent shell casing. The brass casing seemed to pop out of the Model 70 slowly at first, glinting as it caught the last rays of the sun cutting through the trees, before speeding up and arcing into the brush. Chevalier did not move the muzzle of his rifle away from the body of Dumont while the other officers holstered their revolvers. Their heads darted around looking for unseen threats.

"That him?" asked one officer.

Daniel answered, "Yes."

Chevalier glared at Daniel. "He didn't ask you!" Then his words softened a bit. "Yeah, that's him."

"You can get up now," he coaxed him. Daniel didn't move. Still tense, Chevalier glanced over at his deputies. "Fan out and look around for her."

"She's here," whimpered Daniel, struggling to make the words come out of his mouth. Death had been a sliver away from taking him only to turn left and tap Henry Lee Dumont on the shoulder. "He said 'leave her alone.'"

Chevalier ducked into the chapel and immediately whistled. Two other deputies followed Chevalier.

"Got her." Daniel heard Chevalier's growl and his muscles loosened fractionally. He didn't know if Caroline still lived. His answer came quickly. Chevalier carried the broken and dirty frame of Caroline out of the chapel as if she was a loaf of bread. Her arms and legs dangled limply. Daniel's eyes were drawn lower. One of her feet was bare and had a small cut and on the other foot—a bright pink sneaker—its laces still tied in a double bow.

The Dale

Caroline rocked between consioness and unconsciousness. The hazy and undefined moments in between stretched out, twisted back and forth, and then around again. Her perception, no more than a leaf drifting down a stream. She bounced in and out of eddies of time and space for a while before being sucked under into blackness. Caroline Sullivan existed and nothing more, simply floating between the two states of the human mind.

After a while, a light flashed intermittently here and there. The light passed in front of her and then disappeared before she could react.

She did not know her name or if she had one.

Feeling followed and sound returned. A chill swept across her. The stiffness in her legs and back begged to be stretched out. From deep within her came an urge to move. A light, more yellow than white, flashed in front of her again; sound became louder, sharper. She moved, not knowing how, toward the light and the chaotic noise.

Sound metamorphosed into words. All of them familiar, she didn't understand why. She, aware that sound was something she should know, searched the limited space of her mind but couldn't figure it out. Fatigue engulfed her. She stopped moving and rested.

Bright light startled her to consciousness and then she jumped when the sound became much more intense. It was right in front of her and loud. She realized someone shouted at her, which confused and upset her. Nobody enjoyed being shouted at. Her nap must have done her some good because it was obvious now why she knew the sound. Clear and distinct, someone was calling the name *Caroline*.

She realized slowly that if someone called her name right in front of her, she was no longer alone. She rallied with a sense of relief. She no longer wanted to be alone. Then, her next sensation was one of being lifted into the air by a powerful, thick pair of arms and pulled out of the darkness. She opened her eyes as wide as she could make them and noticed that she was missing a shoe and her sock. People and voices mixed with light and feeling.

A man carried her, and that knowledge unleashed a torrent of dread so fierce she twisted and clawed, desperate to be out of his grip. Caroline pummeled him across the face and shoulders. Her small balled-up fists did nothing to the man. He allowed her to punch away until her strength failed completely.

"I've got you, Caroline," he said. She then saw his hat, a funny little hat like only…police officers wore. The dread fell away, replaced by heart thumping anxiety, and finally a measure of calm. The police. She knew her rescuer, Assistant Chief Chevalier.

Safe.

Chevalier carried her among other officers. She stopped struggling, leaden exhaustion dragged her head down to his shoulder and she wept. She didn't know quite why she wept. The action steadied her thoughts. Chevalier held her tighter as he walked, then unexpectedly turned back to the ruined structure of the church. Her head bounced off the assistant chief's thick collar bone. As her nose stung and she tried to breathe, she lifted her head over his shoulder and quickly jammed her face back into the meat of his shoulder and bicep.

Caroline tried to shut out the image which seared its way into her brain. A man lay dead on the forest floor. His gray eyes stared right back at her. His thin mouth hung open. Dark red blood pooled and glistened next to his head.

She remembered nothing. Only knew one thing: she was in The Dale. She did not know why. Her last memory was of the house on the common. Now, she was here. People swarmed her. A policeman huddled around her and covered her with a blanket. A man who called himself a doctor, he had a name too—Dr. David Nash—asked her questions. He asked her questions she could not answer.

What happened? How did you get here? Did he hurt you? Did he touch you? Caroline shook her head each time the questions were asked. She'd seen something malevolent. Vicious. Cruel. Even in the arms of a policeman she didn't feel safe. Terror rocked her body. Even as she processed her encounter only one word came to mind.

Evil.

But as she tried to grasp onto the memory of it, the memory faded, quickly slipping from her grasp and leaving her with a pit in the center of her soul. She had no way to push away from it or push it out of her. Even as it wound around every neuron in her body, she wanted it out.

Dr. David Nash left the hospital room of Caroline Sullivan looking for his friend Father Andre Bequette. He found him in the lobby speaking to Caroline Sullivan's father and the parents of both the Lane and Wilson boys. A crowd had gathered around the priest.

"Father," he said. "A word?"

The sixty-year-old priest followed him to a quiet corner in the busy hospital.

"I came back to the hospital for her," said Dr. Nash and then he paused for a moment. "I have given her something to help her sleep and get through these next few hours. But she is going to need something more."

The priest looked back at him and then nodded toward Caroline's room. "You got a pill in that black bag of yours that lets her instantly process this trauma and fast forward her life for six months?"

Nash chuckled for the first time all day. "No, what are you thinking?"

"She could wake up tomorrow and pop up like a daisy as if nothing happened. But that is highly unlikely. She is going to need counseling."

"Agreed," replied Nash.

"But we can't force it on her or she will reject it," added Bequette.

"Are you suggesting we wait?"

"Perhaps. She will come to either her father or me, and then I can proceed as carefully as humanly possible. She will be fragile."

Nash didn't want to admit it, but Bequette was right. A ping of professional jealousy bounced around in his mind. Caroline would go to Bequette and not him. He was not a man of any faith. Father Andre Bequette could give her something he, as an atheist, could not. Counseling from the perspective of a man of faith. Caroline Sullivan, he reasoned, an altar girl, believed in a God that loved the world. She believed in a world that was mostly good, and that evil cowered in the view of the good. "Are saying she is going to want answers in the context of her faith and her family. She will trust a believer more than someone who does not?"

"Yes. No offense. However, you are more formally educated in the field. Do you want to take on that task?" asked Father Bequette.

"You know I can't in that context. Besides it's too soon for to me to do anything except prescribe her something. She isn't doing anything that would get her admitted to the psychiatric ward."

"I can work to begin counseling with her tomorrow then," replied the priest.

Dr. David Nash shook hands with the priest and decided to trust his judgement. Bequette had been modest in his assessment of his counseling abilities. Father Andre Bequette had received extensive psychological training and had been working with adolescents across New England for longer than he himself had been a psychiatrist. "If you get in a jam, I know a guy," he chuckled.

"If I can't keep her out of your wing, then it might be time for me to retire."

Father Andre Bequette thanked him and returned to the families. As Bequette drifted away, Dr. David Nash wondered if perhaps he should have taken a stronger stance. After a moment, he rejected the idea. They'd worked together for ten years in cases very similar to this. Father Bequette, he thought, was the best person to work with Caroline, for the moment.

Four

Cold Springs
July 1985

SOMETHING DID NOT ADD up about Caroline's story. The more William thought about it, the less her story made sense. He had seen Caroline heading toward town. They found her deep in the Quabbin. William worked through the timeline in his head. Walk to the common and spend time in her old house. Walk back home. Then, walk into the woods. Next, she had an altercation with Dumont and endured his horrible atrocities. Finally, Caroline passed out and woke up when the deputies entered the church in The Dale. The timing didn't work. There was not enough time for everything to happen. So, she was at the house on the common and only at the house on the common, or she went to The Dale and only to The Dale.

Maddeningly, Caroline insisted she'd entered the house on the common even though the timeline was impossible. All the memories whizzing around in her mind were echoes of the house on the common. Nothing about The Dale—other than waking up and being there.

He and Daniel convinced their parents to let them out of being grounded for an hour and take their bikes to church today. William wanted to help Caroline grind down the possibility of ever being there.

William Lane approached the yellow Victorian house on the common in which Caroline once lived from the rear. He laid his bike down beside Daniel's Redline. They stood at the side of the dormant and abandoned home, out of view of anyone from the street. Neither of them made a move. Thinking about sneaking into a haunted house and going into the house were two different things. "Caroline went in from the front door."

"We can't. Someone will see us."

"Do you think the side door is open?" Daniel took a step to the side door and grabbed the knob. It had been secured.

They moved around back and tried to get in through the covered rear entrance. This time, they made a little more progress. The screen door opened, giving them hope. That hope died when the inner doorknob would not budge. "This isn't how she got in," Daniel replied.

William grunted and looked through the windows. The dirty windows offered a poor look inside the house. He could see a kitchen but not much more.

"The basement window is open a little."

They moved out of the shelter of the back door and over to the basement window, which sat open just a crack. Daniel squeezed his hands between the frame and the window and pulled it open a little more. The church bell tolled to gather the last people to their seats. Daniel stepped back to slide the window all the way open. In one motion, Daniel slipped through the opening and into the basement. William followed him.

Once in the basement, they made their way up the stairs to the first floor of the house.

"It's an empty house," said Daniel.
"Nothing Caroline described is here," replied William.
"There's a more obvious sign she never came here," whispered Daniel, looking around the abandoned home. "Not a single footprint."
William could see Daniel was right. Nothing disturbed the fine layer of gray dust on the floor or the cobwebs resting on the large oak front door, which was where she would've entered.
"Caroline," offered William, "hasn't been here. Nobody but us has."
They exited through the back door and out of the house on the common. Minutes later, they snuck into the back of the church just as the congregation moved from standing to sitting.

House on the Common, Cold Springs
Caroline walked toward town on Monday morning. She'd been unwilling to believe what the boys told her during their short visit yesterday after church. They didn't have enough time to check the whole house out. She was grateful that they used their thirty minutes of free time to see her. They'd been grounded after lying to their parents and Assistant Chief Chevalier when she'd been kidnapped. Her walk to the town common felt longer than a mile and, in the late morning heat, tougher than normal.
She needed to get away, so she left the house shortly after her father headed off to Boston for the day. Caroline promised Daniel's mother she would have lunch with her and stay at their house until her father returned from Boston.
As she walked in the heat, she simmered in anger. The world nursed a continent-sized grudge against her. Her father had been distracted. Divorce and the breakup of the band had sucked the life out of him. She could not even focus on her mother. Each time she tried to sort through the clown car full of rotting emotions dancing around her head, her brain ground to a halt. Allyssa had dropped off the face of the planet. Caroline overheard the lawyers talking with her father, and they needed to know her mother's plans. Would she eventually come home, want Caroline to live with her, want to divorce? Each question

spawned another chance to upend her life and spin her further off her axis. But Allyssa disappeared with Niles, and until her mother blazed back into her life, nothing could happen.

She made it all the way down Old Enfield Road and crossed Berkshire County Route 9, stopping only to look over the small bridge railing above Jabish Brook. Now at the edge of the common, she noticed all the businesses on both sides of the common were open. People moved up and down the sidewalks. A group of elementary school kids crossed Jabish Street. Summer campers dropped stakes in the middle school program. Some of them held homemade kites created from green, red, yellow, and blue tissue paper glued to sticks.

As she walked past the rec center, a wail of despair echoed across the street. She glanced back to see a boy holding the two pieces of his now-crashed kite, the striped one. Too bad, she thought, that one had pizzazz.

Finally, she stood at the side door of her old house on the common. In five minutes, she could prove to herself what happened and then move on. That was it. Take the possibility of being here off the table.

The side door opened easily today since the boys had used it for their exit. It banged shut behind her as she stepped into the house on the common. Nothing moved. Only a few more steps to nab her answer. If the room looked like the boys described, then she'd be forced to accept that they were right, and she'd never been here. By "they," she meant everyone that she'd told her story to over the last week. A terrifying prospect, which implied that what her brain told her happened—did not.

Caroline moved into the barren living room area. Just like the boys said, dust blanketed the floor. Cobwebs stretched between the stained-glass windows. She had *not* been here. Her shoulders relaxed unbidden. A boogieman didn't burst out of the closet and attack her as her memories told her because she had never been here. She ventured farther into the house, heading slowly toward the back of the house where the shapeless monster thing had attacked. She could bury the image as a nightmare, or as Father Bequette called it a coping mechanism. He'd told her that her brain didn't know how to react to

Dumont and shut down. The brain, being a wonderfully efficient and imaginative machine, spun up and created images she could understand and react to. Her brain kept her from seeing the brutal reality of her encounter with Dumont. William had told her that Dumont had said, 'Leave her alone,' while beating Daniel. And those words made no sense at all. Why would Dumont ask Daniel to leave her alone if Dumont did horrible things to her? Just as importantly, the question nobody had asked: *What the hell was Dumont doing in The Dale in the first place?*

Either way, her brain did its job and protected her. Certain of the truth now, she could walk back to her home, knowing that beyond any doubt, she was with Dumont. The horror in the house on the common existed as an illusion. Just an element of her mind trying to protect her.

She looked into the room, about to turn and leave when something caught her eye. It lay in the corner just out of reach of a beam of sunlight streaming in. Caroline looked again as curiosity turned to uneasiness, and uneasiness morphed into the first shivers of dread, which shimmied their way up her spine. Another pace in, and the hair on the back of her neck stood up in a full-scale five-alarm blaze of terror. She took a sharp breath in and held it with her hand clamped hard against her open mouth.

Deep in the far corner of the empty room sat a pink sneaker. Her sneaker. The one lost somewhere during the ordeal in The Dale.

She'd been here *and* the Dale—impossible. Everything she thought she knew was wrong. Everything she wanted to believe was also wrong.

She screamed.

Five

Cold Springs
July 1985

CAROLINE REMEMBERED SEEING THE sneaker and screaming. Then, she burst out of the house in a terrified sprint. Her dash across the common scattered the children gathered there, then through traffic before being caught by Assistant Chief Chevalier on the steps of the library. Next, days of confusion and embarrassment overwhelmed her. Everyone in town must've known what had happened. She hid in her room again and refused to come out. There was no way she could logically reconcile being found in The Dale and finding her pink sneaker in the house on the common. The house, truly a mystery, existed as the place that had pulled the ultimate magic trick by putting her in two places at once. A hoax, she hoped. The house could not pull it off a third time—at least she didn't think it could.

Assistant Chief Chevalier had taken her to the station to call her father, who, of course, was in Boston. Her memory of running stayed cloudy, but he'd said she'd had a near miss with a car as she ran into traffic. He'd calmed her down, and she'd told him everything. Everything about the boys going to the house of the common, her insistence on going again, not remembering The Dale or Henry Lee Dumont, and most importantly, the sneaker she'd left at the house on the common. In the absence of her father, she knew that Assistant Chief Chevalier would help her. After she'd fallen asleep on his couch, he'd gone back to the house to investigate. He'd said her sneaker was not there. It's not as if she thought Chevalier would lie, but maybe he'd missed her sneaker.

She wanted to go another round with the house to find the pink sneaker Chevalier hadn't seen. William refused to come with her and Daniel. He'd fought with them and argued until he'd stormed out of her house and vowed that if there was a funeral, he would not go. She never imagined a day in which William would tell her no. Or even mildly disagree with her. But he'd raged ferociously and nearly came to blows with Daniel over it. That she had seen before. William and Daniel would take their aggression out on each other all the time. Daniel's powerful muscles battled William's blinding speed to an even draw most times. The agreement they kept was no face punches. That way parents wouldn't question the bruises.

But, she decided, one more round with the house, a round that did not end with her either miles away in the middle of the woods or running away screaming, *had* to happen. This round required her to leave freely when *she* wanted. Anything else, she thought, would trap her in the same miserable status quo. Unfortunately, it would happen without William.

At least he promised not to tell anyone.

Daniel walked silently beside her. The house looked the same this afternoon as it had on the other occasions she'd been there. This time, the town common lay empty, baking in the late summer air. They dropped their bikes at the side of the house. Daniel lifted the back window and slipped into the dark basement. Caroline waited close to the side door of the house, not wanting anyone to notice them hanging around. She was not as calm as she imagined she would be, and after Daniel did not return quickly, the first drops of sweat dampened her skin.

The door opened, and Caroline stepped back. Blood rolled down the side of Daniel's head. "I bumped it in the basement. Am I bleeding badly?"

"You're not gushing." She reached up and stanched a runnel of the wet, sticky blood on his cheek with a rag she had pulled from her backpack. "Let's go," she said as she pushed past him into the house.

Daniel followed her through the house, feeling woozy. He thought he cracked his skull against a low-hanging beam in the basement, but it was so dark down there he wasn't sure. The flashbulb like impact left him unsteady. The drip-drip-drip of his blood hitting the concrete floor of the cellar focused him. But seeing Caroline standing at the door almost as if she anticipated a ghost, while telling herself she wasn't, troubled him. Her face twisted into something ugly at the sight of his bulging, bleeding goose egg. But like a flash of electricity in the summer sky, her compassion evaporated. He expected her to be a little gentler when she compressed the cut. He acted heroically. Now he's the hero, right? He grabbed her hand to guide her, but she wriggled free and moved in front of him.

They ventured deeper into the unnervingly still house. The front room sat on the left of the side entrance, and she practically stormed in before stopping in the middle of the huge living room that dominated this section. There were four sets of footprints: his, William's, Caroline's, and Chevalier, which were far bigger than any of theirs. No fifth set, which would have been Caroline's if she had been there twice. He stayed one step behind her as she moved out of the dining room and to the sunroom that faced the common. The thick dirt and grime-marred glass prevented them from seeing anything outside. Ancient, faded red carpet, worn down to the nap in the middle, covered most of the room. Caroline gave him a tour of her memories. This was the room where she had played house with a room full of dolls, her favorite a cowgirl, then a toy box full of Barbie dolls. She turned and marched into the living room, looking back at the front door.

Caroline sighed and said, "The room is exactly like I remembered from my last disastrous visit." Then, she wandered to the back room, and Daniel stood so close they touched. He wanted to comfort the anguish clearly stamped on her face.

"This," Caroline waved her hands, "it's nothing more than an old, vacant, dusty square." Daniel remained silent and puzzled by her outburst. Her footprints were there and nothing more. No pink sneaker. He felt her anger well up as she turned and threw open the closet to reveal nothing.

"Ready to go?" Daniel shoved his hands in his pockets, knowing she wouldn't want him to touch her.

"I am going upstairs first."

He nodded, and they walked up to the second floor. The stairs creaked as they went. Like the first floor, the second remained silent and empty, except...

"Stinks up here," she giggled.

"Like an elephant barfed up a skunk," added Daniel thoughtfully. At least the awful stink broke the tension between them.

William's promise to keep quiet lasted about an hour. In terms of teenage promises and secrets, an hour might have been a world record. Worry gnawed at his gut. Worrying about the possibilities of the day, the largest and most painful thought orbited around his worry over losing his friend forever. Equally balancing that fear, his anger bubbled. Daniel, his best friend, knew the stakes, and he did not stop her.

William's mother had gently explained how Chevalier had rescued Caroline from darting into oncoming traffic. His mother also explained his most important job as her friend was to protect her from herself and destructive impulses. A medical professional had examined Caroline and felt she needed psychiatric care. Her father had refused. But if anything else pushed her over the edge, it might be out of the hands of Caroline's father. Daniel knew this and still took her to the house on the common.

As he sat at the lunch table with his mother and father, the words held back by a cocktail of pride and malice gushed out of him.

His father listened to the whole story and then looked thoughtful for a moment. He spoke aloud but seemed to be talking to himself when he asked why John Sullivan couldn't send someone else to Boston so he could focus on his daughter.

"How long?" his father barked, and William realized the question was for him.

"Long enough to get there," replied William.

"Good lord," snapped his father. "Get into the BMW." William briefly wondered why his father never said *car* or *station wagon*. Always *BMW* or *Ford*. He always referred to the brand names. William walked out of the house but turned back to see his father pick up the phone and dial.

William sat in the front passenger seat of the BMW as his father drove toward the common. They said nothing. Caroline would know he had failed to keep her secret. It was the right thing to do; he knew. William hoped that both she and Daniel would understand. Whether or not they did, he knew he'd done the right thing. Even knowing he did the right thing didn't clear the cloud of dread that encircled him.

William and his father pulled up behind the police cruisers, and he could not for the life of him figure out why the policemen were there. He went to open the car door, but his father grabbed his arm.

"I have to go help," he cried.

"You're better than that," replied his father, his voice cold and empty. William sat stunned. He had never heard his father say something like that about either of his friends, other people sure, but not Daniel or Caroline. His father's grip held him, and he stared at William intensely. William sunk into the passenger seat and realized his father was not here to help; he came here to watch the tragedy.

House on the Common

Caroline had enough, and now she wanted to leave. She wished William would come with them to see this, to allow his worry to fall apart like hers. Maybe her brain did her a favor by shielding her from what happened with Dumont. She could deal with this place. Just a house full of empty rooms and dying memories, not haunted or evil. She took Daniel's hand, smiled, and moved down the steps toward the door.

They were at the door and ready to leave when Caroline had a thought. She hadn't gone down into the basement. It was creepy enough when she lived here that she didn't go down into the dark, damp basement. The deep guts of the house, she thought, did not project to be a bright and welcoming place. Even as she let go of Daniel's hand, she felt a shimmer of hesitation, but she knew she needed to take the last step. Just a house, she reassured herself, a house where she had some of the best times of her life, wasn't it?

After two steps into the darkness, Caroline felt afraid. She remembered that there were six creaking steps. She willed her feet to move through the final three and waited a minute before moving again. Her eyes needed to get better acclimated to the darkness, and as they did, she moved downward. With her next step, she expected to find the floor but did not. Her foot found nothing but a black void, and into this void, she fell.

In a heap on the floor, Caroline gathered herself. Seven creaking steps, not six, she thought while rubbing her knee. Daniel stood in the doorway. He started down when he heard her fall.

"I'm okay, just stay up there." Rattled and sore, Caroline stood up. She needed to do the last part alone. The basement looked like all old basements, dim and dusty. She made her way toward the back of the cellar. Just a few quick steps, she thought nervously, and she would be out of the house. She wanted to touch the wall on the far side of the basement and then turn back.

She never made it.

In the corner, something moved. Through the gloom, near the old coal furnace, Caroline noticed a shape glide to the far corner. The basement brightened in a soft yellow glow. Caroline moved closer, and the shape revealed itself to be a girl. Younger than she and dressed in a child's clothes. A slight whimper escaped her lips.

The glow around this girl intensified slightly as the girl turned and sat up; her eyes blinked twice before staring at Caroline.

The small girl with short hair appeared just like Caroline at seven years old. The young girl held a doll made of cotton. She looked puzzled at first, then her expression morphed into one of fear.

Caroline gasped and tried to take a step back, but once again, the house locked her in place. The girl held up the doll so Caroline could see the ragged hole in the center. The girl's lips moved, and a sound came from her. The girl's words were garbled. After a few moments, the words finally settled into a pattern Caroline understood. As the girl spoke, Caroline could see the edges around the hole in the doll were seared black. Even the doll's fluffy inner stuffing had been scorched.

"It will take the whole thing now," she whimpered.

"Take what?" Caroline wasn't sure that she wanted to know. The girl grimaced in pain. Caroline saw the blackness that a second ago occupied only the edges of the hole at the doll's center now spread out behind a thin line of a crackling red heat until the figure grew all black. Then, the doll flared a bit, and the fabric turned to ash, falling through her small fingers as it did.

"Drop it," was the only thing Caroline could think to say, but it was too late. "Drop it now." The girl's arms began to turn black, and they dropped to her sides, resigned to her fate.

"Siege, Caroline. It's a siege." The rest of her skin turned oily black. Like the doll, she flared briefly into a bright white flame, then to ash. The basement grew dim again, and glowing motes of the girl floated in the space in front of her like fireflies.

Caroline stood in the basement watching. She was wrong and William was right; she should never have come back to this house. Whatever lured her here now snared her with a sure grip and would never give up. She caught her breath and shut her eyes hard before attempting to steel herself against the evil haunting this house.

Evil lived here, and she had to do something about it. Caroline had prepared in case the trip to the house went badly. She pulled her backpack off and dropped it to the floor and reached in to grab what she needed to stop this house from taking her. Several rags came out first, and she stuffed them into a pile of wood, paper, and other debris near the furnace. Next, she rummaged around the backpack and grabbed the can of liquid her dad used all the time and would notice if this can was missing too long.

"Caroline!" She heard Daniel's panicked shout but did not answer. "Do you need more time?" She ignored him.

Caroline heard the pounding on the side door where Daniel stood and could almost feel vibrations from the pounding of a fist.

"Chevalier's here," yelled Daniel. Silence.

"What is that smell?" Daniel bellowed, his voice filling the crevices of the room. "I locked the door when I saw him and now it won't open. Caroline, get back up here!" She could no longer block out his frantic voice.

She took out a box of matches and then dropped it into the darkness. Daniel continued yelling at Chevalier that he couldn't get the lock open. That disappointed Caroline, but it changed nothing that would happen. The chessboard was set, and the outcome decided. She groped around the floor for the box and found it. The first match she struck flamed out and ignited nothing. Same with the second. Finally, she grabbed several and struck them all together. Without hesitation, she dropped the matches on the pile of rags and debris soaked in lighter fluid. The smell, bitter and sharp in the enclosed space, left her gagging.

The lighter fluid did its job, and flames crackled to life, burning the rags first before igniting the pile of wood underneath. Caroline felt the euphoria of victory surge through her, and she watched the flames move off the pile of debris she had created and lick at the basement rafters, which were dry and tinder-like after a hot summer. She turned up the stairs. The first step broke when she put her weight on it. Reaching up with her right leg to reach the second step, it broke too. This time shards of wood slashed her leg, and she fell to the ground; the flames were everywhere now. The house, she thought, fought back. As the heat from the fire began to burn her back, she tried for the third step, and it broke. The fire did not have a preference either way; it would take them both. She wanted to live but recoiled at begging the house for mercy.

House on the Common, Cold Springs

William bounced his knee against his hand, furious, and, after a few seconds, decided that he would not stay in the BMW. He would not sit by and do nothing. When his father reached to turn on the radio, he bolted out of the car and headed toward the house. He made it to the side of the house and could see Chevalier pulling on the knob with all of his might and Daniel Wilson pushing forward. The window in the door had a crack but was not yet shattered. From the basement windows, he saw a flash of light, then a pall of smoke welled up, blotting out his view of Daniel.

At the same time, the door broke free, sending Chevalier flying backward when the knob broke off. William could see Chevalier as he fell, a look of utter astonishment on his face, as smoke poured out of the now open door.

Chevalier had lost his balance and hit the back of his head on the ground hard enough to knock him out. William thought he should stop but moved past the assistant police chief to the rear basement window of the house. William ran past the unconscious police chief. Chevalier was on the ground with the doorknob in his right hand. He knew from Daniel's yells that Caroline must still be down there. He opened the window they had used to get into the house less than a week ago. He had exactly half a second to feel good when the backdraft thumped him hard. The suction from the imbalance in the air pressure when the window opened yanked him the rest of the way into the basement.

All he could think about was Caroline trapped in the basement. The fire flared up and covered a quarter of the basement. He could see she had no direction to escape the raging fire. William staggered to his feet and moved toward her. She stumbled to close the gap to him.

The movement caused William to crack his head on a low-hanging beam. He went down hard but refused to let the fire, this house, or whatever else was working against them, kill them. Summoning whatever inner strength he had left, William rolled over onto his back and then flipped back up to his feet. Without words or ceremony, William grabbed Caroline roughly and dragged her to the window. The smoke hung heavily, and the fire blazed, getting hotter, so hot he thought he might already be on fire. The fire left just enough light to see the open window through the heavy gagging smoke, and he pushed her through. William vaulted up and out right behind her, rolling onto the grass just a few feet from the burning house.

When Caroline stood up, William noticed she didn't look right. Something was wrong with her. She was not reacting to the black soot covering her or her smoking shirt. She turned toward him, and he could see it. Her eyes were wide open and manic, and she giggled frantically. William could barely breathe after being in the punishing basement fire for less than thirty seconds. She'd been down there for a lot longer, and she was practically doing somersaults.

A loud, harsh, whooshing sound chased the unnaturally long howl of despair from Caroline's direction. Her face changed again, drowning in anguish with the same irrational fury he'd seen in the eyes of Henry Lee Dumont in The Dale.

Caroline glared at the gush of water with a feral expression that scared William. His eyes darted to the house as a cloud of steam boiled up from it.

"No! Nooo! Noooooooooo!" Caroline screamed as she kicked a flaming piece of wood knocked off the house with the first blast of the fire hose.

"It has to burn! I need it to burn! It has to buuurrrrn!" Caroline's voice hit a high-pitched peak and then trailed off as she grabbed the previously burning piece of wood and rushed the firefighters. William surged forward to intercept her, but Daniel got there first.

"What did you do, William?" yelled Daniel as he grabbed onto Caroline and used his thick, muscular body to pin her down. The smoldering wood dropped out of her hand and into the grass. She wormed her way toward it in vain. Daniel caught a puff of her perfume through the acrid smell of the smoke.

"You did this!" William lunged at him but stopped. Daniel realized William could not hit him without striking Caroline.

"You told!" Daniel screamed, pushing away the guilt of bringing Caroline to the breaking point.

"You didn't listen," William yelled at him. "She started this place on fire! Why didn't you just leave it alone?" Tears of rage streamed down William's face.

Daniel knew William was right and hated him for it. Caroline had ceased to be herself. The look on her face and the way she'd stretched out the back end of the word *burn* seemed to be the shattering of her sanity. The fault for the consequences she would suffer landed squarely on his shoulders. Someone else pulled Caroline away from them. Daniel resisted for a second until he saw they were paramedics. Another bloodcurdling howl from Caroline helped things along for Daniel.

Daniel could not control his regret, and the blame in William's eyes sent him over the edge. There were no words to be spoken. Almost simultaneously, they swung at each other. No longer cautious or holding back. He wanted to knock him out. William was swinging just as hard as he was, some connecting with flesh, others cutting through the air. They rolled around on the ground between the firemen, police, and paramedics, all of whom were trying to do their jobs as they fought. Grunting and swearing, Daniel's seething anger burned as intensely as William's, encompassing everything that had built up; things unfinished, things in the woods, and things in this cursed house fueled them.

Daniel's rage peaked at the same time as the fire in the house, which had rallied one last time. Even adults pulling them apart did not stop him—because it was not over. Wayward punches hit both Chevalier, who made his way to his feet and back into the battle, and William's father, who had left the BMW. Daniel's shame kept him swinging, unaware and heedless of the consequences, still raging at William over Henry Lee Dumont, The Dale, and the agony in the torrid screams of their friend, the death roar of the fire, and the shattering of their small, priceless fellowship of three.

Dr. David Nash argued with Father Andre Bequette across the street from the still burning house on the common. He came at the priest far too hot, but Bequette had failed, and David decided that the priest did not want to admit it. Their egos could hold up to some criticism. "You should have told me she had not progressed. At least I should have known about her disastrous visit to this house."

"It," replied the priest hotly, "has only been a few days."

Nash's chest burned in anger. "It happened *last week*. I only know about this because Chevalier called to tell me. Which is something *you needed to do*." He had made a mistake conceding counseling to Father Bequette. They both used the same process, the only difference being faith. And in this case, Bequette clearly failed. Faith did not matter. The mental state of the girl did.

When Chevalier called him last week, he nearly intervened. Instead, he trusted Bequette, something he'd done countless times before. But he worried his closeness to the family would interfere. Caroline never reached out to Bequette or her father. "Instead of a qualified professional like you or me, she reached out to her two best friends."

"And you never saw that coming," snapped Father Bequette.

The retort only angered him further. "That's not fair."

Bequette stormed away and then immediately turned back. "There may be more to this."

Nash hated the thought. His temper flared "Admit it, Andre! You have failed this girl."

"I counseled her as we agreed to."

"No, when she started displaying signs of instability—which you should have recognized—you needed to reach out to me! But your ego wasn't ready for failure, and you ignored it."

"*I did not.*"

"You didn't see the breakdown coming, and you were too arrogant to admit it. Even now. She is on her way to the psychiatric ward."

"A week with you might help her," admitted Bequette. "But you need to open your eyes as well."

Bequette had pushed all his chips in on one extraordinarily remote possibility. "I see clearly here, Andre. She needs help you can't give her. I will deal with this from here."

It was Dr. David Nash's turn to storm away from his friend and colleague. With any luck, when both of their tempers cooled, they could talk this out. Nash walked to his car and headed back toward the psychiatric hospital just a mile down the road from the common. While he drove, he realized that he had no idea if Bequette would see it his way. They'd never disagreed on a case.

Six

Pediatric Psychiatric Ward
Cold Springs, Massachusetts
May 1987

FATHER ANDRE BEQUETTE SAT and did not speak. The Catholic priest watched Caroline draw on a sheet of paper. She should be a sophomore in high school. Instead, she rotted here under the care of Dr. David Nash.

He and David Nash worked together for over a decade in his office as exorcist. David, an atheist and exceptional psychiatrist, had been the perfect partner in his job. David examined and treated patients who had 'come to the attention of the diocese.' In all but a few of those cases, he had diagnosed each patient with some form of mental illness or incapacity. Bequette supported the patient theologically and Nash medically.

It worked since almost always the problems that faced these patients were of a psychological nature.

Only twice over ten years and across the entire northeastern quadrant of the United States had they encountered something darker, malevolent, and evil. Nash left the first of those cases to him, Bishop Martin, and Father Gene Wright. On that night he waited in the kitchen of the farmhouse, comforting the family of a young father who had lost his faith and then lost his way. They faced the unspeakable and walked out victorious.

Bequette's first act after the exorcism had been to open a bottle of red wine and pour glasses. It was their ninth time in his forty years in the office facing the supernatural, but only the first with Dr. David Nash.

The other case ended their friendship and their professional working relationship. When once they had worked seamlessly together to determine the course of action, in one case they could find no common ground.

The girl in front of him, Caroline Sullivan, divided them. Dr. David Nash insisted that her mind fractured into schizophrenia. Bequette believed she had been possessed after the twin trauma of her parents' ugly divorce and her subsequent kidnapping by Henry Lee Dumont. Their disagreement over her care came to a head after Caroline nearly burned the house on the common to the ground.

Dr. Nash committed her on an initial seven-day hold on the day of her meltdown on the common. He insisted what she saw in the basement had been a hallucination and she needed a different kind of care. Bequette agreed but wanted her to be able to return to school in September to start ninth grade.

Caroline spiraled despite his and Nash's best efforts, and she did not even make it until Columbus Day. Her principal suspended her three times: once for insubordination, the second time for trashing a classroom and destruction of property, and finally, for an incident with a razor in which she slashed a fellow student. She hadn't meant to, but that did not matter.

Each incident divided him and David further; David's once charming arrogance flared, and his own stubbornness hardened until they no longer spoke.

The evening of the slashing incident Caroline came to his office for counseling. He'd broken through her defenses and briefly saw the face of the evil infesting her. Dr. David Nash burst into his rectory office with Assistant Chief of Police Glen Chevalier and personnel from the pediatric psychiatric ward and took her into custody.

Caroline Sullivan hadn't left the facility since and had only worsened.

Now, without the support of Dr. Nash, he could only come here and work with her under the terms of her care.

Father Andre Bequette returned his thoughts to the present and looked on, fascinated by the lengths Caroline would go to antagonize him. Bequette studied her careful strokes as she penciled the edges of her picture. A villainous smile crept across her face as she worked. Once she had the outline and shading done, she added details.

The Sunday afternoon summer breeze ruffled the dark curtains enough that a brief beam of light penetrated the dark room. The only other light in her room, on the third floor of the pediatric psychiatric ward, came from a lamp with a skull print on the shade.

"Almost done," she said cheerfully.

"Outstanding," said Bequette. But the priest knew there would be no actual cheer once the girl had finished. Her attempts to drive him away were as relentless as they were predictable. Caroline's regression under Dr. Nash had been evident after almost two years here in the psychiatric ward. In his mind, he saw her as a collapsing supernova star. The once-promising girl was brilliant and bright but now a core of stellar mass collapsing on itself. The gravity, as he said once to Dr. Nash, or pull of her self-hatred, which hauled her down and inward, could lead to only one ultimate end—a child lost. A lifetime in the psychiatric ward. A life of spectacular promise destroyed.

He prayed each night for a miracle. Perhaps the laugh was enough of a moment, a cry for help. It would be an angle he could use.

Bequette suspected the source of her problem. Nash could not help her solve this problem. He also suspected where the problem originated. But he could not prove his theory. He simply had to wait for an opportunity to help her further. An opportunity, he thought, which would not come if she lived in the psychiatric ward in the care of David. Bequette steamed at the thought. His eyes scanned her room and settled on her long-term pebble project. Each day she went outside during her exercise time and aimed to find the perfect small stone or pebble for the day. Once back inside, she'd glue it next to the previous pebble. She marked the days with those stones, but it did little to help her leave the ward.

"Done," she said and interrupted his train of thought.

Caroline jabbed the paper at him upside down. Bequette had to turn it over. "A coffin," he observed blankly. Not only a coffin, but one with his name scrawled across the top. The crucifix on the cover of the coffin—inverted.

"Hope you like it," Caroline said as she focused on his face in search of a reaction.

Bequette refused to let her see anything. Bequette tilted his head and stared at the image, gray, white, and black, on the page. "I need your pen," he said to her and held out his hand.

Caroline did not respond immediately. Bequette did not move his hand nor change the blank expression on his face. Caroline blinked once, and then curiosity took over. She handed him a black pen.

"Thanks. I see you have studied St. Peter," he said. She attempted to watch as he scribbled alterations to her coffin. He shielded his changes with an exaggerated turn of his body.

Bequette took his time. Caroline peeked over his shoulder, and Bequette turned away.

"Done," he said, and then turned the paper back over so she could not see his work as he handed it back.

Caroline flipped it over. He'd stretched out her lines and made the coffin cartoonishly bigger.

"I'm fat," he said, "the only thing you can fit in that coffin is a horse jockey or a couple of Schrödinger's house cats."

Caroline giggled. Her eyes sparkled, and her cheeks flushed red. For the shortest fraction of a second, she had come to the surface and existed as she had been before The Dale, the house on the common, or Henry Lee Dumont. Caroline Sullivan, the starburst, broke through and glowed bright. Then, as fast as she had returned, that relic of hers disappeared, and in her place came something wicked. A malevolence he'd only been exposed to briefly once or twice before. Each time so fleeting, he could have easily imagined it.

Now he saw it for sure. Bequette, through a little unexpected joke, the antithesis of the anger that roiled just under the surface of the girl, scored a direct hit. He gave her joy. And now, whatever malevolence held her soul flashed back and roared at him in its fury. Her face darkened, eyebrows arched, and narrowed into pure feral wickedness. Joy was not allowed. Bequette did not flinch. Nor did he allow his focus to leave her face. They locked eyes until the priest eventually stared her down. "I know who you are," he said. The words were loud and bold. "And you don't get to have her." His head ached at the pressure.

The malevolence said nothing in return. As if it had accepted the challenge and went back to work.

Caroline blinked, and the malevolence vanished from her face. Vanished, thought the priest, but not gone. The girl who drew the coffin occupied her face, the manifestation of schizophrenia and the host of disorders that Dr. Nash ascribed to her. Caroline turned her back on him and rose to sit on her bed. She opened a book and read it aloud.

He listened to her as she moved from page to page. Caroline purposefully ignored him. Yet, he did not leave. He would not exit her room on her terms since they were not actually hers. Something else infested her soul and burdened her. Leaving at this moment would mean abandoning her. The fraction of a second of joy would be costly to her.

Bequette knew what he had just seen, and he would stay for a while. Occasionally, she stumbled over a word. The priest did not correct her; rather, he sat and listened. She read for over an hour. Eventually, she stopped, now tired, and laid her head on her pillow.

The room was quiet again.

Bequette listened to her breathing to settle into a slow rhythm, then he stood up and left. Caroline's infestation required intercession. He would need to take the next step, and Dr. David Nash could be damned for all he cared. By the end of the day, he could have made progress.

He thought about speaking to Dr. Nash but declined; a waste, he thought, and then left the building.

Dr. David Nash dragged his bone-tired feet to the first floor exit from the psychiatric wing. The afternoon shift had been murder, and the relief nurse came in two hours…no, he corrected himself, two hours and seventeen minutes late. He covered the two hours until the relief nurse arrived. He ensured that the relief knew how he felt.

Father Andre Bequette had visited her, and Caroline had pounded on the door of her room for over an hour after he left. It was long past time he refused his former friend and colleague access to the girl. Bequette believed her problem was one of the soul, not of the mind.

But that was something for another time. He wanted to go home and crawl into bed. 1:35 am. The number rumbled across his tired mind. The head of psychiatry, and now, he thought, back-up nurse, came to a stop when his outstretched left hand hit the stainless-steel door handle and slipped off, skidding up the cold glass of the exterior door of the main lobby.

Clink.

He looked down, realizing the nursing station master key still hung from his neck. Damn, he thought, knowing he had to go back upstairs and drop it off at the station. Without it, the overnight nurse would not be able to lock down the floor or either door, which led to the wing. He had left in a huff and now faced the embarrassment of not being all that nice to the girl who relieved him. He had to do the walk of shame and give her the key.

Dr. David Nash turned around and trudged his way back to the stairs and worked his way up the flights of stairs to the third floor. Their station was empty, but he could hear something scuffling down the hallway near the last room. Dr. Nash dropped the key onto the station counter as he passed on the outside of the station and moved toward the sound.

The overnight nurse shuffled uneasily back toward him.

"Dr. Nash?"

Helen, the overnight nurse, looked back at him, horrified.

"She's not in her room."

"Who?" he replied, knowing it did not matter which patient was missing, no, not missing, briefly unaccounted for, he reassured himself.

"The Sullivan girl."

"I've been gone five minutes, Helen," snapped Dr. David Nash.

"Check every room," he said, suddenly far less tired than he was a second ago, directing Helen with a slightly calmer voice. "I'll call downstairs." Helen did not move, and Dr. Nash knew why. He knew what she was worried about. "It's rainy outside. She won't even try to leave here," he said. Helen nodded and pushed through the doors from the wing to the primary hospital and vanished.

Alone, Nash whisked away from the station, quickly checking each room that Helen had already checked. The doors were locked from the outside, so all he had to do was turn the handle and peek inside.

Once he realized Caroline was not in any room there, he ran back to the nursing station, picked up the phone, and dialed security. They picked up on the second ring.

"This is Dr. David Nash, head of psychiatry, at the third-floor nursing station—we have an unaccounted-for patient..." Then he glanced and saw it.

Not only was the girl gone but so was the master key.

Dr. David Nash steeled himself and prepared for the worst. Nobody could find the Sullivan girl. He worked his way down the service stairs at the back of the ward. The nurses and every available person on the night shift had been searching for her for over twenty minutes. The entire psychiatric wing had been locked down. Worse yet, if anything happened to the girl, it could be pinned on him. He had been the one who left the master key on the nursing station counter.

Even once they found the girl, they could not be certain of getting her to go into her room. She had no power, he thought, other than the power to deny his requests. And she used that power, fighting even the smallest request from anyone in the building and was legendary in the annals of patients who resisted restraints. She broke restraint straps with ease and not only the bones of the orderlies tasked to get her back into the room but also her own. Those breaks never seemed to hurt her as badly as anyone else.

He made it to the bottom of the stairwell and checked the steel door leading to the outside of the hospital.

Dr. David Nash never actually saw her.

Instead, Nash followed her after he turned a corner and stopped in front of the first-floor maintenance room door—the one two steps from a secluded exit from the building. The same loud voice, which also told him when to take a second look at the intersection before driving, practically screamed at him to turn the handle of the maintenance room door. It should be locked.

It was not.

The door opened.

Caroline stood inside with a flat expression on her pretty little face. Beautiful and evil, he thought. She stood back in the far corner of the nearly dark L-shaped room. Dr. David Nash considered turning around and yelling at the top of his lungs until help came. The thought died when he realized there were no lights on in the room. The shape moved and split in two. One of the dark humanoid shadows turned itself into a fifteen-year-old girl, and the other dissolved away.

Nash stared at a spot right in front of Caroline Sullivan. There, in front of her, a tight, glowing, diamond-shaped exhaust glowed blue in front of her. Caroline Sullivan had found a propane torch, lit it, and now advanced toward Nash. The hot blue flame twinkled brightly in the young girl's eyes.

Dr. David Nash realized he was the only thing between Sullivan and the steel door leading to the outside world. Caroline had stolen the master key from the top of the nursing station counter—she could go anywhere she wanted if she got by him. His heart hammered off his ribs as he realized she had trapped him.

It was him. He had to keep the girl from getting out of the building.

"Stop," offered Nash. He willed the growing terror out of his voice and rammed authority into it.

"Get out of the way." Caroline all but growled her words.

The torch hissed a scorching blue between them and Dr. David Nash wondered just how badly he wanted to get between Caroline and freedom.

"It's late, Caroline."

Then the girl turned to her left and moved the flame toward some steel shelving. The shelving housed at least a dozen propane canisters.

"Do you think this gets hot enough to set one of these off?" Caroline asked as she moved the flame to the canisters. The hot blue flame licked against one of the green steel canisters.

Nash licked his dry lips and took a deep breath. His legs weakened as Caroline grazed the flame over the other propane. His mind screamed at him to move back and leave this alone; let her go. He stood frozen in place, unable to even take a single step back. His eyes stared no longer at her but at the blazing fire heating up the canisters of propane. Nash closed his eyes and gritted his teeth, waiting for a white-hot flash ending to everything.

After a second, he opened them, stunned to be alive. The flame flickered against the propane cylinder for a moment before unexpectedly changing from an angry blue color to an increasingly yellow one. It flickered some more, flared reddish-orange before dying altogether as the last of the propane in the tank burned away to nothing.

Caroline glanced back and forth between the fading red glow of the metal end of the torch and him standing in the doorway. As he stood marveling at his good luck, Caroline launched herself at him, knocking him to the ground with almost no effort at all. Once on the ground, Sullivan swept the hot end of the torch, searing Nash's shoulder as it streaked by. He groaned in agony.

Sullivan made it to the door and had the key in the handle when security showed up en masse. Nash rolled over and dragged himself up to his knees and spit out blood pooling in the bottom of his mouth and attempted to gasp for air.

The Sullivan girl, barely a hundred pounds and not even five-foot-tall, held three burly men at bay with whirling arms and sharp elbows. He watched the brutal, grinding, and dirty affair, his shoulder flaring in pain as the adrenaline rush receded.

They secured the girl. Now simply five feet of dark, deep, guttural cries, whirling arms, and pointed knees. Her tearing metal-pitched screams left Dr. David Nash's blood frozen like lace in his veins. And as they dragged her away, the realization Caroline was screaming for him crept up from behind, punching him in the gut. Kicking and fighting the men, Sullivan's head poked out from the flurry of arms and legs, her eyes boring right through him, begging Nash to save her.

He gathered himself after they dragged her away. He knew one thing: Caroline Sullivan would never be able to rejoin the normal world. He promised himself to never let her leave the psychiatric ward.

Seven

The Pediatric Psychiatric Ward
Cold Springs, Massachusetts
Spring 1988

D R. DAVID NASH HURRIED from the parking lot to the front entrance of Cold Springs Hospital. A large, three-story red brick main building with its front entrance grandly adorned with four imposing Doric pillars. The pillars rose from the ground and supported a wonderful white triangular pediment. Under the pediment, a double door led to the main lobby of the administration building.

The left wing of the building housed a small hospital and an even smaller emergency room. The right side housed the pediatric psychiatric wing of the facility. The only long-term psychiatric care facility for pediatric patients in western Massachusetts. Deep inside the building, senior staff members waited for him to begin the morning meeting. They, he knew, would not start without him. He was in charge.

He corrected himself, *in command*. It's the term he preferred. Command. He had never served in the military; indeed, he found the thought of it distasteful. However, the idea of command was something to be savored. Lots of people under him oversaw something.

But command was something different.

Dr. Nash had almost made it to the glassy entrance when he heard the distinct sound of an object smashing onto concrete. Something, he realized, was happening in the psychiatric ward. Moving toward the sound, he saw quite a few things littering the ground. Then, another something whistled out of the window and clattered to the ground. It was an appalling sight, and it needed to stop. He could see now the objects that had been flung out into space were from the last room, the one on the corner, on the third floor. Venturing closer, he could hear the distinct sound of paper ripping. A soft *plunk* as a poster, fluttering in the air, hit the ground in two pieces.

"Hey!" he yelled up to the window. Nobody responded. Instead, a book spun out of the window, smacking the ground near him. He did not need to get a verbal reply to know who was chucking things out the window. Nor was it the first time anything had been ejected from that particular window. "I'll lock that shut."

Dr. David Nash resisted the urge to simply ignore the obvious, attention-seeking behavior. The Sullivan girl did not seem to ever track toward leaving the hospital. The trend was to move patients away and into either group homes or outpatient services. But she had history, a history which would keep her at the pediatric ward for the foreseeable future.

Relief swept over Nash when he noticed her action was not fueled by rage or any aggressive sound of hysteria. Rather a slow, deliberate tearing—an action of someone deep in thought, echoed down to him. He knew she was a thinker, smart with a keen intellect not common for her age group.

Her intelligence manifested itself as a nonstop challenge to his authority as well as countless attempts to escape. Nash sighed, knowing his morning meeting was not going to happen.

Nash walked up the steps of the administration building, the nerve center of the institution. Once through the doors, he passed the offices of the doctors, nurses, and other members of the medical and psychiatric staff. Admittance forms, files, records, and all forms of paperwork cycled through the building on the way to steel gray basement cabinets.

He entered the third-floor pediatric psychiatric wing and walked to the nursing station looking for a report.

"Good luck," said the young overnight nurse, pointing to the last room on the wing. "I've left you some notes," she added and then moved away from the station quickly.

"Sure thing." Nash did not really look at the overnight nurse. A low-level commotion from the Sullivan girl's room grabbed his attention. Nothing major, he thought, but still the thirty-eight-year-old psychiatrist resolved to wait a few minutes to see if whatever was happening in the room would settle down on its own.

Crack! Something else broke.

Not this time, he thought, his head tilted back, and he dropped his lunch on the nurse's station counter. Dr. David Nash took a deep breath, more to calm and steel himself from whatever he would face when he opened the door for the last room on the left.

Caroline Sullivan had been keenly and inexplicably freed. The jolt from one existence to the next forceful and efficient, leaving no room for arguing or consent. In the impossibly small fragment of time between the nightmare maelstrom of wickedness and her new daybreak, the normal world snapped back into place. Once, a long time ago, her life had been bright, and then a malevolence seized her soul for its own, or she lost her mind. She could not be sure which.

She stood shivering in her room, overwhelmed by the power of the hand tearing her from one plane of reality to the next.

Caroline crept toward the bed from which she had leaped out only a moment before. Then, sitting gently on the mattress and reaching for the still warm blankets, she processed what was happening. Her sharp eyes, measuring her world, revealing itself as new. Not that anything in her room looked physically different. She saw her belongings as they were and summarily rejected them as vestiges of *yesterday*, or rather, *before*.

They were relics of the room in which Caroline burned through three years of seasons. In that time, she'd created a room and a life. In this moment, her life was wasted. She fought to hang on to the memories of who she was just a few moments ago as they tumbled away and faded. Caroline struggled to visualize the lost years when she'd destroyed everything around her: classrooms, school assemblies, even a hospital Christmas party. A pleasant, bright opaqueness stood between her and those memories, which effectively blocked them.

But, she thought, in the pure light of morning, she did see *the now*. This whole room boldly stood as a relic. Instantly, between clicks of the clock, things changed, and this space no longer reflected her at all.

She hopped out of the bed, a movement driven by a feeling of confidence and the newfound energy sparking every neural fiber in her being.

She had an opportunity. A door had opened, and she wanted to walk through it before the twister roared back through, sucking the opening closed.

A renovation-level change needed to happen.

Nothing could stay.

The thought popped into her brain like a cork driving to the surface of an angry sea. She dwelled on it, which made her smile. Yesterday had blasted away, shaking the ground and leaving behind only a swirl of dust and a dying wind. Again, her brain sent her the same thought. Nothing could stay.

She moved to the clock on her nightstand. A green glow in the dark skull with the minutes and hours illuminated in each dark empty eye socket. Inspecting the glow, she wondered whatever possessed her to want it. Caroline jerked the power cord out of the wall with a quick flick of her wrist and then opened her window to toss it out through the decorative yet functional wrought iron bars. She waited for a second to make sure she heard the satisfying crack and scuttle of little pieces scattering.

She looked out onto the vast and carefully kept grounds of the hospital. In the morning mist, she saw deep greens contrasting with the crisp blue skies and found a beauty she had somehow missed. A small pond snuggled up to the edge of the woods, and a few mallards paddled their way across, their ripples buckling the calm surface.

Nothing escaped her now careful eye; swaying branches of the dense oaks nearest to her, the shades of green in a large estate-like lawn surrounding the hospital dipping and rolling outward to the surrounding forest, and cars in the parking lot glittering in the morning light. All appeared remarkably detailed as she gazed out. She leaned against her window frame.

Energy injected into her body left her restless and overpowered by the need to change the scenery around her room. It needed to match the outside. Her head and heart fell quiet except for the crackle of electricity begging to be used. The tornado of destructive emotion which greeted her every morning now spiraled away somewhere. Done with her and done stealing years out of her happy life. It had to be more than the clock. Yesterday, she saw the room as a running expression of her certainty that all things ended badly; today, it just looked like it needed more white paint than the local hardware store had in stock.

The next victim of her hand—a poster that no longer fit her mood. It did not fit the vibe she planned for her room. On the face of the large glossy black background, a young, powerful warlock held up a golden cup as a gaggle of witches danced around a boiling pot, cackling in glee. Then in one motion, she ripped it off the wall. One by one, she tore through the rest of them.

The posters and construction paper, which hung on the walls for so long they'd faded to muted tones of black, purple, red, and crimson, now powdered and crumbled as she ripped them in half. The dust settled on her arms, and she brushed it off.

The bright morning light poured into her room. Caroline tried to identify the feeling. Then it came to her, the word was normality. Normality—the way things used to be. She pulled the drapes back farther and let the light into the room as skull-tipped silver tassels sparkled in the sunlight long enough to catch Caroline's attention. Her room badly needed light.

"Maybe new colors in here," she said cautiously.

Caroline started to think of the colors she could use when the first shadow crossed the room. Dr. David Nash stood in the doorway. She was still smiling when she saw him, but he did not look happy.

Everything stopped.

Maybe Dr. Nash just didn't like the way she went about clearing out her room. Only good things from here on out. She squeezed her hands into tight round fists. Her psychiatrist, looking profoundly disappointed, stalked into the room.

"But we have come so far," he said, shaking his head. A large sympathetic frown rippled across his face.

"You don't understand. I am different. Today everything is new." Frustration welled up as she realized she wasn't getting through to him. She could not form the words to describe what happened to her. He was not seeing this the way she did. Somewhere in the back of her head, she heard a rumbling and roaring of wind, and it closed in. The doctor nodded to the two orderlies who appeared behind him, one of whom held restraints in his beefy, thick, sweat-slicked hands.

Caroline became a gazelle cornered by a bloodthirsty carnivore. The doctor smiled his lion smile, still blocking Caroline's way forward, and calmly began to describe what would happen next. "For your own protection, we will put these restraints on you for a few minutes to make sure you do not hurt yourself or anyone else."

"This is wrong. I'm telling you I am different now," she said, backing up, knowing that the black cloud that had miraculously left now defied physics and began spinning back toward her. Caroline had closed her eyes and then reopened them; everything was the same except that the orderlies were closer.

The way out was blocked by two orderlies with restraints and a doctor wearing a lion of the Sahara smile.

"But I have changed. I don't want this anymore," she whimpered.

"No," said Dr. David Nash. "No, you have not." They closed the gap and restrained her as she let out a howl.

Part II

Eight

Cold Springs, Massachusetts
Summer 1994

It was as if the demolition crew had waited for her to arrive and watch the obliteration of her room in the pediatric psychiatric ward. Caroline Sullivan rested her hands against the temporary fencing. She *needed* this to cement the past where it belonged. No more treading water or falling backward.

Six years ago her world popped back into place. The person who she was during the years between her kidnapping and her time in the pediatric psychiatric ward vanished between ticks of the clock, leaving the Caroline before the kidnapping and divorce in her place. Father Andre Bequette called it a moment of Grace. Her last memory in the ward had been of the moment an orderly approached to sedate and restrain her. Seconds later her father and his lawyer stormed through the door. Within five minutes, they whisked her out of the building never to return.

Until today.
Until this moment.
She never wanted to return.

She ran away until the gravity of Cold Springs did the one thing it did to everyone who ever lived there; it pulled her back. Except for her, she thought there was a reason. An important one.

A man counted down from ten over a bullhorn, and the assembled crowd cheered. At zero, the mayor of Cold Springs pressed the ceremonial igniter, setting off a series of explosive charges set deep in the building. One ten-thousandth of a second later, the superheated gas balls expanded so fast that the leading edge of the fireball compressed into a shockwave powerful enough to rip through and pulverize the steel beams and concrete pillars holding up the structure.

Caroline expected to see a flash of red and plumes of billowing flames. Instead, a simple ear-splitting crack rumbled out from the building as it collapsed in a huff of gray-brown smoke.

Nothing. No relief. Nothing that would change any of the horrors which haunted her in one way or another—always there.

After a few seconds, she looked back at the hunks of concrete and steel, which had once been the old hospital and pediatric psychiatric ward. Her eyes moved slowly to her right. Only the back rear corner of the psychiatric wing, rising three stories above the piles of rubble, still stood awaiting the wrecking ball. In that corner, only one window remained unbroken.

The one at the far corner.

Her window.

Caroline took a moment to convince herself that fate had not nursed a grudge against her by leaving her old room still standing. She had to see it destroyed for herself. She gripped the fencing tighter, refusing to lean on William Lane or Daniel Wilson, each standing on either side of her.

A large crane swiveled toward the room. At the end of the crane a five-foot-long metal bit rapped the brickwork under her window four times before the last wall of the ward cracked and moaned before it dropped in a cloud of dust.

Gone.

But the room wasn't the problem, really. Before she'd burned through three years of her life in that room, she'd seen evil. The time in the pediatric psychiatric ward had been meant to crush that encounter into a powerless singularity. To return her life to the starburst of color and hope it had once been. A decade on from the kidnapping, little in her life changed. Her trajectory bent increasingly downward, twisting into the gravity well of the horrors laid upon her by Henry Lee Dumont. A relentless tug at the threads that held her together steadily unwinding since the summer she'd turned thirteen. She'd come back to Cold Springs to find answers and close the book on that part of her life—to break away. To live. The last time she tried it she lost three years of her life to a pediatric psychiatric ward.

Afterwards, fate had not been kind, or she hadn't the strength to safeguard a freedom once taken for granted. She stepped back from the fence and turned to the new Reliant Medical Building across the street—the one with the glistening new glass and a state-of-the art psychiatric ward—and wondered if the next steps she took would lead her to freedom or back inside the newer, prettier psychiatric ward.

Daniel Wilson didn't like the way the thrumming of construction vehicles bounced around his lungs, or the smell of burnt diesel fuel. The steaming heat of the noon sun baked everyone who still watched the demolition crew work. Yet, despite his discomfort, he stood quietly by Caroline's side. The happiness of having her suddenly and completely back in his life after she spent almost a decade away overwhelmed his desire to get away.

He could stay here chatting with them as long as they needed to. The two best friends he ever had suddenly unexpectedly dropped back into his life last night. He hadn't come down from the high all night or even into this morning when they met up for breakfast at William's parents' home.

Daniel's mind returned to the moment. Thick dust slowly drifted across the campus. Caroline's room and the whole psychiatric ward where she wasted away for three years no longer existed. At least in the physical sense.

"Wanna get out of here?" he asked William and Caroline, thinking about where they could go for lunch. His eyes lingered on Caroline. Small and pretty, still sporting a modified version of the short bob cut she'd had since she was thirteen.

Home was the last place he thought he'd see them. Both left right after graduation. He'd planned on going too, but Cold Springs never let him. He found, like others before him, the town functioned as a whirlpool that sucked everything toward the center, and only the lucky were flung out. But somewhere, somehow, something still dropped a grudge on him and trapped him here. Here he stayed and watched as others moved on. Or at least that is what he told himself. Deep down he knew one thing. He knew what the lifers knew about Cold Springs and now loved living there. He never wanted to leave. He loved it even more now that Caroline and William returned.

"Yes, let's get out of here." Caroline smiled at him. "But there is something important I need from you first." She glanced at William first, almost as if she needed reassurance. He reflexively tensed his shoulders waiting for what she would say next.

"I…" said Caroline with trepidation, her hands clasped in front of her. "William has already agreed and I-I just think it would be best if you came. We were…we need to be all there. Together."

Daniel couldn't imagine what he could do for her. She, or at least her father, sat on a mountain of money made as a musician a decade before. William had agents negotiating a new major league contract for him. "Anything…anything you need Caroline."

Daniel listened as Caroline described what she wanted to do. His stomach lurched. Bile burned his throat. His face reddened in anger; anger directed at William. "Are you out of your mind?!"

Caroline held his hand in her small ones and begged, but he could not bring himself to say anything other than what came out. "Good God, *no*!" He regretted how forcefully he said it. Caroline placed her hands on her face.

Daniel Wilson watched them turn and walk away perhaps for the final time. The joy of the past twenty-four hours drained out of him, leaving him leaning against the fence. Caroline wept as William guided her to his Jeep, his arm around her and her head tucked into his chest. Jealousy replaced anger. Remorse, regret, and loneliness welled up and hit him hard as Daniel tried to think of any sane reason they would want to go back to The Dale.

NINE

Quabbin Wildlife Management Area Gate 5A
Cold Springs, Massachusetts

COLD SPRINGS BARELY HELD back the old-growth forest surrounding it. Just before six-thirty, Caroline glanced back toward her house while William lingered with her. They stood in front of the gate at the end of their street. A sign with white lettering which *read GATE 5A Quabbin Wildlife Management Area. No Fishing. No Hunting*, hung from a triangular gate.

The road past the gate had crumbled. Still Old Enfield Road, but after the gate, only a path of cracked and heaved asphalt wound down into the forest. Crabgrass and dandelions poked up through the broken pieces toward the dim light which penetrated the heavy overhead canopy.

They'd entered the realm of the Quabbin: a massive reservoir rimmed on all sides by an even bigger heavily forested wildlife preserve. All marks of civilization quickly vanished as they walked along the road, a lone sentinel between them and the forest.

"Caroline," called out a voice behind them. She looked back to see Daniel walking around the gate as they had. Seeing him quickened her heartbeat and stole her breath. "I found a canteen." He offered it up for them to see. The initials BSA 507 stenciled on its side marked it as his Boy Scout Troop 507 canteen.

Caroline could only wonder what made Daniel change his mind as she ran back. She knew that spending time today with William and Daniel left had her in the best mood in a long time. Stonehill was her third college in four years. Law school seemed to be a pipe dream now. Yet, she had to be here—right now. Compelled to go back and face Cold Springs and The Dale.

She had to come back.

She had to see it for herself. Caroline needed to see that a secret nook deep in the forest remained just that. But she never banked enough nerve to do it.

Then, two weeks ago, Daniel's mom had sent her a little clip from The Sentinel. The demolition of the psychiatric ward would commence on Wednesday and conclude on Friday. That act of kindness inspired her to come. A trip she planned to do alone morphed, by fate alone, into one with William and Daniel. She witnessed its demise. Now she needed to see something else to move on.

"You came," she said, almost in wonder.

Daniel nodded and smiled at both. "Well, as long as we are about to do something really stupid..." he said. Then they walked deeper into the restless wild and headed for The Dale.

Caroline trudged next to them in the summer heat grateful Daniel had come along for her mission. The three chatted away the silent dread which accompanied them on their walk downhill until they reached the water's edge. The road continued for miles, except the rest of it lay underwater. Sunk decades ago, when the Swift River had been dammed to create the Quabbin Reservoir. A small granite obelisk lay on its side. The number 32 had been carved into the top of it. They never knew what it meant.

"32. An archaeology question," chuckled Daniel as they hiked along the shore before the trail ducked back into the woods where a small stream tumbled into one of the countless coves and inlets of the reservoir. He mimicked Caroline's voice. "But not like Indiana Jones…real, digging kind of archeology." The three of them huffed along a series of puddles and damp mud which had been a stream. The sun sped downward as day shifted to dusk.

"Oh, shut up." Caroline laughed, then stomped into a puddle of stagnant water soaking Daniel's leg. She didn't need to be reminded of her first and most unfortunate choice of majors at her first and most unfortunate choice of a university—Brown. "This is way further than I remembered," she said, changing the subject. "Did we miss it?" asked Caroline as her legs ached from the effort. A long downhill walk, followed by a trek along the shoreline, and finally into the thick forest.

"No, we didn't miss it, but I know who missed a bunch of cardio classes." William grinned.

"Both of you guys… just suck." Caroline shook her head and concentrated on her footing as she crossed the muddy stream bed. She swatted away bugs and held her breath, not wanting to go further. Caroline stopped and looked around in the forest, wondering what the hell she was doing here. She'd momentarily lost her nerve. William and Daniel waited. She nodded to both and finally tromped forward in silence for a little longer before they reached a rise of thick trees which overlooked The Dale.

And there it was.

Caroline stopped and gazed at it—halted by the ominous trepidation, as if evil could reach out to her once more just by taking another step. Until now, going to The Dale had been nothing more than a fantasy. But facing the rotting buildings near the edge of the water, she could not decide whether to go on.

They made their way to the center of The Dale, a ruined chapel. Inside, there were a few hickory pews that had not succumbed to the forest.

"What do you want to do?" asked Daniel. "We're here."

Caroline had not considered doing anything. During long sleepless nights, the times when she imagined this moment she simply stood in place and relief washed over her unbidden. "I don't know." Finally, she lurched forward to the doorway of the church. "Maybe we sit?"

William nodded and then entered first. Caroline and Daniel followed. For a while, they sat. Caroline closed her eyes and waited for the relief she expected. The tension in the chapel intensified, and she could not place the reason. Still, no relief came, and then she opened her eyes. She stood up and took a slow walk around the inside of the church and finally through the open front door.

Almost immediately upon walking outside, she saw a pile of decayed clothing sitting underneath a snarl of weeds. She glanced first at William and then at Daniel. Both saw it too.

Caroline took a step toward the tattered roll. This part of the church had been a crime scene. She wondered why the police hadn't taken the clothing or at least picked it up.

"Don't," said Daniel.

She barely registered his voice or that anyone had spoken. She moved closer to the pile. But the clothes were not what pulled her forward. Caroline could see it under the clothing. She pulled away the scraps of blackened denim and cotton.

And there lay a pink sneaker.

She froze, staring at it. Daniel and William were already standing by her side. Each of them reached to hold on to her. "God," she said as she clapped her hand to her mouth.

"Holy…" added Daniel.

William said nothing.

William Lane could not take his eyes off the pink sneaker. Caroline had peeled back the roll of fabric. Most of what she touched fell away in her hand, wet, brittle, moldy. But the sneaker, protected from the worst of the elements, appeared all but pristine.

"All this time," said Caroline. "I never really believed. I would swear the sneaker was in the house on the common."

"The police…and us, found you here. Not on the common," offered Daniel. "I saw them pull you out of the church."

Caroline Sullivan could have only been in one place when she had been kidnapped: her old house on the common or The Dale, not both. William knew she never believed it. Most importantly, she still did not completely believe she had been here rather than her old house on the common. Of all the proof which had been drilled into her over the years, the shoe nailed it shut. There was never enough time for her to be in both places.

Caroline long insisted she had been on the common. The problem had always been she did not remember anything besides being in her old house on the common. She remembered being attacked by something malevolent there. Nothing could convince her otherwise. But now she saw the proof she had to have been in The Dale. The attack in the house on the common could not have happened anywhere but in her mind.

It mattered to William what she thought. It seemed to be the only thing that mattered to Caroline. He believed she thought that if she could solve that problem, life would go on. Stone cold proof right in front of her face.

Something else seemed to hold her up though; as if she hadn't told them everything.

"I didn't walk all the way from the common to here without a sneaker," she concluded.

Grateful for the opening, William followed her line of thought. "You must've had a struggle with him, and you lost it close enough to here, and he put it there before he…" William could not finish the statement. Then he raged at himself for even opening his mouth. The only mercy in the entire wretched affair was that she couldn't remember anything that happened in The Dale. Nothing…including whatever Dumont did to her in the chapel before she had been rescued.

"I remember your foot," added Daniel. "It wasn't muddy or dirty. Just a cut on the side of it. You could've only ever been here."

William searched Caroline's face for understanding, or at least acceptance. Facts were facts. Her sneaker here, the condition of her foot. He wished she could accept what she remembered was not what happened to her.

Caroline walked around the side of the church, her eyes searching. William and Daniel watched her grab a long stick and thrash the brush near each of the three remaining buildings.

Daniel looked as puzzled as William felt, trying to figure out what she was doing. "Can we help?" asked William. Caroline shook her head; a clear no. Full dark embraced them all before she stopped.

"No. I'm ready to go," she said finally.

"What were you looking for?" Daniel asked.

Caroline didn't respond. Instead, she started to make her way out of The Dale and back toward the forest road. "We better get back before my dad starts to worry."

Daniel exchanged a glance with William and asked her, "Do you believe, Caroline?"

"I want to," said Caroline. "But all the evidence points to it but… but I don't feel any better. No different."

The shoe should have nailed the case shut. But it didn't. She needed more. Maybe more than they could give. "We can help."

Caroline nodded and smiled at them both. William saw right through the smile. Under the surface his friend ached for some kind of peace, and she didn't get it today. They went to The Dale together and just like their trip to watch the psych ward get bulldozed, it gave her no comfort—even though it should have. There waited a longer journey ahead for her, possibly if she wanted William and Daniel to come, for the three of them.

Whatever she was looking for in The Dale a few seconds ago, something that she would not tell them, had to be a part of the puzzle in her head. Maybe that was the something. For now, it could be her secret, the thing she left out. Sooner or later, she would have to fess up. He hoped it would not be too late before she did.

Caroline breathed a sigh of relief as she, William, and Daniel made it to the shoreline of the Quabbin Reservoir. She looked upward to the gleaming stars, brilliant in the way a dry, crisp New England evening could reveal. Sharp points of blue, red, and white glowed against an increasingly blackened sky. The forest at night no longer held the mysterious excitement it once did for her.

"Acceptance and belief are two different things," offered William as they walked, breaking her away from the thought. "I think you believe it. I am not sure if you accept it."

"That," offered Daniel, "might take some time."

She'd come back here to see the end of the psychiatric ward and then confront The Dale, so why couldn't she put to bed the last thing that she couldn't reconcile. She didn't have an answer for herself, much less Daniel and William. But her one clue, the one she didn't share with anyone, didn't match that. All she knew was she wanted to accept it—to understand it from a logical point of view—but she didn't. She knew it was irrational. Irrationality could be a symptom of madness, she thought. Great.

She glanced over at William. He'd come here to support her. A sprained ligament in his elbow would keep him out of the line-up for three more weeks. William climbed up the ranks in the minor leagues in New Orleans, the top of the Milwaukee Brewers farm system. He'd told her that the Brewers didn't want him to see a doctor in New Orleans. He'd flown directly to Boston General where a canceled appointment had left him with a few days to visit home in Cold Springs while he'd waited for his next appointment. That's when she'd seen him standing in his driveway, taking out his parents' garbage. He'd waved and she'd hugged him and said almost nothing other than "I missed you." Nothing else needed to be said. Fate, she mused. Had to be.

She knew Daniel came because he remembered his mistake and hated the idea of them making it again, and she loved him for it. She thought back over the years of lost friendship. Most of a decade had gone into the books with little contact, and as she walked with them, they had all slipped into their roles. Had they known about the crash that headed their way the summer before high school, she doubted they would have ever tempted whatever malevolence lurked in the shadows of her doubt. The one that shattered their fellowship. Back then, she had to know. Back then, she didn't get an answer she could remember. Now she needed it to move on.

    She marveled at the semi-normality of today. Friends were supposed to do things like this. If it had not been for her mistakes, they'd still be doing this. She didn't find what she wanted in The Dale. She didn't find peace in the psych ward demolition. She needed to look somewhere else for relief. She had one last card to play. One last hope. In the morning, she would find Father Andre Bequette.

Ten

St. Francis Rectory
Cold Springs, Massachusetts

"WILLIAM," SAID FATHER ANDRE Bequette, studying Caroline in the bright morning light, "I understand, has gone back to Boston?" He sat across from Caroline in his cramped yet comfortable rectory office.

"He's leaving today," said Caroline.

He gazed back at the girl, her eyes glowed brightly when she mentioned William's name. "He is going back to Boston for his appointment. I spoke to his father. His elbow is not okay, and he is seeing a specialist."

"Yes." Caroline looked down and then out the window.

"He is going to need some support. You know," he paused, hoping she would realize the lifeline he offered was for her, "Stonehill College is, in fact, in Easton." He hoped she would pick up on what he suggested. Bequette liked the idea of Caroline in a small private college. He loved the idea of William being close to her for at least a few weeks. "Close to William," he continued.

"I can't." After a few heartbeats, she added, "Yet."

Bequette leaned back in his chair now and did not say anything for a full minute. He wondered if Caroline had said everything on her mind. "So," he began, "you don't want to see him again?"

She sat and said nothing. Instead, she slowly shook her head no. Bequette frowned and guessed at what the issue might be. "You don't want to overdo it. Too much could ruin everything." It was, thought Bequette, a logical and common reaction. He'd counseled young men and women for almost forty years.

Caroline nodded this time. Her face reddened and her lips tightened. "I'm driving back as soon as I leave here," she said, changing the subject. He waited for her to say something else. "I'm fine."

He knew she was not. Her journey here had made things worse. The girl who had lived with the unthinkable sat across from him explaining the two things she had done which she thought would finally free her. This troubled Father Andre Bequette.

"Would you answer his call?" asked Bequette. "Or Daniel's call if they reached out to you?"

"I'm not sure."

"They clearly are still willing to be friends and even…"

"I know," she said, exasperated. "Maybe I should just let it sit for a while and then plan the next time we get together a little better. Maybe," she sighed, "without any mention or reflection on…" She didn't finish.

Bequette held up his hands as if to tell her to stop. Caroline Sullivan had planned everything in her life. She'd been that way since she could walk. Homework, playtime, television time, friends time, all planned down to the minute. He knew Caroline had been freed from the psychiatric ward. Freed didn't mean free. Something else lingered beneath the waves and dragged her under. It hurt him to know that Caroline had yet to grasp that she had the entire world in front of her. Henry Lee Dumont and the psychiatric wing were in the rearview mirror. A mirror which Bequette believed she stared at each day despite the image moving ever further away from her.

He had thought that Caroline watching the demise of the psychiatric wing and facing The Dale, where Henry Lee Dumont had taken her, would ease some of her burdens. Two of three down. But the one last question was the big one. She fixated on the apparent conflict between where she had been found and where she remembered being. She at least acknowledged that she could have only been in The Dale. That demonstrated progress.

Father Bequette viewed the event as an obvious short circuiting of the software which ran her mind. Her wonderfully efficient brain had protected her and spared her the true memory and shared with her something she could process—if she chose to. Bequette decided the real question she needed to answer was: why? Her same efficient brain needed to resolve the conflict between her faith and the anger at God for allowing this to happen to her, or she would not find peace.

He suspected she wondered how God could be so hands-off and allow her to experience the horror of Henry Lee Dumont. It made a mockery of the ideas of faith and God she had adapted since her first communion. It, thought Bequette, was a hell of a lot easier to explain it on a macro scale—until it hit home. Why did a child suffer from cancer? Why did God allow Henry Lee Dumont to unleash his vile desires upon her? Those, *those* questions were hard to explain. At least, he thought she had some closure with William and Daniel. Who knew, perhaps they would reconnect and find their fellowship of three.

"There has to be more to The Dale," she said.

Bequette stayed impassive. "That would be an archaeology question."

"Nice try, but I'm serious about law. I can look into some classes as a minor."

"I can only hope God intercedes again for you." Bequette chuckled. He liked the idea of her working in archeology. She had a mind for piecing disparate ideas together. Except when it came to her encounter with Dumont and The Dale. He took a deep breath and sat back and circled back to the idea that she thought there was more to The Dale than she knew. "Why do you say that about The Dale? More to the point, why does that matter?"

"I don't know." Caroline frowned now. Her brow furrowed. "I went there, and nothing happened. I saw the psych ward drop. I didn't feel any different. I know for sure I could not have been at the house on the common. There must be something else."

Something else. A troubling idea that clearly allowed Caroline to linger in the mystery of The Dale and not move on. To deny her the idea would be to cement it in her head. Kind of like a parent telling their son to stay away from 'that girl.' He decided to try and put her brain to work in a positive way. "It's my understanding that there are at least eight universities in the area between Boston and Providence, Rhode Island. They're bound to have libraries and research labs."

Caroline brightened to the suggestion which Bequette hinted at but did not say aloud. "Yeah." She stood up and moved toward the door. "Thanks." She embraced Bequette before leaving.

As she left, he added, "I know the chaplains and I will know if you are skipping mass...*God already knows.*" The screen door had already clanked shut behind her. He settled back down at his desk and watched her walk to her car. Her question left him restless. Naming the town would only partially answer the question. Perhaps allow her to move on. To really know the history of The Dale she would have to know Metacomet's Barrow, and a second far more malevolent hell she endured for three years, of which she had no memory, and he hoped she never would.

Eleven

New Orleans Zephyrs Practice Facility
October

WILLIAM LANE WALKED TO the pitcher's mound trailed by two coaches. He'd seen the doctor in Boston and lied to him. He'd told him the pain was minor. He'd told the doctor he could do things he could not. William had no intention of staying on injured reserve for the entire off season. Injured reserve meant that he would not get a new contract. No new contract meant insecurity and that someone could come up and take his spot. He'd rehabbed his elbow and now he knew he could pitch, mostly. He just had to prove it, and time had run out. William needed two more weeks to be perfect. Those two weeks would not be granted. He only had a limited number of days left to show the team he could play this offseason in the winter league. He hid his reluctance. A clutch of players stood on the third baseline, with the rest sitting in the dugout shuffling their feet, burning off nervous energy.

Nodding to the catcher, Lane let the ball rip at three-quarter speed. The general manager and head of scouting leaned against the fence near the dugout and watched as well.

"I'm not looking for fastballs," offered the coach just behind him.

"Just warming up," replied William.

The coach grunted but offered nothing more after he watched William zip another five fastballs. William knew the coach waited for him to deliver a curveball. William had to adjust his grip and add a now painful hard quick motion, almost like snapping his fingers, at the end of his delivery. The motion would strain his elbow, and he hadn't even attempted the pitch since his injury.

They called his bluff.

William wound up, snapping his wrist at the end of the delivery and to his surprise, there was only a limited amount of pain. He held up his glove and waited for the catcher to toss the ball back, but the catcher did not have it. Instead, the ball had sailed three feet over the catcher's head.

"It slipped," offered William, feeling sheepish. "It was a brand-new ball." William grabbed the next ball and worked it with his hands, attempting to get any sheen or sweat off the ball.

The coaches remained quiet.

The second attempt went wide and the catcher dove to his left to block it, sparing William the embarrassment of another passed ball. Electric tingles raced up his arm and he called for another ball. William held up his glove one more time. The catcher looking at the coach threw him one.

Once it was in his hands, he prepared to let it rip.

"William," offered his coach.

"I got this."

William reset himself while his elbow flared white hot. He'd waited years to get to the top of the pyramid in minor league baseball. He was at the end of his contract. An injury could set him back months and the playoffs were days away. Play well and he'd make his case to go to the major league and get a new contract. A big one. Surgery meant being out for nine months and letting a sliver of doubt enter the mind of the organization and it all evaporates. A lifetime of work in ruins. The pitcher ignored the coach. He needed to deliver fifty pitches to secure a win. That was only twelve to eighteen pitches an inning—mostly fastballs and a smattering of junk-balls.

William reset and ignored the electric pain in his arm. Then a soft *thunk* of a sound caught his attention. To his horror, he realized the ball had fallen from his hand. William had been less than a second from attempting to throw a ball no longer in his grip.

Even worse, he no longer felt his hand at all.

Stonehill College
Holy Cross Dining Center
November

Caroline Sullivan had left Cold Springs behind her. She'd driven east on the Massachusetts Turnpike in late August and hadn't looked back. Each time William or Daniel poked up in her mind, she crumpled up the thought and stowed it away.

She stood in the Holy Cross Dining Center located just off the main quad at Stonehill College. The late fall colors burned yellow and red on the trees of the heavily wooded campus.

Fine.

Things were fine between them and maybe *the fine* should have some time and space to harden. Time to keep the memory of the walk down to The Dale, and the few days afterward, warm. Happy. Content. Like they could ignore all the days in between.

They saw her as normal, like the days when they trampled through the forest unbound by The Dale or Henry Lee Dumont. They saw her once again as Caroline. Not Caroline in the psychiatric ward.

She wanted them to see more of that Caroline Sullivan.

But one unnerving phantom from the past troubled her. It had been a beautiful, unseasonably warm day when her father suggested a quick trip. Perfect and relaxing. Then a phantom had snuck in and roared across her mind as she dozed off on a Cape Cod beach, while her father strummed his guitar next to her.

Dark as The Dale.

The malevolent phantom had whispered those words to her, bringing her fully awake in terror. Until those words stopped ringing around in her head, she would not be fine—and her relationship with both boys wouldn't be either. She'd tried to forget about that voice for months. Months of pretending a phantom from the past hadn't reached out and tapped her on the shoulder. Caroline couldn't pretend anymore.

She needed the four words, which rippled by, front and center in her consciousness, to go away. Then everything would be fine. Caroline knew she couldn't risk asking anyone from the psychiatric ward to help her. That would be a one-way ticket back to a newer and improved depression cave at the new and improved psychiatric wing.

Caroline held the flyer from the Student Services table in her hand. It offered a little bit of hope. Maybe she could talk to someone without the risk of going back. She scanned the flyer.

Stressed?

Black, thick letters commanded the top of the flyer. Yep, she answered loudly in her head.

Do You Want Help?

Who the hell wants to hear voices of dead people in their head? she asked herself. *Well, maybe, they're dead.* She read the rest of the blue heavyweight paper, tearing the top corner absentmindedly as she did. At the bottom of the page was an office number and an invitation to walk in at any time for help.

She thought about it for a few more minutes. She could make it to the office before they closed for the day. Or she could go back to her dorm and call—just in case she wanted to bail on it. Bailing would not help her. Caroline headed toward Denton Hall. If, she thought, she could just drop off the request form, then they could call her. The form would be simple to fill out. Three questions.

Name
Easy. Caroline Sullivan.
Reason for Visit.
Damn. Don't write zombie voices. End of session stress. Grade Issues. *Don't want to fail out of a third college*

Contact Information:
Caroline wrote down her dorm phone number then entered the counseling office.

She tapped the blue paper as she placed it in the basket labeled Request for Services. She turned away and headed back to her dorm thinking of what she might say to open the door to a solution without explaining exactly what was wrong.

Boston General Hospital
November

William paced around in the small orthopedic surgeon's office at Boston General. A man he'd lied to just a few weeks ago. He had to face that lie and the consequences.

He ruminated in the ruins of a chaotic summer. The first trip to Boston to see an orthopedic specialist turned into a weeklong ordeal in which his appointment was canceled. That cancelation turned into a three-day trip back home to Cold Springs. While there he'd run into Caroline. He'd seen her coming out of her father's house. The sight alone stopped him cold. She'd stared at him for an excruciating period before she wandered over to him like a cautious puppy. Then, raising her hands and placing them on his upper arms, she whispered, "I missed you." Words that snuffed any remaining resentment he'd felt. Then, after he'd tried to help her put a stake in whatever spirits rolled around in The Dale and the psychiatric wing, she'd left without saying goodbye.

Bad decisions sprouted from his mind like spring daisies. He nearly scuttled his baseball career in an ill-advised attempt at getting back onto the mound.

After those bad moves, he sat in the office of a surgeon without a contract and technically without a roster spot. At any time, the club could release him with an injury settlement and that would be it. He didn't have nearly enough money set aside to start his next career.

Despite that uncertainty, his mind drifted back to Caroline.

Throughout the days after the loss of their friendship, he imagined their reunion. Often, she'd scream at him to leave her alone. Or he pictured Caroline merely putting her arms around him and bawling at how much she missed him. William even imagined a scenario where they would bump into each other and he would pretend not to notice her. The scene finished with him walking away and leaving her standing alone in some parking lot at the Hampshire Mall or Cumberland Farms. She would be left wondering what she needed to figure out to regain their friendship.

He'd seen Caroline in Cold Springs felt her warmth against his chest as she embraced him and held on. Yet, he sensed the tension in her muscles. A storm that still raged just below her surface. She'd broken out of his hold a few minutes later and she'd told him why she'd come. His heart sank briefly when she'd told him about her plan to see the psychiatric hospital.

William's connection with Caroline sparked across his mind for days. He'd patched things up with Daniel. For two days the overwhelming contentment of the return to normality with Caroline and Daniel had boosted him into happiness.

Too happy, too confident, he thought. The next thing he did was all but end his career as a major league pitching prospect. He anxiously waited for the orthopedic surgeon. The damage to his elbow had been worse than anyone knew. His attempt to prove he could play had disastrous consequences. He not only looked selfish and hardheaded for trying to pitch but also made his injury worse.

A torn ulnar collateral ligament in his right elbow had not just a small tear—it had been shredded. Surgery loomed in the windshield and worse, a nine-month recovery could end his career one step below the major leagues.

He'd come to Boston to save his career and still, all he could think of was Caroline. Her loss in high school used to haunt his restless nights when sleep would not come. Early on, he reached out to her. He wrote. He called. He stopped in to see her. She did not respond to him.

Shortly after *it* happened, he'd wandered into her room at the psychiatric hospital. He'd leaned against the door frame just a few feet from her. He was fifteen then, and she'd refused to even look at him. She'd left him to stare at her back as he breathed in her light perfume. Without a word, Caroline had dropped all the blame on his shoulders.

He could barely handle the thought now. But then, half a step into his teens, it crushed him. The only time she'd spoken to him in those ten minutes in her room was to ask about Daniel. He and Daniel had stopped speaking. She'd kept her back to him even as she'd spoken. It seemed to him she'd done it out of spite knowing it would hurt him. Knowing was the key word here. She'd known he'd wanted to speak to her to work things out. Maybe bring things back to normal between them. She'd *known* refusing him would hurt him.

She'd made a conscious decision to do it. She had to *think* about it, then *do* it. Caroline had looked at the letter or seen the note showing he'd called and then rejected him. It burned. It ached. Finally, he'd realized he had to be the one to take a break. For his own heart, he had to leave her behind. And that guilt never went away. He'd known she was alone and scared and yet she'd rejected one of her two best friends. He couldn't process it or make sense out of it. So, he'd done the only thing he could and tried to move on with his life.

She'd visited here and there and came and went, but only in his daydreams. Then he pushed her away and attempted to replace her. But only one Caroline Sullivan existed. The one and only starburst he knew vanished and their deep friendship evaporated, leaving nothing behind. By the time Caroline wheeled off the rails of sanity and tried to ignite propane cylinders at the psychiatric ward, he'd known the time to do the unthinkable and heave her out of his life had arrived.

"William Lane." The surgeon walked into his office carrying a file. Surprisingly, he did not look as angry as he expected him to. "Let's get back on track."

Things can change in an instant. Hope trickled up his body. Enough hope that William decided he would call Caroline once he knew about surgery and the recovery. He could rehab anywhere. His season was over but his time with Caroline could just be starting. He decided to make a bold move—he could work on his degree nearby while he recovered. William Lane decided he had a love for history.

Twelve

Stonehill College
Easton, Massachusetts
November

D R. TARA ROSS SCRUTINIZED THE data housed in several reports that sat neatly on the top of her desk. The pile of twenty-one reports, each resting in a manila folder, sat in a crisp stack on the right-hand side of her desk. Once she completed her work on the file, she would close the folder then sign and date the front. She used a word or two to describe what she'd done then slid the file to the top of the neat pile to her left. Her last task of the day would be to return the files to a gray steel cabinet in the corner of her small office.

At least she had a window. She'd hoped that the new title, Lead Psychologist: Stonehill College, would carry the weight of a better office. It did not. Tara supposed she was lucky Stonehill added an entire department for mental health services.

Tara closed the last folder, signed it, and wrote the words FURTHER COUNSELING UNNEEDED. As she rose to file the folders in the cabinet, the sound of heels clicking down the hallway stopped her. She listened as the sound increased in volume. Finally, the secretary stuck her head in the office.

"I have one more for you," offered the older woman.

Tara did not smile or respond to the sheepish shrug from the secretary. She turned back to her desk and dropped the folder in the center. She stood for a moment, wondering if she could just leave it until tomorrow. The secretary walked away. However, she knew the lone folder in the middle of her desk—something out of place—would bother her all night. As a psychologist, she knew the irrationality of feelings. Being irrational didn't make it any less real.

Damn.

Tara sat back down at her desk, the leather seat still warm, and opened the folder. She looked at the file, a blue Request for Services paper. Ross glanced over the form and then at her calendar. Torn at the top, anxiety?

Caroline Sullivan. She looked at the name again and winced. A scan of the rest of the document closed the deal. It had to be her.

As with every student request, her secretary pulled the most basic student information: age, year, status, and hometown. Tara did the math in her head and the age was right. It could not be a coincidence that the name, age, and hometown all matched. This girl was John Sullivan's daughter. Accessing student records to confirm it would be a violation of the ethics code. She knew in her gut it was her.

Her heart snapped to a stop and then restarted. The anger flared and died quickly. Other emotions roared up and burned like lava bursting through cracks in some hellish tectonic subduction zone. Even a decade later, the lie John laid on her still burned.

But Caroline was not John. She could treat the girl. Hopefully. John Sullivan had changed Tara's life. He altered her possibilities. Limited her options. Tara could forget the request ever crossed her desk. She could hand over the girl to someone else. But there really was not anyone else but her. She didn't want to turn the light on in the dark hallway of that past. The one that included John Sullivan, musician, lover, *coward*, liar.

A door clanged closed down the hall and the sound pulled her back to the present. The rest of the offices were probably empty.

Tara needed to help his child get through some silly, girl-who-has-everything, stress. But it was the school psychologist duty to help Caroline Sullivan.

Perhaps she could put aside her feelings. Helping Caroline might be the cosmic symmetry of closing a circle opened by John Sullivan and closed by Tara Ross.

Perhaps not.

Stonehill College
Denton Hall
Easton, Massachusetts
November

The slight girl who sat across from Dr. Tara Ross did not appear to be a threat to herself or anyone. Caroline stood barely five feet tall, and Tara wondered if she even broke the century barrier in pounds. The glasses the girl wore gave off a slight nerd vibe despite her naturally attractive features. Tara had been called statuesque by her mother. She liked the height. She'd started for the varsity volleyball team as a sophomore and by then she was already taller than most of the boys in her grade at five-nine.

She waited for the girl to settle into her seat before pulling out her question sheet. She took on Caroline because she was currently the only licensed psychologist on the soon to be growing staff. There were several standards of protocol that a student would have to fail before seeing Tara on a regular basis. Dr. Ross convinced herself that it was her professional duty. The conversation she planned would appear to be open and free form, but it was a tightly controlled initial assessment. She wanted the girl, if she needed help, to trust her and open up. If she did not, then there would be little success in counseling.

"So, what is the difference between a psychologist and a psychiatrist?" asked Caroline.

She smiled and gave her normal answer. "Well, psychiatrists are angry, little, arrogant men who give you a pill while you are strapped to a gurney and congratulate themselves for thinking they have cured their patient." Tara paused and leaned forward in her chair and handed over a packet of M&M's to Caroline. "Psychologists, on the other hand, listen to what you think your needs are and then give you the tools to deal with the inevitable potholes life throws in front of you."

Caroline smiled and brightened up. Interestingly, she lacked the normal nervous twitches and body shifts she saw in most students venturing into her office. She didn't quickly glance around or display any curiosity about the diplomas or motivational posters which hung from the walls of her office. Nor did she have any curiosity about what would happen next. Odd, she thought. Then, she realized something. Caroline was comfortable here. It wasn't the light conversation or the chocolate candy she handed over from her secret stash. She tightened her thought—*Caroline was used to it*. She's been in a counseling office before.

Tara waited for Caroline to respond to her explanation.

"So," said Caroline, "you keep people off the gurneys in the first place."

And she was smart. "Yes." Tara paused. "What brings you here?"

Tara waited out the silence as Caroline leaned forward and said, "I need help with something."

"You look like the kind of person who knows how to find her way." Tara had used those introductory words often. Birthed from a conversation long ago on a coastal Maine boardwalk. They were the first words that changed her life. Perhaps they could change someone else's life too, she thought. Then added, "Tell me about yourself."

Caroline explained to Dr. Ross how her charmed life had collapsed into a pile of smoking dust and rubble over the next forty minutes. Tara knew Caroline would start slowly and save the worst of it for later.

Thirteen

Stonehill College, Winter Session
January 1995

"12:01 P.M. ON APRIL 28, 1948, the four towns of Dana, Prescott, Enfield, and Greenwich all ceased to exist," Professor Declan Healy announced. Caroline decided that his voice sounded as solemn as he could muster after teaching three previous classes. Even now, two classes into this winter session course, she hadn't stopped finding new posters of world events, leaders, or student work which covered every space on the walls of his classroom. George Washington crossed the Delaware on the back wall and Jefferson stood, Declaration of Independence in hand, guarding the door, while Lincoln watched the room from the front in silent judgement. He carried on, "Those towns and generations of family history vanished for good when the final retaining dam in the Swift River Valley was blown by civil engineers. A wall of water forty feet high roared through the breach in the retainer dam, down the valley, and buried the remains of those towns under as much as a hundred forty feet of water."

Professor Healy, squat and heavily bearded, swiped his shock of hair to the right as he spoke.

Caroline Sullivan copied the words and definitions into her notes.

Quabbin: *Nipmuc word, meaning "meeting of the waters."*
Towns: *Dana, Prescott, Enfield, and Greenwich.*
Reason: *Boston needed water, and the Swift River Valley was a good but not an ideal spot. Four poorest towns. They could not stand up and fight the powers in Boston.*

"What we need to ask ourselves is this," Healy continued. "Was it right or wrong to remove two thousand people from their homes? Homes lived in for generations for the benefit of over a million people. Was the creation of this reservoir and the accidental wilderness that came about, for the greater good?" Caroline scribbled furiously, taking advantage of Healy's dramatic pregnant pauses.

Was it right or wrong/greater good? She lagged. A poke at her shoulder irritated her. She scowled at the unseen and unacknowledged offending finger.

Poke.

She ignored it again. Winter session classes only lasted two weeks and roared along.

Poke! Poke! *Poke!*

Caroline snapped her head to face the person poking her.

William, his left arm in a sling, sat two seats behind her.

He waggled a notebook, one that looked full of notes, with his same big, stupid, goofy, ridiculous grin. She smiled back and blushed. The moment stormed in unannounced and beamed bright.

What are you doing here? she mouthed silently.

William passed a note to her. *I had to come all the way here and sit through this awful class just to get you to—maybe—talk to me. Lunch. Holy Cross Dining Hall. Great burgers. See you then!*

She held the note tightly in her hand, relaxing for the first time today while enjoying the rest of the discussion. Even better, she added something to it.

"Caroline," yelled William.

Caroline, drifting with the sole intent of entering the Holy Cross Dining Hall with no one noticing, wished he hadn't yelled. Less than twenty-five hundred students attended Stonehill College. Five times the size of Cold Springs High School.

"What are you doing here? Shouldn't you be in New Orleans recovering with the team?" Her voice was harsher than she had intended. She'd been happy to see him but suddenly wondered about his motives.

"I can recover anywhere. It just so happens a fantastic doctor has a practice here in Easton."

"That's not what I meant. What are you doing in my class?"

William gently gave her shoulder a shove with his good arm. "I wanted to explore the minute details of the history of Western Massachusetts."

"My dad told you, didn't he?" demanded Caroline. She'd only spoken to William once since seeing him in August and only for a few minutes. He'd just had surgery, and she'd promised to see him. She never did.

"Back to archaeology, I knew it was going to happen," William teased her some more, ignoring her first question. He pulled a chair out for her, and they both sat down.

"Father Bequette?"

William touched his nose. "Bingo."

Caroline still didn't know why William ended up in her class this morning. However, it meant less by the moment as to how he got here.

"I still have money from my contract with the Brewers. So, with my forced time off, I decided to take some classes. Father Bequette told me you were here for winter session." Then his voice hardened. "He told me you're interested in finding out more about the land and the area of The Dale." William paused as if waiting for Caroline to respond. Her mood darkened.

"Are you checking up on me?" she demanded.

William frowned. "No," he said. "But I have nothing to do right now. I thought since I haven't seen you since the summer, maybe I could help."

Caroline eyed William suspiciously. "How did you know which class I was taking?" She again suspected her dad had something to do with it. The thought of three men, Bequette, her father, and William planning to save her from herself stoked the fire inside her.

William's shoulders slumped forward. "You don't get too many good friends in your life. It doesn't make sense to let go."

"Or" snapped Caroline, "you don't trust me enough to live my own life." Caroline stood, her petite frame rising only a few inches above William in his seat. She hung there and steamed through ten more angry responses to fire at William. Finally, she decided to storm away and leave him at the table.

She belatedly wondered why she went out of her way to hurt him.

FOURTEEN

Stonehill College, Denton Hall
January 1995

"IT WAS THE WAY everyone stared at me," Caroline said to Tara. Caroline sank deeper into her chair. She found the first session with Dr. Ross so helpful she decided to sign up for a second. "Twenty-five freshmen in the room and it's dead silent." She could still imagine the sound of a small tin pot that had dropped off a shelf and clanged to the ground causing half the class to jump.

"What about the teacher...Mr. Graves?" asked Dr. Ross.

The poor man, she thought, guilt welled up and constricted her throat. "'That is not acceptable,'" she tried to replay how she mimicked his deep voice in class. She'd swept her hand over the black hard surface of the table, scattering a microscope, pens, papers, and notebooks onto the floor.

Her partner had reeled away from her. "My partner had a look of abject terror in her eyes. She had the look. The one where you know her mother told her to stay away from me." Caroline reflected on that one. "Her mother had warned her about me, and the poor girl learned the hard way that mothers could sometimes be right."

Even about me, she didn't say those words to Dr. Ross. She did not need to. Caroline knew she'd already said way more than she'd planned.

She needed to stop but the doctor prodded.

"I know this is difficult, Caroline. You can tell me the whole story."

Caroline waited and closed her eyes. The words, loud and harsh, echoed back into her ears even though it had been a solid three-quarters of a decade. "Then I yelled at Mr. Graves, we called him gravy because he was so nice." She paused as the memory of whirring around to the next table and whipping her arms across the surface, clobbering the next data set, which earned grunts from the two boys who watched their labor's annihilation.

She'd moved to another table, and a boy wrapped his arms around his work.

"This boy," she said. "There was this boy. Paul. Very smart and always did the best science projects, loved this one microscope. He even put a small sticker on it so he would know which one it was. Everyone left it for him, even when they were in different classes. He said it had the best picture. When I approached his table, he put his body between me and the microscope."

Caroline wondered what kind of dread crept up the spine of Tara Ross as she told the story. "I *like this one, it's the best*," Paul pleaded. "I responded to him with fury. I could feel the tingle in my hand after I slapped him across his face." The welt had been angry and red. "How about that. Another boy I liked. That was the burning shame I left him with. We worked on stuff together. I'd been to his house for birthday parties and Halloween."

"Did you get a chance to make amends?"

"No. That's not something you can fix." She couldn't fix what she had done. "Still, it hurt. Paul had sped off to college on a science scholarship and would most likely marry a beautiful young woman who could manage not to drop out of two colleges.

"Then it was over. As the last of the metal cups crashed from the shelf, I spun around and saw the room was empty except for Father Bequette calmly sitting at a table. He sat all nonchalantly, telling me how glad he was that I didn't tear up the weight room."

Dr. Ross did not speak for a little bit. She closed her eyes and leaned back for so long Caroline wondered if she had fallen asleep.

"Where did this end, Caroline?"

Caroline held back. "Five-day suspension."

Tara shook her head. "No, Caroline. Where did it really end?"

"We went back."

Tara tilted her chin up. "We?"

Caroline shook her head. The memory welled up inside her, real is if she had been standing in the house on the common. "They told me not to go. I went alone at first. Then…" she trailed off.

Portland, Maine
June 1985

Tara Ross listened to what the doctor told her, yet the words seemed to bounce off her head and rattle to the floor. She could only grasp a few clutches of comprehension here and there. "No heartbeat," and "I am sorry," struck home, and then furthermore, words like "Damage and scarring of the fallopian tubes," left her silent.

Her father held her hand, but she could not find the warmth which normally radiated from his small rough hand.

She walked out of the room; her father made her next appointment for her. She stood in a long, dark daze. Less than six weeks ago, her trajectory angled straight and true toward a man named Jake. Then, John Sullivan. She could not face it. It was over. Everything was over. Her baby was gone. Her future gone. No possibility that John would want to be a part of her life. The helpful woman on the pier all those months ago had been right, partially. But she, Tara, made the rest of the decisions. As her father drove her south on I-95 back toward home, she realized she needed to see that woman again. Tara wondered if she could find her.

Emotions metastasized into pictures. Pictures of her, Tara Ross. She was standing outside of the concert hall. At the front of the crowd—probably because she was taller than the rest of the women—near the tour bus. She yelled out to John as he sauntered out of the back entrance to the tour bus. John, the rock-God, noticed her among the other hundred fans and waved her over.

He said he was mesmerized by her and invited her onto the tour bus.

They sat and talked in the back away from the after-party.

He told her she was beautiful.

He asked her to stay for a day or two.

He'd never connected with anyone as quickly as her. Afterward, not sure how much time had passed, they walked along a boardwalk near Boston, then New York. She'd never experienced so much joy and excitement. He'd made promises and plans with her.

And him. All of him. All his attention.

John Sullivan had lied about everything. He used her and threw her away. The hot, raging embarrassment of the encounter left her humiliated and her confidence shattered. He'd cheated her out of a child. Her failed pregnancy left her unable to carry another child.

When the band imploded a few months later at the end of their world tour, no explanation came with the end. The music press wrote an elegy to a man who had no redeeming qualities. The band's agent must've done a superb job putting a lid on it. That was fine with her. She'd lived with and made peace with the idea that maybe she'd lit the fuse that blew up John Sullivan's life and that was her revenge.

But Tara Ross decided that was not enough. No revenge could fill the hole left by the loss of her one job as a woman, to bear children. Again irrational. Society had evolved from viewing a woman's sole purpose as procreation. But she felt it instinctively. She longed to be a mother. She'd been cheated out of a child by John and could have no other.

Stonehill College
Denton Hall
December 1994

Dr. Tara Ross did not think her third session with Caroline could get worse. "You threatened your science teacher and the principal with a scalpel?"

"No." Caroline shook her head. "At least not at first. I held the scalpel the wrong way. I didn't threaten him. It just looked that way."

"Are you telling me everything, Caroline?" Tara held the image in her head and everything leading up to that moment. Caroline had told her that two weeks after the incident when she trashed a classroom something worse happened. Her father had been under tremendous pressure to get real help for Caroline, but he'd resisted. Caroline told her she kept getting worse and even she thought maybe a few days under care would help. But Caroline said she had not quite been ready to concede her life to the psychiatric ward.

"It had been such a good day. Class was over and Columbus Day weekend was a bus ride away."

"Then things went off the rails?" offered Tara.

Caroline launched into the story of how the class used sharp scalpels to cut into clay to prepare them to dissect frogs later in the month. She just needed to put away her equipment and get on the bus. Caroline looked wistful as she remembered feeling so good. Good enough that she'd forgotten about carrying a sharp object. Good enough she'd missed the sheet of paper on the dusty floor. Caroline recited how even as she sat on the ground after falling on her rear end giggling, she felt good. Until the first gush of blood cascaded onto her dress. She looked up in horror to see Paul staring at a neat slice cut across his bicep. Pulses of thick red liquid drained out of the cut, down his arm, and all over her.

"On the way down the blade caught Paul."

"The microscope kid? God help his future girlfriends." Tara covered her mortification with a laugh.

"I remembered Mr. Graves was screaming at me and at Paul. Paul's odd little smile made me wonder if he wanted to show the other boys in class he was strong. Then, Graves shouted at the kids to go get help and Paul was slumping forward onto his desk, fainting at the sight of his blood. Kids were running. I hid in a corner, scalpel out in front to keep the blood away. I don't know why I didn't drop it."

Tara heard Caroline talk about how things got out of control. That she remembered shrieking and waving the scalpel around but then nothing. For the first time in the sessions, the prickle of unease worked its way up her back and into her arms and hands.

"The principal said I couldn't come back," Caroline said. Tara noted the desperation in her voice. She thought, just a girl reaching out for answers and finding nothing and grasping at anything.

"They gave up," she said, flopping her head back on the chair in which she sat. "I went to see Father Bequette to see if he could help. He could make anything right. There was a pounding on his study door. Before he could say anything, several people poured into the room without waiting for his permission. Father Bequette stood up to protest and then saw the medical officer from the hospital and several others standing in front of Assistant Police Chief Chevalier."

"They broke into the rectory..." That alone sickened Tara but she could at least see why it was done.

"Chevalier apologized over and over to Father Bequette, not to me, but to Father. Then Dr. Nash took me to the psychiatric ward. And I stayed there until..."

"Until?" she prodded.

"Until they got me out." Caroline sighed. "I was fine and life went forward again. Father Bequette told me it was a moment of Grace."

Tara realized that again Caroline had left something out. She didn't believe in moments of Grace. At least not since she had been in high school. This seemed to be a change in medication or body chemistry. The girl had not told her everything. Caroline may have thought she had changed but the reality, the objective reality of where she sat at this instant, said otherwise. "Caroline, I can help you, but I need to know more." She treaded carefully here. "Do you remember how you were treated or what medicines you were prescribed?"

Caroline shrugged her shoulders. "No."

Tara wanted to get a look at the treatments that Caroline's psychiatrist used. She could not outright call her previous physiatrist. She had no cause to do so. However, if Caroline gave her permission, then she might make some headway. The request could have the opposite effect. Most kids did not want anyone prying into their past treatment. Unless, Tara thought, she could give her a compelling reason to do it. She might burn some trust capital, but she needed to take the chance. "Caroline. I need to know the methods and medications that, what was his name, yes, Dr. Nash used with you. Perhaps that knowledge can help you dig out of it. I can request them but only with your permission."

Tara could help Caroline. She had no idea how bad things had gotten for the girl after the kidnapping. Anger bubbled up at John for not doing more to help his own daughter—anger at the stigma attached to mental health issues. She, for the first time, now could separate Caroline from John.

Tara didn't see anything change in Caroline's expression. Then, Tara added a slight almost imperceptible nod of her head. Subliminally giving her permission to say yes.

"If you think it will help."

Ross smiled and sat back. "Caroline. There is something else." Ross slowly rolled her next few words because her request held some weight.

"What?"

Tara eased into the request. "I know you are taking courses based on the history of the Quabbin and the towns around it. One of those places you call The Dale. It's come up a dozen times in our conversations. I also know you think this will help you. Perhaps answer the questions we are asking in these sessions?"

"It's the place where everything happened. It's the mystery. That's where I went sideways. But there was a short time where I was saved."

"Saved?"

"While I was in the pediatric psychiatric ward Father Bequette came to me often. He disagreed with Dr. Nash about my treatment. Dr. Nash thought I was a schizophrenic, but Father Bequette believed in something else. They fought about it until the day I left, and they never reconciled afterwards."

"What did Father Bequette think?"

"He believed that I had been freed from a supernatural oppression in a moment of Grace."

Grace, thought Ross. That meant that God himself came and ripped something supernatural out of the soul of Caroline Sullivan.

"Father Bequette used to tell me 'even God lost his patience with Nash.' After that moment I came back to being myself between ticks of the clock. All the memories of my time in the ward and almost everything I had done before vanished," said Caroline. "Every bit of anger and violence. The desire to be a destroyer evaporated in one tiny fraction of a second."

"Do you believe this, or do you believe that the medications finally caught up to your brain chemistry?"

"I do not know," said Caroline, sinking into her chair. "All I do know is that one minute I am the demon child and the next I am myself again. Nothing Dr. Nash did helped. Only Bequette helped me. But I am falling backwards again. So, I don't know. I am either losing my mind or losing my soul."

There, Caroline thought, it was. All her problems in a single nutshell. Losing my mind or soul. Nothing that anyone did, save for Bequette and even he didn't help last time, could answer the question. She had once thought that the answers could be found in Cold Springs and even in The Dale.

"But," said Dr. Tara Ross, "here you are again. In another medical office. I believe you must have spoken to Bequette when you were home, and he did not help or give you answers."

"I trust you. I hated Nash. I can talk to you. But Bequette gave me avenues to find the answers. Now you are asking me to stop following those avenues. I believe I can find the answers there."

Ross took a breath and crossed her legs, to Caroline she appeared to be weighing what she said next carefully.

"That is a fair point. That's what makes you lean toward Father Bequette's theory."

Caroline decided she had gone to the point of no return. She needed to tell Ross everything. The last bit of evidence she had supporting Bequette's theory. Once she trusted Assistant Chief Chevallier and he listened to her, so did Bequette. She liked and now trusted Dr. Tara Ross.

"There is something else. One thing I have never told anyone."

"What?"

Caroline closed her eyes, trying to find the courage to take one final step in trust. To let Tara Ross into the same tier as her father, William and Daniel, Chevalier, and Bequette. "On the day I was released I went from being one second away from being sedated and restrained to being completely free and out of the pediatric psychiatric ward. When we left the hospital, we had to pass the common and I asked him to stop at the lot where our house on the common had once stood." Caroline reflected on how happy she had been that he had said yes to her request. "I stepped onto that recently graded ground and felt my nightmare to be truly, finally over. But in the morning my father had asked me where I wanted to go. 'Any place in the world' he had told me, 'Anyplace you want to be.' San Francisco, Rome, Dallas, all of them beautiful and busy. But I wanted something else. 'Cape Cod,' I told him."

"That's something every New England girl would have said," laughed Tara.

Caroline smiled back at her, her confidence growing. "My dad and I packed up and were there in just a little bit. We found a place to stay, and he got me clothing at the mall. And nobody recognized him. We ended up at Coast Guard Beach off Route 6."

"Did something happen?" asked Ross.

Caroline struggled to frame the importance of the event in words. She closed her and tried to pull the details from her mind. The sun had been close to setting but the sand was still warm enough to sink her toes into the warm late spring sand. The beach was all but deserted this afternoon and she sat happily with her dad. He sat next to her reading *The Count of Monte Cristo*, swearing at the circling gulls.

They had a few bright towels spread out under a large yellow and green umbrella and a cooler full of food and drinks. A small fire burned, and the smoke hung low to the ground and then blew away with the breeze over the dunes. Terns squawked and, occasionally, a seal rolled over and grunted in the surf. The ocean was still too cold for a swim, but the sun felt great on her arms and legs. Occasionally, she would get up and wade up to her ankles, frigid salt water and all, reveling in the day. The sand and gravel moving restlessly underfoot in the tide.

"So, I dozed off and as I did my mind wandered, settling into comfortable thoughts about the future. In the here and now it looked very bright. The idea of similes drifted across my thoughts, bright as the sun, bright as a supernova, bright as Rudolph's nose on Christmas Eve, and then…" she said.

"Then what?" asked Dr. Ross.

Caroline relived the horror of the moment. "Then a voice of a girl, a young girl, and she said, 'Dark as The Dale.'"

Dr. Ross said nothing for quite a while. She sat with her chin resting in her steepled hands.

"So, the day after you are released from the ward and really less than a day free from what Father Bequette determined to be a demon in the form of a young girl, that same demon spoke out to you." When Ross said it that way it seemed less horrific.

"Yes. Father Bequette believed I had received a moment of Grace in which the demon was expelled from me."

"And yet the next day she knocked on the door of your soul."

Caroline nodded again. "Yes."

"And that rattled the confidence in Father Bequette's assurance that you were free."

It wasn't exactly what Bequette had said to her, but Ross was close enough not to argue against her point. "Yes, but he told me it was up to me to stay free. To constantly reinforce my faith."

"And did you?"

"I'm here," replied Caroline. A wave of shame rolled over her. "It doesn't make sense. How could the same voice that tortured me be the one that warned me? Like there was more to come. I just want to know and be ready." Father Bequette had done everything to save her, to free her, and yet she just gave away her happiness. "Dark as the Dale meant something. I haven't quite figured it out. These projects and learning about it help me. Or at least they get me ever closer to putting this to bed and really moving on."

"Indeed. But I need you to take a break from it. At least until you can deal with what you learn."

"But the answers are there," she protested.

"Maybe, but what if you don't like the answers? You keep getting answers. What if you don't like the next ones either? I believe the answers are here with me and you. Not in some empty lost town in the woods."

"But—" Caroline's voice sounded more like a whine. A desperate hollow whine of despair. Ross held up her hands and cut her off.

"Caroline. Promise me. As your therapist, I care about you. Stay away from it until you are better equipped. Just a few more weeks. Spring is just a couple of months away."

Caroline's head ducked down to her chin and Tara waited.

Caroline searched for something to say back. Eventually, the best possible response crossed Caroline's lips. "Fine."

"Promise?" Tara cocked her head and moved closer to her. She placed her hands on top of Caroline's. She normally did not touch a student. Caroline had been different from the start.

"Yes." But the words *dark as the Dale* still haunted her days.

Fifteen

Stonehill College
Easton, Massachusetts

Night had long ago fallen, yet Caroline turned restless and uncomfortable, unable to sleep. A sharp ripping noise rattled her dorm room. She waited. Steadily, the warmth of her blanket drained away. She decided the sound could not have been real or, if it had been real, it had only been a coed tripping in the darkness on his way to the bathroom.

She lay still, reminded of walking along the bone numbing cold ocean shores of Cape Cod on the day she'd heard the voice. The new chill reached up into her chest and thighs, freezing her fingers and toes.

Rip!

The sound was a combination of a hammer clanging off an old gray pipe followed by a long shearing of metal. Caroline did not move. The sound, now real and emanating from beyond the foot of the bed.

She begged silently for her dad to come charging into the room. But her father slept in his house in Cold Springs, seventy miles away from Easton. Caroline sunk deeper into the blankets as the unpleasant smell of burnt air wafted through her room. Her arm lay in something wet.

Bang! Rip!

Hammer on metal, harsh and piercing. The cold moved to her neck and lips. She needed to move before the cold locked her in place for good.

Bang! Riiiiiiip!

The last sound got her moving with a sense of rebellion. She flipped over and sat up, her anger flaring inside.

The covers fell down to her waist. As her eyes adjusted to the darkness, she saw something in the room with her. The wild hope faded to nothing when she saw it.

A girl stood at the foot of her bed. The girl she had encountered on the day of the fire on the common. Except the last time she'd seen her, in the basement of the house on the common, the girl had burned to ash in front of her eyes. She still held her cotton doll. The hellishly misshapen girl now just clumps of grayish-white cinders, raw skin blighted by spidery black patches, topped by winter straw hair. Stretched black tendrils, a tangle of forest vines, wound around her body, interwoven between her shoulders and legs. Worst of all, the black oily tendrils branched out along the floor and wheedled up on Caroline's blankets. That was the wetness she'd felt. The girl opened her mouth to speak and found nothing but the harsh sound of ripping metal.

Caroline recoiled at the puppet of a human before her. Fear gripped her tighter than her survival instincts. When she'd last seen the girl, Caroline had stood on the edge of spinning out of control. She squeezed her eyes shut and gripped the bed.

When she opened them, the girl was still standing at the foot of her bed.

Caroline took several deep breaths. "Why are you here?" The girl said nothing. Memories of the day in The Dale and the afternoon on the common came flooding back. The house is in flames. The blackness inside. The girl glowing red hot, burned to ash.

Dark as the Dale, thought Caroline. The girl in front of her was the voice from Cape Cod.

The girl shuddered in obvious agony. She bent forward, racked by some unseen blow, then dropped to the floor. Caroline slipped out of bed to help, her hand hovering over the paper-like shoulder of the girl.

The girl made of fire whispered, "He's here."

Caroline wailed. "He can't be here! He's dead!"

The girl gathered herself and stood. Caroline backed off and sat on the bed.

"Not, Henry…him." The girl looked behind her, then back to Caroline. The girl opened her mouth to speak again but again, it was that awful, ripping sound. *Bang! Rip!*

Caroline winced. She'd pressed so hard against the maple headboard her shoulders were searing in pain. She focused on the girl's eyes, dark and pleading, terrified.

The girl heaved with effort. "Caroline, siege." Behind her, the air shimmered in the dim light. The girl closed her mouth. An ugly, harsh glow flashed, revealing something hideous. A wicked wave of malevolent emotions swept over Caroline, dragging unwanted memories from the long-buried shadows of her soul. She tried to resist, but it disarmed her effortlessly.

Spidery black tendrils moved off the girl's cheek and wiggled in the air. More sprung up instantaneously from behind the girl, thickening and squirming, rising above her head then bending toward the ground. Dozens formed. Each time they did, a spark of green light popped and shook the darkness. On the floor, the thick, muscular tendrils intertwined again and again. They laced themselves into long spikes, which then slammed into the tile floors.

Caroline jumped out of her bed and raced to the door. A flash so bright, it burned her eyes. In it, she'd seen what she wished she hadn't. From the middle of the puppet girl's back rose a shiny black humanoid form. Its parasitic head was triangular and not fully formed; black tendrils were still combining. She'd seen its face. Cold, vicious, and most horrifying of all, it seemed to be enjoying itself.

The dark malevolence was holding onto the girl while she was trying to tear it from her body. The vicious, writhing, and twisting battle reminded Caroline of a snake chasing its tail. The two nightmarish creatures crashed out the window and thudded to the ground.

Caroline rushed to the window, needing to see the end. Black, oily looking tendrils were slithering between the darkened buildings. They thinned out as they ran along the lawn and squirmed up the side of a house. The girl from the house on the common, now hopelessly ensnared, still struggled while the malevolence dragged her toward the pines. The girl stole one final glance at Caroline before falling into a roiling mass of tentacles, which rolled into the trees and disappeared.

Caroline rocked back and forth in her bed, not being able to remember walking away from the open but unbroken window. She stayed awake for a long time, terrified by the possibilities dancing across her mind.

William Lane's apartment
Easton Massachusetts

William awoke to a pounding on his apartment door. His small ten-unit apartment building held the sound. He sat up and slipped into a sweatshirt and then headed for the door. After a few months in the city, he still knew few people. Nobody he knew would pound on his apartment door at 3:37 a.m. He sniffed the air wondering if perhaps there was a fire. In his freshman year at UConn, a fire alarm emptied out in the dorm. It turned out to be a bag of popcorn left in a microwave too long.

He doubted anyone in the apartment building would do that. The door had a peephole and a deadbolt. He opened the door after looking through the peephole.

"What if I am right?" Caroline looked like she'd risen from a nightmare. She wore a heavy parka and a wool Red Sox winter hat with a pom-pom on top. She stayed at the threshold of his apartment and asked the question again.

It all swept over William too fast to really think about it. "Right about what, Caroline?"

Caroline rolled her eyes and stepped back from the door with an exasperated harrumph.

"Wait," replied William, desperate to keep Caroline close. "That you'll find peace," he said. "To drive the last nail in the coffin before you bury it?"

A smile crept across Caroline's face. She wasn't leaving. At least, not yet. Relief unknotted his muscles. He waved her inside and for a moment she hesitated before entering the dark apartment.

"Sorry about lunch," she said but William already knew that. He'd seen the confusion as she walked away from him in the dining hall. "I have a plan," she announced.

He clicked on a light and sat across from her as she settled in on the couch. He wondered how she found him. Probably his mother. She'd always liked Caroline. It was slightly embarrassing how she'd referred to Caroline as her daughter even though William was an only child. That was the secret looming in the Lane house. She'd desperately wanted more children but it never happened. She'd told William once that he should marry Caroline. His mom never gave up on Caroline, even when she was in the psychiatric ward. His mom told him she'd rise from the ashes, and they'd reconnect. Her steadfast belief clung to him even now.

"Wait. I thought you were doing pretty good now. Second year at Stonehill. You have a major…"

"It's an illusion any college student can pull off," she said. "Just show up to class, go for help, enough to get a "C" or "B," and nobody really notices. Talk about your direction. Take courses but once you're a junior you must declare a major and then get accepted. Right now, I don't have a chance of getting into pre-law. I'm in my third college and I have lost track of how many majors I've tried. I am not getting into pre-law. The best I can hope for right now is to graduate with a humanities degree."

William decided she would tell him the truth.

"Okay," he said, his voice soft in the deep evening. "I'll follow you."

"Anywhere?"

"Yes."

Caroline got up from the couch and wandered to the refrigerator and rummaged around until she found a bottle of water. "I have to tell you something."

Nothing about this night had settled William's fears for Caroline. They had reconnected over the summer and that inspired a wild gambit in which he, after staying in Boston a month after surgery and well into rehab, reached out to her to say hello. They never connected—even though she'd promised to call him soon. He'd found out that she was taking winter classes at Stonehill College, and he needed electives he could transfer to UCONN once his playing days were over. Once he saw the selection of courses, it did not take a Rhodes Scholar to figure out which classes she would take.

"What do you want to tell me?"

She sat down again. This time next to him on the love seat. "When I was in the basement of the house on the common, I saw a girl," she began.

The statement immediately troubled William, but he didn't interrupt her. The entire episode that sent her over the edge was because of a hallucination. Instead, he continued to listen.

"Then at the beginning of this semester, my dad and I stayed in Cape Cod for a few days. I heard a voice speak to me as I lay in the sun." She placed her hand on his. "I heard her voice," she said. "The girl whispered, 'Dark as The Dale.'"

"Christ, Caroline!"

Caroline shook her head. "Please listen," she demanded. "It gets worse. I saw her again. In a nightmare. Tonight."

William listened to her tell the story. For a moment he believed.

"She called out to me and begged for help. Do you see it now? There is something more here we don't know. I'm being haunted.

Chased. She's pulling me back to The Dale. We missed something there. Something we must know and that's why..."

William cocked his head. "What if you are wrong?"

"You said you'd follow me!"

William nodded in agreement. He wanted to see her return to being Caroline Sullivan. He knew Father Bequette had encouraged her to do the research. Hell, it could be something he could get into. It was a fascinating question. What the hell was The Dale? As kids, they'd thought no one knew about it. But really no one wanted to talk about the hidden buildings in the woods. What could it hurt? he thought. But he did not anticipate the hallucinations that now haunted Caroline.

"I said I was in," he offered quietly. "I'm in. Just have you thought of the letdown if you're wrong?"

"If I'm wrong, then I am already halfway back to the psych ward."

William cringed at the thought of her institutionalized again. For a brief time, this summer, their relationship had flickered to life and now she'd come to him. He wondered whether it would flash into a wicked winter and Caroline would spin away forever. "Shouldn't we start with a map?"

Sixteen

Stonehill College
Dr. Tara Ross's Office

D R. TARA ROSS WORKED HER way through the thick file which had come to her from Dr. David Nash. He had sent her far more than she needed. She wondered why, since she had only requested reports directly related to her medication and treatment therapies.

The file left her with a picture of a young woman who drifted between catatonia and violent fury.

An extreme example of schizophrenia. At first, it seemed only an oppositional defiant disorder which expressed itself in educational settings. Perhaps, Caroline as a child, who had never been told no, spiraled off into the wastelands of depression and finally broke mentally after Henry Lee Dumont didn't listen to the word no. Tara could see her using the word to gain control of her life, then losing control of her ability to say yes, or agree to anything—no matter how rational.

It ended in the pediatric psychiatric ward, and she stayed there for three years. There were dozens of incident reports, all of them horrific. She had broken bones of orderlies, destroyed her room so many times they'd bolted down the furniture, she'd even escaped her floor only to be found in a maintenance room trying to ignite a stack of propane canisters with a torch. There were five torches with full canisters of propane in the maintenance room. She'd grabbed the sixth, which was all but empty. That choice had saved her and Dr. David Nash, who found her, from instant immolation. Dr. David Nash described Caroline's efforts to fight off the orderlies trying to sedate her as 'savage' and 'malevolent.'

Then everything stopped. A light switched on and Caroline Sullivan changed back to the girl she'd been before Henry Lee Dumont—just like Caroline had said. The file noted her priest insisted it was a moment of Grace. Dr. Nash refused to believe in 'faith healing' and had insisted she stay in the ward. Then things got interesting, her father used his money and influence to discharge her from the pediatric psychiatric ward. No more incidents.

Until now. She'd reached out to Tara. She wanted help.

Nash had done an admirable job—a job he himself did not believe was complete. His dedication to making Caroline healthy had been admirable. Honestly, she did not understand how Caroline could've been released with her extensive behavioral issues. But now she could finish the job. Tara decided she needed more. There was only one place she could get answers. Dr. David Nash.

She called her psychiatrist of record and waited for him to call her back. While she waited, she decided to read every document in her file.

An hour later the phone rang, and she answered. "Dr. Tara Ross."

"Tara Ross, this is Dr. David Nash. The Head of Medicine at Reliant Medical. You called about Caroline Sullivan."

"Yes."

"We need to talk in person. Soon."

Boston, Massachusetts
January 1995

I have business in Boston this evening. Dr. Tara Ross reflected on the way Dr. David Nash said the words. They were an invitation. One she had accepted. Not because she wanted a date. Dating was easy for her. Despite being single now, she had several prospects if she decided she no longer wanted to be single. The idea this might be a date did not cross her mind until she noted the restaurant David, not Dr. Nash, had selected. Quiet, high class. Men wore suits and the dresses on the women…holy. It was the type of place where they cooked one-hundred-dollar steaks and served twenty-dollar glasses of wine. A place that even after several conversations with him over the past week she did not expect him to choose.

She stepped to the bar and ordered a drink. Technically, she thought of herself at work. The reality of the evening hung low and easily seen. She came to speak about a girl she liked personally, yet one who carried a troubling history. Even after her conversations with Caroline, she didn't know the scope of Caroline's issues until she read the reports. Issues that might endanger students at Stonehill College. Since she held the title of Lead Psychologist, the responsibility for the actions of Caroline Sullivan fell on her shoulders. Tonight fell into a mushy area. She came because she knew Dr. Nash would fill in the details she needed to know before moving forward.

She didn't break a rule by coming here but, she thought, she bent it since she didn't tell Caroline she planned to meet Nash. It happened all the time. Rules were rules but institutions had their secrets. The biggest and most devastating secret fell across her mind—institutions did not always follow the rules, and nobody could do a damned thing about something that could not be proven.

Dr. Nash thought the problem was big enough to come here tonight. She hoped to find a way to stop hating John Sullivan while she fixed his daughter.

A gentle hand fell on her shoulder. "Tara?" When she turned the man in front of her looked nothing like a psychiatrist. Instead, he looked like a soap star. Rugged face, short trimmed brown beard, and the bruising build of a hockey player.

"Dr. Nash," she replied. "Dr. Tara Ross," she added, not sure if she liked the idea of a stranger touching her shoulder. She decided that it had not been anything but to get her attention and forgave Dr. Nash of the miscue.

"We have things to discuss."

Over the course of their dinner, he outlined the problems with Caroline and his working history with Bequette. Exorcisms, she thought, fascinated, and his break with him over Caroline Sullivan. During that time Tara's worry solidified for both the Sullivan girl, the safety of the people in her dorm, and the student body in general. He painted the picture of a lying, manipulative girl with no boundaries. He feared Caroline actively plotted to harm William and anyone else connected to that day. William, as a student at Stonehill, needed to be protected along with all the other students.

Tara grew concerned by the facts Dr. Nash presented, not the identity of Caroline's father. Tara listened to his plan to invoke an involuntary psychological assessment and then to work from the assessment data and the whole picture it generated of Caroline's mental health. She recoiled at the idea. Dr. Nash's theory that the data generated from the assessment would probably lead Caroline back to the psychiatric ward for a stay of indeterminate time, didn't match up to the girl she met.

Besides, Caroline would never agree to it—right now. Maybe if she saw the ward as something positive, she could be persuaded. If not, there was always the option of involuntary treatment and holds. Those were options but not a bridge she would cross yet. Not until she was sure that Caroline was a danger to herself and others.

"Is she honest with you?"

Tara nodded. "Yes. She holds some things back, but she has told me about her time."

"Little by little."

Tara turned defensive. "She's not going to blast the whole thing out at once. No kid would. Even someone who had not been institutionalized."

"Well," replied David, "she will appear to be doing everything you ask, and then one day she is slipping out the side door of the psychiatric wing with a propane tank in her hand."

"You think she will do that here? What could she hurt?"

"You tell me." Dr. Nash squared his shoulders a bit. "Does she talk to you about The Dale?"

"Yes. It's a thing with her. She believes she'll find answers there."

Dr. Nash looked back at her. "It's not 'a' thing with her. It's the only thing. The night she nearly vaporized half the wing she intended to leave the building and finish burning down the house on the common. Anything connected to the events of the night she was kidnapped in The Dale are dangerous to her. That place and the kidnapping have the singular effect of her making irrational, dangerous, decisions and actions."

"She promised to stay away from it. At least until she has some better tools to deal with it." Tara protested David's conclusions, but her words came out without the same conviction as she had when she thought of them.

"Are you sure?"

"Yes, of course."

Dr. Nash smiled at her one more time and placed his hand on top of hers and patted it once. "Please be careful with her."

Tara frowned and didn't want to talk about Caroline anymore. She had read the reports about the girl, and they raised enough concern to have her reach out to David. And he did not have a solution. As the evening went on his theme repeated itself. Get away from her. Get her away from the school.

Later in the conversation, she realized that Dr. David Nash dropped the 'Dr. Ross' and addressed her as 'Tara.' Shortly afterward the discussion turned away from the girl and focused on her. She found that agreeable as well.

Old Orchard Beach, Maine
April 1985

"You look like the kind of person who knows how to find her way." That opening statement had changed everything for Tara Ross who, just a couple of hours ago, had been at a most troublesome crossroad and now walked with the air of someone freed of a difficult load. A load effortlessly lifted off her back, and she stood suddenly, unexpectedly, free. A pleasant rosiness had returned to her fair cheeks as she smiled for the first time in days. Tara walked back toward the hotel with buoyant strides. The ties binding her almost into submission fell limp and dropped away, a casualty of her renewed self-assurance.

Even though Tara faced two very difficult things, she did not feel the power those things held over her. Power held over her as late as this morning. Jake would need to understand that she was a person, independent and individual. Able to make her own choices. She was not a part of him, now, nor would she ever be a part of him. He loved her very much and would have provided her with a good life. But, as the woman to whom she spoke this morning said, who wouldn't give their right arm to be the one who would love Tara and take care of her every need. *Who wouldn't indeed?* She stifled a giggle.

Her glowing smile exuded the confidence missing since, well, missing since she'd met Jake. A fact the woman she'd met on the pier gently pointed out to her. Jake, the man she loved until this morning. Jake, the man who would have been her husband. Jake, the man who she cheated on.

She needed only to make a clean break and end this stage of her life.

The woman with whom Tara had made her acquaintance this morning was a miracle and a mystery. The woman had answered the questions which roared over Tara like the surf below—how could she marry a man who inspired no spark? How could she pretend the child she carried was his? How could she have cheated so close to the wedding? Should she choose the man she loves or the one who will take care of her?

Alone and upset, Tara had stood at the edge of the pier gazing into the great ocean crackling against the rocky Maine shoreline. Then, as if summoned by an angel, the woman stood there, present and engaged for Tara. In a single hour-long conversation, the woman had shown she understood. She'd shown Tara what her world looked like in real light.

Tara's life looked ugly, and after that hour's chat, she knew what she had to do. She'd turned her head to look back at the ocean, now looking smaller and less impressive. Turning to say thank you, the woman had vanished. Maybe the woman had just slipped into the crowd and left her to sort things out. The woman had done her job, and the future opened.

Returning to the hotel, she found Jake sitting on the bed reading a book. She said little but let her actions speak. He didn't need to know why she was leaving. He only needed to understand that she was leaving.

It would hurt him. Jake would deal with it. Besides, his feelings were not the issue here. Hers were. She took the ring off her finger and placed it on the bed. She packed up her things, ignoring his pleas and his confusion, and left.

She did not answer any of his questions. She stopped at the door as he started to follow her only to convey a warning.

"Don't contact me," she snapped. Jake stood shocked at the contemptuous tone devoid of tenderness. *Not one tender word*, she remembered the woman's warning, *it will only give him hope.*

Tara left the expensive hotel room and moved on from what had been a long-planned pre-wedding getaway. Now she had a purpose, sharply focused. Her way to a brave new life led her to a small town at the foot of the Berkshires. The man she craved lived there. A new man. One who could take care of every need she and the child growing in her womb could ever think of. A man who occupied the thoughts of her every waking moment. A married man, to be sure, but certainly available. Most importantly, he was the father of her child.

Seventeen

Stonehill College
Dr. Ross's office
January 1995

D<small>R. ROSS NEEDED TO RECHECK</small> Caroline's story to be sure Caroline hadn't lied to her. She wanted to believe Caroline over Dr. David Nash. She could have a productive relationship with both—but only if Caroline remained honest with her. If Caroline stayed truthful and continued her treatment, she could reject David's notion that Caroline's presence threatened the school.

The relationship between herself and David complicated the relationship between her and Caroline. The intensity and blinding speed at which her bond moved from professional to intimate with David left her turning things over in her head.

She did not know who to believe. Caroline or David.

She never asked Caroline about David beyond the treatment regimen he used with her. She couldn't decide if she wanted to know or not. *How did he treat you? Were you comfortable around him? Did he listen?* These questions wouldn't get Caroline any further along in her current treatment. All were answers that fell closer to want than need.

David's most concerning detail left her pondering Caroline. The one scrap of information that led to the doubt she romanced now. He'd told her that Caroline was 'fool's gold.' She had been on the right track half a dozen times only to implode in spectacular fashion.

The analysis initially turned her off. Caroline did appear to be doing better in her classes. At least she hadn't dropped out. Tara spoke to each of her professors weekly. Tara had one more place to check in. If Caroline passed the test, she would be fine, and David's concerns could be extinguished.

If not. Well, she thought, let's not go there. Either way, David might be right to be concerned. Tara asked Caroline directly if she had stopped researching the place she called The Dale. The center of her psychosis, according to David. She'd been working to find the name of the worthless hovel of abandoned buildings in the woods. The place where a man named Henry Lee Dumont captured her and the dark mystery of what happened there drove her to the pediatric psychiatric ward and in and out of colleges.

Tara had asked the professor during the winter session if she'd changed her topic. He'd told her she did. Then he told her something interesting. The Commonwealth Archives would probably be the only place Caroline could find the name of the land she was looking for.

Tara needed to know whether Caroline had been there. There would be a record since the library required students to sign-in and sign out the maps. Tara called over to the archives and connected to the person at the research desk. A girl named Emily answered, and Tara identified herself and asked her to look up Caroline in the sign-in records.

Emily's voice tensed. "I think I need to check with my supervisor…"

Ross smiled to keep her voice friendly. "Of course. Is he or she in?" Tara deliberately chose late afternoon when supervision would be non-existent. "I am a doctor." Tara could hear the flipping of pages indicating Emily's search.

Emily sputtered a bit then said, "Depends on which time."

Ross paused, confused. "What do you mean?"

"She was here twice. Once before and then again earlier today. She had me pull out the same maps. I guess she wanted to show William Lane and her other friend something she'd found."

"Again? Twice. And *William and another friend?*" asked Tara, fuming.

"Yes," confirmed Emily. "She's here now."

"Now?"

"They arrived right after we opened," said the girl.

Ross did not say anything else. Instead, the idea that Caroline had been to the Commonwealth Archives twice—including right at this moment—occupied every neuron in her brain. *Why would she do that?* The possibilities swirled and tumbled across her mind; it wasn't logical. Kids lie all the time. But this was a big one. Was she lying because she didn't want to disappoint her or something far worse?

Caroline lied to me.

Tara closed her eyes and rubbed her temples. She had misjudged the girl. Caroline indulged her obsession and Tara bought right into it. Caroline, as part of her counseling, had been clearly instructed to avoid all topics relating to The Dale until she had the tools to handle what she'd repressed. Once she had the tools, she could meet the truth.

To rush in and try to find answers and then drag her friends into the mix. It was more than a simple obsession—it seemed clinical, acute, to her. It could be the return of psychosis.

David was right. Damn. He *could* be right.

She decided she wanted to ask Caroline about it. Perhaps she had misunderstood what Caroline told her. Maybe the girl had been confused. She wanted to reassure David that Caroline had progressed and left the need to lie, subvert, manipulate, and destroy behind her.

Tara stopped and willed the part of her brain that wanted to believe in Caroline to succumb to the rational part of her mind.

It wasn't a small white lie. *I have put The Dale behind me, and I won't go looking for more information*, Caroline had said. It was a worthless lie, yet one that could easily be checked.

Tara had a tool that could determine Caroline's mental status and whether she was a risk to herself or others. Tara had the right as the lead psychologist of the school to do a complete assessment of the girl's state of mind. The assessment would scientifically prove whether Caroline needed psychiatric help or not. She'd let science answer her. But first, she had to make a call. Perhaps Dr. Nash was right. David was already coming to Boston to spend time with her this weekend. He could stop at the archives and could confirm Caroline was there. She picked up the phone and called his cell phone.

Cold Springs, Massachusetts
April 1985

Tara Ross rolled past the house but parked her aging sedan a few doors down—closer to the gate at the end of the street. *Clicked.* That was the word that the man who lived in the A-frame house had used. The word yanked her forward, out of Maine, and down the Massachusetts Turnpike. To him. John Sullivan had told her about the sound of his heart as it roared in his ears—and that feeling only happened when she touched him.

Tara stayed in her car for a few minutes, not because she needed courage, but rather because she wanted to take every moment of today and internalize it—save it and savor even the air. She sat in her car and watched John kick a soccer ball toward his daughter. Tara knew her name, Caroline. She remembered every detail about her. Caroline stopped the ball mid-air with the side of her foot, let it bounce once on the ground, and then drilled it back to him. They worked out on the grass next to the house. He never looked Tara's way. His attention raptly intent on whatever move his young daughter would make next. The girl did not look like a teenager yet.

John's first complaint about his wife, Allyssa Sullivan, rolled through her mind. *Allyssa is not good with my daughter*, followed by the second, *Allyssa doesn't want me anymore.* But Tara did want children. Tara wanted lots of children with John Sullivan.

She took a deep breath, opened the car door, and stepped out into the warm late spring air. Tara took one step before a voice from behind startled her.

"Where are you going?" asked the voice, female, savage, cold.

Tara spun around to face the voice and whatever response she thought of died before it reached her lips. In front of her stood one of the most beautiful women she'd ever seen. Allyssa, willowy and blonde, the petite woman with stunning green eyes and a perfect oval face, took a step toward her. Her yellow sundress followed the perfect curves of her body as she moved.

"I..." replied Tara, dressed the way she had when she'd met John, in jeans and a T-shirt. She glanced back toward the man and his daughter playing soccer in the grass less than fifty feet away. She could not get her bearings; she couldn't speak. Tara merely stood there.

"You don't think you're the first...do you?" sneered the woman.

Hot shame inflamed Tara's face. Still, she fought to speak. Everything she had planned to say in this very situation wilted in the presence of the formidable wife. Finally, she gathered some air. "I need to see," she stuttered out. "I mean, I am here..."

Allyssa held up her hand and raised her eyebrow. "I asked you if you thought you were the first. The first to come here after he made you feel like you were *the one*?"

Tara braced herself on the car for support as she gathered her courage. She looked back. "John," she called out. Her voice was desperate and flagging. John did not move toward them, recognize her, and sweep her off her feet, then send Allyssa away.

Allyssa glanced back at John now too. Tara saw how she looked at him and, in a flash, steeled her nerves. "He's going to divorce you," she spluttered.

Allyssa moved closer, her expression stern and deadly. "That's his line. He's unhappy with his wife, she doesn't love him, or his daughter."

A line. It couldn't have been. He'd said it with sincerity and heart. Enough so that she'd chosen him over Jake. "He's leaving..."

"John says that. But look at what you see. He knows who you are, that you're here, and he never even glanced over here. Not once."

Eighteen

Commonwealth of Massachusetts Archives Annex
Boston
January 1995

CAROLINE STARTED WITH ONE map and William with another. She wished she could remember which map she'd found information about The Dale. Information she didn't share with anyone. They labored in the Commonwealth Archives. Her eyes started to blur. The headache she'd been nursing thumped louder in her head.

Maybe she should tell William the truth.

William's couch wasn't comfortable at all, despite how it looked. Caroline couldn't bring herself to return to her dorm after her encounter with the seemingly wicked and the hopelessly damned.

They'd only had a light breakfast, and her stomach growled, and she felt the crankiness work its way up to join in an unholy alliance with her headache.

"I called Daniel to join us."

Caroline turned to William. "Why?"

William stopped and looked up from his document. "He's part of this too."

Caroline stared back at the map in front of her and digested the idea—and despite having a decision made for her, she smiled back at William. "Thank you." She settled back into the pile of maps, census figures, and photographs from the building of the reservoir. Most of the maps were made after the construction of the Quabbin Reservoir. Other maps, which were completed well before the construction, didn't have the information she needed. It was laborious searching for a survey of the land done in the exact time frame they were looking for.

She brightened when Daniel showed up with snacks fifty-five minutes later and they all sank into a deep quiet with the seemingly endless piles of documents and maps for the next several hours.

Finally, William called out to them. He stood over a surveyor's map of the Quabbin so large he had to move it away from the main pile and open it up on the next table. It covered a five-by-five table and hung over the desk. William kept his eyes glued to a spot. "Do you see it?"

She and Daniel shuffled to get closer to him and get a look at his spot.

William moved his hands away from the map and gave her a better look. His enthusiasm over whatever he'd found clear.

"It's an image of the towns without the Quabbin Reservoir. We've seen several already," she said. Strange, she thought, to see the area without the Quabbin Reservoir. To her, the man-made lake looked like a large dragon head arching backward. The boulder shaped cranium reeling back, ready to strike out.

Losing herself in the large map, her eyes wandered over the dotted and fading yellow lines. The lines marked the boundaries of the towns. Each one centered on an oval common area marked in green. Other solid black lines showing roads spread out like tire spokes from the common at the center of each town. On closer inspection of the map, tiny gray squares marked major buildings such as churches and town halls or even a factory.

"We were looking at the town of Enfield on the map," Daniel said, finally figuring it out. Enfield was one of the four towns buried by the reservoir. "But Enfield is not The Dale."

"Right but look closer," William said.

"But..."

William slid his finger to the town of Enfield in the lower left corner of the map closest to Cold Springs. One road stretched from the border of the Enfield common, a faded green oval, to almost the far reaches of the drawing, and stopped near at the edge of the document. Where the road ended was a faded number 34 etched in, so lightly lettered that she had to stare at it for a few moments to make them out.

"34," she said out loud. "How does that help us?"

William explained Enfield sprouted up in what would be the lower jaw of the dragon's mouth, way too far to be anywhere near dry land so Enfield never worked as The Dale. The mapmaker stenciled the number 34 far in the map's corner and connected to Enfield by several miles of paved road. The paved road split: one section heading up toward Cold Springs and the other started as a paved road then ended as a dotted line—a seasonal road. One road went right past all three of their homes and into the center of Cold Springs. The split section of the first road stretched out to the number 34 and then stopped.

Then her eyes flicked back over to their road—Old Enfield Road. She ran her finger down the road toward Enfield and stopped at a number. "32," she said aloud.

"Yeah," replied William.

"That's the granite marker at the edge of the water," Daniel said as Caroline clapped loud enough to draw a glare from a staff member.

Caroline loved the symmetry of it all. "We never knew what it meant. 32. It's a survey marker."

"If 32 is the marker at the edge of the water at the end of Old Enfield Road, then 34 has got to be The Dale. It's in the right spot but there's no indication of a town there. It's the only road that pokes out of the water of the Quabbin for miles."

All of them went back to the material in front of them with new eyes and perspective recharged by the discovery. Electric excitement rolled over Caroline's entire body.

Two more hours produced nothing new and while the excitement faded, she still drove forward. They piled the remaining maps onto a circular table and each took one and passed it to the next person. The system didn't even have a chance to start working before her heart lurched. She asked for William's magnifying glass and studied the town road, her breathing quickened. Then, she traced the path back along the road with her finger, willing it not to shake, until she reached 34 and stopped.

Something else was there.

She glanced back at both boys; they were occupied with other documents. "Hey," she said.

Both William and Daniel turned to her. She pointed to the 1905 land survey in front of her. One of two they'd found; the other land survey had been dated 1936. Before the Quabbin had been a reservoir or a wilderness.

"South Enfield," she said in triumph. "The name of The Dale is South Enfield." Caroline stepped back and grinned, and unbidden joy welled up all over her body, leaving her skin in goosebumps. "Look," she added.

Daniel moved over to her and smoothed out a new map over the clean portion of the table. On this map, the road from Enfield to the 34 marker only showed up as a dotted seasonal road. In 1905, the road had not been paved yet. There, instead of a simple 34, the tiny icons for a church, a common, and several buildings lay in faded ink on the map. Inscribed in even lighter small letters the words: *S. Enfield*.

They all stared at the name. Nobody spoke. Caroline drifted back to The Dale, 34 for a few hours, and now its true name, South Enfield. She envisioned it as it once existed. The town quiet, green and young, now alive; then a shadow crossed her daydream. A flash of fire roared by, leaving it in ruins tangled by strangling tendrils of forest waste. Except the tendril of the vines and brush did not look like wood and cellulose, rather black, slick, and powerful oily tendrils which strangled life out of anything good.

"Caroline," said Daniel, with his head tilted slightly to the right.

"We could take a walk down there. Confirm that there's a marker with the number 34 somewhere in The Dale."

The suggestion shook Caroline. She'd already thought of it. She'd thought of it the first time she found the marker on a map over the summer. But she didn't tell anyone then. She hadn't even reconnected with William or Daniel yet. When she'd received a letter from Daniel's mother with the clipping about the planned demolition of the pediatric psychiatric ward, everything had welled up inside her. Old questions demanded to be answered. A trip to the Commonwealth Archives Annex, just to look, maybe, at a map. Get a peek, maybe an answer. But instead of an answer, she found a clue. A bread crumb that demanded more research, a marker with 34 on the road right where the water's edge would be. Then, then she knew 34 was The Dale. She needed William and Daniel. But their trip to The Dale didn't reveal a marker and the first map didn't give up the secret of the name of the town. She didn't even tell them what she was looking for.

Today gave up the name of the town. Tomorrow she could end the quest.

Caroline left Cold Springs, her home, the minute she had been released from the pediatric psychiatric wing. No new place relieved the lingering tension or sense of dread. Father Bequette once told her that to name a struggle gives you power over it. She had the name; she could see the next step.

Go there. Touch the survey marker. Say a prayer at the church. Spit on the ground. Leave everything behind. Move on with her life. Done.

"Are you both in it with me?" she asked.

"Yes," offered both.

"Let's do it."

Daniel grinned as Caroline said, "Let's do it." He watched her walk away to return the maps and speak to the librarian.

"Do what?" asked an unfamiliar voice. A voice whose cold, angular timbre inspired dread. The rugged looking man with glasses and a trimmed beard dressed in a dark suit walked toward Daniel and William.

"Who are you?" asked William, straightening his posture to his full height.

"You must be William," replied the man. "I am rarely surprised. Considering the feelings Caroline harbored for you... I am."

"Surprised by what?" demanded William.

Daniel liked nothing about this man. An air of arrogance clung to the man. He'd seen the man's eyes glance over each of them.

"That either of you would accompany Caroline here." The man dropped his coat on the nearest table with a huff. A sheet of paper fluttered down to the floor. "Considering," he added, "how she treated you both."

"Who are you?" Daniel asked.

"Dr. David Nash," he replied flatly. "I treated Caroline in the psychiatric ward. I'd like to know what the three of you are doing here. And where did she go? Dr. Ross informed me Caroline was here."

Dr. Nash's smug self-assured voice grated against Daniel's nerves. "Nope, she's not."

Dr. Nash pointed to the piles of maps and documents on the tables. "Maps of the Quabbin? Near your houses? That place left Caroline hospitalized for three years. Thirteen-year-olds running around in the middle of the woods." He clucked his tongue. "If Caroline's not here, why are you here? Why go back?"

"She can do whatever the hell she wants," Daniel snapped at Dr. Nash. "She's not under the care of anyone."

Undeterred, Nash picked up the magnifying glass and spun the handle between his fingers. "So, she is here." Then, he nodded at Daniel. "Indeed, she can. I vigorously opposed her release. Her father paid for her way out. Her case is officially open. If she becomes a danger to herself or others, she can be returned to the psychiatric ward."

"She isn't a danger to anyone." The words came out hot.

"The doctor paid to express that particular opinion... retired. You boys, tell her she needs to listen to Dr. Ross and stay away from here and The Dale or suffer the consequences."

Daniel stood side by side with William as they watched Dr. Nash leave the building. "We must stay in Boston tonight. I have an appointment at Boston General, and she has a meeting with Professor Healy. We can be back in Cold Springs tomorrow by three," said William.

"I'll be there," replied Daniel. "Do we tell her?"

William shook his head. "She's come this far. She isn't going to stop now."

Nineteen

Stonehill College
Dr. Ross's office

   TARA DRUMMED HER FINGERS on her desk as she dialed Caroline's dorm room. She hoped Caroline was staying in her dorm. She'd bent yet another rule to access the swipe codes and discover Caroline did not enter her dorm for a few days. However, she swiped in last night.
  Tara had followed the rules and had tried to contact John to express concern over Caroline's mental health. She'd left no message, hanging up as the answering machine had picked up. It would've been too hard.
  "Hello?" Caroline's voice sounded wary.
  "Ms. Sullivan," said Tara.
  "Yes," replied Caroline.
  "This is Dr. Ross. I need to see to you," she said. "As soon as possible."

"I'm going out of town in a couple of hours."

"Good, I am glad I caught you before you left." She let out a relieved breath. "Stop by my office before you leave."

Tara knew to wait before saying anything. Then, after an uncomfortably long silence, Caroline knew the trick as well. The lack of eye contact and her shaky voice told Tara a lot. Caroline was nervous and off balance. Maybe even guilty.

Caroline broke the silence. "I didn't set up an appointment. Did I miss one?"

"No, Caroline. I'm concerned about you."

"Wait. I came to you for help." Caroline seemed confused.

"Yes. And that is *really* good. It shows you are taking charge of your psychiatric issues."

"So, you think I'm on the right path," Caroline replied.

"I hope so." Tara changed her tone, now she spoke more directly, allowing firmness to enter her voice. "But in our conversations and in conversations I've had with other professors, we have some concerns."

"What concerns?"

"Your fixation about your past. We've been working well together—until now. You need to come face to face with the reality that Father Bequette has set you on the wrong path."

"He hasn't. I don't see how my past has anything to do with now," countered Caroline.

Tara gave a sympathetic curl of her lips. "It shows a pattern of irrational behavior."

Caroline glanced nervously at the door. "Wait. What did you mean, before when you said until now?"

Tara smiled and placed her palms flat on her desk. Caroline had taken the bait. From this moment on the conversation could only go one way. "After we settled in on a course that would lead you to success and build on our relationship, you lied to me. You went to the Commonwealth Archives to find answers about The Dale. That hurt me, Caroline. Why do you have to know the name, Caroline? That place is only hurt and anger for you. You don't know how to deal with it or fight back."

Tara waited for Caroline to deny the charge. She didn't. Nor did she acknowledge the accusation. The last ember of her fight to take Caroline's side died right there. It hurt Tara. She moved on to something else, ignoring the lying. Tara remembered that Dr. Nash often noted her lack of empathy for others. By ignoring her accusation and the caveat that it hurt Tara and their relationship she proved one of David's points. Her lack of empathy for others could be a pointer to the onset of psychosis.

"I am going somewhere today." The words sputtered out of Caroline's mouth. She sat unsteadily in her chair.

Ross tilted her head. Caroline hadn't been specific about where she was going. "Where?"

The girl stood up. "I'm going home."

"Two nights before your final and project presentation for Professor Healy?" Caroline displayed another characteristic Dr. Nash had warned her about: confused thinking. To leave school didn't make sense. She'd need a big reason to leave, something that would draw her away, an irresistible force. A marker of her unwinding mind. A characteristic Dr. David Nash warned her about. Caroline, he had said, lived on deception and would never tell the whole truth.

Evasive.

Argumentative.

"I forgot something."

"Must be important. You said you were going somewhere. In my experience, and looking at your file, your aggression toward me now tells me that you are a student who is struggling with letting something else get in the way of school. What is it that you are letting get between you and success in school?" Ross rolled onward.

"I'm not being aggressive," replied Caroline.

Tara held up her hands and decided to push the small girl harder. "You must put your encounter in The Dale in the right context and away for good. It's a trigger causing you to deteriorate right now.

What Father Bequette called Grace was nothing of the sort. Even if it was, where are you? Are you ready to put that behind you?"

Caroline shook her head. "I'm not dangerous, I'm heading home to see my dad."

Tara let off the pressure. She didn't want Dr. Nash to be right about Caroline needing a mandatory assessment, but he was and now she had enough information to execute it. She decided to send the girl on her way. "Remember, my job is simply to keep the campus safe and keep you safe. When you return, we will work together to complete an assessment of your mental condition. This will be a formal process which includes several interviews and testing."

Caroline glared back at her, but Tara expected it. She did not expect the next question to wound her. "Why would you do this to me?"

Tara's first instinct was to remind Caroline that her own choices had done this. But the answer, while correct, stayed inside her. Caroline hurt her and she did it deliberately. As many students as she had consoled in her career their lies always rubbed her raw. She wanted to see success and lies broke the back of her trust. Once broken, the bridge would be difficult to fix. She decided not to answer the question. "Since you are subject to a psychological assessment, your prior history now legally has become part of the decision. When you consented to let me look at the files, you opened the door. Your file contains some evidence of issues that could've excluded you from campus in the first place." Ross again paused before speaking. She decided that it rattled Caroline. "You slashed a young man in high school with a scalpel. You threatened and harmed several of the medical staff at the psych ward. There was even an incident with propane tanks."

"Fine. What do I have to do?" asked Caroline.

The question caught Tara off guard and gave her momentary pause. Most students under the threat of a mandatory assessment would argue and fight and vigorously deny they needed the help. Caroline had already done that, and she'd expected her to keep fighting. Instead, she saw resignation on the girl's face. Dr. Ross brightened. "One, you *must* complete the psychiatric assessment. Two, while I am setting this up, convince me that you are ready to continue here as a student."

"How?"

"Stay away from anything that would trigger any psychiatric episodes. For example, The Dale has a powerful effect on you. I am *certain* that has the potential to trigger an episode. Stay away from The Dale. Stay away from Father Andre Bequette."

A pout curled across the young woman's face as she nodded her agreement.

"Remember, when you left the care at the psychiatric wing your doctor did not sign off on your release, so you have an open case. That was a requirement of your release. Stay away. That applies to this college as well as your personal life. I don't want to see you devolve like you did years ago. We want the same thing, your peace of mind. If you face your triggers, you might not be able to stop your descent, which could result in being recommitted."

Twenty

The Quabbin Gate 5A
January 1995

WILLIAM HAD THOUGHT IT all the way through. He'd dropped Caroline off at her father's house and then set up a late lunch with Daniel and Caroline but never showed up. He was not going to wait for Daniel or Caroline, nor would he expose either one of them to one more encounter in The Dale. He would find the marker in The Dale, then take a picture to prove its existence before heading home. William left his house shortly after three o'clock on foot. The air sat still under a clear, bitterly cold sky. Hardened snow crunched under his boots at each step. He could not remember the Quabbin Reservoir freezing over this early in the season.

He knew he probably should've told Daniel and Caroline where he was going, but he wanted to surprise them with some pictures. He also didn't want to burden them with this task. Caroline had obvious reasons for not returning, and Daniel had nearly died there. He needed to take care of this for all of them.

William knew Caroline would be pissed when she found out. If she was mad—like push him away forever mad—at least she could go down there with Daniel.

However, he mused, unlike Caroline and maybe Daniel, he no longer feared The Dale. After the battle with Henry Lee Dumont in The Dale, nightmares stalked his darkened room in the dead black hours. After each dream, he awoke suddenly, fully, jumping out of his bed ready to fight the hooded shadow in the corner by the window. Furious swings chased the black tendrils of the phantom away, but not before it flashed its tusks and pulled a murky cloak in front of his face, vanishing in a whisper.

Left with only the sweat that covered him and the hammering of his own ragged heart, he would settle back into bed and the fitful sleep of the damned.

Over time, things changed, he felt better. Before he'd left town for college, he'd confessed to Father Bequette about the anger he'd felt toward Daniel. He never took Father Bequette's advice to solve it. After the events on the common, they had not spoken. Losing Daniel had been remarkably easy. By the time his anger cooled, there was something else in the place Daniel once occupied. Daniel worked from the time he was a freshman and enrolled in Pathfinder's Vocational High School Program, then off to UMass. Even their deepest connection, baseball, ended for Daniel the day Caroline had been kidnapped. The summer everything fell apart. The summer before ninth grade. He threw one last pitch, with two outs and two strikes, a fastball that Darren Light launched over the fence and off the concession stand. Light got to live the rest of his life knowing he hit a walk-off little league championship home run off a guy who almost made the big leagues. William heard Darren sold insurance for Prudential and kept the trophy and a picture on his office wall as proof.

Daniel never played another inning. Their friendship fell away, and they no longer crossed paths. Like the road under his feet, it crumbled. There had been no contact since the fire on the common.

William knew he'd already dealt with the aftershocks of Henry Lee Dumont, and the previously seen horrors of watching one friend come apart at the seams, and lose another in a fight at the house on the common.

So, he reasoned, going to the place where it all started did not bother him. To prove the true and proper name for The Dale would hammer the final nail in that coffin. Father Bequette said it best, name something, and it can no longer have power over you.

Heading out with a backpack and his dad's camera, he would put dirt over the blackened wooden casket. The Dale and South Enfield were the same and nothing more. He would find the survey marker and prove it today.

He walked past Gate 5A and onto the Quabbin. Despite the layer of fresh snow, he had no trouble finding the way. By the time he made it to the shoreline, his confidence in the whole mission peaked. William stopped at the first survey marker and snapped a few pictures of the number on the short granite obelisk. Then after he trekked up the shore, he paused at the creek which quietly drained into the cove. Finally, unbidden, his legs carried him on, following the tumble of frozen water up for a while until he found the path which led to The Dale.

The woods were quiet after a snowfall and as the glow of the late afternoon sun spread across the horizon in hues of pink and amber, William reached the ridge that overlooked The Dale. In the still silence, he stepped from between two bare oak trees and looked down. A shallow coating of crisp snow glittered in the last shafts of light spilling across the ground.

He pulled out his father's Canon again, clicking the wide-angle lens a quarter turn before snapping frames. Then he made his way off the ridge toward the structures. From the ridge, he noted a single pane of stained glass on the east side of the church windows held on against the wind and rain. William glanced around the ruins and did not see a marker.

He continued until he stood between the church and the road, amazed that the steeple rising thirty-five feet above the road had yet to fall.

"Still hanging on," he said, breaking the silence.

The small cement block building across the road with the collapsed roof and circled by a hopeless tangle of frozen sumac and thorn bushes, slumped under the weight of winter looking just as menacing as the last time he saw it.

Steadily, he clicked away before changing out the first roll of film. He turned on the flash as the pastel colors of sunset began to fade and its color transitioned to deeper shades of blue.

William spotted it through the viewfinder first. A spark of recognition welled up and a wave of adrenaline flooded through his system, spiking his heart rate, which he commanded himself to steady while stepping toward his prize.

William lowered the camera. Close to the side of the church, near some snarled frosted undergrowth, and almost exactly in the place where Henry Lee Dumont nearly ended Daniel's life, an unnaturally sharp edge of rock jutted out of the ground. As he drew closer to the gray weathered clapboard church, his eyes focused intently on a two-foot length of white stone, he halted. A shape like any other chunk of broken concrete in this discarded place, he thought, but now, he knew what he was looking for. There on the ground and partially covered by frozen underbrush a marker lay sideways. A marker, he thought, taking in a breath, meant nothing. The number did.

William dropped to the ground. He pushed his hands through the snow and ice then wrestled away the thin, twisted branches and thorns, sweeping the hard angled sides of the small obelisk clean. The action tested his surgically repaired elbow. He'd been without a sling for a week now.

The moment disappointed him.

No number.

At least not one on any of the three sides he could see. He put one hand on it and again pushed. Still nothing. The side above ground didn't have the number so he'd have to dig it out.

The marker would not budge out of the ice-hardened ground. He pushed again, and again, powering into it with his good arm and both legs before finally it budged slightly, sounding like a branch bending at first then wholly with a resounding crack. He flipped it over in one slow lurching motion. Right at the top of the marker, the crisply carved number *34* glistened in the light. William did not even need to brush the side clean.

The hard evidence glinted wetly in the dusk. He raised his camera to his prize and stored it on film. The marker number matched. He stood in the ruins of South Enfield as the first person to stand on the ground and call it by its proper name in forty years.

The joy of the discovery faded quickly. Alone and cold, he regretted the decision to come here without Daniel and Caroline. This, he thought glumly, is something Caroline and Daniel should've been here to see and share in the excitement. He took a last look around before gathering his will to leave.

As he rounded the front of the church for his walk home, he noticed something. Something he had never seen before. Above the church door, he saw letters scrawled into the wood. It was a single word and not, as far as he could tell, in English or French. It did not appear to be Latin either. His fascination with the language he first saw in words painted along the walls of his own church ended when he struggled mightily with the Latin grammar book given to him.

The carving itself did not appear fresh. He noted the faded appearance of the cuts. Old but not original to the church. The cuts were sharp, and the color was far lighter than the gray wood around it. William could not be sure the Canon would pick up the carving, so he considered another option. After he took a picture and packed the Canon away, he pulled out a pen from his pocket and wrote the word on his arm.

Εισβολή

William looked around, ready to leave the church, when he felt *it*… and *it* stopped him cold. Something lurked in the quiet behind him. Carefully, and slowly turning his head back to look behind him, he saw *it*. Just a shadow, out of place in the forest, between two trees. The black and cruel shape then moved closer.

In the gloaming, he heard a single word erupt from the center of his brain, which exploded from that middle point and touched every single cell in his body and blasted out of him. It was a command, and he needed to follow it. Just one word filled his universe. *RUN*.

And he did.

He ran for less than three seconds.

Because William ran the wrong way. A few seconds ago, he stood calmly on the center of the road in front of the church and now he wobbled on thin ice covering the cove.

The shadow glided back into the forest and vanished, leaving him in his predicament.

The ice bent first and then cracked and began to give way under him. He had the sensation of being on a trampoline for a moment and then he fell through, arms in front, his head arched back to avoid the inevitable. His momentum carried him under the water and past the hole he created as he broke through.

Only his face felt the burning bee-sting of the ice-cold reservoir water as he went under. For another second his jacket, boots, hat, and gloves protected him before the onslaught of cold hit him. Water sped in through his collar then his swamped his ski jacket sleeves as he fought his way to the surface.

Water sogged everything on him and drove him deeper as his cramping legs buckled under the cold. After a reflexive gulp for air filled his lungs with water instead of air, the real panic began. He struggled, conscious of being underwater and of the desperate need for air to fill his aching lungs. William, fully aware he was drowning, could do nothing about it. Then, his boots struck the mud at the bottom of the reservoir, and his legs bent under his sinking weight. He gave a push off the bottom and moved to the surface with a *whooshing* sound bubbling past his ears. When his head struck ice on the way up, he gasped again, allowing more water to pour down inside of him. The ice trapped him, and he knew it. Bouncing off the layer of ice covering the reservoir and with his waterlogged clothes pulling him down deeper into the water, he spread his arms and legs out wide like a skydiver in flight. He could see himself hitting and setting in the debris on the floor of the reservoir. Everything burning and tingling, he could sense his hands and feet burrowing into the mud as he came to a complete stop. Out of air and out of strength he thought, *dear God my family*, before sinking into the murky blackness and entering the company of a thousand intertwining dark shadows.

Twenty One

The Lane House, Cold Springs
January 1995

DANIEL COULD SEE CLAIRE Lane deep in a novel through their large picture window when he rang the doorbell. She had the luxury of working from home, which his mom always envied. He could also see the half empty glass of red wine next to her. She looked up in surprise and confusion at the sound of her doorbell.

Her surprise made Daniel even more uneasy. William had dropped Caroline at her house to visit with her father. He'd left to take care of something else. Caroline and her father then walked over to Daniel's house to visit his mother. They were supposed to meet for a late lunch, but William never showed up. Caroline had theorized he might have forgotten or misheard where they were supposed to meet. Daniel had deeper misgivings.

Daniel shrugged off the cold while they waited. When she opened the door, she smiled at him and Caroline.

"William's not home," she said, disappointed as if she wished they would stay. "Would you like to come in out of the cold?"

Neither he nor Caroline moved as if they were bound to the outside by another force.

Caroline leaned forward and spoke. "He never met us for lunch. And he didn't call."

Claire listened and slowly processed the words. Her gaze stayed on both and did not change.

"Do you know where he went?" Caroline asked.

"He'd asked me to sit with him for a few minutes." Mrs. Lane looked down as if trying to remember. "He'd grabbed his father's camera and had lunch with me. I...he left. Something about a project you were working on together."

"When did he leave?" Daniel asked calmly.

Worry crept over her face. "He left at three o'clock to take some pictures for his part of the project. I had a call." Mrs. Lane turned away from them and walked back into the house, waving them to a table so she could look at her notes. "3:17 p.m.," she said. "I took the call at 3:17 p.m."

Daniel shot Caroline a look of alarm which was returned.

"My project?" asked Caroline.

"Yes, the one about The Dale you're doing at Stonehill?"

"Did he," asked Daniel hopefully, "take his car?"

She looked out the window and didn't see William's Jeep in the driveway and then to the key rack. Both sets of keys hung there. Panic, real fear, physically jolted her body. "No, it's in the garage," she responded, her voice fading. "Wherever he went he walked." Mrs. Lane's voice rose an octave. "Why is that important?" she asked.

"We discovered our place, which we call The Dale," said Caroline slowly and carefully, "might be a town named South Enfield. We made it the centerpiece of my, our, research."

"Why would you ever want to go back there?" she asked, her voice shuddering.

Daniel ignored her question and then did the math. "The Dale is a thirty to forty-minute walk, he left almost three hours ago and it's been dark for an hour."

The lines on her face deepened and her jaw slackened as the realization sank in. Her voice was a hoarse whisper. "Even if he stayed an hour and a half, he should have been home by now. We should call the police," she added, attempting to sound hopeful.

Daniel watched Mrs. Lane stumble down the hallway. He dimly heard what happened next as she dialed the police. "My son is missing. Please help me." She hung up after a quick conversation.

Caroline sat down on the couch, but she instantly popped back up. "Can you find him?" Mrs. Lane asked Daniel.

"Yes."

Caroline stood in the corner of the Lane's living room with Daniel.

"I'll find him," announced Daniel. He wore a heavy parka and thick gloves. He'd said it twice. Mrs. Lane would wait for the police and Daniel would head out into the winter night to search.

"Me too," Caroline said, not nearly as well prepared for this as Daniel.

"No! Someone needs to stay with Mrs. Lane."

"I am just as much…" replied Caroline. "She's handling this well. She is tough."

But Daniel touched her arm lightly and stopped her. "Only you and I know the path we take to get there, stay back and wait for the police so you can guide them."

Caroline despised this idea. It meant waiting and inaction. She would bet a semester of tuition that Claire Lane also hated this plan. "But you said Chevalier knows where it is!"

"What if he doesn't come?"

Caroline, irked he was right, stood, thinking of a way to make it work for everyone. She felt a driving need to go. She wanted to go right now and knew two people searching would be better than one.

Then another voice entered the conversation and said something unexpected.

"You two are not the only ones that have been to The Dale," said the voice with gritty authority. "I know where it is too." Caroline and Daniel both spun around to see Father Bequette standing behind them wearing a long heavy navy coat and blue winter cap.

"What are you doing here?" she asked.

"You're late for our appointment," replied the priest, pointing back to her house. His breath fogged out of him as he spoke. "Get a flashlight from the garage, as a matter of fact get two and then go." It was the voice of someone used to commanding and being a leader. No shrillness or arrogance, just a simple, clear declarative *sentence, go find him.*

While she had forgotten her appointment with Father, she remembered quite a few people were there in The Dale on the day of her kidnapping. It had spoiled the secret. Who could say how many people had been there since? She suddenly felt a little foolish investigating it—a place where apparently people already knew its name. Except them. Then she reminded herself, people that also do not speak the name. Maybe they didn't think it was The Dale. Maybe only they did.

She moved down the short driveway to comply with his directive. Bequette put his hand out to stop her and, looking at her feeble jacket and thin gloves, took off his own coat and gave it to her.

"Mrs. Lane…" she offered, not quite knowing what to say.

"Is one tough woman. But she's also smart. If there is a search, she will be in it. I'll wait here for the police and guide them there," he replied emphatically. "But you must go! Daniel," he said as the boy returned with flashlights, "you remember your cold weather Boy Scout training?" The priest did not use the word hypothermia.

Daniel nodded.

Then a set of headlights lit up the street and a 5 Series BMW rolled into the driveway. William's father had arrived.

"Go," implored Bequette. "This could be nothing, but you go make sure it is nothing. Help is behind you."

Without another word, both Daniel and Caroline turned away, then ran as quickly as the snow and ice clogged road allowed. Two bouncing cones of yellow light jittered off the trees and glistened in the snow as they jogged away.

They descended in the darkness along the road that once led to Enfield, one of four towns sunk below the completely frozen surface of the Quabbin Reservoir.

Soon Caroline slowed down to a fast walk, and she could feel Daniel's annoyance. But she did not interrupt the silence for several long minutes. "Something's gone wrong," offered Caroline. She slowed more.

"We only know William didn't get home, and it's late," replied Daniel sharply. He doubled his pace, leaving Caroline two steps behind before slowing down again for Caroline to catch up.

"I can't," snapped Caroline, stung by the harshness of the tone, "think of a good reason, short of a disaster, he would be late!"

Daniel started muttering, mostly to himself, seemingly working through the facts. "William left with his camera three hours ago and hasn't returned even though it was dark. He wanted to spare us going to The Dale again." Now it was Caroline's turn to feel Daniel's horror.

The snow had blown off the road in some places, leaving only bare asphalt speckled with ice. Caroline could barely see her feet to ensure her footing. Then, she was down on the ground on all fours. One moment she was walking and the next, her front foot hit something soft and solid while her rear foot kept right on going. She hit the ground hard.

She worked up the best curse she could manage in the cold and tended to her ripped right glove and scraped palm. When she sat up, she heard Daniel gasp. Her flashlight had landed pointing up the hill. Gravity pulled the heavier front of the light downward until the beam of light stopped. When it did, the beam shone across the object which tripped her.

Then, she gasped too. Caroline had tripped over William.

Caroline knelt at the body of William lying on the ground as bile rose in her gut. Her friend lay on his side and when she touched him his green and white ski jacket made a soft cracking sound. The jacket was almost completely frozen around him as were his pant legs. Stifling a scream, she shined Daniel's light on his face and his hair. The hair clung solid and stiff with ice to his head, leaving his face a ghastly white. William's eyes were closed.

"He's dead," she cried out—more than a question, a declarative. Caroline didn't need to say it. She knew he was dead and shuffled back.

"Oh Christ," said Daniel as he dropped to his knees and immediately began to pull William's jacket open and then off.

"What are you doing?" she gasped.

"Even though it's cold, we have to get the wet frozen clothes off if William is to have any chance at survival." Daniel then took off his own coat, still warm with his body heat, and put it over William. He struggled to put it on William's stiff and cold limbs. "Help me rub his arms and chest," he said, doing his best to get heat into William's body.

Caroline snapped out of her momentary daze and took off her gloves and rubbed William's cold chest and arms as fast as she could.

"Not too hard," snapped Daniel, "you can damage his skin and muscles. He needs heat." William shuddered for a second in response to it and then went still. Both stopped and waited for another sign of life.

"Keep going," implored Caroline now that the first sign of life sprung from the icy flesh. "And pray," she added.

"We need to get him to a hospital." Daniel looked frantic as Caroline imagined his mind working through the time frame and statistics.

"We have to let them know."

"If help is already at the house, he could have a chance," Daniel said, tears welling up in his eyes. He stopped for a moment, his friend motionless at his knees.

"One of us has to go back," Caroline whispered. If they both stayed here, and both worked to warm him up, William would run out of time before anyone found them. If one of them went up the hill back to the house, the lack of a second pair of hands to warm him up would leave him dead just as quickly.

Either option had serious risks. Either option could leave him dead. She did not want to leave him.

"We gotta decide."

"Nobody knows where we are," Caroline said as she frantically worked to rub life into the cold skin beneath her hands.

In the few minutes after they found him, Daniel kept glancing back up the road hoping for a sign that help was on the way. "Take a light and run back to let them know to come here. I'll stay here with him."

"I don't want to go. We both need to be here," she said, her protest lingering. Even though she'd suggested one of them had to go back, she really meant Daniel.

Daniel just shook his head.

"Stop arguing, Caroline," Daniel shouted, his hands leaving William. "He's dying."

Caroline briefly froze in place. Daniel had never raised his voice to her even once. Twice in five minutes he snapped at her.

"I know he's dying." Wounded, she stood up, dreading the impossible uphill run. The reality of leaving, in what may be his last moments, tore into her.

Caroline let her gaze linger for a second on William who faded faster than she could warm him. Without a word, simmering in anger and snatching her flashlight from the ground, she set off. All the while she stewed, pledging silently to avoid speaking to Daniel if there was a funeral for William.

Caroline had not run, except years ago, in her hopelessly short sprints from hospital personnel with long steely needles. Her small lungs burning, legs useless after only a couple of hundred yards held her to a pace only slightly faster than walking. She never exercised because she had a high metabolism. She did nothing to help her cardiovascular health. Father Bequette's oversized coat also impeded her progress.

The icy road stretched into a long, steady uphill climb from the edge of the water to the gate. In the middle section, just as she passed the fire lane where the power lines ran and industrious beavers had been building a dam, the grade became very steep and punishing. She slowed to a crawl despite her desire to drive forward. Caroline wept in frustration as her body continued to betray her will.

Caroline trudged on, her lungs in flames, arms and legs worn to barely moving stumps. She saw flashes of red light reflecting through the tops of the trees far in front of her. They scared her at first, because she did not realize how close she was to the end of her run. Given the history of the place in which she travelled, she did not understand what they were. A red flash in the dark forest rarely boded well for anyone unlucky enough to see one.

She reached the gate and wormed her way through. When she was less than a hundred yards from his house, she started a final sprint along the icy road and began yelling for help. However, nobody responded. Caroline yelled louder and waved her hands.

Her sprint desperate, she sped up faster and faster nearly losing her footing in the snow frozen road. Still, no one moved toward her high-pitched calls as she pushed herself even harder. Frustrated, she realized the problem. The engines. She ran toward them but on the wrong side of the idling ambulance and police cruisers for anyone to hear her. The loud diesel motors were blocking her cries for help. So, she did the only thing she could while she was running, she yelled louder, and she pointed her flashlight at a police officer standing only two hundred feet away.

The Quabbin
Forty-five minutes earlier

William Lane moved toward the road barely able to see or even feel. His motions were stilted and clumsy as each painful, miserable step seemed to take longer than the last. The two numb clubs that formed his hands hung limply at his sides hemmed in place by a jacket stiff with ice. His recently operated on elbow throbbed relentlessly. Still, he lurched forward, feeling the steady push of the presence behind him. He could not see or hear what or who had encouraged him to swim for the surface and flop onto the ice. Thin ice, which had broken time and time again until he finally fought his way to shore. Someone in the desperate quiet had pushed him forward.

The cold had worn down and stiffened his joints and he'd lain on the ground for a time until the urge to go forward manifested so urgently, his need to curl up and stay motionless bowed to the impulse to walk. As he stumbled through the forest, unable to summon the energy to even think which way to go, the presence, a simple consciousness, leaned into him, driving him through the pitch dark of the frozen woods. His anger flared when it kept him from stopping as he begged. He wanted to just stop and stay still. Yet, William did not because of the steady push, and he went forward painfully slow and miserable, freezing the whole time.

William faltered at the edge of the road and took a few more wobbling steps before dropping to the ground. He rested and waited for the relentless push to drive him to his feet before he realized that for the first time since he broke through the ice, he was alone. A moment of panic stabbed through, driving William to his numb feet, and he staggered forward beginning the long uphill climb knowing he did not have the strength to make it on his own. He needed push, and it had left him. Without hope, he dropped to his knees. William took one look up into the clear and brilliantly starlit night before again sinking to the ground with a whimper.

He lay with his head on the ground, facing uphill, dreaming that he walked. William woke up with a start. In the distance, he could see two small stars moving slowly toward him. As they came closer, he tried to catch one.

The stars passed over him, and he reached to touch one. When he did, his side blazed in pain as a weight dropped across his chest. The pain was too much, and he drifted back into the blackness dreaming of warmth and starlight.

Twenty Two

The Lane House
Cold Springs

FATHER BEQUETTE WATCHED THE ambulance from Cold Springs' Vigilant Fire Company roll in behind Assistant Police Chief Chevalier with lights on, siren off, and diesel engines roaring. He caught sight of Chevalier with William's parents, all huddled in a tight circle of neighbors. The lights from the emergency vehicles flashing painted the trees in a roving, restless, red and white glow.

William went back to The Dale, thought Bequette, and the evil that brought him there had not let him go. The temperatures were well below freezing and the boy had been missing for three and a half hours, which ticked away after dark.

Bequette listened to Chevalier instruct everyone in the neighborhood to look for the Lane boy. Chevalier told his deputy that William had missed a meeting with his friends and unless he was asleep in an attic or under his bed, he must be in the Quabbin.

Father Bequette listened to Chevalier command his deputy to call another car for backup, when he caught a flash of light in his eyes and heard someone yelling at the top of their lungs. He turned toward the high-pitched and loud shouting, a cone of light from a flashlight blacked out whoever ran toward him. Then, he saw Caroline running toward the emergency vehicles shrieking for help.

Chevalier turned and intercepted her before she ran right by him to the ambulance. Father Bequette calmed the urge to intervene, he could see the terror on her face as Chevalier tried to stop her progress.

"Caroline," Chevalier said, still gripping her shoulders tightly. "I've got you."

"We found him, we need to go!" Caroline was yelling right in the assistant chief's face. "We need a doctor."

"Where is he?" Chevalier growled, grasping her elbow but not able to get a firm grip through the heavy, oversized jacket.

Father stopped Claire from grabbing Caroline. "Where is William?" she demanded, her voice rippling in fear.

"He's lying almost frozen on the road beyond the power lines almost to the water." She gasped as the lack of oxygen created by her sprint and the further demands of speech seemed to catch up to her. Claire dropped to her knees, wailing as she fell. Bequette glanced back at her husband, torn by the sudden clash of urges, one to run to his son and the other to hold his wife in her wash of grief. He grabbed her and held on as Chevalier started barking orders for a rescue that did not include William's parents.

Father Bequette looked on incredulously as the bolt cutter brought out of the trunk of a squad car appeared to be too small to cut the bolt holding the gate closed.

Chevalier hopped into the ambulance with a paramedic and waved everyone forward. Bequette watched Chevalier direct the ambulance into reverse. Then, backing up ten feet, they drove the boxy vehicle toward the gate. Seconds later, two police cruisers followed it with lights blazing.

Once near the gate the ambulance never slowed, and the four-ton red and white vehicle hit the gate at twenty-five miles per hour. The gate bent under the impact and with a resounding crack, blew off the mooring posts whirling off in the dark forest. The paramedic could not help his smile. A second later the grin cut to terror when they noticed the man running up the middle of the road.

Daniel worked desperately to heat William up with his hands. Steadily rubbing William's chest and arms failed to warm him. William had only the faintest pulse.

He decided that these actions wouldn't be enough to help. He had checked for breathing and a heartbeat as soon as they stumbled over him and found a weak thready pulse and shallow breathing before he sent Caroline for help. The former Boy Scout knew hypothermia victims go from bad to worse quickly and didn't know how long William lay on the ground before they'd found him.

William would not die here. Daniel did not think it was a coincidence that they were the ones to find The Dale or to figure out the name of the place. After the night they saved, or rather tried to save, Caroline, he vowed never to step foot in these woods again. But he'd ventured back twice. And what they found did not bring peace to him or his friends. He could've gone the rest of his life without ever coming back down this road. He foolishly gave The Dale and whatever evil snarled there a chance to take him and his two best friends and then made the same mistake three weeks later on the common. Daniel decided the Quabbin and The Dale might kill William, but it was not going to be the place where he took his last breath.

Caroline ran for help a few minutes earlier and he settled on a new plan of action. He could not wait for anyone to come to him. In one swift move, he lifted William's hundred and eighty-pound lean frame onto his broad shoulders and began to plod his way up the hill. His thick powerful legs drove onward occasionally slipping on the snow and ice-covered road, a road barely there in the best of conditions.

His legs worked for two hundred yards without fatigue. Then as the adrenaline wore thin, shots of pain danced up his legs. He pushed out his first dead breath— the one he usually took after running a quarter of a mile. All the available glucose in his blood would be expended and he gasped out the last of it in the form of carbon dioxide, oxygen, and water.

A minute later the path turned far more treacherous. Steeper uphill with almost two hundred pounds of deadweight on his shoulders. He puffed again now as his legs threatened to cramp. His body burned muscle for power while his mind turned hard inward on the only goal that mattered—getting William up to the top of the hill for medical attention. Years lost between them had not been enough for the wickedness that threaded its way around every tree and rock in the damned forest. He decided that the malevolence did not get to win. It did not get to take the best friend he'd ever had.

Daniel heard the ambulance before he saw it. Its red lights and growling diesel engine roared, and he was sure it was getting closer. He heard the crash at the top of the hill and then headlights filled his entire world. Tires screeched as the ambulance fishtailed on the ice. Lights and people surrounded him. A fireman pulled William from him and thrust his friend into the back of the ambulance. Out of energy, he dropped to his knees then to a sitting position looking up at the stars wondering if his friend would live.

Twenty Three

Reliant Medical Emergency Room
Cold Springs, Massachusetts

When Caroline's father reached the entrance to the hospital, Chevalier stopped him, but she kept going. Her father kept glancing at her while he spoke, never really looking at Chevalier.

William still languished in the ER and Daniel had been taken to a room to be examined by the medical staff. She could hear him. Daniel demanded to see William and her. That outburst from Daniel left her chest warm and her fingers with a vague tingle.

The bustle from the emergency, which had swallowed her outside the Lane home, spit her out and left her alone while everyone focused on William. She wondered what to do in this next stage of the crisis. She barely remembered anything after being rescued from Dumont. The aftermath only a blur did not help her now.

Despite living in a hospital for three years, she had no idea what to do as a visitor. She stood in front of the nurse's station silently wondering who to ask about William.

This problem had a brief life. Her father excused himself from Chevalier and swept in and motioned to her to follow him through a set of automatic sliding double glass doors. The doors led to a hallway from the emergency room to treatment rooms with more sophisticated equipment. The hall with clean industrial tile floors led to another waiting room directly across from these rooms.

Caroline stuttered to a complete stop upon seeing William on a gurney and engulfed in a flurry of medical activity, one member of the medical team stopped her cold. Dr. David Nash appeared to be supervising the operation.

"He's the head guy here now," said her dad.

After seeing Nash the hope she had for William a few minutes ago evaporated.

A flurry of sound announced a clutch of families coming in from the street as they crashed into the room at the same time.

Her head turned back to Nash, and she ached to say something to him. Maybe, he should leave this to the professionals or someone who knows what they are doing. She queued them up in her head, her frustration with William, Daniel, Dr. Nash, and men in general boiling over until a gentle hand grasped onto her elbow.

"Caroline." She spun toward the owner of the offending hand clutching her. It was Daniel's mother, Julie, gazing impassively at her. Caroline yielded to her warm, soothing touch but still seethed inside and with nothing else to do, Caroline lofted an unpleasant scowl in Nash's direction.

Caroline orbited in the hallway just outside of William's room waiting for a chance to see him. Her father sat in the waiting room halfway down the hallway, talking with Julie Wilson and Daniel, who had finally convinced the staff that he'd live until morning and reluctantly agreed to be wrapped in a thick, heavy, white blanket. Caroline's chance came as William's mother left the room. She jerked to a halt as the next person came out.

Dr. Nash stepped out of the room gently guiding a haggard Mrs. Lane. Her effortless regal stature was gone, replaced by the slump-shouldered shock of the day. A woman staring at the reality of the pending death of her only child and wondering if the hood and scythe would turn away alone with a sweep of his rotten cloak or take her onlyborn by the hand.

Caroline could hear him whispering to Mrs. Lane. As they passed, Dr. Nash turned and glared at her. "Dr. Ross will know by morning," he said, stalking past Caroline, pulling William's mother along. Caroline stood up to the stinging rebuke. Dr. Ross would know Caroline disregarded her warning and would come at her hard. When Caroline returned to Stonehill, Dr. Ross would come knocking on her dorm room door sooner than later.

Caroline shook off the hideous thought and stepped into William's room. After several hours of waiting, she finally got her look. The gaggle of focused doctors and grave faced nurses elsewhere.

William lay on a bed raised slightly at his head. Heavy blankets wrapped around him up to his shoulders. An IV line dangled from a bottle of clear liquid and sunk into his arm. To his left, a large oxygen tank pumped air through narrow hoses, which hung over his ears and in front of his nose. Monitors beeped evenly in the corner of the room.

Caroline moved closer and reached her hand under the blanket to gently rub his arm. The room had the familiar smells of alcohol, cotton, and body odor.

"That was not fair," said a voice behind her. It was a soft voice, but she jumped when she heard it. "Not your fault," added the voice. Turning, she saw William's father.

Caroline had been so focused on William she hadn't noticed his father sitting in a chair to her right. He stood up slowly and timidly, like he'd been in that seat for a long time, like a man who had also been thinking and turning things over in his head.

She knew the look.

He must not have even stirred when his wife left the room. He stood next to her in his dark blue suit, white shirt, red and blue tie hanging loosely around his still stiff collar. They both gazed at William in bed. The tone of his voice eased the stress of the day.

"We haven't talked in a while, but" she said, wanting to comfort him. "But…"

He waved her off.

"Do you know why he went back?" he asked.

"It was the marker," answered Caroline. "He went back to prove The Dale was a place called South Enfield. To find a marker we saw on a map," she said, and then added the thing that bothered her, "I don't know why he went back alone." Her hands tightened into fists.

For a while, the only sounds in the room were of the heart monitor beeping steadily and the hissing of the oxygen tank.

"No, you wouldn't," said William's father, finally breaking the silence. "The marker and the project were an excuse," he whispered and placed his hand gently on her small shoulder. "He went back because whatever evil infested that place had already beaten him twice. Once with Dumont in The Dale and again on the common with Daniel and you. He wanted to show himself that the evil that lingered in either place couldn't beat him again. He sought it out."

His words were a light clicking on for the first time in her brain, illuminating a hallway darkened by time and denial.

"The map and the marker were just excuses?" Caroline bit her lip and wondered why she hadn't seen this. Then, something else hit her. "William hates to lose. It's a loop we're stuck on and can't get off. The best we can do is get far away for a while before we get sucked back into the loop. We can't ever totally escape."

"Yeah."

"That pull will never go away. It knows it can beat us and make us come back for more. But maybe it wants something else. Something that it does not yet own. Or possess," she said as the adrenaline wore off and she began to feel weak and exhausted.

"No, the pull won't go away," he said in as much of a matter-of-fact way as he could muster in his current sadness but then softened up. "Not for a long time. He never let it go… and you know what? I taught him that, to never let a loss hang around, to go back out and get it off your chest." William's father shook his head slowly, almost ready to weep. William's chest rose a few degrees with his breathing. His father ran his hand down William's arm. "It seemed like a good idea because he had a gift, you know." Mr. Lane sighed. "I did that too. I purposefully embedded this trait over time in my son, and I did it so effectively that William thought the idea was his and his alone." His hand stopped around William's heavily wrapped elbow.

"Can he play again?" asked Caroline, wondering what else could go wrong today.

"It doesn't matter, for now, maybe it's the price to pay to be alive," he offered, "maybe." William's father's voice broke.

The lines in his handsome face deepened. She saw him as a man staring losing his only child in the face. A man who seemed to vacillate between a dazed blank stare and the frenetic, almost obsessive, study of the dials and numbers on the medical equipment attached to his son.

He pulled her close, a little roughly, a moment of near panic appeared to rise in him and then fell away leaving him only to say the last words on his mind.

"I know you will want to go back and figure this out, and you have no reason to trust me." He stopped and looked her in the eye. Caroline saw he and William shared the same stunning blue eyes.

Those eyes were begging her to listen. "But for the love of God… let it go. You have an entire beautiful life ahead of you and you deserve that life. Please stay away from that place, it is nothing but evil. It has taken enough from you." His hand slid off her shoulder and he turned and left the room.

To her horror, Dr. Nash stood in the doorway staring at her. She wondered how long he'd been there and if he'd heard their conversation. His smirk as he left unnerved her.

The emotions welling up inside of her were too much and she needed to leave. Before she did, Caroline noticed William's arm. She pulled away the blanket covering his arm.

There were words she did not recognize written just below his palm in the middle of his wrist. Impulsively, she took a pen and pad from the table next to his bed and wrote down the word before sliding the scrap into her pocket.

Twenty Four

The Quabbin Gate 5A

FATHER ANDRE BEQUETTE WALKED past the tangled remains of Gate 5A purposefully and without fear. The moon was down, and he had only starlight to guide him. He was still without a coat or hat and yet he continued in the dark.

The Catholic priest had been walking for a while down the road, bracketed by the forest of hardwood and conifer, on either side, when ahead of him he saw a dim yellow glow, barely perceptible even in the umbral dark. Bequette stopped and assessed it before moving toward the light.

A small glow, stationary and weak. When Bequette stooped down to touch it, the cold burn of metal surprised him. Still, he picked it up. One of their flashlights, he thought, the battery all but dead. In fact, the bulb was only the barest spark and only visible because of the depth of night in the forest. He clicked it off and on absentmindedly before leaving it off for good. His eyes now attuned to the low light noticed something else on the ground.

It was a camera case. William's mother had mentioned that William had been in the forest to take some pictures of The Dale. Bequette picked it up but in the dark could not see much of the camera beyond the flecks of ice on the case, glinting in the pale light of the night.

For the moment, the camera could hardly be a curiosity. He would deal with getting it to William's parents later. Bequette then turned toward The Dale and stared off into the blackness long enough that he started to shiver. He did not fear The Dale or even whatever lurked there. However, Caroline, William, and Daniel did not know what twisted and scurried its way among those ruins that should terrify them. Caroline did not display any of the faith he prayed time and time again she would accept. Without it, she'd be helpless against the malevolence. He turned back up the road and began to plan. He needed to consult the bishop.

She'd been freed in one moment of Grace. It was the only explanation. Three years of psychiatric care yielded nothing. He had been approved to do an exorcism on the girl after a long process of documentation and medical examinations. After Dr. David Nash, the arrogant ass of a psychiatrist, yielded nothing from his hopeless treatments.

Bequette knew his reputation. A man married to his powerful faith and his intellectual wattage white hot. Assets clear to anyone. In his youth, his career beamed bright enough that his superiors used words like *Vatican* and *bishop* in his presence as if the result had been a foregone conclusion. And then, over forty years ago, he'd shown a talent that few priests possessed.

Possessed, he grinned at the irony of the word. He *possessed* a talent to determine the real deal from the pretenders. A talent which proved to be valuable, critical to the faith; his unbendable faith needed to face down true evil and live to face it over again. He'd agreed, obedient from the first, even as the dreams of young men fade slowly. Bequette's career screeched to a halt in Cold Springs. More accurately, he thought, in South Enfield, and from that moment on he'd stayed put. He worked the day-to-day existence of a Catholic priest. Except, he and two other priests also excised evil that infested souls. Exorcist, he thought. A rite looked at with contempt by some in the church and as a Saturday afternoon movie trope by the public. The reality of the rite existed as simple authority and expulsion.

However, he would've needed to discuss it with Nash since it was not likely Nash would let him perform the rite in the psychiatric ward. He needed to find a way to get her out of the facility for a day or two. He could neither perform the rite she so desperately needed or even get her out of the building. He had the tool to help her yet stayed hopelessly caught in an endless frustrating loop. He'd been stuck until the moment she had been freed. Then, he knew God intervened. Even *He* got impatient sometimes.

The malevolence had infested her, broken her soul, and shattered her faith, crushing her so far down that she drifted for years in a psychiatric wing. Her body had been there but the bright starburst that was Caroline Sullivan had vanished. The malevolence had replaced her with a Caroline who broke bones of orderlies and devastated everything around her.

Bequette had discounted every other explanation for the obvious one. Suddenly and completely the malevolence which had infested her soul had been ripped away and tossed aside. Nothing other than the intercession of God himself could do that.

In one moment of Grace, she had been freed from it. Even with the malevolence that infected her soul gone, she still sought answers.

Twenty Five

St. Francis Rectory, Cold Springs
January 1995

DANIEL WILSON DIDN'T KNOW why they headed to the church rectory. Caroline said she had a hunch. He wanted to go to the hospital to see if William was any better, but Caroline insisted that they do this first. Ultimately, Daniel decided that going to a church could do nothing except help their cause. Besides, he thought, Caroline was driving, so he didn't have much to say about it. He turned to look at her bundled up in a blue ski jacket, gray mittens, and a Boston Red Sox winter knit hat. She squinted out the window of the Explorer as she drove. She'd met him in his classroom as soon as his final class ended. The buses were not gone, and people still crowded the hallways. All he knew was Caroline had popped her head in and said they needed to go to the church rectory, and she would drive. She had a way, he realized, of saying something that was a command without it being an actual command.

She'd told him about the threat that Dr. Nash made but so far, he had not followed through. Before they went into the rectory, she grabbed a large jacket from the back of the SUV. Mrs. Ventura opened the door, welcomed them, and led them to Father Bequette's study.

"Thank you for coming so soon," said Father Bequette.

Despite the office being overloaded, Daniel didn't feel cramped in the large space stuffed with books covering a whole spectrum of interests; biology, medical ethics, theology, a thin mathematics text *Mandelbrot's Fractal Geometry* that looked wildly complex. On every flat surface were more and more books. *Orbital Mechanics Third Edition*, and *Astronomy: A History*, and still more texts than he could catch the names of in that short time. Also, he noticed a small section dedicated to the history of Western Massachusetts. Watercolor paintings and at least a dozen framed pictures of Bequette with his friends dotted the walls. The priest who was still standing waiting for them to settle in noticed him lingering near the bookcase nearest the large bay window at the back of the study.

"I thought," said Daniel, pulling an astronomical mechanics text off the shelf, "you guys just had to read church stuff."

Bequette chuckled when he finally sat down. Daniel knew Father was smart from talking to him at mass each Sunday and the many times he saw him at the Sullivan house, but it never occurred to him to think about what Father did in his free time. Apparently, he did a lot of reading. And from the pictures on the wall, he traveled. He looked at pictures of the Middle East, Europe, and what looked like a squalid place in Central America with red clay soil. In each picture, people, mostly young people, he realized, surrounded Bequette.

"For over a thousand years after the fall of the Roman Empire the only educated people in the kingdoms of Europe were the priests, monks, kings, and bishops, everyone else was illiterate or barely literate." Bequette leaned back and continued, "So priests continued the hard work of keeping knowledge—and keeping their heads if *knowledge* did not please the king. Think of all the great minds of that millennia; Mendel in genetics, Mersenne and Picard in math, Lemaitre the physicist best known for coming up with the Big Bang, all of them were part of the church. God gave me a brain, so I use it." He looked at Caroline and thanked her for the coat.

"I…" she stuttered, pulling a small piece of paper out of the pocket of her jeans. "Can you tell me what this means?" Caroline handed it over to the priest. "William wrote this on his arm. He must've done it before anything bad happened," Caroline said.

Daniel noted her edginess, but Father seemed not to notice. He was thankful she didn't engage in small talk.

Father Bequette took the paper and looked at it, then rotated it to correctly orient the letters. He studied it before leaning back in his chair.

"It's a word written in ancient Greek," he said in a deep, clear voice, "and the English translation is *epitheon* which means to surround or… siege. Homer used it to describe the events around Troy," he said and then stopped when he saw Caroline's reaction. She had gasped when he'd said the word "siege", and the color drained from her face as if she'd seen something horrific.

Father Bequette opened his desk and pulled out a manila package and removed some pictures from it. He paused for a second and then spread three pictures out across his desk and all of them centered on the same thing—the word Εισβολή… *epitheon*. The word shown carved into the wood of the structures of The Dale in its present state. William had taken pictures of the carvings. Against the black wood the carving looked fresh. "I found your flashlight last night and his father's camera. Both near the edge of the road. This morning, I had the photographs developed and saw these last three pictures. The image was distorted because the camera had been exposed to the cold and probably submerged."

Daniel wondered again why they had not gone directly to the hospital. While he listened to Caroline indulge her questions, he sat restlessly. He wanted to see William and not revisit the relentless terror which occupied every moment from the time they realized William was missing until the time the doctors declared him stable. However, the question was a good one. He had already thought the only way William could've gotten that wet and icy was to have fallen in the reservoir. Neither of them had been in any hurry to go back to The Dale to confirm the theory.

"He must have seen the carvings and then not only took the picture but had the presence of mind to write the letters just in case the film did not show them," reasoned Father.

"What does that mean?" asked Daniel, not grasping the significance of what he was looking at but knew from Father's face and Caroline's reaction, the impact of the knowledge reigned over them.

"It means that you have a bigger problem."

"What could be a bigger problem?" asked an exasperated Caroline. William clung to life in the hospital, stable but not well, nightmares had left her dorm room a tangled mess, and fear danced across her midnight hours. However, despite her distress, Caroline calmed herself upon seeing the seriousness creased in Father Bequette's face.

"The other word," he said, pointing to the picture, "is a problem." William had taken several pictures, there were two different Greek words carved into the church. He turned the picture around so he could see the second word better. The second word was faded, and you had to strain to see it. He tapped the Greek lettering,

εισβολή

"The second word is also written in ancient Greek, in our lettering it would be *eisbole*." He wrote the word on the paper in neat, clear, Arabic letters. Then added somberly, "Which translates as *invasion* in English." Bequette let it sink for a moment.

"Invasion," said Daniel incredulously.

"Siege," added Caroline, trying to wrap her mind around the words as they collided and twisted into each other uniting into an understanding she could grasp but did not want to accept.

"It is a warning. A loud, unmistakable one at that." Bequette looked out of the window as a whisk of snow blew by. "To answer your question, I believe it means you. You are under siege, and the invasion is here," he said, pointing to both of their heads. "Evil never stops looking for a way in, but you two and William have been attacked, invaded, or laid siege to."

"Who would write the words, in Greek using Greek lettering, on the face of the church in The Dale?" asked Daniel.

Invasion.

Siege.

Pieces were clicking into place for Caroline. The siege of her mind stopped, and the invasion pulled back in what Father Bequette called a moment of Grace three years before. That moment of Grace allowed for her release from the psychiatric ward. The malevolence in command of those operations crashed back in that Grace but was not completely gone. The happiness she now had was something for which she had to fight. She realized the battle never ended; evil kept tempting her back toward despair. She'd been freed but still faced the prospect of the same evil seeking her out. And she foolishly allowed it back into her life. Maybe she didn't need to know the name of the town after all. Perhaps that was a snare.

An idea that she had been fighting roared forward, unabated despite all her defenses, and burned past the roadblocks and bulwarks she had erected and stopped only when it had her full attention and stood dead center of her mind. Whatever was in The Dale didn't just want her, it wanted them all. The idea of something evil in that place had been limited to the actions of Henry Lee Dumont. An idea neatly placed into a tight little box marked MENTAL ILLNESS or JUST-A REAL-BAD-MAN. Evil in that event was concrete and limited to her understanding of the world. But now, Bequette's translation and William's pictures demanded her to face something more. A malevolence wound into the fabric of the forest and the roots of South Enfield. A wickedness that explained the nightmares and dark horrors burned in a basement. Evil which reached out from the deep-frozen woods and into her bedroom.

It was real.

And from The Dale, it locked in on the three of them. Only Daniel had been spared. She wanted the luxury not to believe in the supernatural, but the evidence sparked in front of her mind and glowed stronger.

"I have something to tell you," she said barely above a whisper. "Something important." Caroline took a deep breath and told them about the girl in her nightmares, and the encounter not only in the basement of the house on the common but also in her dorm room. A secret she'd been keeping. The story came out of her quickly, ending in a long silence.

"I will suggest," offered Father Bequette, "the next time you have an experience with the wicked and the damned… lead with that."

"Only William knew. I think he agreed to help me because of that." A sense of relief left her fatigued. Odd, she supposed telling him would bring her comfort.

"The same girl keeps haunting you?" asked Bequette. "And she's the phantom voice from the beach?"

Caroline nodded. "William was right," she said finally, "it was always The Dale. All this time I just thought it was me. My psychosis. A stubbornness and tantrum I couldn't control; horrible actions I unleashed on others. Feeling like the impulses came from an evil part of me." Caroline wanted to latch onto the theory that she wasn't a terrible person. That her vile acts before her time in the psychiatric ward and those while she lingered there were not of her making. She desperately wanted it to be true. But no one made her do those things. She did it all. Dr. Tara Ross told her that she must take responsibility for her actions. "How do I know it's not me. It still could be me. Right?"

"No," replied the priest with a dismissive wave of his hand. "The Devil's greatest skill is to hide in plain sight. To allow someone to look at his work and not define it as his," replied Bequette, his words kindly.

"That's why you saw the girl as evil rather than the true malevolence attacking you."

"Well, how should I look at her?" Caroline demanded. "She is the person from the house on the common and my room!"

"As help," offered Bequette. "After all, according to your own story, she suffered horribly, barely able to get out those two crucial words of warning. Upon any sort of reflection, she is help."

"Is she trapped by something?" asked Daniel.

"No. Only God can allow her to be bound. The malevolence in The Dale, the demon, does not have the power to keep her there if God does not want her to be there."

"She has a purpose," concluded Caroline as the idea began to firm up in her mind. "She wants to be there. Or is there by choice. Why?" Caroline dropped into thought about what purpose the girl could have. Why would she risk the living hell which Caroline saw, and Daniel could only imagine? The hell in which William possibly drifted?

"You said you knew how to get to The Dale, and you would guide the rescue units there," Daniel said carefully. "You couldn't have remembered just by following the police one time on the night Henry Lee Dumont died. How do you know about The Dale?"

The winter sun set, drawing shadows across the town common as a few people scurried about their business, and a clock chimed the hour. Mrs. Ventura steadily tapped away at her keyboard in the next room. The air in the room was warm and filled with the smells of dinner cooking. A thin line of condensation had built up at the bottom corner of the window. Both Caroline and Daniel stared at Father Bequette in silence, awaiting an answer.

"I know about what you call The Dale because I have been there. Not just on the night of your encounter with Dumont, but a long time ago. Before the Quabbin existed."

"What were you doing there?" asked Caroline, her imagination flared with the idea that Father Bequette had harbored this secret for years. Then inexplicably she sensed the warm first light of anger banging away at her ribs. She realized something else. She was angered because Bequette knew about The Dale. He hadn't told them about it when she had been rescued. Caroline squashed the feelings and gave Bequette the benefit of the doubt. But it was a big thing to keep from them.

"The bishop," offered Bequette. "I was staying a few days at his residence on some other business when he received word of a troubled young man. The parish priest in Cold Springs was nearly deaf and borderline senile so the bishop dispatched me to meet the boy."

"Back then the town had all but dried up. South Enfield had a tiny common and a few businesses dotted around. A few families clung to the edge. Everything had been condemned or taken over by the state in preparation for the construction of the Quabbin Reservoir and South Enfield sat deep in the surrounding forest.

"They were already in a crisis when I met them… the Evans family. They owned a successful mill that supplied lumber for businesses in other towns. They were not strangers to tragedy since a year earlier, the mill had burned to the ground, taking their young daughter, Hannah, with it. Grief stricken, the father, Lester Evans, drifted away from them and occupied himself with rebuilding the business. The mother, the strongest, held up Lester and kept the house together. Their son, Henry Evans, previously a jubilant young man, was the problem for her. She watched as he struggled to do the job his father had given him. He sullenly wandered the forest looking for stands of trees which teams of lumberjacks could harvest for his father."

"Was he depressed about the loss of his sister?" asked Caroline A flash of emotions whirled over her as she tried to envision the loss of a sibling. William, she thought as the electric grief jolted her.

"Of course. Both Lester and his wife were concerned," replied Bequette, "because Henry's behavior changed so rapidly and completely. It was far more than grief, which is seen in stages, denial, anger, bargaining, etc., the boy displayed aggressive, savage tendencies, acting cruelly. Cruelty that had never existed in the boy before in his previous twelve years on earth."

"Is that why they called you?" asked Daniel.

"Yes. But not until his father followed him into the forest," replied the priest.

The scrolling picture of an angry boy heading into the dark forest around the town briefly stiffened the hair on the back of Caroline's neck.

"The boy would leave the house and wander, at first for an hour before returning, then two hours, half a day, until he'd be gone for a whole day, and then, alarmingly, days at a time."

"Where did he go?" asked Daniel.

"His father thought he was searching for stands of good lumber. Times were tough, and the good usable stands of hardwood were harder to find in a forest choked with pine and ash trees. He never returned with new locations of trees. Fed up, one day his father followed him into the woods. The boy walked into the forest, which as you well know, is thick and filled with short valleys and sharp ridges, and hiked into one of these valleys. Lester snuck into the forest behind his son, carefully and quietly he tailed him. He followed him through the woods and to a valley not far from the town. He followed him even as the boy wandered up a stream. At the very end of the valley where the stream emerged from a solid rock wall and drained down the steep face, the boy sat down. After a period, the boy got up, then looked around before picking up a large stone from the floor of the valley. Finally, he placed it onto a pile of other stones already there in the middle of the pool."

Caroline jumped at the description. So did Daniel. "We know this place. We found it. He just put a single stone upon an ever-growing pile." Caroline, her mind dazed by the smack of the image. Stones, an ever-growing pile...*just like mine.*

"One stone at a time each day for months. A whole day, used up in the box end of a narrow valley without so much as a thought." It was a compulsion, she realized, he had felt a need to be there.

Caroline didn't like where this was going. She, at first, had been terrified of the pile of stone. So much so that she could not wait to leave. Only then and the days later did she encounter the overwhelming urge to return. "Why did the boy so desperately need to be there?"

"Lester Evans asked himself the same question," replied the priest. "He traveled back to the place for several days, watched his son repeat the process over and over. As he watched, he searched for whatever might draw his son to the valley. He thought he had come up empty, he did not. Lester did not recognize his son had found and disturbed evil. The malevolence was lying low, slowly circling, gently pulling them closer to its center."

"How do you know the place was evil?" demanded Caroline. It was fully dark outside, and the streetlights powered on, leaving the falling snow to glow like winter fireflies. A fresh, slim white coat of snow smoothed out the edges of the common.

"It's not the place which is evil, again simple Saturday movie nonsense. Evil waits on a weak spot to open to enter your life. There in the place Henry Evans named Metacomet's Barrow, his defenses failed. Like yours did in The Dale. He marked it stone after stone and day after day. Just as you marked your days in the psychiatric wing."

Father Bequette took a deep breath and leaned forward. The furnace air, warm and dry, rumbled through the vent near Daniel's feet. Caroline wished her own feet were closer to it.

"Faith," said Bequette, "is the effective counterstroke which crushes evil. If the two of you do not understand the power you hold… things will go badly going forward. Going to church on Sunday is one thing but *acting* in faith and an understanding of the power of that faith is quite another. Henry Evans had none at that point in time and he crumbled.

"I counseled the boy," continued Bequette, "and attempted to help him make some progress. I stayed in residence with the bishop. Then, the Great New England Hurricane dropped a bullseye on Cold Springs and the rest of the Pioneer Valley, and everything fell apart. Heavy rains tumbled down the slopes into streambeds dry for a decade, one of which undercut the foundation of the Evans mill. What had been nothing but a ripple in the land, now revealed itself as a creek bed. A fifty-foot-wide, boiling brown, roaring waterway racing down from the head of the same valley Henry had named Metacomet's Barrow. The torrent cut away the land under his mill. Lester tried to change the inevitable outcome. His land had been taken from him. His business was being taken from him, his daughter had been taken and now his son. His last desperate act was to try and hang on to something. Lester was last seen waist-deep in the roaring water angling a wooden support beam into place as the back of his mill collapsed around him. Utterly foolish since the mill was slated to close because of the reservoir."

Caroline raced to the vision of another loss. Except this time, she shook it off and pressed Father Bequette for another part of the story. "What about the boy?" she asked.

"He lived," said the priest, "a troubled life and died in the valley."

Pity rose in Caroline's heart for the young boy. She, like Daniel, knew what it was to yearn for something that they couldn't have. She wanted to know one thing about him. It seemed he had a cruel life, and she hoped that maybe his death had not been cruel.

"What happened to him?" Daniel asked quietly.

"You should know," replied Bequette. "You were there. He died in The Dale."

Caroline tried to think of something to say, but the overwhelming sadness crushed any thought.

"What?"

"The boy's name," said Bequette, "was Henry Evans. After the death of Lester Evans, his mother never remarried. Not long after her husband perished, she disappeared and left Henry alone. He later took his adoptive father's name. You knew him as…"

"Henry Lee Dumont," whispered Caroline.

Twenty Six

St. Francis Rectory
Cold Springs, Massachusetts

THE MAN HAD HAUNTED Caroline's restless nights and drove her to an asylum during the fruit of her teenage life. Dumont, who viciously tried to beat Daniel to death before being struck down by rifle fire, and who marked his days in stone—so much like she did, except instead of tiny pebbles on her desk in the psychiatric wing he used small stones. "Henry Lee Dumont," she said. Images of the man who never escaped and suffered as endlessly in The Dale as she did in the wing tore through her mind.

"Did Dumont," Daniel asked, "carve those words into the church?"

"Yes," said Bequette. "Part of his education was the study of ancient Latin and Greek. Much like the battle you witnessed with the girl in your room, somewhere the soul of Dumont still reached out for salvation." Father Bequette moved next to Caroline and placed a comforting hand on her shoulder. Caroline felt her face twist into a grimace. "This," he gently said, "is the connection that you seek Caroline. The boy disturbed an ancient evil, and it ruined everything in his orbit. He allowed that malevolence to overpower him. To oppress him for his entire life. You met him once in The Dale and came face to face with that evil. The malevolence could not hurt the three of you when your lives were happy and whole and together."

"And Dumont was alone."

"Yes," offered the priest, "and yet he had one lucid moment in which he fought his way out to the surface and carved the words screaming from the bottom of his soul."

"Christ," moaned Caroline.

"While you were weak in the aftermath of the horror in The Dale, the divorce, and the abandonment by your mother, the malevolence came for you. He forced his way in and held you captive without you even knowing it. You believed that your thoughts and actions were your own. But they were not. He pummeled you into submission. He shackled you as he did Dumont."

"And now..." said Daniel slowly, appearing as if his mathematical mind was snapping everything into place.

"It's coming back for us," said Caroline, leaning forward to prop herself against the desk before sinking back into her seat. The threat of falling backward into the hellish state of mind which led to a stay in the pediatric psychiatric wing loomed dark and dreadful. She traced a whip straight line from the moment Dumont set foot in Metacomet's Barrow, through his death, then to her psychiatric nightmare, years of fumbling around in college, and finally this moment. There did not even have to be a bogeyman to torment her, the world around her, everyday emotions and actions, could reign the same terror down upon her. As they sat here, Dr. Nash and Dr. Ross could be planning to lock her away. Caroline feared she wouldn't be strong enough to fight it off.

Father Bequette gazed back at both and then gave them the simple, honest answer. "Yes," he said.

Cold Springs, Massachusetts
August 1948

    Father Andre Bequette sat and listened to Leigh Anne Evans describe her nightmare of a life. Leigh Anne visited him often. He decided that she needed someone to listen to her. Reassure her. But he had been so very wrong.

    Evans could still hear her deceased daughter Hannah's graceful voice, and it did not surprise Bequette. She'd been lost in the horrific fire that had destroyed the family mill. Despite being a few years out of the seminary, he had completed a significant amount of counseling. He knew the memory was a gift from God bestowed upon her.

    The sweet clear voice ringing throughout the house is what Leigh Anne remembered most about her daughter. Now, Leigh Anne confessed to him that her greatest fear was that one day she would not remember the sound. Then her daughter would be truly gone.

    Before, when Leigh Anne teetered on the edge of the shadow zone between sleep and waking, the sound of Hannah's voice came to her. She dreamed of fire and burning, but Hannah had disappeared. Abandonment, thought Bequette.

    It was her new hell until last night when Hannah's tune was strong and ringing in her ears and miraculously calling out to her. She'd burst awake and opened her eyes in anticipation of finally seeing her again but what she'd seen in front of her was not her daughter, but her son. And he'd spoken to her in the voice of her dead daughter.

    A cruelty unleashed upon her by a son who had also lost his way. However, young Henry had something far worse at his core than grief. Henry enjoyed her pain.

    Father Bequette needed to study the boy further.

Cold Springs
The Sullivan House
January 1995

Father Bequette sat in John Sullivan's living room along with Assistant Police Chief Glen Chevalier. Caroline slept in her room—overcome by the stress of what she had learned earlier in the evening. They disagreed on how to move forward with Caroline. Clearly, Chevalier did not agree that Caroline should have been allowed to seek answers for herself. Well, mused the priest, Chevalier was neither a counselor nor ordained. The issue was out of the assistant police chief's expertise—for now.

Bequette decided Chevalier did not see the evil she faced or did not want to see it. Both Chevalier and he had encountered the same evil there, twice. Bequette had come out of it with his soul intact. South Enfield, that odd little place. Neither hurricane nor a flood had put it away for good. The waters didn't bury it—they just pushed it aside for a while. Chevalier never fully understood the level of evil there.

Dumont had settled south of Cold Springs in the town of Agawam a few months later. Then his forty-year slide into hell ended in The Dale—South Enfield. Chevalier thought he'd ended the evil a decade ago when he shot Henry Lee Dumont as the man raised a boulder with the clear intent of crushing Daniel Wilson's skull. That should have ended everything. Caroline proved over the years that it had not ended. "Why would you want her back there? What does she gain?" Chevalier demanded.

John stayed silent while Bequette spoke. Knight's irritation was clear but he didn't care if Chevalier had been angered.

"Because," snarled Bequette, "she is in just as must peril whether she is in her dorm room or sitting in the middle of South Enfield with a ten-foot-wide Ouija board." It was Bequette's turn to be angry. Both John and Glen believed the evil would be contained in a specific area. If only that were the case, Caroline would have been settled half a decade ago.

"I will never argue with you about theology, or the hand of God, and the existence of evil. It doesn't make sense to tempt fate and jostle the evil there every time Caroline feels the need to know more," added Chevalier. "I thought you told me she'd be fine, and that the moment of Grace saved her soul."

"It did!" replied the priest. "But now it is up to her to keep it. There are questions she needs to answer. She thinks the answers are there. Are we to stop her from trying?"

"Isn't a psychiatrist the best way?" snapped Chevalier. "We are talking about real consequences here—not ones of faith."

John piped in, cutting off the priest's answer, "Nash ruined my daughter."

This seemed, to Bequette, to snap Glen Chevalier into a calmer state. "There are other men or women to do the job." They'd been in the Sullivan home for less than five minutes, and they were already at each other's throats. "They want to force her into treatment whether you or Caroline want it or not." Chevalier sighed.

"I haven't told you the bad news." The assistant police chief's words echoed through the living room. "Twenty minutes ago, I received a phone call from Dr. Nash and both of you need to hear the details "A woman…Dr. Tara Ross. She's the school psychologist at Stonehill College and she has ordered a mandatory psychological assessment of Caroline. It will determine her future at school. She could be pulled back into the psychiatric wing—recommitted if this assessment goes sideways. John…they only need one parent to do it."

"Allyssa," added John sharply, "has not spoken to or been around Caroline since the day she left."

"John, it does not matter," said Bequette. "You don't think Allyssa is going to take Dr. Nash's side here? She has been punishing you for a decade. She isn't stopping anytime soon.

You," said Bequette, his words glum, "better believe Nash has Allyssa on speed dial. If he doesn't, he'll find her to prove himself right." Then he added something they didn't know. "Caroline confessed to me that both Ross and Nash warned her to stay away from The Dale, what Daniel, William, and Caroline discovered to be South Enfield.

But further research is forbidden because Ross believes it to be a trigger. A match to light the dynamite so to speak. A place she should stay away from at all costs if she wants to remain free."

"And," said John, "she didn't stay away."

"No," replied Bequette.

The room stayed silent for a while until John broke it. "There is something you need to know. It's about Tara Ross."

Twenty Seven

Sullivan House, Cold Springs
April 1985

A LINE, THOUGHT TARA. IT couldn't have been. He'd said it with sincerity and heart. Enough so that she'd chosen him over Jake. "He's leaving…"

"John says that. But look at what you see. He knows who you are, that you're here, and he never even glanced over here. Not once."

Tara noted John was close enough to see her, but he didn't respond when she called his name. "I'm pregnant. He's…"

Allyssa turned away from Tara, her shoes ground into the pavement with a crunch. "Prove it," she said. Tara's brain slowed to a crawl, burdened by her labored breathing. The front door of the Sullivan house closed behind Allyssa, and the yard sat empty of father and daughter.

Tara stood in the shock of the last ten minutes. She sat back in the car and turned the ignition. John didn't leave the house by himself or with his daughter. Tara sat alone in the idling car, then finally shifted the Nissan into gear and drove away. Tara could prove it, and she was determined to have him.

Dr. David Nash's Home
Route 9, Cold Springs
January 1995

Tara could not get comfortable despite the obvious time David had taken to make her so. The ride from the Boston suburb of Easton did nothing to relax her. Instead, each mile she drove west wound up her anxiety. She arrived in Cold Springs by midday and parked in the driveway of Dr. Nash's large home. A modern structure that showcased several floor-to-ceiling windows, which glittered in the clear blue sunlight. This could be her home too. She opened the back door of her sedan and pulled out the suitcase.

Later, as she sat at his dinner table, she decided she could wait no longer. "David," she said as she placed her hands on the table.

David glanced up and nodded. "Tara." He held a small basket containing a loaf of bread from the oven.

"There's something I have to tell you."

David didn't stop setting food on the table. He didn't even respond to the introduction of her confession. It irritated Tara. She required every bit of his attention. No distractions. No opportunity to miss the scope of what she needed to say. What she needed to tell him demanded it. Once she spoke, he needed to judge her so they could decide whether their relationship would continue. One side of the conversation held the amazing now and the other only hazy uncertainty. From the beginning, just a few weeks ago, she found herself attracted to David. Strong, principled, and dedicated to those he served. She rarely fell for any man. If she did, the fall would be a prolonged and halting arc downward. Never fast. This time it happened without her even realizing it.

Only one thing stood in the way of her happiness and eventually, it would have to come out. Without this confession, the sunken mood of inadequacy held her down. He needed to know before they went any further.

"There," replied David, "isn't anything you could tell me…short of 'I'm married' that could change the way I feel about you." David chuckled then went back to the task of bringing dinner to her. "Besides, you have nothing to do with William Lane lying in a coma at Reliant Medical."

His gentle reassurance and task focus made it worse. She knew she wouldn't be held responsible for William Lane. Why would he bring that up? "David," she began again. "I'm not married. This could…It's bad." Tara's eye twitched involuntarily.

David stopped and held her hand in his. He didn't look at her though. "Have I moved too soon? We could cancel the ski trip and do something less…around my friends."

Again worse. She wanted the ski trip badly. She didn't even know how to ski anything more complex than a bunny hill. Tara had only a few close friends and fewer knew each other. She preferred to go out in pairs. Yet, she longed to meet a group of his friends in an uncomfortable social situation. Tara gripped his hand as if what she would tell him would end with him ripping his gentle hand away from hers. She decided to simply get on with it. But she let his hand go first and hoped he would take it again after she told him. "David…a long time ago. A long time ago," she repeated, willing the strength to say the words and make it real again. "I had an affair with John Sullivan. I was going to have his child. When I went to tell him, his wife confronted me instead. He never even looked my way or acknowledged I was there. He used me and threw me away. I miscarried." Tara found the strength to look him in the eye. "I can't have children because of him."

David held a bottle of wine and stopped his attempt at pulling the cork mid-twist. To Tara, he seemed to stop in mid-motion and freeze. After a long pause, David looked down at the bottle and returned it to the rack. He pulled out another bottle—whiskey—and poured her a drink.

"We are going to need something stronger," he said

Twenty Eight

Cold Springs High School
February 1995

        ANIEL WILSON RESENTED THE calendar. More particularly he resented each of the days which scrolled by without the slightest improvement in William. Caroline had gone back to Stonehill College; this time she called before leaving. It'd been three weeks since William's accident and he'd heard that the doctors had already approached William's parents about moving him to a long-term care facility in Amherst. The day after the accident Claire Lane sat with Daniel next to William's hospital bed. She'd brought a large envelope containing a new contract proposal. Mrs. Lane explained the Brewers general manager had sent it before the accident. She had to call the man back personally. Normally she would have contacted William's agent, but she liked the general manager. She'd told Daniel he'd been to their home and took walks and ate dinner with the family after drafting him. So, Mrs. Lane left a pen for him to sign it. It would be the first thing he saw if he ever woke up.

Daniel had not seen Father Bequette except at mass since Father had revealed what he knew about South Enfield. The knowledge did not upset him in the way it grated at Caroline. He got it. Bequette never knew that they had found The Dale. He knew both Caroline and Dumont had faced the same savage evil. Nothing more. That knowledge in Caroline's hands would have demanded that she explored it more. Caroline had reluctantly gone back to Stonehill College to start the semester. She spoke with him before she left but the painful realization that their link, the thing that bound them, was William and The Dale, hammered into Daniel. There was nothing new to say about William and he dared not speak of The Dale.

The ordeal had even put his job in jeopardy. The day after the accident his principal called him into the office to get the story directly from Daniel. The principal had told him not to worry about anything but proceeded to ask how Caroline Sullivan had become involved. Daniel had offered only the sketchiest of explanations. He'd left out most of Caroline's role in the affair.

The principal had warned him to stay away from Caroline, stating Cold Springs had a very conservative board. The same men and women had been on the school board for a decade and a half. They knew Caroline and her history. They wouldn't want to grant a teacher tenure who might bring a catastrophe to the school.

The warning was clear, stiff, and direct. If he wanted to keep his job, he would need to steer clear of Caroline and anything to do with The Dale. Principal Shaffer needed to be careful as he moved forward. The best friend he ever had lay deep in a coma and the on and off again friendship with Caroline had been the main cause of that. He didn't tell her no when he should've ten years ago. He didn't tell her no over the summer. He didn't tell her no when she wanted to swim in her obsession with The Dale.

Still, a word bothered him. A word he needed to investigate, the lingering nettle which dug into the sensitive part of his mind. Metacomet's Barrow. It didn't seem right. Today, he saw his opportunity. He had to see the history teacher, Shaun Gilinsky, when no one else was in his classroom. Daniel was new, and quiet rumors filtered around the school that he had caused the accident which left William Lane, hometown hero and rising baseball star, in a medically induced coma.

Reliant Medical
Cold Springs, Massachusetts

    William Lane no longer felt like a heavy, thick sheet had been dropped over him. No longer alone, he realized. Except this time, the surrounding presence was not a welcome one. He hung in a Netherworld, two places at once, a place where hell overlapped and touched his normal reality. Unlike the relentless desperation that had wrapped around him and drove him forward on his journey to the road, William now withdrew from what he sensed in the darkness in which he wandered. The normal world faded and more and more of the hellish one crept in.

    Wickedness and cruelty emanated from the overwhelmingly malevolent entity that had joined him. William wanted to be as far away as possible from what seemed to make its way closer to him. Worse yet, he recoiled in his fear, which rapidly metastasized into terror as he realized that the malevolence seemed pleased by his frightened, crippled state of mind.

    The young pitcher realized why something pushed him so furiously away from The Dale and back to the road and it wasn't just the danger of the cold and ice. He got pushed to get away from the silky menace that rolled toward him now like a midsummer morning fog off the Quabbin. He understood the guttural urgency in the emotional pull of his first companion.

    William hung alone with something evil. He drifted in the twilight between consciousness and unconsciousness; in the forgiving light and punishing darkness, nothing in his mind revealed a way out.

    William yielded to the relentless pull back toward the center of the malevolence. As he closed in on the core, an equally restless tug away from the center split him into two. William spun in the raging ocean surf, surging once toward the land of light, almost reaching it, then violently pulled back out to the freezing swirl of the dark sea. This tug of war between two worlds continued, and since he had no reference for a time, the battle filled his entire existence. The middle ground was a hospital room that faded in and out of the gray misty curtain which wrapped around him. For a time, he drifted unsteadily until the gray twilight moved in.

Pulled toward the dense, cold evil he saw flashes and pictures, in motion for a second then frozen and fading to nothing, of events of which he had not been present. He see-sawed and moved deep toward the malevolence. As he did the flashes increased in brightness and intensity. Raw emotions bound to cruel visions spinning past overwhelmed him. Eons of loss and betrayal welled up as a bright bloom of color and then at the peak of the emotion, he would see a picture, image, or a few seconds of some hellish moment. All of them threaded back to the malevolence closing in on him. Framing each moment—a ring of satisfaction and pleasure. Drawn closer to evil, he realized it wanted him to see these moments—and those moments gave it pleasure. The malevolence he encountered now lorded over and manufactured these experiences on his own. Without a doubt, malevolence owned him now.

A word burst into his mind unbidden: trophies. Much like William had a mantle full of baseball ribbons and plaques, the malevolence had captured the raw, bitter emotional foundations of the worst moments of people's lives and fed on them. The malevolence broke countless people over eons of time and bathed in the joy of the destruction which he wrought. Much worse, as William felt great pride in his ribbons and trophies, so did the malevolence.

Then another word welled up; a word which formed a better picture of the malevolence, and the word demon fit. The demon had its trophies too. They were the raw, wrecked emotions of the damned piled high around him as it sat on a throne of the shattered, burned, and splintered bones of their bliss.

Another pulse of pure satisfaction looped around him. The presence was feeding on his fear and while he instinctively knew it, and felt drained by it, he could do nothing. Abject terror trapped him in the dim Netherworld.

Flashes and pictures.

Every moment from the first encounter between this evil which surrounded him and his subtle attack on a boy angry he could not be with his father, and to the moment in which he saw this boy watch his sister reach out and beg him to rescue her from the fire, and then to the enormous cruel acts the boy heaved upon his mother. To the battle. A battle with the faithful priest that left him wounded, and the years of tortured anguish unleashed on the man until the moment he died. And a soul which did not completely belong to the malevolence.

The images snapped into reverse and pulled him back further and deeper into the pool of savage emotions. William reached out to hold them back only to be sucked into the deepest, darkest socket of the well and the center of the evil. And the horror of this betrayal erupted inside him so fiercely that it was painful. He sank into the pit with the high smooth walls made of emotion and cried out to the only one who could help him.

Twenty Nine

Stonehill College
Denton Hall
February 1995

THE WOMAN WHO SAT across from Dr. Ross dropped her face into her hands and wept. Tara waited patiently for the woman's emotions to cool.

David, no, thought Tara, he is now Dr. Nash—at least for a while. He'd guided her through this mini crisis. Things would change later. At least she wanted to believe that. They would stay professional, and she had to believe things would work out for the two of them. After she confessed her affair with John, David told her he would think about what they should do. His answer came the next morning when he told her she needed to leave his home—just in case anyone had seen them together. He'd told her they shouldn't see each other or contact each other for a while. He'd reach out to her when he felt it was alright to do so. He'd warned her they both could not only lose their jobs, but their licenses. The heartbeat of their careers was in jeopardy. Nobody could know they had worked together or shared information about Caroline. It would appear they held a grudge and that tainted their professional judgment.

He still helped Caroline. He'd even given her the big prize. Allyssa Sullivan's telephone number. One that worked.

"I didn't know," Allyssa said before she lifted her head to meet Tara's eyes.

"She came to us last year after a troubled time in her previous two colleges," Dr. Ross paused, shook her head, and frowned. "Her father is blind to her struggles."

"I don't know what he's thinking," she replied.

"That's why I reached out to you. It was very hard to find you, but Dr. Nash helped. I need to let you know how serious her illness is and how we need a medical intervention to help Caroline. Just for a short period of time to get her back on track." Dr. Ross believed that a few weeks under the care of Dr. Nash would do wonders for the girl. With new medications carefully managed and outside influences eliminated, her stress would evaporate.

"I'll do anything that you need." She took a breath.

"I know you want the best treatment for her." Tara smiled at Allyssa and took her hands. "Let me make a call to her dorm room." Tara dialed the number, blissfully the woman sitting in her office did not recognize her.

Fifteen minutes later, Caroline appeared in the doorway pale and visibly shaking. Caroline did not look good. Dr. Tara Ross wondered briefly if the stress of her actions finally caught up to her. Ross took a deep breath and waved the girl into the room. Here was the time. Caroline had to be held responsible for her actions. William Lane still lay in a hospital because she could not heed Tara's warnings, which were in her best interest.

When Caroline broke eye contact with Dr. Ross, she saw the other woman in the room and Caroline stopped cold. Her lungs visibly deflated as she struggled to come to terms with what she saw.

"Hello Caroline," said the woman as she stood to embrace Caroline. "I am here to help you understand how badly you need help." She paused and offered a warm smile. "Dr. Ross and Dr. Nash are just looking out for your best interests."

Caroline's mouth opened and closed several times before she said the word she'd given up ever saying again, "*Mom?*"

Thirty

Stonehill College
Denton Hall
February 1995

CAROLINE EMBRACED HER MOTHER as if Allyssa Sullivan was a rarely seen uncle. The gulf of time between the last time she saw her, kissing Niles Sparrow, and now shrank to nothing. Two points, wildly variant universes, touched. Then: blissful, thirteen, the world sunny and promising. Now: now sucked.

Allyssa's presence left Caroline weak and barely able to stand so she sat, without being bidden, into the nearest chair. Caroline noticed that her mother had retreated to the far corner of the room. Dr. Ross stood up from her desk and poured Caroline a cup of water from a water cooler.

Allyssa spoke while Caroline took a careful sip, "I can't stay here long. But I came to…"

Caroline decided not to let her finish. She didn't have the right. "Why would you? It's been almost a decade." Caroline saw her not as her mother, rather as a selfish woman. Separate. Not part of her. The fantasy had already shattered.

Allyssa's gaze had not left her daughter for a single moment since Caroline entered the room. "That's not fair." Allyssa glanced at Dr. Ross then pulled a chair next to Caroline. "Dr. Ross has taken the time to find me, and she and Dr. Nash have asked me to help. To try and seek some path of healing for you."

"*I have a path*! And who the hell are you to tell me anything?" Caroline demanded. "You have been gone!" Caroline slipped down to the edge of her control, and her mother didn't respond to her. Her mother just clenched her jaw tightly. Guilt bore its way into Caroline.

"You were in a psychiatric ward for years. Not talking to anyone. Destroying everything around you. How do you think that feels for a parent to see that? And...and you're sliding back to that place again."

Caroline gasped and searched for words. The epicenter of her mother's world was not her and never would be. "It's not about YOU! You didn't see it. I was kidnapped while you were gone, and you never came to help. You never put your anger at Dad aside to come back to me. Don't you see, you should have come for me?" demanded Caroline.

"I didn't want to give you hope," Allyssa whispered and dropped her head into her hands.

"*What?*"

"Hope that your father and I can work things out. I had to stay away for your own good." Allyssa took Caroline's hands in hers. "I didn't want to hurt you. Everyone needed time. Then you were committed and Dr. Nash assured me you were getting the best treatment possible. I didn't need to come. Going to you wouldn't change anything." For the first time, the expression on her mother's face broke. As if saying the words, long whispering thoughts in her head, no longer convinced her or anyone else.

Caroline could hold back no longer. Rational thinking no longer controlled her mind. "There are hotels, Mom. There are motels you could've stayed at. You didn't want to come. You did not want me." Tears rolled down her red and angry face.

Allyssa didn't respond. Instead, she released Caroline's hands and moved away to another chair. "It's not that I didn't want you. It's the life I didn't want."

In the long silence that followed Caroline recovered enough to take a tissue from the desk of Dr. Ross who sat quietly until breaking the tension.

"I feel that we need to move forward. The professional opinion of both me and Dr. David Nash is that Caroline needs psychiatric care for the safety of herself and others. The accident with the Lane boy really was the clincher for me. We need an adult signature for an involuntary hold. But for everyone involved, I think you need to volunteer for this Caroline."

"I am not a danger to anyone," snapped Caroline.

"Caroline, you are, and you don't see it," said Dr. Ross. "Was your trip to the Archives in Boston the only time you went there?"

"Yes."

"Are you certain?"

The warning flashes lit up in her mind. She stuck to her story except the affirmation came out weaker this time. "Yes."

Dr. Ross leaned back in her chair and then turned to Allyssa. "I know this not to be true."

Caroline felt the blood draining from her face. How did she know?

Ross continued. "She went there twice. Once in the fall and once over winter break with both boys."

Allyssa frowned and shrugged. "Why is this important? I don't understand."

The question gave Caroline a momentary thread of hope. Hope that was extinguished when Dr. Ross explained the path Caroline had taken over the last few months. She lined up all the pieces and then laid them out for Allyssa. "First, she heard about the demolition of the psychiatric ward from Daniel's mother. Her obsession must have been rekindled. Next, she went to the archive and found maps with information regarding the place she was kidnapped. After that, she attended the demolition and walked to The Dale with William and Daniel. My source tells me she was looking for a land marker that she didn't find. So still the burr of The Dale jabbed at her—relentlessly. She enlisted William in her quest." Then Dr. Ross added the throbbing painful piece. "Caroline knew about the marker and what it meant. She needed closure but didn't want to do it alone. She lied to everyone—even her best friends. She could have been honest. If she had, William Lane would not be in a coma."

Anger flashed across Allyssa's face. "Caroline?"

Caroline said nothing. Ross didn't have everything in the correct order, but she had everything. She resented the way her actions were wildly smeared into something ugly. She'd trusted Dr. Ross to help her and find closure. Dr. Ross betrayed her. Caroline judged her worse than Dr. Nash, who never pretended to care. The fact of the matter is that the last few months had been cathartic; like little parts of herself clicking into their rightful places. Something organic. Natural light shown on the dark, damp places. Until…until William fell through the ice.

"This is what we mean by a danger to herself and others," the doctor added. The snare Dr. Ross built tightened around her.

Caroline dropped from the chair to her knees. "I couldn't do this myself. I had to know. I only knew about the marker. Nothing else. Daniel found the name."

Dr. Ross pulled a set of papers out of her drawer and lifted the phone on her desk. "Security to my office."

"Don't tell them," begged Caroline irrationally. "Please don't tell anyone."

Her mother seemed to ignore her words and then turned on her once more. "Please listen to us Caroline and make the right choice. Get help for yourself." Her mother's voice strained with irritation. As if the meeting had been an inconvenience to her. Something she had to do because her father would not.

"You can sign this order if she does not. Either way. I think we know what is best for her right now." Caroline heard the words again and struggled to keep up. The events spun away from her with breathtaking swiftness.

"Don't tell them," Caroline said it again.

"How can we not?" replied her mother.

"Caroline," said Dr. Ross. "Will you sign this?"

Caroline sobbed on her knees, out of energy. Out of time. Hopeless. Yes. The word scoured deep into the grains of her mind. Yes, I'll sign. Wrong. Evil. Then one word screamed from the bottom of her soul "No." She shook her head. "I won't."

Her vision was now blurred as her mother took the document affixed to a green clipboard from Dr. Ross. She clicked the top of the pen and signed her name on the involuntary hold order. "You need to heal, and you can't heal with secrets."

Caroline saw her mother sign the document which would involuntarily commit her to an institution. As she did, a flood of memories long absent roared back and buried her. The torrent choked off her air, leaving the horror of a blackout imminent.

She hated her.

"Security will be here in a few minutes," said Dr. Ross. "Caroline. Please sit down and take a few breaths. Help is on the way."

Caroline shot a look back at Allyssa and saw the annoyed look punctuated by a glance at her watch. Then adrenaline shocked her nerves into action. Caroline stood up and took a final look at her mother and Dr. Ross then turned and sprinted out of the room.

Part III

Thirty One

Stonehill College
Denton Hall
February 1995

Caroline confirmed she knew about the mile marker. But she fled." Tara waited for David to respond. Instead, she heard nothing. David overhearing Caroline's conversation with William's father was a stroke of luck and one more nail in her coffin. The morning spiraled out of control so fast she struggled to keep everything set straight in her mind. The key takeaway of her morning: Caroline Sullivan had vanished. As soon as her mother had signed the recommitment paperwork, Caroline had raced out of the office, down the stairs, and away from school.

She'd chased Caroline all the way to the parking lot and then watched in horror as Caroline squealed out of the parking lot in her SUV. Her mother had never moved from the chair in the center of her office.

Tara knew she had to find Caroline. Second, she needed to end her day employed. Her first call, to Dr. Nash, might have been a mistake. He'd told her not to call and barely spoke when she did. She considered the idea and then rejected it after realizing someone would need to go through the work of getting her phone log. It would be determined that calling the previous psychiatrist who treated Caroline was good practice. No one would ever know how much deeper their relationship went beyond professionalism.

She'd never tell. David wouldn't either. It'd be career suicide for both. Mutually assured destruction.

Tara did not understand Allyssa Sullivan. She hadn't recognized Tara. Allyssa stayed in the office for less than ten minutes and then left for her hotel room in Boston. Tara decided Allyssa couldn't handle the stress and she bailed on her daughter and those who wanted to help her. *I've done all I can,* she had said before she left.

Tara dropped her head down and waited for David to speak. She reviewed all her actions and knew her intentions had been good. She'd overstepped normal protocols but all with the end goal of treating Caroline. Her past with John Sullivan did not affect her treatment of his daughter. She put that aside long ago.

When Dr. Nash finally spoke she had to ask him to repeat what he said. He did. "She may not be gone for long. She has only one place to go. Cold Springs. Most likely, she will go to her father's house. The pre-knowledge of the marker means she may be far further gone than we had realized."

The logic of it seemed sound. A band of tension squeezing her forehead loosened slightly. "It makes sense," she replied.

"There is something else," he added.

"What?"

"William Lane is awake."

Tara smiled for the first time since Caroline had blazed out of her office. The nightmare scenario of an unstable girl on the run had offered a new outcome that could save her job. David was right. Caroline had to be headed to Cold Springs and even if they didn't find her at her father's house, they could still find her. William would be awake in bed at Reliant Medical Center. A lure Caroline would not resist. "We can have the police set up a patrol car at both the house and the hospital. You said Chevalier will play ball, right??"

"Yes."

Tara refocused. Campus security did not exist as a proper police force. She had to take the next step, contact the faculty dean so he could consult with the Massachusetts State Troopers and contain her that way.

The faculty dean of Stonehill told her to stay put. Inside, her heart thumped away in her chest. She did not relish the conversation. Tara knew she'd pushed the girl too hard and instead of bracketing her into peaceful compliance, she'd created a mess. There will be an inquiry. There were questions she could not answer truthfully. If she lied and the lie was discovered, she would never work in the field again. If she told the truth, she would never work in the field again. Tara decided not to stay put since finding Caroline would help her cause. Heavy cloud cover had rolled in, and a storm had boiled its way up the East Coast, threatening all of New England.

Just as she made it to the exit of the building, the faculty dean intercepted her.

Thirty Two

Reliant Medical Center
Cold Springs, Massachusetts

CAROLINE HAD RUN. HER mother had signed the paperwork to recommit her. In one action, Allyssa Sullivan drove a spear through the heart of her once favorite fantasy. A normal life with her best friends by her side. Allyssa now existed as someone she used to know. Dr. Nash would drug her, take away all of the things she cared about, and she would be lost to the outside world.

Her biggest question remained, one which she couldn't find an answer to in the psychiatric ward. Why did she see the *ghosts*? Ghosts of the past which came back to haunt her tortured present. First, she saw the girl in the basement of the house on the common and again in her dorm room. Hallucinations. Or as Bequette insisted. Warnings. Caroline disagreed that the warnings delivered by a ghost were helpful.

The droning buzz in the back of her mind screamed out and cried *NO*, every time she tried to open the door to see what happened in The Dale, also known as South Enfield. Why would she remember a memory in her old house that didn't exist and not Henry Lee Dumont? Knowing his tortured life story did nothing to open the memory to see what he had done to her. Each of her discoveries over the past few months took her a few steps further along the path. Caroline stood in front of the door of the main mystery.

She'd found out about the marker and thought if she could find the proper name for The Dale it would lose its power over her. But she hadn't been able to find the marker in The Dale or the name by herself, Caroline had desperately wanted William and Daniel with her when she did. Their friendship, the fellowship of the three as Father Bequette called it, had been reborn. She was terrified of losing it again. Her life had been empty without it.

Dumont lived almost his entire life as either a criminal drifter or a man possessed by a malevolent evil. Why were those answers critical to her happiness? Only the dark hidden space in the back of her mind knew the answer. Dark and hidden, like The Dale. But those questions were the phantoms that rattled their chains in and across her mindscape. She'd fought for almost a decade to forge ahead without them, now, today, as the gloom of a winter storm hung low over the Berkshires, she was going to find out.

Caroline drove to the safety of her father, his influence, and the only place where she could gain her answers. She parked her SUV in the large visitor lot to the right of the Reliant Medical Complex. She had first gone home and didn't find her father. She waited for a half an hour and then decided to drive to the rectory. Once there, she'd found Father Bequette had already left the building. Mrs. Ventura told her about William and both Caroline and Mrs. Ventura assumed Father went to the hospital to see William and his family.

Nobody knew she was here. She wanted to see William before the world caught up to her and he found out that she'd lied to him. Lying to him had been bad, her impending institutionalization was worse but not having the light at the end of the tunnel that was Daniel and William was the hardest of all.

She took a deep breath and said the words, just above a whisper, "I lied to them."

The building, while modern and glassy, still resembled the footprint of the old Cold Springs Hospital. She brushed the ghost of the psychiatric ward out of her head and walked into the airy and open lobby, past the front desk, and headed to the elevator.

Caroline didn't sign in, hoping she would be ahead of the Massachusetts State Troopers and any news that she was a fugitive for all intents and purposes. If Dr. Ross would get the troopers involved, Caroline felt like she would but could not be sure. Nobody but family knew that William had woken up so nobody would think of looking for her there.

Moments later, she entered the elevator and headed up to the third floor. She stopped in the doorframe to William's room as she watched the doctor examining his arm.

William sat on the edge of his bed while a doctor checked his vitals. "I think they've done this at least a dozen times in the last five hours," he said as he waved her in.

Caroline ran to him and the doctor backed away to see other patients. William looked pinker in the face, hair flat and greasy, his muscles slack. Caroline hugged him tightly. "You are an idiot," she said, and then recoiled back. "And you smell like body odor mixed with Lysol." She breathed in the moment and then met his eyes. "I have some things to tell you."

Massachusetts Turnpike
Palmer Exit

Dr. Ross could only guess what the plan would be once she made it to Cold Springs. She knew she needed to link up with David and ensure they were on the same page. They needed to look professional. She needed to play the role of concerned caretaker. A friend by her side. There would be a chance that David would have things under control and the police would be in place waiting for Caroline to show up. They only needed to catch up with her and execute the involuntary placement order for psychiatric care. Reliant Medical Center had a psychiatric care unit and David was the director.

Dr. Ross glanced over at her company in the car, the faculty dean, the boss of all bosses at Stonehill College. The man decided to join her on the ride to Cold Springs. The faculty dean explained that he needed to be on the front lines of this problem. Even he had bosses to report to.

As they drove the dean asked questions in a calm and pleasant, almost casual voice. "So, she started to express certain behaviors, after she filled out a Request for Services form?" he said, picking up on his questions where she had left off. "Behaviors that are inconsistent with a successful student at Stonehill College."

"Yes."

"Can you be more specific?"

Tara hoped not to have to reveal she compelled Caroline to give her access to her previous mental health records. It's not that her request was unethical, but it wasn't common practice. If her affair with Caroline's father came out, it could hurt her professionally. "I came across some troubling documents in her file. She agreed to give me access to them. We'd established trust."

"After you found those documents which you found 'troubling' you initiated a mandatory mental health assessment? Seems awful fast." The faculty dean's concentration on her felt unnerving.

Tara waited for a semi-truck to clear her rearview mirror before exiting the turnpike onto Route 202. "Yes."

"Well, it *could* be reasonable to a board of inquiry. I think. After which, I suppose more behaviors exhibited themselves?"

Tara relaxed. The tension in her shoulders loosened and her grip on the steering wheel eased. Tara knew the risks to both Caroline and, secondarily, to the college. Caroline Sullivan now was his problem too. Tara detailed four or five examples of Caroline's behaviors that concerned her. All of which she could argue before a board of inquiry were correct actions. The tip-off from Nash, any cover-up later of that action, and their affair would be seen as grounds for termination. The faculty dean did not know any of the problematic sordid details of the Caroline Sullivan affair.

"But," replied the faculty dean after a pause, "these seem to be problems that could have been managed." He adjusted his seatbelt. "It should have been managed by you and never have gotten to the point where we are now. I'm troubled that this spun out of control. You reached out to both parents and raised your concerns to them?"

Tara was ready to respond. "The father didn't respond. She had already spent three years institutionalized. *He refused to see the gravity of the situation and return my phone call.*" Tara inflected a devoted concern to the tone of her voice then shook her head as if in disbelief. "Mother had been out of the picture. I thought she might be able to reason with Caroline. I took a shot. Maybe she could get through to her daughter that she needs help."

The faculty dean's tone changed immediately. More avuncular, empathetic. "Again, thoughtful and reasonable. I didn't say you were at fault. Simply that I would have expected this to be managed by our protocols. Obviously, they are flawed."

Tara listened to her companion speak. The faculty dean didn't speak carefully. "I wish I could have handled this too."

The faculty dean nodded. "I am impressed that you would drive through this weather to make sure this girl gets the help she needs," he added. He further complimented her dedication and told her it inspired him to see that kind of devotion to her job and the students.

Tara smiled, now totally relaxed. "She's a sick girl and we can make sure she gets the help she has long been denied." Then she added, this time a little playful, "And look at you heading into the snowstorm with me to track her down."

"I am not as altruistic as you might think," said the man. "I have a good friend that lives there. Father Andre Bequette. College roommate. He asked me to pull some strings to get her into the college." The man then turned to her and gazed directly at her. "I spoke to him before I left."

Tara shuddered in the knowledge that the faculty dean might have more knowledge of the past than she did. Father Bequette came up often in her sessions with Caroline. And worse, the dean might believe that everything she'd said to him over the last hour and a half was a lie.

Thirty Three

The House on the Common
Cold Springs, Massachusetts
1948

FATHER ANDRE BEQUETTE STOOD on the porch of the Evans' home. Leigh Anne had decided she needed help for Henry. She'd received a settlement that was large enough to purchase a new home in the center of the growing town of Cold Springs. It sat across the street from the common and a few doors down from the church. She also had enough money to live for years to come, but that did not fix her son.

Father had met with her several times about her young, tortured son. Henry had rejected all her attempts at comforting him and outright shunned her and unleashed moments of ever more creative cruelty.

She had called Father Bequette at his home, not the rectory, in desperation this morning after she woke to an exquisitely painful sensation on her chest. She'd explained through hitched sobs she had jerked up out of bed to her feet and several glowing hot coals rolled off her and onto the floor. She had seen Henry standing there impassively. He had not moved to help her or even show any sign that he had noticed her predicament.

In horror she'd noticed the tongs from the fireplace hanging limply from one of his hands. Henry had placed the hot coals on her blanket and watched as she'd leaped out of bed in agony. Henry clicked the tongs together a few times before walking out. As the pain from the burns flared, she'd realized he'd gone to the coal furnace, gathered a few orange glowing embers, and dropped them on her.

It had stuck with her that after he sang in Hannah's voice at the edge of her bed, he did it with a smile. He'd known he was hurting her, and he did it anyhow. He'd left the room humming then looked back once to get a last glance at her pain and shock.

Leigh Anne found him falling further away from normal sane behavior and moving toward a joyful cruelty which she could not understand.

Even a trip to see a doctor had not changed his behavior or explained his actions. The physician in town had found nothing wrong with him. He'd referred him to a psychiatrist for psychoanalysis. After several appointments, the chief of staff of the hospital had declared that the boy was mostly healthy.

Mostly, she'd steamed, mostly healthy.

Leigh Anne had followed him to the basement and found him burning Hannah's doll, a low guttural joyless laugh rolled out of him. Whoever was in the basement was no longer her son. Whatever squatted down by the furnace boiled in evil. She'd closed the door and locked it. Next, she'd done the only thing she could think of doing. She'd called him.

Bequette had no doubt that Henry had encountered something malevolent. A supernatural entity infested the boy's soul and crushed whatever was left of it into a small dark corner from where the boy could find no escape.

But, thought the priest, there was no place in the universe which could not hear the voice of God. It was long past time the evil which had ensnarled the boy learned the lesson.

Cold Springs High School

Daniel leafed through a book from Gilinsky's bookshelf. He struggled to make sense of the dense academic language. Then something occurred to him. What if the battle in the valley happened in the same place Dumont lost his way? Maybe that's why he called it Metacomet's Barrow. Barrow, in this case, a grave instead of a hill. He had to tell Caroline and Father Bequette.

Before he could further explore the kernel of thought, the phone rang in his classroom, jousting him from the reverie. Something far more important stole his attention.

"Daniel Wilson?" said the unknown male voice.

Daniel, unhappy about the disruption in his thoughts, offered a short reply. "Yes."

"This is Dr. David Nash." Daniel knew the name and the vision of his threat to Caroline in the Commonwealth Annex assaulted his senses. The doctor's words came out smooth and oily. "We met briefly in the annex a few weeks ago."

Daniel grit his teeth. He did not need a record of personal calls at work. Especially ones related to Caroline if he wanted to keep his job. He breathed out the single syllable, "Yeah."

"I am not sure if you are aware, but Caroline Sullivan is missing. Have you seen her? Perhaps you know where she is? Been in contact with her?"

Daniel decided he didn't want to tell Dr. Nash anything. "Why the hell would I tell you anything?" Daniel leaned back and waited for a response. His heart rate slowed down, just the way it did at any big moment in his life.

"You know Daniel, she's been to the annex twice," said Dr. Nash. "Once with you and William and once by herself. Before she reconnected with the both of you."

Daniel did not understand the statement. Caroline only went to the archives after she reconnected with both. Not before. Nash was dead wrong.

"So, what if she did," he snorted back at him as the implication of her being there twice crept to the forefront of his mind.

"Daniel, I remembered speaking to you at the common on the day of the fire. Caroline spoke about you often."

The words jabbed into Daniel's heart, but he shook it off. Nash angled in on his unresolved feelings for Caroline to open the wound and leave him vulnerable.

"You nearly died. Dumont held a boulder above your head and only the intercession of Assistant Police Chief Glen Chevalier saved you. And yet, I suspect, nobody asked you about that. Nobody told your mother, and you did not either."

In the aftermath, Daniel spoke to his father first. His father asked him to leave that detail out of the story. The fight with Henry Lee Dumont would be enough. Since there wasn't a trial and barely an investigation that detail could be safely lost. William had been facing the wrong way and in a heap on the ground to his left, so he never saw that moment.

"She did not need to worry," Daniel regretted saying the words immediately afterward. His decisions were not the business of Dr. David Nash.

"No," replied Nash. "Of course not. Then the two best friends you ever had vanished from your life—who asked how you were?" Nash paused and let the words hang in the air. "She came back and used you and William to help her. Then, like vapor, she's gone. I am sure she kept you up to date and called often now that you reconnected. Right?"

Daniel could see why Caroline hated this guy. He oozed arrogance and left him constantly looking for the next spot Nash would attack. Feeling like he was a step behind Nash. The impact of the questions roiled his insides. He'd asked himself the questions before. Daniel didn't need to hear them from Nash. "Caroline and William had their own lives and people grow up and move on," added Daniel defensively. Nash hit a nerve, and he didn't want to let him know.

Nash continued, less subtly. "You are the good soldier, the good son, and the good friend. It's gotten you where you are. Someone must be left out. Or in your case, left behind."

Daniel didn't care for the sarcasm any more than the arrogance. Nash's attack burrowed deeply into him. The night of the demolition of the old psychiatric center flashed back into his mind. Caroline had poked around the brush for something and never told them what she'd been looking for. His heart and chest compressed in one painful wallop. The memory of her thrashing a stick around the high grass and thorn bushes around the church. Looking for something. Damn. She'd been looking for the marker. *Caroline knew about it the whole time.* Daniel let the wave of horror pass and then closed his eyes to refocus. He allowed the lumbering anger to surface. New anger at Father Bequette for keeping Caroline away from the knowledge of Dumont and The Dale. Rage at Caroline for selfishly running down the rabbit hole and taking William with her. Fury at himself for his inability to change a damned thing. Everyone had their reasons, everyone thought they were doing the right thing, and nobody listened. The shit hit the fan and now everyone was running for cover.

She must've wanted to go but didn't have the courage. So, she enlisted the only people on the planet who would go along with her. Caroline never let go of The Dale. It still haunted her and now she was missing. "I don't know where she is," he said.

"Fine," replied Nash. "Please contact me if you see or hear something." Nash rattled off a phone number and added one final item. "Be aware, now that William is awake she may try to get to him."

"Awake?"

"Yes. Hours ago. I supposed someone in your caring friend group would have told you. They didn't?"

Daniel didn't know why Dr. Nash would say that to him. He simply grunted and hung up the phone. William was awake and that was all he cared about. Seconds later he slid into the driver's seat of his ten-year-old cream-colored Volvo wagon, and he was off into the cold air of a stormy afternoon.

THIRTY FOUR

The Sullivan House
Cold Springs

JOHN SULLIVAN RETURNED HOME to a red light blinking on his answering machine. Next to the blinking light the number "2" glowed from the message counter. He ignored both. Instead, he headed to the fridge and took out a bottle of light beer. Odd, he thought, to want a cold beer in the middle of an early February snowstorm. Still, it went down easily, and he opened the door and rummaged around for leftovers and a second beer.

The light still flashed. Maybe it was her.

Caroline had been back at school for several weeks and she called him every day. Stonehill College had proved to be the magic bullet for her schooling, and he had brightened at the thought of her finishing something.

Dr. Ross and Dr. Nash had vanished from the picture. Even after Chevalier and Bequette told them about Nash's plan to readmit her nothing happened. Perhaps it stalled out. Maybe he'd bluffed and failed. Ross could mess with some other girl.

He struggled to remember Tara Ross's face. Tall, curvy, dark hair, but her face was a blur. John didn't remember much more than a few flashes from the weekend he'd spent with her. He wished he'd treated her better. They were all supposed to be anonymous. Then, one was not. One came to the house. But Allyssa had intercepted her, turned Tara away, then used the affair to hammer him into submission. She'd dug the needle deeper. She'd made him pay for everything. She'd picked the one man in the band who would piss him off the most to have an affair with. The band had broken up, so had they. Then, Allyssa vanished.

Now, years later, Tara Ross came back to bite him in the ass.

The woman he'd rejected. The woman sent away by Allyssa. A woman he'd admittedly had feelings for once roared back with a vengeance, and Caroline might be the one who paid the bill. He opened the second beer and pressed the button to play the two messages.

"*John, this is Father Bequette. William Lane is awake. He and his family are here. He has asked for Caroline. Perhaps you have a number? See you soon.*" A welt of joy rolled up inside of him. Of course, he'd get the number to him. William had been a rock for Caroline since they'd reconnected over the summer. Then another thought popped into his head. William would already have Caroline's number. They'd been talking for a couple of months. Why would Bequette be asking him for the number? Worry crept up inside him and wiped away the joy from a moment ago.

Trouble. Bequette sent him a warning without using the word. A clever man. He stared at the blinking light and pushed the button to play the second message.

The machine beeped again. An unfamiliar voice boomed out of the speaker. "John Sullivan this is Blaine Walker at campus security please call me back as soon as you can." John wrote down the number and called back.

He waited for Blaine Walker to answer the phone. When Walker explained to John that Caroline was missing, all the joy he had felt evaporated. He hung up knowing the Massachusetts State Police were looking for his girl. Dr. Ross and Dr. Nash had sprung their trap.

That was what Father Bequette wanted him to know. He couldn't break the law or his oath by telling him directly. However, he could tell him to be aware and that trouble was imminent.

John squeezed his eyes shut and took a long breath. He had one play. Inside his Rolodex, he found the name of the attorney he used whenever Caroline and her mental health were in question. The man even had a cell phone. Something he'd avoided. Now, however, he decided he needed to have one. Caroline would be scared and need to find him. If she had the brain, he thought, she would want to get to him and an attorney. The attorney didn't answer. He left a message and begged him to call him back.

Caroline was somewhere, rattled and scared, driving in the middle of a snowstorm. She was going to need more than an attorney to help. She would need Bequette to help stabilize her. He called the rectory.

"Mrs. Ventura," he said when the long-time church secretary answered the phone. "Do you know where Father Bequette is?" Without really knowing why he said it, he added, "Caroline is in trouble. She is going to need him."

"Mr. Sullivan," she began. "I believe Father is at Reliant Medical Center. But…Caroline was just here and left. She's probably going to the hospital. Should I call the police?"

Police. The word rocked him. "No." He hung up and grabbed his coat and headed out.

Before John had made it three steps out of his front door a green sedan pulled into his driveway. Father Bequette rolled down the passenger window and waved at him to get in.

"John," said Bequette. "Where is Caroline?"

"Isn't she with you?"

The priest shook his head and grumbled out the next four words. "Damn it. Get in."

Sullivan wheeled around to the passenger side of the high-end luxury car. Sullivan had never seen Bequette drive anything other than the plainest most economical vehicle and here he was in a Lincoln Continental the size of a boat. The car even smelled brand new. John made sure to kick the snow off his boats as he entered, then broke the tension. "When did you get all fancy and buy a Lincoln?"

"I was thinking of ways to honor the greatest president…" Bequette shot back. "Mine broke down in my sisters' driveway. This is hers. Don't break anything, I can't even afford a tire on this thing. Where is Caroline?"

John had been grinning but turned serious. "I don't know. Campus security called. She is on the run. That's all I know."

"Bad news. Dr. Ross got together with Allyssa…"

The news jolted John hard in the stomach. "She can't do that. Caroline is over eighteen," John argued.

"With the recommendation of a health professional after a health assessment she can," replied the priest.

The second wallop bent John over in the car. "How?"

"I'm not sure how they found Allyssa, but they did. There was a meeting in Tara's office." Bequette put the car back in park to have this conversation. "I don't know what happened in that meeting. But Allyssa was there in person. At the end of it, Caroline ran out and sped off in her car. Allyssa signed the paperwork and left town."

John shook his head "How do you know this? Campus security only told me she was missing, and the state troopers were looking for her." Everyone else seemed to be in the loop except him. He needed to know if Bequette had solid information.

"Caroline," said Bequette, "went to Stonehill College after I pulled in a favor from the faculty dean. We did our undergraduate work together. Same fraternity. He told me everything earlier today."

John grunted. He'd assumed that she'd been admitted because of his fame. Not because of anything Father Bequette did. Bequette knew lots of people too. "I already called my lawyer." The air blowing out of the vents heated the car until it was uncomfortable, and John looked for the switch to turn it down.

"We may need more help than that." Bequette shook his head as he spoke. "We know Dr. Nash and Dr. Ross coordinated this. Caroline is still at risk. Allyssa's signature is all they need to recommit her. We need to find Caroline," said Bequette.

"I think I know where she's going."

"Me too," offered Bequette as he rolled out of the driveway, but the car skidded to a stop in the snow. The flashing lights of Assistant Chief Chevalier's police interceptor blazed white and red through the rear window of Bequette's sister's car.

"Damn," cursed Bequette as he shifted back into park. "We might be too late."

John stiffened against the wave of nausea which rumbled up from his ribcage and squirted bile into his throat. He needed to find Caroline and get her out of Massachusetts. Assistant Chief Chevalier blocked his way and slammed the door on his effort. John sat quietly and waited while Chevalier knocked on the driver's side door of the car. Another officer, one he knew from town, Lt. Conway, stood a few feet back and to the rear of the passenger door. Lt. Conway said nothing.

"Can I help you, Glen?" asked Father Bequette.

"Funny," replied Chevalier, "I was just going to ask you the same question. Follow me." Chevalier and Conway reentered the squad car and pulled away.

"Can we just," asked Sullivan, "say we lost them in the snow?"

"Maybe, but I suspect we are going to the same place."

John knew Glen Chevalier did not particularly like Dr. Nash, but the situation made him anxious. He had no idea if the assistant chief knew Dr. Ross or what Chevalier thought of her. He suspected that Chevalier wouldn't want Caroline sent back to the psychiatric ward.

They followed the squad car down Old Enfield Road and up to where it turned into Route 21 near the center of town. He prayed the assistant police chief would turn right on 202 and head to the opposite end of the common to the police station.

Chevalier did not.

The police chief continued along Route 21, past the Clapp Memorial Library, through the only light on this side of town, and down toward Reliant Medical. John's heart sank as they pulled into the parking lot and parked fifty yards from the main doors.

Chevalier rolled down his window. "Nash has me by the short ones. If we see her, I must take her into custody. We'll wait here."

John jabbed his finger out to Chevalier "Not if I get to her first."

"*John*," thundered Bequette, "don't make it worse."

John's emotions were too raw. He sulked in the passenger seat of the Lincoln while Bequette made small talk with Chevalier.

They sat with the windows open, their engines idling and the fan blowing hot air across the windshield kept it clear. Once every thirty seconds or so the wipers brushed away the wet snow falling from the sky. John wondered if he'd be able to swoop up Caroline and convince Bequette to drive away without Chevalier noticing. John was losing his mind.

"Shouldn't we be further back?" Lt. Conway asked Chevalier. "If we don't want to spook her?"

"No." Chevalier's answer came out short and curt.

"We are in a police car," replied Lt. Conway. "It's not like she'll miss it."

They had been sitting in the same position and John needed to do something- anything- to help Caroline.

"There are," replied Chevalier, "five other places I'd rather be right now. This is not my idea, but Nash asked for police assistance weeks ago and now he's pulled the trigger. If I see her, we'll take her into custody. It will go better for everyone if you two are here to help."

A small figure hurried across the parking lot from behind them. Caroline, thought John. Everyone stopped talking and stared.

"Hey," Lt. Conway barked. He pointed to the small girl hurrying up the sidewalk toward the front door of the complex. Lt. Conway had been the one who handed off Caroline to Chevalier in the chapel in South Enfield. John believed Conway didn't want to be here either.

His daughter had a *strut* when she walked. It looked unmistakable in that it looked identical to the way he strode forward onstage. The figure that hurried to the door had to be her. He said nothing and tried to gauge the distance to have a fighting chance of escape. He decided she would have to be near the doors of the hospital.

"Is that her?" asked Lt. Conway.

John unbuckled his seatbelt and put his hand on the door, but Father grabbed his arm. Caroline had come to Reliant Medical as Nash predicted she would. *Damn. Go home.* She'd come to see William.

"Is that who?" asked Chevalier.

"Is that," asked Conway, "Caroline Sullivan?"

Assistant Police Chief Chevalier looked out across the lot toward the main entrance then back to Bequette and John. "No. I don't see anyone. Lt. Conway. Do you see anyone?"

Lt. Conway stared out at the girl and then nodded back at Chevalier. "Nope can't see a damn thing in this storm."

John froze in stunned silence.

Bequette reacted better. "Perhaps we should check to be sure."

"Come back," replied Chevalier, "if it's her. I can't do anything until I see her."

Sullivan decided Lt. Conway didn't like Dr. David Nash either. This would only buy her a little time. Nash, Ross, and God knew who else would be closing in on Reliant Medical quickly and Caroline needed to do whatever she came here to do fast.

Thirty Five

Reliant Medical Center
Cold Springs, Massachusetts

WILLIAM FINALLY FELT SEMI-NORMAL since he'd awakened from the dreadful Netherworld hell in which he'd endlessly drifted. Eight hours later he was ready to go. However, the physician on duty also determined that he couldn't leave for the next day or two. So, his friends had to come here. He'd asked his father to reach out to both and then he'd waited. He needed to speak to Father Bequette as well. They were all trapped in this hell together.

Hell. The perfect and only word for what he had witnessed in his state of semi-consciousness. While everyone around him celebrated his awakening, he smiled and hugged but knew he had a far more difficult task ahead of him.

Caroline came first. She looked like she'd been on the back end of a three-day bender. Her short bob was frizzy, she wore no makeup, and dressed in jeans and an old slouchy sweater; William loved it. She locked him in an embrace, his weakened body could do little to resist even if he wanted to.

Daniel came in before Caroline could expand on what she needed to tell him. They briefly hugged. "I don't want to break anything on you," said Daniel as he broke away.

More medical personnel came into the room but gave them a few moments of privacy. As soon as they were gone, William turned serious. Caroline watched as his expression switched from grateful to concerned. "I've got to tell you something," he had said. Caroline had something to say too but when Daniel came in the words died on her lips. William needed to share what he knew. What he'd experienced in a place he could only think of as a Netherworld. Hell on one hand and the present on the other.

William held something back from the medical staff and his parents. Even though awake and brimming with energy, emotions still untethered, un-sifted, and welling up in his mind, landed in a massive pile held back only by his inability to deal with them all at once. Slowly, they leaked through and crept to the surface.

Caroline kept her hand on him as he moved from the bed to a standing position. He felt his face twist as his emotions cycled from concerned to terrified, he had a hard time getting the words out of his mouth.

"There's something you need to know," said William. "It's not Dumont..." he paused. "He's not the one. His memory, the time in The Dale, it's something else entirely."

"What are you saying?" asked Caroline.

"Guys," William declared, his voice dry. "I felt it. I saw it. It's going to come after us. It's been reaching out to us since the first day we set foot in The Dale."

Caroline looked dazed for a moment before she refocused. She had turned away from him when he first spoke but now leaned into his words.

"I saw it all," said William, exasperated, and then he told them about his experience in the coma—every moment from the time he broke through the ice and crawled out of the reservoir. All the way to the encounter with the demon lording over all of them. Everything from the word on the chapel, the feeling of two presences, one which held him there and another who helped him escape, the endless time in which he wanted to wake up but couldn't, all the way to the sinister evil and the thousands of afterimages leftover from his encounter with the malevolence. Even now as he spoke, they were still spilling out and flooding his mind and it was an enormous feat of concentration to even speak to his friends.

"I saw *him*," offered William. "Better yet, I felt him. He is not alone."

"Who is he, and why a Netherworld?" Daniel had unconsciously taken a step away from William and immediately felt the shame of it. "And who is with him?"

"I don't know," he replied, "but he's something wicked. The other presence just pushed me away from him."

Caroline moved back and embraced him again. "Thank you, William."

Daniel held back wondering why she would thank him. Then, he understood that for the first time Caroline could connect with William because they suffered the same trauma.

"We," said Caroline, "learned some things too." She filled in William and explained what they knew about South Enfield, Henry Evans, and the word William had written on his skin.

One thing still bothered Caroline. "The name seems wrong," she said finally. "If Evans/Dumont named that area, why would he give it a name that made little sense? Especially," she wondered aloud, "if he unearthed something outside the realm of nature. The word barrow means hill," added Caroline. "I looked it up. The place Father Bequette and Evans were talking about is a valley."

"It can be something else," said Daniel slowly. "I found a history book that said a barrow is a hill or mountain only in English and typically it names hills or mountains in England." He stopped and looked between William and Caroline. "There is a less common usage, a barrow can also refer to a high mound of stone over... *a grave*."

"Nobody died there," countered Caroline. "Did they?"

"Maybe no person," offered Daniel. "But Evans/Dumont marked his days there, maybe he marked the perceived death of his soul with a pile of stones in a pool of water at the head of a brook, a mound, or better said a barrow. *Metacomet's Barrow*."

The House on the Common
Cold Springs, Massachusetts
August 1948

Father Andre Bequette found Leigh Anne Evans near the front door of her house on the common waiting for him.

"It's far worse, and that..." she pointed her arm low toward the basement, "is not my son." Her normally strong and powerful voice trembled. "Do what you can to save him. Please help him." She turned away from her house, her son, her life, and stepped into the back seat of a waiting car. She did not look back.

Nobody, Bequette thought, was too far gone for salvation. The Holy Trinity is a mighty power. But the treatment and the counseling that Henry received had been a failure.

A thump from deep in the house snapped him out of his musings. *Crack!*

The impact on the locked door to the basement strained the hinges and rattled the doorknob.

"Henry," he called out to the boy. The next impact splintered the middle of the door and knocked off one iron hinge. "God still loves you, Henry," he offered. It was silent just long enough for the priest to think he might have gotten through to him with that well-placed shot.

BOOM!

An unhallowed roar thundered from the basement and the door blew completely off its hinges and spun into the living room.

Bequette expected to see the boy lying on the steps. Instead, he saw him standing coolly at the bottom looking back at him. Henry looked uninjured. He could not see a mark on the boy. *What the hell?*

"Come up," offered Bequette calmly. "The door is open." He reached a calm hand out to Henry and did not betray the alarm rising in him. Henry slipped out of view and went deeper into the basement. Bequette called out to him but instead of a reply, he heard another crash so loud that it shook the floor, sending a cloud of dust rising in the afternoon sun. The priest lost his footing but steadied himself on the door frame. Next, the house shuddered under the sound of a whine and twin booms a fraction of a second apart followed by an ear-splitting crack. Father moved toward the sound on the main level to the last room in the house. There he saw the closet doors pushed open. Evans had gone through the basement ceiling and emerged from the closet. His impact blew debris from the flooring and joists into the room.

"Holy Christ," said Bequette out loud when he saw a second bigger hole. Evans had also smashed his way through the side of the house.

Father tracked Henry in his car until he had to continue the chase into the woods on foot. He feared he knew where the boy would go. Father Bequette persisted until dark, tracking the boy all the way to the place he'd named Metacomet's Barrow. However, the boy had slipped away in the darkness, leaving the priest to stare glumly at the pile of stones in the middle of a pool of water that marked the center of the Barrow. Bequette needed to circle back.

Hours later Father Bequette watched Henry in the morning light, dodging low-lying brush. He kept enough distance, so Henry didn't run.

Bequette watched as a sapling tangled Evans momentarily before he wandered into the arm of a bush. Henry did not seem to suffer any fatigue as he passed a stubby, three-foot tall stone wall that looked like the worn fossil spine of an ancient dragon rising from the ground and disappearing in the distance.

Henry leaped from the top of the wall in a graceful smooth arc but then the boy lost his orientation, spun wildly, and thumped with a painful yell into the ground. Father Bequette, seeing his chance, leaped out from cover and pinned him to the ground. The fight left Henry. Bequette rolled over onto the ground panting and exhausted while the boy next to him snarled and snapped at him with his teeth. He had witnessed the supernatural strength of the boy the previous day and wondered how he had wrestled a boy, who had blown through two walls, into what amounted to submission. Bequette looked around and saw the church steeple rising through the trees and knew the time had come. The bishop had already approved his plan after ruling out psychiatric conditions.

They worked to organize the rite and called for two other more experienced priests who Bequette would assist. He had not planned to do this by himself, unfortunately, he was alone, trapped in the woods with a possessed boy. There were two things that he needed to begin the exorcism of the boy. One was the express permission from the bishop, and he had that.

The other: his faith.

He looked back at the gleaming white clapboard steeple of the church with the sun glinting off the stained glass and it gave him hope. He picked the boy up over his shoulder and began to walk toward the church as the boy continued to wail, snap, and curse him.

Thirty Six

Reliant Medical Center
Cold Springs, Massachusetts
February 1995

FATHER BEQUETTE HAD FORMULATED a plan with John; get Caroline and get out of the state. Bequette knew her problem could not be solved in the psychiatric wing.

"John," said Bequette, "I have an extra set of keys." Bequette handed him the keys. "If we get separated and you have Caroline, take the car and go without me."

Sullivan looked back at him and slapped on the sticker given to him by the receptionist. "You got an extra set of keys? For your sister's car?"

"I said my car didn't start," he said as he punched the button for the elevator.

"Is it even your sister's car?"

Bequette didn't answer the question and instead hummed along with the elevator music.

Father Andre Bequette entered William's room and John followed. John embraced his daughter and held on to her as long as he dared. "We have to go right now."

"I can't leave."

John had wrapped his arm around his daughter, wanting to guide her out of the door. He kept stealing nervous glances into the hallway. "Why?" John asked.

"Because this evil is real," she said. "William saw it or him and he's never going to go away until…"

"John," interrupted Bequette. "Go get the car. I'll have her out in a minute."

John Sullivan looked at his daughter and then back at Bequette. He nodded once and then sped out of the room and shut the door behind him.

Bequette shook his head, taking a long look at each of the three before him. Battered and beaten, separated and alone for a long time but through the grace of God, they were friends again. Caroline risked an immediate involuntary return to the psychiatric ward every second she stood there. But he knew her, and he knew that look. She was not going to change her mind until her concern for dragging William into her nightmare was addressed. Caroline's search for an answer to her mystery took her to the realm of the supernatural. But the supernatural had no power in the realm of men—unless it was given to them.

He sent John for the car because he planned to address her problem quickly.

"Whatever happens next you need to know this," he began. "Be strong in your faith. If you know it and live it, you will be safe and nothing this malevolence can dream up can hurt you. He is pushing back. Except," said the priest, "he is pushing back much harder now."

"Are you talking about possession?" asked Daniel.

"No," replied Bequette. "If anything, you are dealing with oppression. The possession comes later. The malevolence possessed Evans.

It once possessed Caroline while she was deteriorating in the psychiatric ward. A possession is ownership, an infestation. In Caroline's case, God himself intervened and cast him out. Possession is severe," answered Bequette, "but it can look like any medical or psychiatric problem. People brought to the attention of the church with worries about being possessed are normally medical or psychiatric issues. A doctor can treat them. That's why Dr. Nash was so convinced he could fix you. A possession, however, has a weakness inherent to the evil of bringing attention to that person. They act out of character. Evil, vicious, reckless, with cruelty that had not been a part of their personality before. The evil inside can only be evil and that brings the attention of the trained faithful. The single role of the exorcist is to send evil back to hell for eternity. Which is why exorcism, while rare, is a nasty, vicious, and dirty fight. Oppression is something different. Often hidden under the banners of a bad day, depression, or tough luck. All the things that came together to pull you apart from each other and from God. It is sinister and cruel and coldly effective."

"He never let Henry go, did he?" Caroline looked weighed down from the revelation. He knew she had spent years hating the man. "Henry could've freed himself but chose not to," Caroline said as an affirmation of understanding seemed to overtake her. "Henry allowed it to own him."

"Do I need an exorcism?" asked Caroline, now alarmed.

"Seriously Caroline?" asked the priest. "We are out of time, but no you don't. Unless you let him back. Evil, an unclean entity, whose only desire is chaos and pain, has reached out for you in a half a dozen different ways." The priest felt the mood in the room plummet. "He is trying to intimidate you. Break you down further and feed on your fear. Once he does, you will open the door for him and then he *will* possess you. Don't let him do it. Now let's go!"

"How do we stop him?" Daniel asked.

"You don't," replied Bequette, pulling Caroline to the door. "Men have no dominion over the supernatural only God does; however, the hand of God can work through us and our works."

"We do nothing?" cried Caroline incredulously.

"No." They were almost to the door of the hospital room. "You keep your faith. But you can't go barging into The Dale or Metacomet's Barrow and demand he leave because he is not there. Dumont is dead and you are free."

"I want him gone from my life now," whispered Caroline with a look of non-acceptance, as if he'd asked her to do nothing but sit and wait for the demon to take her. "Can't we beat him?"

Bequette, troubled by the idea she still did not understand what she faced, turned to Caroline. They needed to leave right now. He preferred to discuss this in the car, but Daniel and William needed to hear this too. "*Christ on the cross was beating him.* Your only job is to live and not go all bullheaded and give it another shot at you. If you don't know that, then you will need to get a better handle on your faith because that is the only thing that will free you from this oppression," replied Bequette, losing patience, seeing her resistance boiling up.

"If you try to face an entity which has existed since the beginning of time with intelligence far superior to any of us in this room, including me, you will lose your soul. You are doomed to fail if you directly confront him in your state of mind. You likely could not distinguish reality from whatever lies he pushed down your throat. Just like when you thought you were at the house on the common, but you were in The Dale. That's him. He would never allow you to even reach for your most important shield—the only thing that could save you in this fight," snapped Bequette.

"What is the shield?" demanded Caroline.

Bequette never had the chance to answer the question. The door of the room sprung open. Dr. Nash and a host of others, including Dr. Ross, flooded into the room. Caroline could see that he held a slip of paper in his right hand.

"Caroline," said Nash, "I am glad you are already here. We will only need to go down a floor to get you settled into your room."

"No," snapped Caroline. She tried to go back deeper into the room but an orderly who'd slid through the crowd locked her arms in place. She'd been living in fear of this moment since the day they had released her. Caroline struggled against the orderly until she weakened as the stark terror of the moment overwhelmed her. Her knees buckled as the orderlies dragged her away.

Caroline's heart sank further with her knees hovering just above the tiled floor. Her new life was over as she headed back to the dead years. The tornado which destroyed her life and left it as a three-year blank space of depression and loneliness had never left, it had roared off, circled back, and now touched down right on top of her. She tried to remember what Father Bequette had told her only minutes ago but the noise in her head became too loud.

Caroline watched as Daniel squared up with the orderly but kept jerking his head to the left and the right looking for more danger among the many adults in the room. He reached out to Caroline but an orderly, large and beefy with a brow covered with sweat, gave him a shove. Caroline saw it and gathered enough energy to call out to warn him off. He'd suffered enough and so had William.

All their suffering was because of her and a friendship in which she never gave enough and asked them to do far more than any friend. They'd followed her to The Dale on the first day of the trouble, fought the evil and lost, survived the fire in the house on the common, and then came back to her when she'd asked as if a day hadn't gone by. They took her back without question. Calmed her every stupid worry about The Dale. William nearly died there twice, and all of it based on the black cloud which hovered over her and her bottomless pocket full of why's.

Enough already.

"Daniel… stop!" she cried as the orderly eyed up Father Bequette whose glare was boring holes into Nash.

"Back off," warned the orderly. The orderly scowled at Father Bequette then manhandled Caroline out of the room while everyone else, now held at bay by another orderly, watched. Caroline twisted her head to see Bequette motion for the boys to stay in the room and he followed her.

As the orderlies ushered Caroline out of the room, they gave Daniel one more push. It was hard enough to drive him back into a heel first stumble, only brought under control when his left hand hit a table behind him—knocking William's father's coat on the floor.

Out of the coat spun a lighter and a set of car keys.

He and William were alone in the room since everyone else escorted Caroline to the hospital equivalent of a jail cell.

William, no longer in a hospital gown, wearing jeans and a UMass sweatshirt, bent to pick them up but then Daniel held his hand up to stop him. In one moment, he picked up the keys and lighter. In the next, he flicked the lighter, which produced a clean blue flame. He then jumped up on a chair and raised the lighter to the sprinkler head on the ceiling of the room.

A second later the fire alarms screamed to life, red painted sprinklers on the ceiling of every room began spraying water over every square inch of the hospital. Daniel hopped down to the floor under the unexpectedly heavy shower of water and flicked the keys to William before they both hustled out the door.

"Your dad's car is in the corner lot. Meet me at the east side door," yelled Daniel. "I'm getting Caroline."

"Wait," said William, pausing for a moment as he looked at Daniel.

Daniel stopped; the water pelted him as the fire alarm wailed. "What?"

"How many cats do you think the shrink from Stonehill College has?" William asked as he slipped on his father's coat.

Daniel simply snorted out a laugh before turning to chase Caroline through the heavy knot of people. Daniel hoped William would find his father's car in a hurry.

Thirty Seven

Reliant Medical Center
Cold Springs, Massachusetts
February 1995

D ANIEL WOVE HIS WAY through the nurses, orderlies, doctors, and patients. A haphazard swirl of soaking wet humanity blocked Daniel's view of Caroline. He continued to fight through the dizzying throng of people which were moving in every direction except the one he wanted to go. While he couldn't see her, he could see the two orderlies that were escorting her to her second-floor room. They'd stopped in the middle of the hall, frozen in mutual indecision. Dr. Nash, Dr. Ross, and the others with them had scattered away from Caroline, seeking shelter from the freezing fire suppression. Only the orderlies remained around Caroline Sullivan and their orders were to get her to her room, but the fire alarm and remarkably efficient sprinkler system left them standing in the middle of the hallway.

Daniel worked his way toward Caroline. A lane to her opened along the wall and he quickly passed the orderlies. Caroline's face twisted into a wild snarl as she tried to fight her way free from their stiff, clamping grips. He wanted to get in front of them and distract them long enough for Caroline to break free. As they passed the third-floor nurses' station, he scooted up to a nook in the wall, a spot between a silver fire extinguisher and the stairwell. He had no idea how he would spring her, and he had only seconds to create a plan.

Another idea popped up.

He would need his luck to hold a few seconds longer for this to work. The next moment he realized that Caroline's father stalked the orderlies from the rear. Except he was moving smoothly and fast. John Sullivan reared up to strike.

Caroline's arms burned as the rough grips of the orderlies squeezed her flesh almost to the bone. As if a malfunctioning blood pressure cuff was crushing the blood flow out of her small arms and sending thousands of pins to prick her simultaneously. Cold water venting from the sprinklers made everything worse.

Both orderlies attempted to maneuver through the throngs of patients and staff intent on exiting the building.

"Shouldn't we just get her out of the hall?" said the meat-handed orderly.

The mouth breather didn't answer him. Instead, they turned into the crowd and headed for the back stairwell. Caroline realized they were avoiding the crowd that migrated to the main stairs by the elevators. Trudging through snow to the next building, it seemed, would be better than standing in the screaming fire alarm and frigid spray of the sprinkler system.

"That hurts," Caroline snapped. Mouth breather grunted and in a smooth shift of posture, raised his hand above his head to smack her.

"Stop resisting," he said, using the keywords which allowed him to use more physical force.

Caroline focused only on the big meaty hand raised high above her head and the nasty grin on the face of the orderly as he prepared to strike her. She turned her head into his shoulder for cover and in a flash of inspiration, opened her mouth as wide as she was able and bit down into his thick muscular shoulder with as much force as she could muster.

Caroline felt like she was being dragged deeper and deeper into the thick, dark, muck in which she'd struggled in all the years she'd been in the psychiatric wing of the old hospital. She unleashed one wholly satisfying bite. She didn't even realize someone had slapped her, but she saw her father heading for her, his eyes burning in wrath.

Caroline only heard one thing as she wiggled free from the orderlies.

"Run!"

She took two steps before things went from bad to worse.

John Sullivan romanced a single thought, not my daughter. He almost made it to the orderlies holding his daughter when two things happened in quick succession. The sprinkler systems stopped spraying water everywhere, which made everyone glance up, and then look at each other to point out that the sprinklers stopped. Before anyone had moved beyond that moment, an enormous white cloud erupted in the faces of the orderlies.

Then, the lights went out. John had to assume the hospital had some sort of emergency backup system. The system would cut the power so no one would be electrocuted with an abundance of water then the generators would kick in to restore emergency lights and equipment. He had to act fast.

John did the only thing he could, lunged forward into the crowd and grabbed Caroline and hustled her in the dark toward the stairway. He made his way down the stairs toward what he thought was the front door.

John was talking to his daughter, trying to calm her down, all the way through the cold, wet, claustrophobic, and dark journey out of the front door of Reliant Medical. The emergency lights kicked on, glowing red as he hustled her through the stainless-steel framed glass double doors and into the glaring harsh lights of the first rescue vehicles on the scene.

Caroline was not with him.

The disheveled woman John Sullivan had grabbed, her white nurse hat askew on her head, pulled away without a word, and worked her way back inside.

He moved to go back in as well when someone else bumped into him.

Daniel saw the bite and slap all transpire in front of him as well as John's reaction to both. Caroline went down but bounced back to her feet standing but still trapped. Daniel stood in frozen fascination as Caroline's father rose behind the two orderlies, his eyes wide, mouth turned downward into a snarl, and body springing forward uncoiling all his pent-up energy. Just before Sullivan struck, Daniel pulled the pin on the fire extinguisher and clenched his fist around the nozzle spraying a huge cloud of white dusty powder into the soaked faces of the burly orderlies and John Sullivan.

The event created a moment of opportunity, and he took it.

He grabbed a coughing and wheezing Caroline more roughly than he intended. He brushed away some of the white powder covering her face. He was amazed that she came with him willingly even though she couldn't see him.

Daniel moved quickly through the darkness to the back stairwell, which led to a side door and out into the cold. He released Caroline and looked around in the chaos of lights, patients, visitors, and staff and scanned for William.

"You could've taken my hand there," said Caroline, rubbing her arms against the sudden bitter cold.

"I…" stuttered Daniel. "I didn't want you to think…"

"What's the plan," Caroline interrupted.

"William's coming with a car," he explained.

He heard Caroline laugh for the first time in days and she moved closer to him for cover against the wind as they ventured toward the parking lot.

Lights flashed at them from a car twenty feet away.

"Come on," yelled William. "We need to get out of here, like right now."

Daniel hustled her through the wind and snow into William's father's BMW sedan, which, while running, had not warmed up yet. "Anyone else here see the problem with William driving?" asked Caroline. "I'm not the one who is eight hours out of a coma."

Daniel ignored her. So did William. The doors closed and William dropped the clutch and popped the car into first gear before roaring out of the parking lot, but he looked unsure of where they would go next. Daniel knew William was the only person in the car who could drive a stick shift, and he assumed Caroline's silence meant she knew it too.

Thirty Eight

THE STEADY THUMP OF the wiper blades cleared the wet clumpy snow from the windshield, leaving twin arcs of clear glass. Caroline refrained from issuing orders and was relieved when William flicked the defroster on and a whoosh of air warmed by the heating coils deep inside the luxury car's dashboard pushed out into the cabin.

Despite their escape, nobody said a word.

Caroline had no idea what to do next and doubted the boys would know either.

They drove up Route 202 back toward the center of town while the snow fell in steady white sheets.

Caroline, momentarily exhilarated by the cold and wet escape, could not get past the feeling their escape would be temporary. The thought embittered her as much as the image of her mother advocating for and then signing her commitment to the psychiatric wing. Why did her mother hate her so much? Committing her to an institution, she would never forgive this.

She turned to the only thing standing between her and hell. Her two best friends and whatever plan they could cook up. They acted brave and willing. However, she realized they may not be up to getting this to the finish line.

"We need to get some dry clothes," offered William. Another fire truck, lights blazing and horns blaring, roared by them heading down Route 202 toward Reliant Medical. "I have some at my house. Nobody will be there."

Daniel nodded but looked unconvinced.

"I think that might be the first place anyone would look to find us," suggested Daniel. "We could go back to my house to get set up and leave. My mom won't be home, and she doesn't know what is going on. To be safe we can use the basement. Then, we'll get you out of town and somewhere far away." He had turned to Caroline, searching her face.

Caroline heard the phone ring at Daniel's house, but he didn't answer it. They'd come into the house through the storm door on the side of the house that led directly into the basement.

She watched Daniel's head turn nervously, like there was more than one thing on his mind. It had to be nerves, thought Caroline. He walked with almost a twitch, in a slow, vaguely circular path to a pile of clothes neatly folded and stacked on shelves along the far wall of the basement. He reached up and handed a hooded sweatshirt and weathered jeans to William and took another almost identical pair for himself. Instead of a sweatshirt, he selected a green thermal long-sleeved shirt.

"My jeans are almost dry," she said, looking at the wall of clothes. "Can I borrow that sweater?" One half of the wall was shelves stacked with clothes and the other half held freshly packed fruit in clear jars. She couldn't remember the last time that she ate.

Daniel nodded then reached up to get it. A nice soft white crew neck, one of his mother's, and after a little more looking he located dry jeans, a heavy jacket, and a suitable knit cap.

They stood in their wet clothes in the corner of the basement and simultaneously realized that they could not all change in the basement.

"Well, turn around," demanded Caroline with a whisper.

"Oh," said William, his face red as he stared at her but slowly turned away.

"Hey, we'll go upstairs," offered Daniel, "and change in my room so you can change down here." He waved William upstairs but didn't follow.

Caroline did not like the way Daniel looked at her. "What's wrong Daniel?"

Daniel's response landed bluntly. "Why didn't you tell us?"

The mile marker. She cringed and took a step toward him, but he stepped backward. "Are you going to tell William?" Caroline asked, looking for some absolution from him. Keeping the truth away from both nearly killed William and almost certainly ended his baseball career. She could see Daniel pushing back his resentment at her. He didn't look at her with his normal unabashed graceful love between friends which rolled out of him easily. She only saw hurt in his eyes.

"Someone will," he replied. "Maybe if it comes from you, it won't hurt so much." He turned and went upstairs.

Caroline wept as she struggled out of her jeans, which were wetter than she thought, and then slipped on the heavy sweater and a well-worn pair of jeans. Now completely alone, reality knocked on the door of her mind. Stuck in a basement in someone else's clothes awaiting capture. Nothing her dad or his lawyers or anyone could do would stop it. Nothing could stop this present madness. She headed into a long darkness, endless treatment sessions, and medications which made her sick. Worst of all, she'd betrayed the best friends she'd ever had.

The truth was Nash would catch them. William and Daniel would resent her. Everyone would be in trouble because of her. It occurred to her she might not be worth it. None of this was worth the risk or pain which had washed over her life once more. As a matter of fact…

William still could not believe Caroline had left. He looked around the basement expecting to find her.

"She's gone," said Daniel.

William only saw the worst of it and pointed. "Her clothes." Several garden stones formed a neat circle. They curbed the urge to bolt outside after her and after a disagreement, made calls to Father Bequette and John Sullivan for help only to leave messages.

Minutes later, William trotted alongside Daniel as fast as his beleaguered body could on the slick icy road. He said little. William saw it differently. His mind stayed on the subject of possession. The wet clothing twisted into a perfect circle was all the confirmation he needed. Whatever evil, and he knew unspeakable evil lurked in The Dale, attacked her soul again.

"I had her," snarled Daniel at William. They chased her into the woods to fight a battle best left alone. "She's crossed over the line, William. We can't ignore this anymore. Maybe she should get help. I'm not saying Nash is the answer, but she needs serious help."

William hated that Daniel could be right. To Father Bequette, Metacomet's Barrow and The Dale were places where faith failed, but to him, there was more. Evil had come to South Enfield from Metacomet's Barrow and left a mark there. The evil which left that mark had been around before the first settler put a stake in the forest around South Enfield still lingered there, and Caroline headed right for it. He saw it while drifting in his endless coma.

They had to get to her first.

"I don't know if we can get her to the Vermont state line," Daniel offered, breaking his thoughts.

"Things can get worse you know," William snapped back.

"For her or for us?" Daniel steeled his voice. "What are we going to do when we find her? Force her to come back with us? She won't. You know that, right? We chase her every time. This must be the last time. She needs help."

William could feel Daniel's rising anger but chose not to respond. He'd beaten evil in his unconsciousness and knew it'd be a battle, but he'd do anything to save Caroline. Saving her meant getting to her before evil took her mind, body, and soul. Then he and Daniel could fight about which to save first, her mind or her soul.

After a burst of energy, he began to tire. They'd discovered her missing and then lived the minutes of horror of seeing the single set of footprints that led from the storm door, down the long driveway to the end of the street and The Dale.

"Save your energy," said Daniel as he tightened his jacket, shrugged his shoulders, and squeezed his hand into a fist.

William could barely see Caroline's footprints in front of him in the darkness even though she only had a fifteen-minute head start. The wind already erased the sharp edges of the prints. The snow had let up, and by the time they reached the shoreline, it had stopped all together. He flexed his hands for warmth and scrambled up the narrow strip of land between the wall of pines and the frozen reservoir. He prayed to God she wasn't too far gone.

Part IV

Thirty Nine

Reliant Medical Center
Cold Springs, Massachusetts
February 1995

D R. TARA ROSS STOOD IN what had been William Lane's hospital room. Water still rolled down the walls and beaded up on every surface. It pooled, held together only by the power of surface tension, on the floor of every room and hallway. Staff hurried from one place to the next desperate to assess the damage and contain the emergency. Backup lighting left the room dim. A white light on the ceiling blinked steadily.

Across from her, Dr. David Nash fretted with decisions as people moved in and out of the hospital room. Chevalier, the Stonehill College faculty dean, William's parents, and several others demanded his attention. To Tara, he seemed woefully inadequate for the task at hand. Not a leader, she thought.

"Here is what we know," began Nash, taking a few precious minutes away from his other pending tasks to address them. "Caroline Sullivan, who is now a ward of the Commonwealth of Massachusetts, assaulted staff members in the emergency event"—he avoided the word fire—"and then in the confusion, slipped away. We have both the state troopers and local police agencies looking for her and both Daniel and William."

The faculty dean broke in, cutting off Nash. "You have told me what I already know."

Ross smirked a moment of happiness in the chaos, Nash recoiled at the tone and snarled back his response. "Well?"

"I want to know how," replied the faculty dean. "How does a young girl who clearly needs assistance does not get help and instead ends up being recommitted? The paperwork to do so signed by, of all people, her mother, who has been absent from her life for the better part of a decade? How did you, who is clearly biased, get reinvolved and why?"

Nash did not conceal his irritation. Tara thought he knew the question could eventually come; however, he obviously didn't recognize the man who accompanied Tara Ross. They came in together but did not speak. Tara had been instructed by the dean to avoid speaking to Dr. Nash when she arrived at the hospital. He must have assumed him to be some other functionary. "Who are you?"

"I am the faculty dean at Stonehill College. Some very serious irregularities in the protocol regarding the counseling of Caroline Sullivan have come to light. I feel they need to be explained."

Dr. David Nash licked his lip and cocked his head, his leveled gaze appeared at its most intimidating. "I treated Caroline Sullivan some time ago for a psychiatric event which lasted for over three years. In that time, she made no progress." He continued, "She was released against my advice."

"Dr. Nash," offered Tara Ross, her voice helpful and measured. She could see he needed help, so she decided to try.

"Don't," replied Dr. Nash, his tone unleashing a wave of hurt on her. She felt the shock must be clear on her face. Her lips stayed half-open as her shoulders dropped. The surprise of the moment blinded her to what came next. "Dr. Ross," he announced, "reached out to me a few weeks ago about the care and history of Caroline Sullivan. She reached out to me because I was her primary care provider for her stay in the psychiatric ward. Caroline had given her permission to release her records to Dr. Ross. I assumed Dr. Ross's concern was only for her patient."

Tara stepped forward, worry crept in as she recognized what he was going to do too late. "David, please don't."

Nash frowned as he continued. She knew he hated being called David in front of the faculty dean. He pointed at Ross. "She asked for the telephone number for her mother, she told me she needed it so she could get an additional asset to help with Caroline. However, she had an ulterior motive. She confessed to me several days ago that she had an affair with Caroline Sullivan's father."

"Good God... *David*," cried out Tara Ross. She should have known he would try to save himself before her. A pair of hands grabbed her elbow, leaving her unable to move.

"She used me to attack Caroline to hurt John Sullivan. John Sullivan rejected her years ago and the grudge polluted her professional judgment. I had no idea how far she would go. Only this morning did I realize how far she would take her revenge. Her actions and her actions alone have resulted in the total breakdown of Caroline Sullivan. I was as shaken as you are now by her behavior."

The faculty dean glared first at her and then at Dr. David Nash. "Do you have anything else to add?"

Nash took another look at her as she stumbled backward and into a seat. No pity, not one tender word. She buried her head in her hands. "She has taken my effort to help her in her treatment of Caroline Sullivan in a wildly inappropriate way."

The faculty dean now took a step between Ross and Nash. "What do you mean?"

"She came to my house last weekend. Unannounced and uninvited. She had packed an overnight bag. I was stunned by the behavior. I asked her to leave."

Tara burned in embarrassment and betrayal, she could not listen to another word out of Nash's mouth. She hated him and hated that he manipulated her. He flung her under the bus at the first sign of trouble for himself. He stomped on her career and did not even care. Her gut roiled in anger, and she would not take another second of abuse from the man.

"David," she said one more time. Her voice hitched a bit as she stood up and walked to him, stepping in a large puddle along the way. Once she reached him her wrath took over. She slapped him hard across his cheek and again on the other side of the face, leaving his cheeks burning red.

She took note of two things as she left the room; one, the faculty dean followed her, and second, the dean told David he was full of shit.

Tara Ross knew she'd made a mistake and now she needed to make it right. She no longer had a job… or even a career. She'd thrown it away chasing a ghost. A target with no more substance than a child's breath. Resentment cooled to embers.

The faculty dean at least had been kind enough to explain to her that a board of inquiry would follow, and she would be placed on paid leave. He had also been clear regarding the expected outcome of that inquiry.

Tara reluctantly told him she would resign if needed to keep things clean for the school. She expressed her desire to go after Caroline—this time to save her—and dropped the dean off at the rectory. She guessed Caroline would head home, or unfortunately, more likely, The Dale. She could not even be sure now that time in the psychiatric wing really made sense. Dr. Nash clearly had used her and manipulated her. Maybe the girl would present differently outside of Dr. Nash's sphere of influence. Tara hoped Caroline would go home but really, she knew the girl would head for the woods the moment that door opened.

Tara knocked on the front door of the Sullivan home first and when there was no answer, she placed her hand on the door hoping to feel something. Dr. Tara Ross knew it was irrational to do so. Tara didn't realize she still held onto the fantasy of telling John she was pregnant. Now racing to save Caroline, she came full circle.

When she looked over at the two homes across the street, she noticed three sets of footprints exited from the Wilson home. And all three headed down the street and into the forest.

She drove down the street all the way to the broken gate, which once would have blocked her from going any further. After she opened her car door and walked out into the cold, she saw several police cruisers and other rescue vehicles arrive in front of the Lane home. David's state issued sedan pulled up as well. A stab to the heart as he looked in her direction.

She ignored him and spun away to start her search, determined to leave Dr. David Nash in her wake.

Tara's small flashlight easily followed the set of three prints for a while. Despite the light of the gibbous moon and the tracks in front of her showing humans in woods, she grew uneasy and wondered why she walked alone. David Nash should be walking alone. Not her. For the first time since she entered the forest and headed down the empty road, she felt a warning tingling deep in her skull, from where the oldest and most primal of impulses emerged.

She stopped and listened. Tara noticed one set of muddled tracks had moved off the road and into the forest. She waited and listened more. Nobody came down the road behind her. Steadied, she willed herself to follow the tracks further and into the dark forest.

Tara Ross headed off the road and carefully stoked her wrath at David Nash just enough to keep the embers a dull reddish orange. It kept her warm. Her steps were slow and deliberate, each motion thought through and then executed.

Ross almost turned back after she stumbled forward into a thorn bush and ripped her jacket. Blood dripped from her arm into the snow.

She trudged through the forest, snow, and ice, following the tracks of a possibly insane girl's desperate escape attempt—driven by her stupidity—through a dark New England winter's evening. "Now who is the crazy one?" Ross asked aloud.

The ground to her right sloped down and away toward the reservoir. The angle, while not very steep, challenged the limits of her stylish impractical boots. Ross had already given up any hope of them looking new after tonight.

Then, she heard the voice.

"You look," it said a short distance away.

Tara jumped, startled, and stifled all but a short yelp of what started out as a scream. She whipped around frightened. However, there was nothing in the snowy woods around her. She, with her heart hammering away in her rib cage, snapped her head left and then right. Still, nothing broke the silence. It took an enormous amount of effort, but she forced herself to slow down and breathe. Slowly and deliberately, she scanned the frozen forest from where she stood in a small stand of dying pines. Her eyes adjusted to the limited light focused on each rock, hump of snow, then there, yes right there.

She had missed it the first time; but barely visible, a figure stood in the shadowy umbra between two dying pine trees.

Tara instinctively recoiled from the mostly hidden figure. The shape, far enough away that she could almost convince herself nothing lurked in the dark. She stared hard, and the formed shadow spoke again.

"No," she said, knowing the words as the woman spoke. Words replayed in her head a thousand times. Words that had warmed her soul and reaffirmed her life decisions ten years ago. Tara retreated several steps until her heel caught the edge of a rock and she flopped down hard.

"You look like the kind of person who knows how to find her way," it said louder this time. Ross froze in place, unable to stand, knowing the voice, unwilling to believe she could hear the low calming words here in the woods. Her heart jolted to a hard stop.

After all this time, she thought. Her eyes opened wider to see the woman in the darkness. She realized the woman did not speak to Tara; the woman just spoke. As if it was a recording or a memory of the event, when a *single conversation* changed the trajectory of her life.

"Please just stop," she pleaded, holding up a single hand while bracing herself in a sitting position with the other. Tara noticed the woman didn't respond to her and, worse yet, recited Tara's own responses in Tara's voice from that conversation on the boardwalk.

The old woman seemed oddly connected to the ground. Rather, she corrected herself, not connected but growing from a slick of black oily slush stretching out from the woman's feet and threading back in the forest gloom. A damning property she hadn't noticed when she first spied the woman.

"Are you really going to let your life," said the woman, "go by without ever trying to become the best you? How is that possible with *him* and a child holding you back?" She continued to speak as if she had not heard Tara, or worse, she shuddered, did not care. Each word a memory, and a *verdict*. A recitation of who Tara used to be and what she had become.

Cold wet seeped up her back. "You're supposed to help me. Like you did the first time! To be there to listen." The idea the woman had a purpose slammed into Ross. Anger briefly flared inside Tara.

"*Don't,*" she cried out. "Don't you judge me," she snapped. "Don't you dare judge me." This time she yelled it out louder.

The woman had come back to collect on the bill Tara had rung up on the boardwalk in Maine. The woman, she knew, had come for her soul.

She rattled on, edging ever closer to Tara. Her words slurred and sounded metallic as she wobbled from the shadows, slogging through the slick and dragging a ragged tendril of the sludge along.

Forty

The Quabbin

CAROLINE SULLIVAN FLED INTO the dark night as sheets of snow whipped and swirled around her. There were only a few inches of wet snow on the ground and as she walked, it became harder and crisper as the temperature dropped. When they'd left the hospital, the snow had been slushy and heavy. Since then, the temperature plummeted, and the falling snow transformed from clunky and sticky to light and stinging.

She raced down the dark crumbling road until she reached the shoreline of the Quabbin Reservoir. Caroline turned left, hugging the tree line, hoping for some shelter from the wind but found little. A quarter of a mile along the shoreline, when she passed the narrow cove, she turned up the mostly frozen streambed, carefully avoiding the black thin spots where a small flow of water softly gurgled. She moved through the silent, thick forest and crossed the ridge which overlooked the ruins of South Enfield, and for the first time since Henry Lee Dumont, she entered The Dale alone.

Caroline stood in the quiet darkness of The Dale just a few feet from the dim void where the door of the ruined chapel once welcomed the faithful. The house of worship strained under the heavy load of snow. A light puff of her frozen breath drifted slowly away, and she pushed back the heavy cotton hat on her head.

She waited alone with nothing but the stillness and the rotting remains of a dying town. The wind had blown patches of the broken road clear of snow but left behind the thin veneer of ice. The chapel stood to her left, and the ruins to her right, which she knew from the maps, was the Evans' mill. The road in front of her ducked below the ice of the reservoir fifty yards away.

She imagined what this had once been like when Evans' mill turned trees into lumber. Perhaps, children moved in small flocks while they whirled and spun, playing games across the lawns of the old houses. The simple chapel, once filled on Sunday with farmers and field men, had been the centerpiece of town.

South Enfield's future was stolen in deference to the greater good. Their clutch of land held more value a hundred feet underwater. These few decaying monuments to hope and faith remained while the forest steadily took them back, leaving only the bones to molder in the wild.

The steady cold leached into her feet and fingers. Despite being here, she wasn't sure what she should do. With the cold came another feeling, not physical but a dull emotional one. Here she noted complete stillness. Stillness, the thought dawning slowly across her mind, in deference to the damned.

When she ran away from Daniel's house, Caroline imagined a conflict here which started with her storming into The Dale and coming face to face with the waiting malevolence. It would wait for her, perhaps with a deadly serious grin on its dreadful face. She would eye him down with a cold determined stare and then they would battle to the death. Because she would not live this way any longer.

Caroline Sullivan found nothing in the frigid quiet.

Even as she waited the truth dawned on her. The Dale did not house evil. It's me. I am the problem.

Fear Caroline once barely held back, blew her foundations to dust. The knowledge she'd caused all her troubles, leaving Dr. Nash and Dr. Ross as right, hammered into her.

The weight of the revelation grew heavy while a new desire rose within. She stomped her feet into the snow to get her circulation moving again. She wanted to confront something. Nothing rose from the darkness to confront her.

No devil.

No possession.

No ghosts.

She yelled out, "Well…?"

Nothing.

The moon brightened as she turned around and moved deeper along the road closer to the ice-covered reservoir. The trees picketed around the town cast shadows in the bright snow on the ground.

It must be part of the joke, she thought, the sick, pathetic joke laid on all of them. Father Bequette had been wrong and so had she. In the cold freezing night, while the rest of the town looked for them, she stood here in an empty, long dead town whose buildings, if they could even be called that anymore, stood out of sheer spite.

Nothing to face here.

Evil, Bequette had said, would come out of the shadows and show itself because it knew it would be on the verge of winning. He'd said evil would crawl out and settle old scores and knew nobody would be safe. It would take the form of the darkest fears and secrets of anyone it encountered, emboldened by the scent of despair. Little did the priest know nothing lurked in even the darkest parts of the forest. She didn't need any of the defenses he'd been afraid she was lacking. No epic battle to guard her faith or steel her mind against intrusion.

The malevolence and the doctors could debate who was right. Caroline was either insane or possessed. She had to know. She realized how she could know for sure.

The evil that entered her life first began with Henry in Metacomet's Barrow. It seemed logical to Caroline that Metacomet's Barrow should be her next and last step. Since nothing faced her in The Dale, there would be nothing in the Barrow, forcing her to go back up the road and turn herself over to the endless time in the psych ward. She would finally touch the basement wall of the house on the common. Something she failed to do years ago. Except now she did not seek a far wall in a damp basement.

Caroline Sullivan wanted Metacomet's Barrow, and she knew exactly where to find it.

Forty One

South Enfield, The Dale
1948

FATHER ANDRE BEQUETTE KNEW at noon a fuse would be lit, and a grand twenty-foot-tall wall of water would come roaring and tumbling into the valley. His level of stress kept climbing because they were not safe from the coming flood. Henry would have to be freed of the malevolent oppressor before he could leave South Enfield. If they were not out of the South

Enfield, they would perish. So, he needed to move faster. The boy would not cooperate, and it took everything he had to move him a few hundred yards.

The Swift River had been filling the basin of the Quabbin Reservoir for months, flooding the remains of the towns that dotted the valleys and plains. Once dynamite took out the center of the retainer dam the entire Swift River Valley, including South Enfield, would be underwater.

The only thing left would be a road that emerged from the trees to his right. The church which held its last mass only two weeks before stood proud. Fifty people attended the joyful mass. Mostly those who attended returned to see the town one last time after leaving years or months before. Having a church intact turned out to be a lucky break for Bequette. He needed all the breaks he could get.

Bequette had secured the boy against a pew, but this time he used a coil of rope to lock him down. The boy had stopped screaming and moaning, reducing his output to mumbling.

CRACK!

The priest instinctively ducked. A heavy oak door of the church, ripped off its hinges, roared over his head and into the altar, shattering into three jagged pieces. Father Bequette snapped his head around and looked back at the boy who shot a nasty grin his way. They locked eyes in the deadly quiet of the church.

"Well, what the hell is it with you and doors," he murmured to himself while wiping the sweat off his brow with the sleeve of his shirt. "Who am I with?" asked the priest, more out of curiosity rather than the procedure he needed to follow. He received no answer.

An exorcism was no simple thing and not taken lightly. Great care and preparation went into the rite. Nobody ever attempted it alone. And yet here he stood alone. The rare rite was a multi-step process meant to separate a person from the possession, obsession, or oppression of an unclean spirit. Bequette believed evil infested the area of Metacomet's Barrow. Henry's body, now held hostage by an unclean spirit, and his soul suffered somewhere deep below the surface.

He pulled a book from beneath his torn black shirt. There was no longer a doubt in his mind that there was a presence. The boy projected the will of the malevolence. He did not even have to move, he simply had to think about it and the door had been ripped off its hinges. The boy had not punched his way out of the basement and house, rather, had been empowered by something fierce and evil which willed a hole in the house. Bequette wondered for the first time if this was bigger than him and if he swam in waters out of his depth.

Bequette knew he faced immense strength; however, he had something infinitely more powerful on his side.

Bequette paused for a second, reared back to his full height, and flexed his shoulder and arm muscles. After a few comforting breaths, he spoke out loud to the boy.

"Henry," he said with a calm and firmness that he knew would need to last. "I will invite a few of my friends to assist us in this journey." The boy looked back at him quizzically and Father began the exorcism by calling out the litany of the saints of the church for help before sprinkling holy water on both. Then he began, "Lord have mercy."

He moved through the rite but the boy with the wicked little smile and the eyes that penetrated deep into the man did not seem at all altered. It was not, thought Bequette, happening quickly. The priest questioned the boy and the few times that the boy responded, he insisted he was fine, nothing was wrong. Bequette completed the prayer cycle twice before the boy broke into raging fits and a fury not seen yet.

"Stop," the boy had whimpered several times in a voice meant to engender pity.

"No."

Father Bequette moved further and further into the rite. Those moments in which the boy appeared to be in gut-wrenching pain and agony had passed and now, and he sat silent. For some time, the boy did nothing except fix his terrifying glare on him.

Bequette tired, no unclean spirit would leave easily or make leaving anything less than agony on the one possessed. Leaving meant returning to hell and the damnation of eternity. The evil he faced seemed no less cruel than expected. Nothing happened in the order he expected, or in the research and planning that he had done. He realized he must be the one to keep the process on track. Off balance, Bequette made mistakes that let the demon control the rite rather than the other way around.

All at once, a crippling thought slammed into him.

Perhaps this had not been the first time the malevolence had encountered an exorcist. The demon controlling the body of the boy and subverting his will kept anticipating Bequette's movements and striking back at just the right time to knock him off track.

The demon infesting the boy played with him. Delayed him. Despite the withering glare and guttural laugh clucking out of Henry, Bequette continued and for the first time during the battle, he knew that he was losing.

"Strike terror, Lord, into the beast now laying waste to your vineyard..." wheezed Bequette but still the boy, seemingly unmoved, fixed his wretched scowl upon him.

The floorboards of the room rattled and shook but Bequette tried to ignore it. But to ignore the supernatural, from even the standpoint of the sheer fascination that it engendered as he witnessed it, took tremendous focus and discipline. His reserves of both were running empty, the demon unnerved him and distracted him enough to make mistakes in prayer and sequence. Bequette understood the strategy but could not do a damn thing to change the trajectory in which they were heading. The demon had played on his sense of urgency, his sense of confidence, and drawn him into a losing fight. He should have dragged the boy to his car a half mile up the road from South Enfield and driven him to the residence of the bishop where two more priests waited.

The entity, sensing his unease, imploded one of the stained-glass windows, showering the pews closest to it with bits of rose and emerald glass. Bequette moved on, this time directly addressing the spirit infesting the air around the boy.

"I command you, unclean spirit whoever you are, along with all of your minions attacking, tell me by some sign your name!" Bequette bellowed, willing strength back into his body.

He heard a groan from beneath him as the foundation shifted. He feared the whole church might plummet down around them. The sky may have blackened, Bequette knew, it may have only appeared to blacken. A sign of strength from the malevolence. The young priest had run out of time, and he needed to dig down deep into his faith and get things back on track.

A yell echoed out in the valley, and it was not from the boy. The sound came from outside of the church. Several voices were calling for the boy. Help came too late.

Bequette turned to Henry, who gazed back at him, a wry smile beginning to cross his sweaty face. The calls from outside were getting louder. The voices increased in intensity and volume, continuing to call Henry's name and his own.

The boy replied, "Please help," a whimpering, painful cry to elicit help and condemn Bequette for inhumane deeds. Father would be seen in a very different light with a boy tied to a pew.

"I'm in here," Henry cried, "help!"

Time was up. It was too late. Chevalier and the search party had found them.

Bequette ran to the door, realizing that he had failed, duped by the malevolence infesting Henry Evans' soul. In a flash he saw it. Bequette had only found the boy less than an hour and a half ago. The malevolence orchestrated the events starting with the incidents at the house, so his mother called Bequette, blowing a hole in the house to escape into the woods, keeping Bequette searching last night and this morning only to run out of the church and be caught minutes later. The malevolence predicted his attempt at exorcism here in the church with no help. Of course, the boy knew Bequette would ask the police to aid in the morning search. Henry could then accuse Bequette of vile acts and get away with it. Bequette knew, while not eternal, the demon was ex-temporal, meaning he could see time at all points of time at once.

And if that ploy failed, the malevolence could destroy Bequette and make his escape.

The priest turned and burst into the open air just outside of the church. Several men came to a stop in front of the church. Glen Chevalier, to whom he had offered the benediction at the swearing-in of the new officer weeks before, stood in front.

"GET BACK! GET BACK! GET OUT!" Bequette yelled and immediately regretted his unfortunate choice of words as the men covered the twenty feet between them in a blink.

Above the grunts, curses, and moans the dark sky was lit up with blooms of red, green, and white bursting across the sky followed by the sharp snap of an airburst. A bright flashing display rippled with light and thunder across the night.

"YOU'RE KILLING YOURSELVES," he yelled as a policeman tried to wrestle him to the police car.

Officer Chevalier held back at the car for a fraction of a second. Bequette, face first on the ground, wrestled his head toward Chevalier and willed the young officer to investigate the church. They could still pull the boy out of the hell in which he drifted.

Chevalier turned toward another sound.

An enormous boom rumbled through the valley, shaking the ground underneath them. The shaking did not stop, rather, it increased in frequency and resonance. The retainer dam had blown, and a tsunami was rushing toward them.

The men released him to sprint toward higher ground. The ground shook so hard it was difficult to stand but they all made it up. Bequette thought only of the boy and turned back to the church to get him out of there. Chevalier followed right behind him and Chevalier's terrified gasp told him they would be too late.

He tried anyhow. Henry stood in the middle of the church laughing with a wickedly satisfied grin. Bequette stole a glance at Chevalier, knowing the officer saw the same look.

Bequette took another step as he heard the water roaring into town. It slammed him against the church and pinned him while he struggled under the pressure, weight, cold, and ultimately darkness.

The boy was lost.

He had failed.

Forty Two

Cold Springs
February 1995

"Have you been to confession?" the priest asked John as they drove to find his daughter. "I'll know if you are lying."

"Yes, you are my confessor," he replied. He typically confessed the same things; anger at Allyssa Sullivan, frustration at himself for not figuring out his daughter's emotional seasons, bitterness over the loss of the small circle of his family which made him whole, the deep and endless doubt triggered by his infidelity. John confessed to the general, gnawing feeling of having everything he'd always wanted, only to watch as it burned into nothing.

"She knows she is facing years more in an institution, and this is her chance to settle the score. To face down the questions that have haunted her," Bequette said.

A quick pass down Old Enfield Road allowed them to see Lane's BMW in the Wilsons' driveway. They saw the set of small footprints in the snow leading from the house toward Gate 5A, which told both Sullivan and Bequette where she went. Twin tracks further apart on either side of hers, the boy's, were those of people who were running. "If they were running," said Sullivan. "It means she must have gone alone."

John wanted to jump out of the car. Bequette held him back. "I have a better way to get there." They drove to the top of the next street north, Juckett Hill Road. "It's quicker," he declared, soothing John's emotions. "Caroline probably realized that William had just beat the malevolence, even if William did not understand the nature of his victory, and she will want a piece of it too. If you look at it from her perspective, things are grim. I'm afraid she's run out of hope."

They pulled to a stop at the top of Juckett Hill Road and parked in front of Gate 5B, a twin of Gate 5A but a quarter of a mile north on a dead-end road.

While Bequette grabbed a black bag out of the back seat of his sister's sedan, Sullivan allowed himself to think of the timeline of events that got him to this place. His wealth mattered less than the snow under his shoes. Without the natural hard-wired connection between father and daughter, he had spun aimlessly through the days after the storm. Then he broke.

In those first days, after Henry Lee Dumont, he'd told Bequette he'd heard her moan and whisper, tearing restlessly beneath her sheets at night deep in a nightmare, searching for a way to the surface and a chance to breathe. He'd lay next to her and held on to, her praying that she would find her way. Even when committed, an action he'd only grudgingly agreed to because he could figure nothing else out, he'd held on hoping and praying but still watched her drift further and deeper into the ocean of doubt and darkness in which she floundered. And he could do nothing. Neither could Nash, who'd insisted he could save her. However, in his care, she fell apart and the heartbeat between them grew fainter and dimmer until finally there was nothing. He knew his little girl had vanished into the ether. Despair, thought John. Dangerous self-loathing. But understandable.

John had blamed himself for trusting Nash. Even with his money and lawyers it still took an agonizing three years, and a miracle, to get her out of there. One day she woke up, coming to the surface as if nothing ever happened. Despite what Nash claimed, he knew his daughter.

Now, Nash wanted her back in the room under his care. He'd convinced Tara Ross to join the expedition. The boys had broken her out, Bequette confirmed it, and were going to take a hit because of it.

True friendship.

Those young men made the sacrifice, twice now, so he would too. There was no way she was going back to Reliant Medical Center or any other psychiatric wing, not if he breathed the air of this wintry earth. What ailed her was not psychosis, but he believed in something else. He believed Father Bequette that something evil had stalked her life. A question about confession told him that what he was getting into was all about ending that evil's grip on his daughter.

Just beyond Gate 5A
Cold Springs, Massachusetts

The woman from the boardwalk lurched steadily from between two trees and out of the shadows. The footprints Tara had followed led her to a confrontation with her past. Tara could see the woman looked just as she did on the ocean boardwalk in Maine. Her posture stooped and frail with rumpled and furrowed skin stretched across her face. A rounded mouth waggled above her slack, unhinged jaw hanging slightly open. The woman staggered, dragging a thin tendril of oil through a layer of hardened snow.

Each step, followed by a wet sucking pop sound, churned the stomach of Ross. The ancient woman then put a hand on her tightly curled snow-white hair before stopping to look Ross in the eye, reaching a hand out, bidding Tara to take it. Her neck stretched out and the vertebrae popped as if it were knuckles. Black oily filth slopped down from somewhere above the cuff of her shirt, draining off her hand and into the snow.

Ross, drawn in despite the horror and building sense of dread, could not resist her. A greater power, curiosity, blocked her efforts.

"Why…" she said gravely and stiff, as if she had woken up after a long sleep.

"Is he worth it?" gurgled the woman, black strands draining out of the woman's mouth and shunted nose. Tendrils of the substance wound their way around the legs of the woman and up under her flowing shirt.

Terrified, Tara could no longer move. But the tendrils did, vibrating as if a string on a cello. Her face shimmered once and stayed that of the woman from the boardwalk. Once more it shimmered, and something else neither man nor woman took the place of the woman. All the while, the black oily tendrils continued to squirm around the arms, legs, and face of the woman.

Strangest of all were the eyes of the woman; deep, dark, and sunken, lacking the glistening fire they held the first time she saw her. The woman leaned within a few feet of her, turning her face toward the moon, and reached over with frail brittle hands, blackened by throbbing veins draining the vibrating black ooze. As the woman spoke bitter bile rose in Tara's throat driven out by her churning stomach.

"Don't you judge…" Tara never finished her plea because in the moonlight she saw tiny tendrils emerge from the woman's eye sockets.

Her shriek pierced the dark, but the forest swallowed the echo.

Tara felt the shriek leave her lungs, but it was not one of fear but rather the anguish of a person who fell for a ruthless deception. A person who saw their deceiver for who they were. Instead of the talcum powder grandmotherly warmth that had calmed the riptide of emotions, Tara glared at the hollow-eyed shell of a person. Righteous fury fanned out of her center. She reached out to latch on and crush the throat of the woman now springing dark tendrils from all over her body. To Tara, she looked like a spider with a thousand slender black legs as she escaped.

Coiled up like a viper Tara sprung forward, her hands reaching out ready to lock onto her quarry but found nothing but air as the woman jumped backward with astounding speed. Her legs snapped and bent in wide circles like a steamship paddle in reverse complete with a wet crunch, pop sound.

Had Dr. Tara Ross been in her office looking at the problem she wouldn't have chased the woman deeper into the woods. However, hate seared through her limited resistance and overwhelmed the logical part of her mind. She moved without caution then, her right foot skidded out. Ross cartwheeled to the ground, rolling down a narrow chute of ice. Nothing she did slowed her movement through the blue-black gloom of trees flashing by her.

She bottomed out and hit the smooth flat frozen surface of the reservoir and spun in a half circle, legs and arms flailing. For a long time, she could not move, but when she did, she heard the ice crack. She had slid fifty yards on the perfectly smooth ice and stopped on the frozen surface of the Quabbin Reservoir.

Another pop, the sound echoed across the ice from shore. She glanced over to see the woman slamming a stout tendril with incredible power, smashing it into the ice, creating a large crack. Tara would plummet through either drowning or freezing to death.

Tara dared to hope as a figure appeared at the edge of the icy bluff. She zeroed in on the figure and had the oddest thought that he was not at all dressed for the weather. His coat was too thin, no hat or gloves, and the way he slipped he wasn't wearing boots but shoes. His head tipped down farther as he tried to find the source of the sounds. And his face shown in the moonlight

David. He'd come back. Maybe…

Tara brushed back the thought. Nothing he could do would change a damned thing between them. But he didn't know what waited for him under the bluff. Tara did, she longed to both warn him and watch him be shredded into nothing.

He hadn't seen her yet. Or at least she didn't think he did.

The woman melted away and no longer looked like a woman.

There was nothing more than a rough silhouette and when the meager light of the evening illuminated its features, they changed even as she watched. The beast flickered. Now roughly humanoid and massive, laced with thick blackened cordlike muscles. The black muscles hung loosely on an iron-sheened skeletal frame. Each image existed as nothing more than a suggestion. There for a moment and then gone. Only to appear more sinister. And whatever it had become, focused its attention on David.

Watching the malevolence and David at the same time she knew she hated him. Dr. David Nash manipulated and then betrayed her, leaving her career and life in smoldering ruins. He stepped closer to the edge and finally saw her. She raised her hands toward him.

The beast stalked him.

"Tara," he yelled out. The tone of his voice, all elements of the arrogance gone, only concern filtered through the one word.

Too late.

She dropped her hand horrified that she caused David to reveal himself to the malevolence and she dropped down onto the ice. She didn't want to watch.

"Hey," he shouted.

"Run," she finally managed. "Run. Run. *Run!*" she yelled, hiding her face in her hands.

The beast lurched up the bluff thirty feet from David. Its long and boney arms rammed like twin ice picks to pull itself up and over the ridge. One arm flopped over and then the next. Thin and sinewy skin hung below each bat-like arm and each claw-like end slammed into the ground, bracketing the terrified psychiatrist.

A rotten rancid odor, like that of spilled garbage emanated from the beast and wafted across the ice.

Tara summoned her courage to stare at the beast. It stood humanoid, towering, the malevolence continued to flicker in appearance. Tara could imagine it whumping one massive arm down upon David in a single life-stealing blow as he quivered in place. David's face betrayed his fear in the presence of evil.

Nash's expression changed. David looked as if he wanted to both run from it and fall before it and beg for mercy he knew would not come.

She locked eyes with Nash. She raised her hands in a useless, last-ditch effort for his help. She'd lose her soul and her life, but she wanted someone with her.

David glanced once more at her. Then ran away. Leaving her on the ice with this monstrosity looming.

"*Still an Asshole!*" she shouted.

She watched as he ran along the top of the ridge away from both her and the beast. It was a chaotic, inefficient run. He slipped, got up, tripped over a log, then ran again until finally, he launched into a full panic sprint heedless of the noise he made or the route he took.

At the peak of the ridge, Tara saw his face in the moonlit glow of the night, sheer dread and animalistic panic pulled his face back into a feral growl. He never took another step. Dr. David Nash slammed face first into a tree at a full sprint and collapsed in a heap. His screams filled the night.

Tara lost sight of the beast. It melted away into the tree line. It appeared to Ross that it hurried away as if something had suddenly, and immediately, grabbed its attention.

Her body sank back down to the ice, and she cried for a few minutes. Part of her was mad, he ran away leaving her alone, another part of her knew why he didn't run to save her. It was the coldest judgment she could think of, in his eyes she was not worth sticking around to save.

Tara rolled over onto her back and looked up at the stars with the realization that there was no way off the ice. Her life: a sham. She had thrown away the best of it ten years ago. A crushing sound moving along the shore toward her forced a reflexive jump. The ice cracked. Wrong again, she thought, she would not freeze to death or drown.

The malevolent accuser had come back for her.

Forty Three

Metacomet's Barrow

        AROLINE MOVED AWAY FROM The Dale and the ruins of South Enfield. She realized she already knew the location of Metacomet's Barrow. She, Daniel, and William hadn't known what they were looking at when they all trampled up the path of the spring fed brook to its source. They'd found the perfectly circular pile of stone at its center. In her conversation with Bequette the day after William's accident, Bequette confirmed it.

    She connected the dots of her childhood adventures to Father Bequette's recount of the mill, Henry, and evil. It all fits, she thought. She headed upstream and over one of the stone walls. She could see they had been little retainers to store water. Maybe to power the mill in the warm summer months before it had been switched to electrical power. Perhaps the sheer volume of water generated by the 1938 hurricane had blown them open all the way down the side of the valley. The water, free to run, had carved out the land under the mill—causing both the collapse of the structure and the death of Lester Evans.

She moved several hundred yards northward, walking slightly uphill through the dense forest. Careful to follow the stream, hidden under the snow, but still visible as a crease in the land which wound its way deeper into the narrowing valley. Here and there the stream bubbled under the snow and ice.

She stopped once and rested after she crossed a low stone wall. Her legs were aching. Caroline took a deep breath and looked ahead, pulled forward by desire and desperation.

Caroline followed the stream ever deeper into the forest. The valley sides steepened the further she walked. She made her way to the dark archway of heavy, snarled branches, hanging icicles, and tangled brush. *Evil might lurk inside.* Or it might just be a dark place. Her skin immediately tightened, and the pit of her stomach churned. Caroline wanted to go on but hesitated because one word roared up in her head.

Siege.

This time, she wasn't interested in what the hallucination of the girl had told her. Since evil did not exist in the way that Bequette claimed, there would be nothing in this place either. Just as nothing met her in The Dale.

From far behind her, she heard a siren and distant muffled voices rolling through the forest. The sounds of pursuit echoed in the night. Instead of flight, Caroline stayed and strode into the deadly stillness of the dark narrow valley and followed the stream up further.

Caroline pushed away the nagging sense that she headed into the forest ready to make the same mistakes she'd been making since the first time she entered The Dale alone. She didn't need answers then. She'd only followed the scent of desperation, which drove her to a place where she'd been content—The Dale. With Daniel and William, she had always been happy. Their fellowship of three had been a home for her.

It wasn't the same anymore. No, she thought, the anger simmering, this isn't the same. She knew what she needed to confront, and she knew why.

Dr. Ross and Dr. Nash didn't want her to do it and Bequette didn't want her to do it alone. Bequette worried about her faith and her ability to fend off a supernatural malevolence that she was certain did not exist. William had been in a coma and hallucinated evil.

The pull toward the center of Metacomet's Barrow felt as irresistible as the need to find the answers she sought. The pull so magnetic, she couldn't turn around if she wanted to.

Caroline heard a noise and turned to see a clump of snow cascade down through the tangle of pine boughs. It hit the ground as nothing more than a thin crystal cloud studded with a few glints of ice that reflected the scant dim light. She stared for a long time before she saw the shape in the tree. Humanlike and out of place high in the trees above her, it slowly crept between the spurs of white pine branches.

It did not, Caroline saw, move of its own will. Something pulled it. A long thin whorl of black twine stretched out from the darkness snarled in several loops around the trunk finally wrapping around the figure on which it tugged. Darker than the surrounding trees and now framed by the midnight sky the form advanced. Caroline intently watched it struggle in the high branches dragged from one tree to the next. She had convinced herself only a few minutes ago that evil did not exist. Yet there in the high branches, some murky human form jerked and struggled in a losing battle as it was hauled deeper into Metacomet's Barrow.

Caroline regarded the scene above her and did the only thing her mind demanded her body to do. Driven forward by the compulsion borne of a force not her own.

She followed.

The dark four-limbed entity fell from the high crown of a pine into the mid-section of the next one over and still deeper into the stream leading to Metacomet's Barrow. Framed by the moonlight Caroline recognized the figure and gasped. Terrified, Caroline watched the girl from the basement of the house on the common, and the girl from her dorm room, turn toward her with the malevolence seamed to her back.

In front of her hung a mass of icicles, which clung thickly to the rock face that fed the pool of water, once clear and deep now lay frozen solid. They gestured to the perfectly circular mound of large stones which rose above the ice at the end of the valley.

Metacomet's Barrow, she thought, the place where Henry Evans' faith had failed, and her trouble began. "But that's not true," she said aloud. "Because you," she said, pointing to the girl, "aren't really there, are you?" She turned as the shape melted into shadows. "I'm insane and I didn't even know it."

She crept across the frozen pool of water and knelt by the circle of rocks at the center. Then reached out to touch one stone, a half circle of black obsidian. She finished the trip to the other side of the basement. Touched the wall.

Again. Nothing.

Nothing, until she looked at her fingers. An oily black smudge stained them. At first she thought it might be dust from the obsidian. Next, she found she could no longer move. From behind her she heard the voices of William and Daniel. She called out but no sound escaped. She closed her eyes, squeezed her fists, and tried again.

When Caroline opened her eyes, the sky was brighter, a soft burnt orange glow that filled the immediate area around her replaced the darkness. Wet, oily cords and tendrils wound around her. Her breath came in gasps.

She could only see out of one eye but then it became half covered as a tendril wrapped tightly around her head. The words which sprung through her mind were the same ones the last time she'd faced the malevolence. She didn't listen to the warning and now she lay trapped in the snare. Snares that whipped out from every direction and latched on to her without her even feeling them until it was too late.

She felt *him* rising above her, towering into the trees, his arms out wide, chest heaving, and head back as if in the middle of a roar. Horrified, she saw that it wasn't a roar, instead hundreds of the tendrils and cords retracted into its wide maw and at the end of each appeared to be a person. A person, as dammed as she, under the heel of this malevolence. Worse yet, she'd invited him in and done exactly what Father Bequette had told her not to do.

Thousands of cords and tendrils which comprised his arms vibrated and wound tightly at its soot-colored shoulders. When she saw the malevolence as a complete figure it was a thick-boned and horrifically misshapen skeletal humanoid.

Snares of souls, thought Caroline miserably, thousands and thousands of snares reached out to latch on to countless souls like hers.

Something had tapped her on the shoulder that day in The Dale and never left her side. In full view of the malevolence, she could see countless others burning under his grip. She watched as he turned, drawing her closer to its mutilated face, wondering why she ever tried to face him.

A single horrific word crossed her mind, and she desperately willed it to go away. Except it repeated.

Home. Home. Home.

She'd been freed in a moment of Grace years ago. But she'd been unable to live in freedom and now her path took her right back into the realm of malevolence, the demon, the infestation. The possession. It had called her back, and this hellish Netherworld became her new home.

Forty Four

The Dale

WILLIAM WAS DOWN TO fumes by the time they made it to the rise above The Dale. Daniel had his arm around him, pulling him forward.

"You want to go ahead?" asked William as he dropped to one knee.

"That doesn't work out very well in the movies," snorted Daniel.

They stopped at almost the same place as when they'd first seen Henry Lee Dumont standing near the church. That was the moment that their lives spun away in three different directions. It was as if they were three different beams of light glowing on the dark side of a crystal prism. Stemming from the same place but separated from each other. He wondered if being here now would change things again, maybe this time for the better.

"The tracks go all the way in," said Daniel, pointing to them. They looped almost to the frozen edge of the reservoir and then back to the church and then out of The Dale. "But they lead back into the woods just past the church."

"She went back to the waterfall," replied William, straining to see further in the darkness. He shivered for a moment, remembering the despair he encountered during the relentless bombardment of emotion-charged flashing images.

"She's looking for Metacomet's Barrow," Daniel said.

"Why?" asked William. He felt as if his brain descended into a fog, and he wished he had more time to recover from his frozen state.

Daniel looked out into the woods to the west. "Because that was where Henry Lee Dumont wandered into the woods and found something evil, and it destroyed him along with the rest of his family. She's probably seeking it out. I'm guessing she wants to know if she has lost her mind or if something evil has been hunting her down."

"Do you think she's lost her mind?" wheezed William.

"I don't know. Maybe. Probably," said Daniel cautiously. "If she hasn't, she is heading for something Father Bequette does not want us messing with."

"I know," he said glumly. "But Caroline didn't give us much of a choice, did she?" William felt the weight of his anger at the grim situation and stated, "You know the malevolence, the thing that possesses her now, showed me everything it had." He stopped, caught his breath, and looked Daniel in the eye. "And if she is there alone, she doesn't have a chance."

William rallied his strength, and they doubled their pace, moving upstream through the forest. William and Daniel followed the tracks. The snow continued to harden as the temperature plummeted.

William saw her first and yelled out. Daniel released him as they both ran the last few steps toward her. Exhausted, William wiped out on the ice and skidded into the pile of stone in the center. She stood on the mound of rocks standing stiffly erect. Caroline's eyes were open and terrified. Instead of speaking, she started to thrash around.

Daniel gave him a look of uncertainty as William reached out to assist her. Caroline began to whip her arms, then brought her hands to her throat, straining forward, coughing a breath of air out, and dropping to the ground. William whipped off his glove, shaking his left-hand several times before the last snap flung the glove off into the darkness. Using his index finger and thumb of his gloved hand to prop her mouth open, her eyes rolled back, then William swept the ungloved index finger into her open mouth. As soon as he did, his hand dragged a long, thick, oily black string out with it.

He repeated the process over and over, each time dislodging more of the strings from her mouth. However, it did nothing to help her. She still lashed back and forth on the ground, her eyes darting frantically all around her as she choked and gasped for air.

Daniel seemed to get his head in the game, and they took turns extracting thicker strands from her mouth, but it was unmistakable, she was fading. Caroline's face, a ghastly shade of white covered with spittle as her tongue lolled out of her mouth.

"What the hell do we do now?" Daniel yelled out to William, but he couldn't answer. William fell to the ground in a panicked hopeless whirl, grabbing for his own neck and ripping his coat off as black tendrils roped out of his mouth and nose then wrapped around his body, causing his fall to the icy forest floor.

"Run for help," William croaked, desperate for at least one of them to escape the onslaught. He struggled for breath, looking up at the once clear black sky now burning orange. He knew he was going to lose, and the panic vanished. He decided he would lose fighting. He didn't have to win this battle. Daniel could escape and they all could still win.

William knew the onslaught heading his way. He prepared for what was to come. And it did. The first strains of it showed up as regret. He'd been pulled back into the Netherworld and worst of all he'd let it happen. He could do little to defend himself against the relentless pounding of the roaring emotions before submitting. Despair came quickly. He knew little more than the twisting agony of the twin assaults of visual wickedness and the punishing crush of tendrils binding his body. The return of those tidal forces of the emotions seared the dread and wretched feelings into his core. He desperately tried to remember how he'd freed himself the first time. Instead, he hung miserably under the attack of the malevolence. An attack so powerful he could not conceive of anything other than the immediate harsh torture he endured. The stout physical beat down defeated every attempt to retrieve the tenuous string of hope buried deep under the assault of the malevolence.

The malevolence showed him more; *it enjoyed this*. He raged through the pain and despair, attempting to gain some free modicum of time to reach back into his memory to remember how he freed himself.

The answer danced at the tip of William's conscious, but he could not pull it to the surface. Somehow, he had escaped this version of hell; and the answer to how he did it faded away. So infuriatingly close, it had something to do with what he was seeing below him, but the brutality of the emotions caused by the vision washed it away. The thousands of atrocious scenes raining down on him crushed the answer back below each time it came agonizingly close to the surface.

Forty Five

*The Netherworld
Metacomet's Barrow*

OF THE THREE, DANIEL remained the only one suited to help. But he could do nothing as waves of despair crushed him in the surf. To the left of him, Caroline choked out her life's breath and gagged for air, and to the right, William thrashed on the ground. There wasn't anything he could do for either of them. Finding help wouldn't make a damned bit of difference.

They should've just left her in the Barrow and figured things out from there. Daniel took one last look and turned away from his friends.

He made it exactly three steps.

It started with an extra gasp for air. Nausea churned up, filling his throat full of mucus he could not clear. Daniel gasped again; precious air blocked by a snake-like body writhing in his throat. He yanked it but his chest raged in fiery pain. As if pulling on the tendril would wrench his lungs out with it. He dropped to the ice, striving just to keep his eyes open as more tendrils wiggled out of his body and wrapped around him. Nothing he did helped, and the edges of his vision blurred.

The trees cracked and shards of wood and branches whipped by them. The crack of concussion slapped him, bending his body backward. He thought of a meteor slamming into the small clearing blowing a fifty-foot crater in the middle of it. The hump of rock and ice which had been the center of the barrow rocketed past him and fell like bombs into the forest and out onto the frozen reservoir.

It revealed itself as it stood massive and thick boned. A sky-scraping humanoid body burned iron black.

Daniel shuddered and recoiled as far inside himself as possible. The malevolence towered over the top of the box end of the valley with one clawed foot in the crater and the other on the remnants of Henry Lee Dumont's pile of stone.

Its muscular tendrils coiled out, binding all three of them. Fear phased from panic to terror as the three struggled to free themselves from the dark slick tendrils. Each suffered as the relentless tug dragged them closer to the malevolent creature.

Daniel could still think and reason despite being drawn in close to the massive creature lording over him. As he struggled to free himself from the grip of the malevolence, it pulled him closer and then dangled him high above the ground. The grasp on him loosened momentarily and gave him a fractional moment of relief with the ability to breathe again. He fell, arms out, legs moving in a cycling motion along with the heart stopping acceleration of being dropped from a great height, followed by the bone jarring whump of hitting the ground hard. He rolled onto his back and struggled to his feet. Daniel, now free, could see the agony of both Caroline and William spinning and bouncing along with countless others attached to the cruel arms of the malevolence.

His anger flared out, willing to fight the evil with his bare hands but as the anger peaked, he discovered that he could not budge his feet. He looked down to discover that his feet were sinking into the ground and each of his movements drove him deeper into the frozen soil and less able to help his two best friends. Daniel thundered out a yell of pure animal frustration seeing the malevolence's true intentions for him, dooming him to watch his friends suffer.

Daniel tore his gaze away from the hypnotic stare of the malevolence because he could hear someone coming. The sounds of someone crashing through the brush as if in a hurry caught him off guard. Locked up to his knees he struggled to free himself as the noise of footsteps along with the unmistakable sound of crying rumbled closer.

"*Get out of here!*" he yelled since it was the only thing he could do. Desperate, he leaned down to pick up a stone and toss it toward the sobbing, but the ground sucked in his hand next to his feet. After a moment of panicking, he freed it, and the stone dropped away. He yelled again.

His warning chopped off as two things happened at once. First, a long, thick, black muscular tendril rose from the ground in the center of the crater, splitting rocks in half as it drove through them, rising fifteen feet over Daniel's head. At the end of the tendril, a three-foot spear-like tip angled toward the sound. Then a girl, Caroline looking much younger, the way he remembered her from middle school, tore down the path and stopped cold in front of the pile of rocks at the center of Metacomet's Barrow.

The sight of thirteen-year-old Caroline paralyzed him. She stood in front of the pile of rocks and refused to acknowledge him. He waved and gestured and yelled and calmly spoke and even begged her to leave to no avail. The girl just stood at the pile of rocks as a tendril the size of a tree trunk slowly slithered her way.

Nothing he said made her run. But then Daniel understood he saw something which had already happened, a memory being replayed as clearly as a movie and the sadness of it enveloped him. *This* is how it began and now they were all trapped. Right there at a pile of rocks in

Metacomet's Barrow, her final defenses failed exactly where Evans'/ Dumont's flamed out. Nash was right about one thing, grief, shame, and anger drove her away from those who loved her. Then, just as it had done tonight, the malevolence took her.

Then more steps echoed out of the woods. His gut tightened; someone was chasing Caroline. From a shadow between two trees, he emerged. Guant, thin, and repulsive. Henry Lee Dumont raced out from the darkness, tracking Caroline down.

Daniel swung at a running Dumont, but his fist blew right through the memory, wrenching his knee. Daniel reared back and with an enormous effort pulled his left leg partly free of the ground. He did not need to see the violation of his friend. He would not let the malevolence make him watch. He powered his way forward.

Caroline fell just past the pile of stone and lay still. Dumont stopped just short of the girl and looked at the pile of rocks which existed as the heart of Metacomet's Barrow. Daniel worked his foot almost free before he saw another tendril rising from the Barrow and was sure it was heading for him. He locked his eyes on the tendril, one which looked different from the others. This one, battle scarred with chunks of it ripped off and grown over, not as slick; it was grayer and had smaller tendrils wrapped around the blunted damaged tip.

Maybe I have a chance at this one. As the words rocketed through his mind, he watched Dumont bend down to pick up Caroline. He pulled his leg out of the muck for just a moment before he was sucked back in.

He roared at the memory vision of Dumont and as he did the damaged tendril snapped forward and struck Dumont square in the chest with such force that Daniel was sure it would impale the man. Instead, it bounced off and dropped to the ground limply and quivered like a wounded snake.

Dumont picked up the girl and sprinted away from Metacomet's Barrow and as he did the damaged tendril rose from the ground slowly, pursuing Dumont through the forest. More tendrils followed Dumont and Caroline.

Daniel watched, not sure whether to feel relief or horror but he knew what he saw, Dumont knew what lurked in Metacomet's Barrow and he had hefted Caroline away from the immediate danger. The memory continued to play; Daniel was being dragged along now, his feet barely glancing off the ground following the pair through the forest. Fifty yards from the church he saw her sneaker get caught up in a snarl of vines and dropped off her foot and onto the ground. Dumont, almost to the church when he noticed it, looked back at the approaching tendrils before bending to pick up the sneaker.

Daniel did not feel guilt. Instead, he saw the bravery of the man he thought of as the center of all his problems. Dumont instead had revealed himself as a flawed man who faced the evil knowing he could not win. As far as Daniel was concerned, Dumont was the first person to try to save Caroline.

He stopped being dragged along now. Suddenly released. Daniel tried to sprint back toward The Dale to where Dumont had taken Caroline. Daniel knew it was useless because he only saw a memory played out as shifting phantoms whipping through the night. However, he could not help himself. He had to follow. Maybe there would be an answer.

The first steps were like walking in quicksand but the farther he made it away from the Barrow, the easier it was to run. He had made it to the rise just above The Dale when he got socked from behind and driven to the ground by a tendril, and as he rose in the air, he could see them slithering into the church.

It forcibly jerked him so that the only thing he could see was Dumont standing outside the church as the thirteen-year-old version of himself emerged from the other side of the church. William, at the same age, ran along the ridge right beside him, a phantasm glowing, trailed by a small whip-like tendril in its wake. He closed his eyes, knowing the tragedy was about to unfold and the end Dumont was about to endure, and he would have none of it.

Daniel refused to watch.

Caroline hung high in the air buffeted by the hurricane of painful portraits of hell the malevolence unleashed upon the world around him. She hung angled downward, looking at the ground with her one good eye. It felt like being on one of those roller coasters at the Big E, which went upside down and hung there for a moment before release. She could suck in a little more air. The endless flurry of hurt and painful scenes which played out at a rapid speed in front of her slowed so only one appeared. The ground below her looked far different; now greener, warmer, and the forest glowed in the dull orange of a sun flaming down and tamed by the hills on the far side of the Quabbin.

She could see something moving between the summer trees above Metacomet's Barrow. It didn't move as much as it struggled, hanging helplessly tangled in the trees. The girl lost her battle. She had only a moment to watch her because then Caroline heard a loud grunting and cracking. Someone else worked their way through the forest toward her.

She screamed when she saw him.

Henry Lee Dumont. Or at least the Netherworld hell version of him that the malevolence wanted her to see broke into the clearing. Lean, exhausted and muttering, he struggled forward carried a figure over his shoulder.

The Dumont below her had her. Except not her now. He dragged Caroline as a thirteen-year-old. The day in The Dale in which he violated her and ended her childhood. The malevolence was going to make her watch what he did to her. The long-shuttered window into her soul shattered. A decade of wondering about the black space where those hellish minutes should be.

Caroline watched open mouthed as the phantom carried her thirteen-year-old self back to the chapel. Caroline waited for the worst of it to begin. A thousand different ways of being violated by the man roared through her mind, each one worse than the next. She screamed again at him. This time not in terror but instead she cursed his name in vengeance.

What she witnessed in the next seconds cut deeper than she could have imagined. Each moment she saw crushed her soul. The idea of joy pulled ever further from her.

Instead of a violent assault, he took her inside and gently shook her shoulders and even pressed water from a canteen to her lips. Yet she did not move and was barely breathing.

No.

She begged the malevolence to stop but again she knew it enjoyed the revelation.

Caroline tried to close her eyes, but the small eel-like muscular tendril bound her eyes open. Dumont looked around the chapel, searching for something that he couldn't find. As Caroline lay on a pew, he carefully tucked a bedroll under her head with a tenderness that evoked an overwhelming tide of guilt upon her.

The tendrils moved toward the church, slowly curling around the entire structure, wrapping the entire thing in their web. The only thing that stood between the evil of the malevolence and her—the desperate courage of Henry Lee Dumont. He had stumbled through a lifetime in a fruitless search for Grace, and the sliver of faith he had left, he used to try to save Caroline from the evil that once took him. Surrounded, Dumont sat down on the pew and tried to figure out what to do next.

She'd been wrong. She'd hated the wrong thing. The evil wanted her to understand her failure and witness the end. Her walk in the woods had done this.

More tendrils wrapped around the chapel. It was only a matter of time before they breached the chapel structure. He stood up once more and took a knife from his pocket and began to cut deeply into the gray wood above the doors. She watched as he worked the knife across the wood, sweating and mumbling as he worked.

επίθεση

Her mind strained to retrieve her more recent memories. She knew the word *Epitheon*, the word that William wrote on his arm before he fell into the ice and endured this horror for the first time. A word of warning that the girl in her bedroom, the same one from the house on the common, desperately tried to make her understand. The word meant siege in Greek. Only one person would know what it meant. Father Bequette. Henry wrote a final note to him.

No. No. N*ooooooooo*! She screamed as Dumont fought Daniel and William. She could see everything as it was. The malevolence manipulated William and Daniel into fighting for their lives, but Dumont, his soul destroyed, desperately fought for hers.

"No." The word more wept than spoken.

The shots were loud and echoed forever through the forest, each of the vibrations shook her. Dumont lay motionless on the ground and the tendril snapped forward, snaring his limp form, ready to pull it away into the darkness; one more trophy for the malevolence. The Dale released the first of its secrets. For years, her mind refused to unlock those events. Her personal boogieman, she saw through the shame and grief of the revelation, had been nothing but a man.

A victory for the malevolence, she knew, hiding the truth from her until it could hurt her the most. The man who tried to save her from his cruel fate died, his destiny sealed by her angry walk in the woods. Guilt bloomed across her heart and the darkness took the remains of the day as her evil bonds tightened again.

As she struggled in the darkness, far below her, she saw another figure in the forest. A young girl that Caroline recognized as the girl from the common and in her room, the girl that had been drawn to this place along with Caroline—except now she was free. Nothing wrapped around her or connected her to the malevolence. The girl hovered around the dead man for a moment before sitting down in the dirt next to him, oblivious to the commotion of police and rescue swirling around her. She took his hand and wept quietly. Caroline watched as the tendrils slid off the chapel and focused on attacking both the girl and the unmoving Dumont. The girl, unintimidated, stood up and kicked the nearest coiled tendril away and stepped on another one, then she disappeared into the gloom for a moment before reappearing near the church.

She gazed up at Caroline hanging high above her, tangled in the vise grip of the malevolence's tendrils. "Siege, Caroline... can't you see it?" Her voice sang out musically and clear for the first time since she saw her, unfettered by the malevolence. The girl wanted some form of understanding from Caroline before effortlessly swatting away one tendril. "*Siege*," she said again before vanishing into the gloom, leaving a gray ashen withering tentacle behind.

As acts of love go, Caroline could think of none greater. Hannah's spirit stayed behind for Henry and then for Caroline. Hannah came to her in the basement of the house on the common, and in her room, and here in the forest. Now she begged Caroline to understand something more.

Caroline still did not understand what the word *siege* had to do with this. The tendril wrenched and a new torrent of horrific images pounded her.

All she knew, and certainly, William and Daniel felt the same, was that at this moment they wanted to be free of the malevolence.

Forty Six

The Quabbin

JOHN SULLIVAN'S BOOTS CRUNCHED down into the snow, and he walked as fast as he could with Father Bequette on the downslope of the narrow forest trail. Nothing disturbed the night, save the occasional voice of Bequette.

The priest slowly and carefully fed him details about Caroline he never expected or wanted to hear. He heard words like *possession, oppression,* and *demon* and listened as ideas like evil and exorcism drifted past him.

It made sense, how else could his little girl spin so far off her axis in such a short time? Medical treatment did nothing, and then one day she was freed. He thought of it as a miracle but now it occurred to him it was more than a miracle: it was a moment of Grace.

The boys were, he realized, not ready to face what had taken her. He was unsure if even he and Bequette were equipped. Bequette warned him they were heading into a fight with evil and victory meant keeping his daughter while defeat meant possibly losing her soul forever.

"What are we going to do when we get there?" asked Sullivan as he tried to keep from stumbling.

"We," replied the priest, "will find your daughter, William, and Daniel and get them the hell out of there. We secure Caroline and you somewhere far away until your lawyers can deal with Dr. Nash."

After a seemingly endless slog through the dark, snow, and ice, Father pointed. John saw three sets of footprints.

"Amazing," John said incredulously. He had not been certain of Bequette's shortcut. He'd wanted to follow the tracks from Gate 5A and surely catch up to them.

"They're all moving in one direction," said the priest, staring intently at them.

"Good shortcut!" John excitedly pushed past the priest and turned to follow the path of footprints, but Father Bequette grabbed onto his arm.

"Stop for a second," he said in his deep voice. It was a voice that boomed out from the pulpit each Sunday morning, clear and authoritatively bringing the hopeful word of God to the assembled Catholics. However, now the tone changed sharply. "Haven't you been listening to me for the last three-quarters of an hour?" His eyes gleamed, looking for an understanding that eluded Sullivan. "Don't go in there half-cocked."

John nodded his head affirmatively, confused by the sudden change in the priest's attitude. "I'm not. My daughter is out in these damned woods looking for answers. Looking to get even."

"What if she finds something else?" he hissed. "I don't know if you really understand the evil or just think you do."

The magnitude hit John, the only person in the woods right now who knew anything about fighting the evil in that place only managed a draw. It was almost a loss from the way Bequette described it.

"William and Daniel are out there right now chasing her down."

"Her friends followed her out of the blind loyalty," offered Sullivan, thinking about their fierce unbridled friendship. Love without fear or the tempering awareness that it can evaporate in an instant.

"Blind is the key word here," said Father Bequette. "Don't go in there blind to what you are about to deal with, John."

Sullivan hardened at the idea. "The boys," added Sullivan, "are chasing her knowing damn well what she will find, and they could not swallow the idea of her facing it alone."

"Neither can we. But we will not fight his fight. It is still God's earth, not the malevolence's. So, let's treat it like that."

The tracks led deep into a narrow valley, forested far more heavily than the rest of the area. It seemed to come out of nowhere and dropped away into the dark distance. If there was an entrance to hell, this is what it would look like. *A dark hole in a bad place.* Below them a stream dominated the bottom of the valley.

"In here," said Bequette as he stepped through the opening. John did not reply. Instead, he nodded his head as they made it to the bottom of the valley and to the frozen stream. They then walked upstream in silence.

John and Father Bequette found the three of them at the end of the mostly frozen stream where it ended as a high wall with a large pool of frozen water at the bottom.

Each standing stiff with unmoving eyes and mouth gagging open. John leaped for his girl, standing rod stiff on a hump of rocks that rose from the floor of the bottom of the valley.

"Stop!" Bequette reached out and grabbed him for the third time in just a few hours.

John, desperate to save his only child, ignored the priest and stumbled toward her.

Sullivan paused with his hands just above his girl, her eyes wide open but unreactive, watching her struggle in some unseen battle, quivering and straining against an unbearable weight. Unbidden, guilt ate him. He hadn't been a good father, often away and leaving her in the hands of others while pursuing his dream—not hers. Even after Henry Lee Dumont, he did not make her the focus of his life.

He'd refused to deal with the reality facing both. Afraid that by facing it he would lose his daughter too. John had lost his daughter anyhow.

Caroline's world had spiraled out of control in The Dale, and in the aftermath, he'd done nothing to bring her back. Instead, he'd helplessly tried everything, begging and pleading for things to change only to fail her. He had failed and failed again. Maybe Caroline would be better off somewhere...

The next word never crossed his mind because Bequette snapped at him.

"He's a clever bastard, isn't he?" asked Bequette coolly.

"*Damn it*," replied Sullivan, now jarred out of his dark reverie. As his hands hovered over her, he felt the ripple of electric tension. The demon which Bequette had spoken of, the one who had his daughter, had lulled him into despair and he hadn't even realized it. *Christ, it had me that easily. Not even here for a minute.* John moved away from his daughter and the two boys, wondering if his act of faith would be enough to give them a chance.

The priest took off his coat and pulled a small brown leather book from his waist while John shook away his gloom. "We have crossed a barrier, John."

"Barrier?"

The priest looked at Caroline, William, and Daniel facing outward from the mound of stones at the center of the barrow. "This is a full-scale assault on your daughter and her friends. Do you understand what I must do?"

"Yes."

Bequette added something else. "John, I have had conversations with the bishop starting after the incident in The Dale. By the time she melted down on the common the talks had picked up and a plan put in place. It was too much of a coincidence for me or the bishop to ignore even in those first days. The malevolence has, once again, reached out for her and Caroline once more has let him in. So has William and Daniel. I must act, or we will lose them all."

"Action," Sullivan repeated. One word flared across his mind. A word that almost engendered a laugh out of him. Exorcism. "You're going to do an exorcism here? Now?"

An exorcism, here in the dark woods at night, with the singular purpose of driving out the demonic malevolence and sending it back to hell. He glanced over at the priest, showing a calm and focus that he wished he possessed. That was the word: *possessed*. A hand reaching out from the darkness and taking control of a person in their loneliest most shattered moments.

Father Andre Bequette began the procedure without flourish or pomp. Under his coat he wore a short-sleeved surplice tunic and over that was a purple stole. Under all of that was a simple thermal shirt.

The priest moved rapidly through the first part of the rite and Sullivan repeated the phrasing when Bequette nodded at him. John's hands shook and his stomach vaulted, and his legs left him unstable. He'd never been a nervous man. Even before concerts in front of tens of thousands of people, he'd never felt this way.

By the time Bequette crossed himself, John, Caroline, Daniel, and William and then sprinkled holy water, Sullivan choked back the bile rising in his throat. *This is real.* He never imagined thinking those words while trying to save his daughter.

The priest moved through the litany of saints over the three who were still unnaturally stiff. But underneath he saw them quiver and strain against the malevolence. Sullivan used the book given to him by Bequette to follow along. He found himself challenged repeatedly as doubts about the need to do this wrapped around him. John struggled to bury them. He felt these doubts thumping against him time and time again, causing him to lose focus. That was him, that was the demon fighting back. He had to believe.

John shook under the impact of evil when Bequette addressed the malevolence directly. More than physical weakness, a mental strain. Did Bequette truly know what he faced? The invisible impact that nearly knocked him off his feet made him believe they were in the presence of pure evil.

"Save your servants," called out Bequette in his deep, authoritative rumble of a voice, "let them find you." The priest stopped for a moment. He called out to them over the noise of the possession infesting each of them. "Let them find you," he prayed. The priest continued. "Let the enemy have no power over them."

The malevolence rocked Sullivan with a mental shot that keeled John Sullivan over and he dropped to his knees as a wave of nausea more powerful than anything he had ever experienced hit him.

"Get ahold of yourself," demanded Father Bequette sharply enough that he stood again, ready to do his part even though he could barely stand.

"In the face of the enemy," coughed out Sullivan, leaning against a tree and nodding to Bequette. Sullivan, keenly aware of Bequette's first warning about the demon's attempt to make him feel small and inadequate, did not recognize until now just how inadequate he would feel.

"Why isn't this working?" asked John as his frustration boiled over. They had been working for a while and nothing changed. He said the set of prayers and demands and still, even though they made those demands there had been no answer. "Maybe we should try something else." He had seen the movie, and this looked nothing like what he'd watched. He wrapped his brain around it by picturing them existing simultaneously from the world of the living and that of the damned. Their physical bodies stayed here while their spirits were trapped in a fight elsewhere. The badly timed question appeared to break the priest's concentration. They had made progress, John knew, but doubt crept in driven by fear for his daughter.

"The exorcism," Bequette said as calmly as possible, "pulls them back to the world of the living and away from the world of the damned. We do this by casting out the demon from this world and driving him back to hell."

Casting out. The term stuck to John. It was a biblical phrase he'd heard his entire life. Cast, as the word implied a violent, forceful action. Bequette's arms drooped in fatigue. "The violent action part of this rite could go both ways." The priest gave a grateful nod as John helped him stand upright. Bequette continued in the moonlit dark.

"Fill your servants with courage," Bequette said. John kept his eyes on Caroline and the boys who were now looser and less stiff, almost unbound. Daniel had even sat up and opened his eyes, *those eyes led to a soul lost in chaos, desperate for courage,* for a brief time but showed no understanding of where they were. In a blink he was dead-eyed, gone again.

John understood why he had to be here. The real reason the priest wanted him in the woods with him. If Bequette failed, then Sullivan could get help, and the fight could go on for another day.

The priest had the power here. He issued the commands, telling the malevolence that he knew the *One* who made him. It was the *One* giving Bequette the power to drive the demon away. The malevolence, however, had an advantage which could derail everything; a person possessed needed to give consent for the exorcism. Caroline, Daniel, and William might not comprehend that evil had infested them. He knew the beast would keep them in despair and keep up the punishment so they could not hear him.

Bequette placed his hands on Caroline's forehead. He flinched, heat boiled off her forehead as if in flames. The priest ignored the pain, and the sensation passed as quickly.

"Caroline," he called out into the night as she squirmed beneath him. Long welts swelled across her face. "Caroline," he called out her name again as her face began to bleed. With his other hand, he grasped hers. "Caroline, I need you to tell me if you want to be freed," he called one last time before she responded with the slightest squeeze.

Bequette didn't wait. "I cast you out, unclean spirit, along with every satanic power of the enemy, every specter from hell, and all your fell companions; in the name of our Lord Jesus Christ. Begone and stay far from these creatures of God, Caroline Sullivan, Daniel Wilson, and William Lane. For it is *He* who commands you, *He* who flung you headlong from the heights of heaven into the depths of hell."

Each time he repeated the word 'He' power rippled through Bequette's fingers. He flexed his shoulders and drove whatever words he spoke out of his mouth at a near shout as his confidence skyrocketed. Bequette, now over three-quarters of the way through the rite, rounded on the demon. He interpreted the small squeeze of his hand as the acceptance of his offer to help and then bullied his way forward.

Bequette saw the way John looked at his daughter. As if he expected a gigantic flash of heat and light, a ground that rumbled or a thunderclap in the sky.

"Is he gone?" John moved closer to the priest. Bequette decided John must be longing to reach out and touch his daughter and did not respond. Instead, he continued praying the rite of exorcism. Sullivan moved glumly back into the shadows.

Bequette roared forward. "God, Creator and defender of the human race, who made man in your own image, look down in pity on these your servants, Caroline Sullivan, Daniel Wilson, and William Lane, now in the toils of the unclean spirit, now caught up in the fearsome threats of man's ancient enemy, sworn foe of our race, who befuddles and stupefies the human mind, throws it into terror, overwhelms it with fear and panic." Bequette crossed each of them. This time on the forehead. The priest struggled to stay focused and upright. The attacks seemed to hit all three and he experienced an ever-increasing sense of weight on his shoulders and back. So different from the intimacy of their last battle, a new tactic caught him off guard. The weight was so great now that he had difficulty raising his arms and even keeping his head upright.

Forty Seven

The Netherworld

WILLIAM WATCHED FROM ABOVE, his waterlogged self rolled from the edge of the Quabbin and to the shore. The fall through the ice weeks ago left him with barely enough strength to move forward. Even though he was out of immediate danger, he faced an even greater one. As he lay on the edge of the water shivering and delirious, a young girl emerged from the woods. She spoke to him as he lay on the ground and as she did, she kept looking back at Metacomet's Barrow. She spoke in his ear with the intensity of burning phosphorus, pleading with him to move out of The Dale and toward the road and help.

The tendrils snaked out from between the trees and wrapped around her as he took his first step onto the road. Once around her legs, waist, and face, she fell in a heap.

The image faded away, and William felt even worse, knowing whoever the girl had been she had suffered the same fate he faced now. Except, she'd endured this hell for far longer.

He noted that things changed again. The ground below him changed into a wasteland with burned and scorched stumps of trees stabbing up at odd angles. Everything stopped and then began again. He heard his name and those of Caroline and Daniel. The malevolence paused and turned its charred head, first toward the ashen sky and then to the burned-out forest.

It was searching for something and moved toward whatever it had found.

William dangled helplessly high above the ground. Without warning, a stomach lurching sensation of being dropped and the tension of the muscular snare loosened. The assault of the horrific images, trophies of the malevolence conquests since the beginning of time, paired with the emotional impact of those images, which had been hammering him into despair, all stopped.

They halted just long enough for one of his own memories to pound to the surface through the assault. When the muscular tendril crushed against him and the images stormed back, the first flame of hope erupted inside him. He had something to use in the fight.

William could hear the voice of Bequette not only calling Caroline but also praying. The effect on the malevolence was obvious. The snares holding him loosened again. Meanwhile, the assault of trophy images and the emotions they inspired had slowed significantly. Slow enough, William used his one weapon against the malevolence. He sought cover in a simple memory of working as an altar boy during Sunday morning mass. It seemed to be the one set of memories that the malevolence could not manipulate or destroy. The memory he had of himself silently reciting mass in his head so he wouldn't forget. It provided a barrier from the malevolence and eventually escape.

The Netherworld

Caroline peered out into the orange gloom and saw all the thousands of tendrils briefly go slack and then snap back in place. When they snapped taut again, it sounded like a soaking wet towel hitting a ceramic floor. The moment coincided with a short reprieve from both the crushing pressure on her chest and the relentless bombardment of the emotion tangled up in horrific images. In that fractional space of respite, she heard someone calling her name. Muffled and distant but without a doubt someone called her. She twisted against the pressure of the cords binding her. She searched, needing the voice.

Caroline heard her name being called repeatedly and despite the pounding she endured and the images of war, poverty, discord, and betrayal the voice offered hope. If someone was calling her name, then a rescue might be possible, hope made the barrage bearable, and the emotion warmed her, counteracting the fierce grip under which she suffered. The grip of the tendrils loosened, and the face of the demon turned toward her.

Caroline felt the largest of the tendrils loosen to where it tumbled away below her. The malevolence defiantly rocked back and forth as all around her the long, black tendrils started turning to ash and releasing their damned souls. They dropped away into the distance, swallowed up in the shimmering band of light cresting over the horizon.

The malevolence itself appeared to be smaller, more brittle, and now snapping its mouth open and shut like a dog chasing a bee. The voice of Bequette was getting louder as each of his words was clearer than the previous one.

The Netherworld

Daniel felt the difference rather than saw it. The sound of his, William's, and Caroline's names being repeated in the distance tempered the more horrific images flashing one after the other in front of him. Courage crept into his thoughts for the first time since being pulled into the realm of the malevolence. Caroline sagged on his left in the same crushing grip of the malevolence while William hung in the ashen sky almost directly above him.

A flicker of Caroline in a Halloween costume, head bent back as a part giggle part snort erupted out of her, splashing cider out of the side of a green plastic cup as she held a half-eaten donut in her other hand. The memory ignited his heart, and the indomitable hold lessened. William, tripping up a set of stairs and face-planting into his lunch caused the grip to loosen again.

Daniel groaned as an explosion of red orange light surged past him as the malevolence regained his footing. Seconds before, after beginning to disintegrate, the tendril suddenly snapped tight once again.

Metacomet Barrow

Bequette cursed as Sullivan flew on top of him in an instant, crushing him onto the ground with a muffled thud. His friend's hands quickly wrapped around his neck and squeezed. In the imperfect light of the moon, the priest recoiled at the sight of John's eyes bugging out of their sockets, neck veins pulsing. Bequette struggled to free himself, lying partly on the toe of Caroline's boot. He hooked his thumb under John's palm and pressed the tip of the digit into a pressure point at the fleshy base.

John yelped, coming to a half stand and half crouch. Bequette seized the opportunity and drove his knee up, catching the musician by surprise. John stumbled and hit the ground with a moan.

Bequette ignored the man and resumed performing the rite. "I adjure you, ancient serpent, by the judge of the living and the dead, by your Creator, by the Creator of the whole universe, by Him who has the power to consign you to hell, to depart forthwith in fear, along with your savage minions, from this servant of God." Father saw John rising, eyes glowing with hands balled into fists.

John Sullivan never made it another step. His daughter drew his attention away from Bequette.

Forty Eight

The Netherworld

CAROLINE FOUND THE VOICE of Bequette as loud as if a jet had passed overhead and her thoughts swirled around happier moments with him. The countless times he'd been in her home or when she'd listened to him in church. His assertion that she should be one of the first alter girls in the area. The smell of the cinnamon apple tea he drank. The emotions related to those visits welled up and filled every part of her being.

Siege, the word ricocheted across her mind unbidden. It was the word Henry carved into the wall of the church in The Dale, and William wrote it on his arm, and it refused to go away. *Siege* was the word that Hannah Evans called out to her not once but twice and now it refused to leave her mind. *Siege... Epitheon*, in Greek, an ancient term. *Siege*, the message to Bequette from Dumont. Everything slid into place.

Caroline had been looking at it from the wrong side. When she heard the word, she assumed it was meant for her. She was under siege under the domain of the oppressor.

As she looked around her, at the turn in fate, she bathed in the joy of those images and the sound of Bequette's voice ringing out across the sky. It was she, for the first time, who lay siege to the malevolence. The demon who tortured her looked small, brittle.

Further, as she searched for Daniel and William, she could see that they were rallying. All around them the world in which they dwelled was crumbing and even the sky looked fragile.

They held the demon's world under siege. A world collapsing.

Every tortured soul living and dead possessed by the demon saw what Caroline saw and rallied against it, laying siege to it as well.

The sky cracked for the second time and the entire body of the malevolence shook as the tendrils slithered and twisted as they turned to ash and blew away like a thin scattered gray hail. The bones of the malevolent demon, iron black, pitted and burned, went next, shattering in the shoulders, spine, and legs, reducing the once towering demon to a cloud of dust as one final sound echoed across the sky. The last black oily tendril lay ashen, shriveling, and dying as the earth swallowed the remains of the demon.

Dantalion.
Dantalion.
Dantalion.

Bright, silvery-white exploded around and through her, blasting away everything in one last flare of light. For a long while, the pure, beautiful gleaming white was all that she knew.

Metacomet's Barrow

Bequette witnessed the change in everyone around him immediately after finishing the rite of exorcism. The weight which had viciously pounded him downward dropped away, leaving him to feel nothing but exhaustion. The seventy-year-old priest slumped to the ground while John remained motionless, taking in what had just happened. Bequette waited and held his breath for some assault that never came. He exhaled and the hope of victory crept into his heart. After a few more moments he allowed himself to believe it.

They had won. The demon Dantalion careened back to hell so it could terrorize no one.

Bequette would have preferred an indicator. Perhaps a bright flash over the sky. He battled to the brink of failure. He'd willed Caroline, William, and Daniel to hear the truth and reject the spitting, slanderous, vicious lies of the demon who possessed them. *You, children of God, named before he spun the universe from his fingertips are the precious, loved, and center of someone's world. You are something worthy* he'd cried out to them. He could not know if they heard, he'd simply had to pray and perform the rite.

By God's Grace, he realized, they'd heard him. Not just him, they latched onto the one piece of knowledge of which there could be no denial. Bequette had told them over and over: God loves them and nothing in the hate and fury of the excised demon, Dantalion, could change that truth.

He knew the moment they grasped the idea because the heavy cloud of desperation and despair, which threatened to overwhelm him, vanished. Suddenly and completely gone. After a few seconds of pure wonder, joy had flooded the space where seconds ago corrosive anguish worked its way toward desolation.

The three survivors stirred in the snow and Father knew he had won for sure. William and Daniel and Caroline lay in a tangled heap of legs and arms. Silence returned to the forest and a single trickle of water dripped down the face of the frozen stone wall.

Sullivan moved behind him. "We gotta get out of here," cried John, gently shaking his daughter.

Father Bequette placed his hand on John's arm. "Give it a minute. You have won." Saying the words aloud made it real for both. In a crisis, everyone involved has their own perception of the event. John had just encountered the wicked and the damned. A malevolent demon named Dantalion had taken a slash at his daughter. The supernatural had invaded the natural world and punched John in the face.

John turned his head back to Caroline and stared at his daughter for some time. She looked as content as she'd ever been. "How do you know?"

"Faith. He would not just let her go. His only place to go once banished is hell. That's why they fight like starving dogs."

Sullivan slid his daughter onto his lap, putting his head to her chest to be certain she still breathed. "Right," replied Sullivan. "Hell. *Christ*. He wanted my daughter."

Bequette knew the man needed some time to accept that his daughter was free from the malevolence. So was, he realized, Dumont and everyone else. "He stole your daughter. You took her back. She came back to you."

John Sullivan buried his face into his daughter's hair and wept until Caroline opened her eyes. "I'll be better," he promised her.

Bequette turned away from them and gave them the privacy of the moment. He made his way to William and Daniel. It was cold and they were at least an hour's walk from warmth. They needed to move, but the three sat groggy and mostly senseless.

One moment the world sparked bright white, and Caroline floated. Then, in the next, she sat upright wrapped in the warm embrace of her father. She flashed back to being three-years old, and one of her first memories. She never willingly went to bed. Her father, tired himself, would wrap his arms around her until she fell asleep, or at least he thought she drifted off. If she still lingered half in dreams but aware enough that he was still there, she would grab tightly onto his arms the moment he tried to move away from her. The moment also reminded her of her first awakening in the psychiatric ward. Except this time no scent of the temporal. No lingering doubt. As she sat up and finally stood, electric shimmering hope filled every nerve and cell in her body. Once again, like her first awakening, she saw the world in the frozen forest as brand new.

Even the memories of the battle faded so quickly she could barely recall any specific thing about it. Except Dumont, she closed her eyes and wept for him for a few minutes. She didn't tell her father why. William and Daniel would know but Father Bequette had not managed anything more than a grunt out of either of them. Dumont had tried to save her and although she felt she should experience guilt, she could only feel relief and joy. Henry Lee Dumont also received the miracle of a soul free from the malevolence.

All secrets of The Dale had been revealed and the last tangled threads which kept her locked firmly in the past crumbled and broke away. She could move on. She'd never been to the house on the common, a malevolent evil had deceived her, but she'd recaptured her faith and shattered its grip on her. The demon now existed as dust and ash.

She lived free.

She remembered one thing, something important. Father Bequette noticed her internal struggle, so he ambled over to her. Caroline spoke to him quietly and explained. But then, even that conversation and its focus faded and a few minutes later she could not even remember why she needed to speak to him.

Caroline absorbed every detail in the forest from the moonlight diamond sparkle which danced across the snow to the tiny movements of the branches of the trees. The sounds of a faraway siren penetrated her revelry.

Sirens.

People were out to capture her. The sirens were for her. Her mother had signed the paperwork to recommit her. That truth didn't dent her confidence. She walked out of the forest as sane as anyone else.

She demanded her freedom from something malevolent, evil, and timelessly wicked, then used her faith to wrench her soul back from it. She won. No one, not her mother, Dr. Ross, or Dr. Nash could change that. Caroline just pushed them aside.

She lifted her chin ready to face whatever lay in front of her. She then led William, Daniel, Father Bequette, and her father out of Metacomet's Barrow and back toward The Dale and the shoreline of the Quabbin Reservoir.

The Quabbin

"We should get home and warm. My mom will be worried." Daniel said the words as if he came to consciousness halfway through the sentence. Dropped from nothing into the middle of a conversation deep in the cold dark forest.

"Sure," replied Father Bequette who trudged along beside him.

Daniel's mother had cooked beef stew the evening before and he wondered if some still sat in a bowl at the back of his refrigerator. He walked on wobbly legs, dazed and not sure about anything other than he'd been walking. He knew they triumphantly traveled away from Metacomet's Barrow, and it no longer served as the domain of the malevolence but rather a memorial to the courage of Henry Lee Dumont.

Memorial. He had no idea why that word jumped into his head. His mind was still a confused swirl of contradicting memories—none of which seemed to be his. Memorial, the thought bound to the surface again. Daniel had fought the nightmares of Dumont standing above him, a second from crushing his skull with a bowling ball sized rock, for the better part of a decade. Nobody knew that. He didn't hate the man as much as feared him. Now that terror, one relived over and over in a thousand nightmares, evaporated in the cold night air. He gained nothing more than understanding and perspective and that was enough for him to release the fear.

His existence narrowed down to the simple desire to go home, shake the cold out of his body, and sleep. As they marched on in silence, he saw the ruins of The Dale and they took a short break in the church. He couldn't sort through the thousands of memories which had walloped him, their pain, despair, desperation, all there but fading quickly. Then they were all gone.

He turned to his friend and bear-hugged him.

William tried to push him away. Daniel didn't let him go.

They ground on through the forest and the knee-deep snow to the edge of the frozen stream, John and Father Bequette poked the edges to find a safe passage.

Finally, after walking in the endless cold they arrived at the shoreline. Daniel thought he'd seen a flash of light near the edge of the water. He kept those observations to himself, worried that he hallucinated. Mr. Sullivan seemed distraught, but Caroline calmed him after an intense conversation. She walked out of the woods first and everyone followed her lead.

Miraculously, the lights were real and with the lights came people and shouts from police and firemen. Daniel's muddled mind couldn't process their presence just that they emerged from the darkness and brought light and heat.

People shouted and pulled at him. Others quickly surrounded him and grappled for his attention. He closed his eyes, overwhelmed by the sudden raft of people around him.

Someone covered him with a blanket, then yelled into a walkie-talkie. Another person, who looked like a doctor, shone a light in his eyes and tugged at him to sit down in the snow and rest.

Nothing made sense. He turned to William and Caroline, he could hold off no longer and the question burst from him, "What are we doing in the woods?"

When he looked to William for an answer, he saw none forthcoming. William's face content and blank. "I don't know," replied William, "my butt is soaked, and my feet are cold."

Caroline pointedly tried to nudge the three of them away from the medical personnel. Medics intended to separate them for assessment, but Caroline held up her hands. They stopped and allowed the three of them to stay together. Caroline moved between them. "Come closer and keep me warm and I will tell you."

Forty Nine

The Reservoir
One hour earlier

TARA ROSS COULDN'T BE sure she wanted to know what headed her way when she saw a light bobbing in the distance. The light meandered along the shore and closed in on her. She tested the ice around her by sliding her knee forward, thinking she may need to get off the surface of the Quabbin Reservoir in a hurry. Six inches later, the ice crackled again, and she stopped and shivered violently, cold and alone.

Damn!

Tara, left with limited options, lay a hundred and fifty feet from shore on thin shattered ice with water of an undetermined depth beneath her.

She wondered if the bobbing light could be David, then dismissed the thought. She saw his face when he ran. Not the face of a man who would lead the malevolence away from her and then circle back to rescue her in the dark. The thing in the woods must've killed him by this point.

A voice interrupted her thoughts. A voice in the distance called out a name, but it wasn't hers.

"Caroline. Don't move," yelled the voice. Dr. Ross knew the gravelly voice. It belonged to the assistant police chief… Chevalier. The first glimmer of a smile cracked across her frozen lips. Chevalier had brought the whole town to the party.

His voice called out again, "Caroline, we're going to help you." Chevalier sounded closer to her than it looked.

"I'm not Caroline," she yelled out through her uncooperative lips and chattering teeth. "I'm Dr. Tara Ross," she cried, overjoyed. She had offered a silent prayer a while ago promising to be a better person and begged for John Sullivan's forgiveness. She'd be fired from her job, but she could still ensure Caroline walked across the graduation stage from afar, if for just one more chance to live. She should've been a guide for the girl, a champion. Not her enemy. It seemed so petty now. However, the past was the past and the only thing she could do was atone.

"What the hell are you doing out there? Is she with you?" asked Chevalier. He had the quiet calmness that she wished graced her voice. For a man into his late sixties, he was fit, portrayed strength, and had the aura of authority that she needed right now.

Embarrassed, she went with the truth. "I slipped. Please help." She sobbed as the enormity of everything washed over her. "Something is out here, it killed David," she said the words out loud, making it real. David was dead.

It took some time before Chevalier spoke again. "There are evil things here in the darkest places. But we are not running."

Like all men, Dr. Tara Ross thought, his attempt to make things better did just the opposite. "I don't feel faithful." She had shown no faith and knew it. Her faith, abandoned on a Maine boardwalk almost a decade ago, evaporated. The woman showed up tonight in the woods to close the ledger on that part of her life. It had not been a woman, she corrected herself, just the same malevolence which tempted her back then, and it had killed David tonight.

She raised her head as Chevalier reassured her, took in his words, and felt like she had a chance. "Okay," she replied.

The Quabbin

John Sullivan halted at the edge of the forest by the rocky shore at the rim of the reservoir. A gust of wind blew a light sheet of stinging snow past his face. He turned back to Father Bequette and jumped back into the tree line. "We can't go this way. Cops everywhere."

Caroline held his arm and shocked him. "I am ready for this."

He turned her, stunned into silence.

Finally, he spoke. "No." He said the words sharp and loud. "We have to go back the other way and head for the Vermont state line." William and Daniel nodded their heads. John wondered if they even knew what they agreed to. "That's the plan."

"I'm not going to hide." Caroline took the final step out of the forest. Out of the shelter and darkness. Her face, pale and soft in the moonlight, left him wanting to grab her hand and run for the cover and darkness of the forest.

"I can't let them take you again. Not Nash or Ross."

"They aren't winning." Caroline's voice calmed him. "I'm free either way."

John looked to Bequette for help.

Bequette leaned into him. "John. Let her take control of her own life. She's strong enough now to do it."

John wanted her home and safe. He didn't want her any further away from him than she was at this moment. He looked once more at Bequette, who stared back at him stony faced.

"Okay," said John. "I understand."

They walked the last hundred yards to the first sign of the outside world they'd seen in hours. Halfway there someone noticed them and pointed flashlights their way. A shout or two echoed across the cove and within a couple of minutes a team of paramedics and policemen were on them.

They handed out blankets, asked questions about how they felt, if they needed medical attention, offered them coffee or hot chocolate from thermoses. He even heard a small celebration when word of their safety rumbled along the shoreline.

Nobody arrested them or took Caroline.

At least not yet.

John noticed a large cluster of the personnel focused on the ice. He saw the center of the storm on the shoreline. A woman sprawled out on the ice fifty yards offshore and nobody could figure out how to get her. A thin strip of smooth snow free ice stretched from where the woman lay back to the edge of the cove. She could only have made it that far if she had come from the high bluff at the edge of the cove and slid all of the way down and out.

Chevalier directed the operation twenty feet away from him. The assistant chief of police nodded to him as an acknowledgment that John lived then turned away to coordinate the rescue.

"Glen," offered Sullivan. "I know the reservoir out that way. We used to sled down that ridge when we were kids."

John's eyes flashed back to Caroline and the two boys.

"I got two ambulances," replied Chevalier, "and two poor patrolmen out here dragging a portable generator through the woods. And a person stuck out on the ice because of you."

"Two ambulances?" asked John.

"Nash went chasing Caroline in the woods. Got lost then lost his mind. Shattered his leg running terrified through the woods and he's on his way to Reliant an incoherent mess. Last I heard he's babbling on about the devil."

"Damn." John's head sagged downward. Then he lifted it up and shrugged. "I am… Caroline needed to…"

Chevalier cut him off. "Glad you found her." He turned his back on John, dismissing him to speak to a trooper. "Christ almighty she will go into shock from hypothermia if you wait any longer," snapped Chevalier at the state trooper.

"We can't take a chance on breaking through the ice. Then we'll have two people in the water."

Sullivan grew angry at the absurdity of the moment. A woman lay on the ice and grown men were having a pissing match about who would get her, when, and how. In the meantime, the woman's predicament only got worse. Waves of energy ran roughshod over him. Fingers tingled and he could not manage to stay still. Bequette hovered around the paramedics who also hovered around Caroline but focused most of their energy on William. They were safe.

Lights bobbed up the shoreline as more people and equipment descended on the scene.

Nobody grabbed him or placed him in handcuffs. His mistake attacking Bequette, the malevolence's last desperate attempt to save itself, wore on him and he needed to make amends. John nearly cost Caroline, William, and Daniel their lives along with Father Bequette. In the worst moment of the exorcism, his faith broke just like his daughter's. When he needed to trust Bequette and by extension his daughter's ability to fight the malevolence he failed—because of his lack of faith.

The malevolence had been cast out, he was not going to watch a woman die while men argued. He could at least atone for his earlier blunders.

One smooth lane of ice, twenty yards wide and two hundred yards long, stood out to Sullivan. Saying nothing, he picked up a coil of rope from the ground and hefted it up in his hand and gave one end to a police deputy before walking out onto the ice. His first two steps caused the ice to break under his feet but ten feet out from the shore it was thicker and firm. Once he felt it give underneath him, John flattened himself onto the ice and shimmied forward so he could reach the woman.

As he continued to shimmy across the ice, he saw in his peripheral vision another trooper had moved down shore, tied an orange backboard to a rope, and slid it out to him. The backboard skidded to a stop close enough for him to grasp the cold plastic in his hands.

John could see her shivering violently. She looked like she was wearing the least effective outdoor clothing. "I'm John Sullivan," he said, reaching out to take her hand. It was cold and stiff.

"Dr. Tara Ross," she whispered between chattering teeth. She pulled her hand back, but he hung on.

Tara Ross. The name shocked him and rattled his nerves. Tara Ross lay on the ice on the edge of consciousness with her arms and legs pulled in close to her body. Her soft black hair splayed out on the ice contrasting her light angular facial features. It was the same way she slept. He'd seen her in the mornings for a weekend a decade ago.

Waves of conflicting emotions crashed over him. She'd made his daughter's life a living hell. She conspired with Dr. Nash. John knew he'd started it all. He'd made the decision to cheat on his wife—again. He'd justified it as part of the life of a successful musician. Allyssa knew about it. But he had always known it was wrong. If he had not cheated, Caroline would've never run into the woods alone.

She never would have endured Dumont. One bad moment in the forest nearly leveled everything in his life for good. Several bad decisions as a husband and then as a father ravaged his life. The shock and hurt evaporated. Corrosive acidic emotions flashed into the inexplicable desire, no need, to protect Tara Ross.

He'd been the problem. He'd known who Allyssa was. What she could do. Allyssa the emotional vampire. She sucked the life out of everything around her. He'd met Tara, electric and engaging. Tara had taken the risk and offered herself to him. He'd lacked the courage to tell Allyssa it was over. He'd lacked even the mettle to look Tara's way as Allyssa ground her into the asphalt with her heel.

He slipped the hat off his head and gloves from his large hands and then worked them on to her.

"We seem to have gotten off on the wrong foot," she whispered, holding onto his arm, and he used his bare hand to help warm her.

"I knew who you were…then. When you came to the house. I blew it," was all he could muster as he gave her his coat.

"I started out trying to help her. I got lost."

John nodded and helped her onto the backboard. Four metal strips extended from the sides of the safety device.

Ross lay quiet for a second and he worried she'd passed out from shock.

"Don't be too impressed with my rescue, the water is only about four feet deep here." He rubbed her arm softly, hoping for a laugh from her. She managed a small smile before her eyes fluttered closed. "I've got you now," he vowed.

Caroline stared, not blinking, as her father dragged Dr. Tara Ross slowly along the narrow ribbon of smooth ice to the safety of the shoreline.

"Got her," he said and then toppled back into the knee-deep snow and gasped in the cold air, white vapor drifted from his lips. A crowd of medics, satisfied William, Daniel, and Caroline would live, rushed to John Sullivan and Tara Ross.

"Why did you do that?" she demanded as she grabbed his cold hand and squeezed. She'd just lived the horror of Dantalion and then watched her father risk his life for a woman who'd betrayed her.

Her father wheezed out another breath. "Because I didn't do it when I should have." A set of arms gently guided Caroline a few feet to the left of the medics.

The words stunned Caroline. "What do you mean when you should have?" He didn't answer. She assumed he'd done it out of misplaced heroism. The idea there had been something deeper spiraled up in her mind and left her confused.

Another look at Ross softened her. Dr. Ross looked younger, prettier, and had lost the normal hardness in her body language. God only knew how long she had been on the ice. Her father had left her side and pulled a high wire act on the frozen surface of the Quabbin to rescue Tara. It must have been something big. She'd need more than that cryptic answer. She would not get it tonight, so she left it alone.

To her right, Father Bequette allowed himself to be fussed over by another medic. "I'm quite fine. I'm cold, not dead. That stethoscope isn't making me warmer," he complained as the young man opened Bequette's jacket and checked the priest's heart and lungs. With a nod from one medic to another, they escorted Father Bequette, John Sullivan, and Tara Ross to a tracked snowcat.

"Let's get them up top," ordered Chevalier, smacking the snowcat with his hand twice.

"Come up with us?" her father asked. There were several snowmobiles there already and more whizzed up and down the road between Chevalier's initial command post at the Lane home and the rescue site on the shoreline of the Quabbin Reservoir. Caroline felt one last wave in the flood that should have buried South Enfield grab her and spit her almost all the way out of the forest.

Before she let the snowcat leave the shoreline, Dr. Ross rallied to discuss Caroline's situation with both Chevalier and the Massachusetts State Trooper captain. In just a few words, she forcefully declared that it was in Caroline's best interest to stay away from the psychiatric wing of Reliant Medical. Nobody had the authority to disagree with her, she was a doctor. Caroline felt tension leach from her body upon hearing the words. Caroline knew she would sleep at home tonight. The relief was immense, but she still couldn't leave.

Caroline shook her head. "I need…I need a minute," she said as her mind tried to formulate what exactly she needed.

People pulled away from her. Daniel started toward one of the snowmobiles. "I'm not walking," he said.

William followed, creating more distance between her and the people she loved. "Wait," cried out Caroline. "Just, just wait a second." She knew she must have sounded desperate enough for Daniel and William to stop, but they did not backtrack to her. The distance had not been shortened. The snowcat with Bequette, her father, and Dr. Ross growled to a start and began its crawl up and out of the Quabbin.

Daniel rubbed his hands together. "It's cold out here, Caroline."

Caroline, still unable to articulate what she wanted to say, reluctantly mounted the snowmobile idling in front of both William and Daniel. A police- or fireman drove each snowmobile in the large caravan. She held on to the driver tightly and they sped up the road. As they neared the last crest near the top, she realized what she needed and how to do it.

Caroline tapped the side of the policeman's shoulder, and they ground to a stop. Behind her the snowmobiles carrying William and Daniel, as well as the rest of them, stopped in a single file line.

She hopped off and stood at the remains of Gate 5A. The lights from the dozen police cars and volunteer firemen's trucks flashed in front of them. The last of the searchers dragged the rescue equipment up the snowy hill. She'd heard Chevalier ordering everyone, including the state troopers, to return together to ensure none of the rescuers ended up left behind.

Caroline took two steps toward William and Daniel and stopped at the edge right where the living road met the dead one. She realized she needed one more moment in the woods. The nerves rattling all over her body told her everyone stared at her apprehensively and probably wondering what she would do.

For the first time since leaving Metacomet's Barrow desperation and insecurity glowed inside her. Not hot, not even warm. There. She needed something. One more thing.

"We need a plan." They looked at her in grave concern. "A plan about tomorrow."

William glanced at Daniel.

Caroline stomped her foot on the ground in frustration because she could not completely form the question. "I'm serious. We need a plan." How do you ask your former best friends to be your best friends again? The demon had taken so much from her, and she would not allow their friendship to be a permanent casualty.

"I don't think there'll be school tomorrow with this storm, and everybody is down here," replied Daniel.

Finally, the words broke out of Caroline, bringing the relief she needed. "No. What time should we meet tomorrow?"

"Tomorrow?" asked Daniel, tilting his head as if she was a puzzle he needed to figure out.

"Maybe," Caroline said, nodding vigorously, "seven in the morning for breakfast? We could have it at my house." Caroline waited for the boys' response. Maybe, the idea flashed across her mind, they just followed her into the woods to save her and nothing more.

Daniel reached for her hand.

William shook his head. "There's no way you'll be out of bed and ready for anything before eight."

"Nope. Not after tonight. Nine-thirty, we'll try to pry you out of bed," replied Daniel with a chuckle. "William, bring the donuts."

Caroline slumped into the embrace of the best friends she ever had. The three of them held fast for another moment, and then William broke away, climbed on the back of the nearest snowmobile, and gave them a head nod.

"In the morning," added Daniel.

Daniel gave Caroline a hug before Assistant Police Chief Chevalier barked at them to get moving before he had to take them to Reliant Medical for frostbite. Caroline waved at Daniel and then William as they zoomed out of the Quabbin.

Epilogue

Stonehill College
Easton, Massachusetts
May 17th, 1996

G RADUATION DAY AT STONEHILL College burned scorching hot and Caroline felt for sure she was going to either melt or begin to smoke if the ceremony didn't end soon. The outdoor ceremony started at noon, and she flitted around beforehand making small talk with some new friends she'd made over the past year.

In March, the realization had hit everyone. Graduation meant several hundred young men and women spiraling away in different directions. Friends leaving.

Girls from her dorm rallied around her after hearing the sanitized version of her near death in the woods. They'd helped her with everything from where to shop for a graduation dress to where to make dinner reservations for after the ceremony. She even got invited to a girls' night out before graduation day. Something Caroline had never done with the pressure to finish her degree.

However, despite the throngs of friends and dozens of pre-graduation conversations, she always knew where Daniel and William were in the crowd today.

Daniel had saved his job and been granted tenure. They'd made him wait an extra year to sweat it out and be sure he didn't stray away from the values of the conservative board. Of all the places in the world where Daniel had dreamed of going, he'd stayed in Cold Springs. A happy lifer. Content to drive each day from his new house on Juckett Hill Road into town and teach at the new high school being built right across the street from Reliant Medical. Maybe it was enough that he wouldn't be occupying the same building from grade nine until retirement.

Perhaps the weeks spent over the summer working in Wyoming guiding trout fishermen placated the wanderlust of his youth. Caroline decided that men like Daniel Wilson couldn't see a life away from the easy contentment, the small agonies, and intermittent joys, of living in a small New England town. He'd told her the new high school felt like a fresh start.

She pictured him fishing the Quabbin at dawn in a steel boat with a ten-horse engine. If she tried, she could see herself in the middle seat and William at the front. They would discuss which pile of sunken rocks held the most fish or which color to use as bait all the while she'd be wondering how to tell them she had to go to the bathroom. Caroline chuckled.

William came today. Fate had determined that the Brewers played a three-game stand in Boston on graduation weekend. William didn't need to be at Fenway Park until five and it would only take forty-five minutes to get there. Before the ceremony, he'd chatted with her father about sliders and cutters, and she had little if any idea what they were talking about.

She'd convinced her father to forgo the massive graduation bash he had planned until next weekend. Tonight, they'd all see William pitch against the Red Sox. She hadn't decided who to root for yet. It all depended on whether William could get her into the clubhouse.

She thought back to the price William and Daniel paid to be her friend. Both spent weekends at Reliant Medical under the watchful eyes of the nursing supervisor, cleaning up the mess they'd created with the sprinkler system. Dr. Nash had limped around offering suggestions about William's elbow as it related to his curveball or Daniel's teaching technique, but he'd mostly stayed away. He and Bequette had worked things out between them. They had lost ten years as friends. Her friends, the people who lost the most around her, still stuck with her.

Father Bequette spoke as graduation wound down. She clapped loudly at his well-received speech. Like most moments graduation was over quickly, almost as soon as she entered and sat down on the soccer field in the rows of carefully lined up folding chairs behind Stonehill College she was already standing up to receive her diploma. The girls in front of her giggled nervously as the winding line headed to the small portable stage where they would receive their diplomas. They called the names one by one until, finally, her name rang out over the speaker.

Later, Caroline accepted the hug offered by Dr. Tara Ross and embraced her. She'd forgiven Dr. Ross in the aftermath of The Dale. If she could forgive Henry Lee Dumont, forgiving Ross would be easy. Her father confessed the full breadth of his failures to her. Caroline understood Tara better. Tara was the chance her father should have taken. Her mother, now long gone and location unknown, hadn't bothered to find out what happened to Caroline once she bolted from Dr. Ross's office. Once again, she'd left Caroline in her weakest and most desperate moment. But Tara Ross did not.

Tara had recognized how her mistakes had been detrimental to Caroline and risked her life to make it right. She'd faced the malevolence and lived with her soul intact. Anger is just a little to the left of love. Some great lost cosmic circle closed when her father rescued

Tara on the ice. Ross left Stonehill at the end of the year and the glowing letter of recommendation written by the faculty dean opened the door for her new position at UMass Amherst.

Dantalion. She had asked Father Bequette what the word meant. It was the last word from the mouth of the malevolence, she could never call it a demon, before everything shattered. The priest told her it was a name, the name of the malevolence, adding it's a powerful act to name that which oppresses you. Dantalion, the malevolent demon who had tortured and oppressed countless, tainted The Dale, driven out of her life. Thousands of tendrils connected him to the souls of thousands of other people shattered all at once, and now they were all free of his malevolence.

She thought back to the moments before they defeated him. And really, that was only how long the switch from being completely routed, William called it being manhandled, to their total victory. Despite Bequette insisting it was never all that close, she'd felt beaten. They were all but defeated before a single opening led to the slaying of the demon, Dantalion, in a remote valley called Metacomet's Barrow. Bequette explained that the moment the fraction of joy she found under the worst oppression allowed her to find her faith. She'd reached out and grasped onto her faith—really believed; the fruits of that faith, hope, love, and joy spread like wildfire along the interconnected tendrils which until that moment had pumped a nonstop torrent of despair and hopelessness into those Dantalion infested. Then the long missing emotions drawn in by hope, roared along those tendrils and destroyed the lie the demon Dantalion laid upon every soul it infested. In the face of that truth, Dantalion had failed utterly and had been banished back to hell. Once Caroline grasped onto her faith in God it took a fraction of a fraction of a second to end the battle. A battle raging for almost a decade for her and eons for others. The Netherworld Dantalion had created, and in which he'd held their souls, imploded, taking Dantalion with it.

She thought about Henry marking the place where his faith collapsed with stones and hoped now, somewhere, he knew those stones would mark the victory over his tormentor.

As they left the stage, she scanned the crowd to find her father. He leaned sideways and sported a tan suit, a short haircut, and stylish sunglasses. Her father caught her glance and smiled back at her. She held on to the hands of both William and Daniel all the way back to their cars all the while wondering what in the world she would do when she woke up the next morning. Most decidedly it would not be archeology. At least not like Indiana Jones. But the possibilities were endless.

www.ingramcontent.com/pod-product-compliance
Lightning Source LLC
LaVergne TN
LVHW021231080526
838199LV00088B/4311